THE CTHULHU PALIMPSEST

Brian Stableford's scholarly work includes *New Atlantis: A Narrative History of Scientific Romance* (Wildside Press, 2016), *The Plurality of Imaginary Worlds: The Evolution of French roman scientifique* (Black Coat Press, 2017) and *Tales of Enchantment and Disenchantment: A History of Faerie* (Black Coat Press, 2019). He has translated more than three hundred volumes from the French, mostly in the genres of *roman scientifique, contes de fées* and Romantic and Symbolist fiction. His recent fiction includes the visionary science fiction novel *The Revelations of Time and Space* (2020) and its sequel *After the Revelation* (2021); the last in his long series of "Tales of the Genetic Revolution," *The Elusive Shadows* (2020); and the comedy fantasy *Meat on the Bone* (2021), all published by Snuggly Books.

SNUGGLY BOOKS

BRIAN STABLEFORD

THE CTHULHU PALIMPSEST

A ROMANCE OF TERMINATION

CONTENTS

In memory of the late Michael R. Burgess,
alias Robert Reginald,
a temporary Pharos in the darkness of my perverse vocation

THE BACK-STORY

THIS novel is something of an afterthought, written to complete and conclude a series of metaphysical fantasies begun several years ago, for a publisher now extinct, although all the earlier titles remain available as print-on-demand books. The series relates a number of adventures of Auguste Dupin, a character invented by Edgar Poe, some of which involve him with characters and entities invented by H. P. Lovecraft, as well as actual historical figures and occasional devices appropriated from other works of weird fiction delivered by the passage of time into the public domain. The adventures are narrated by Dupin's friend and associate, Samuel Reynolds, an eternal bystander summoned by fictitious Fate to bear witness to them. Because the present project wraps up the series, tying up numerous loose ends left dangling in the earlier volumes and necessitating frequent reference to them, a prefatory summary of the earlier volumes might be necessary to make the present one a little less confusing.

In the first novella in the series, *The Legacy of Erich Zann* (2011), the violin employed by the Lovecraftian character in question resurfaces in Paris in the 1840s, and its finder is enthusiastic to find someone capable of playing Zann's magical music on it. The remaining manuscripts of Zann's scores have been destroyed, but Dupin has heard the music played and is blackmailed into attempting to reconstitute a particularly dangerous example.

In *Valdemar's Daughter, A Romance of Mesmerism* (2010), Jana, the daughter of Poe's Monsieur Valdemar, a talented mesmerist who has been perfecting her art in Paris under the tutelage of the President of the Societé Harmonique—who claims to be a reincarnation of the Comte de Saint-Germain and who employs that pseudonym—attempts to involve Dupin, Honoré de Balzac and the latter's physician, Pierre Chapelain, in a swindle involving a supposed elixir of life and the evocation of an entity featured in Edward Bulwer-Lytton's *Zanoni*, the Dweller with the Eyes of Fire.

In *The Mad Trist, A Romance of Bibliomania* (2010), Reynolds comes into possession of a copy of the book that Poe's Roderick Usher and his companion were reading on the fateful evening when the house of Usher collapsed—a book that carries an exotic curse, the unfolding of which has tragic consequences.

In *The Quintessence of August, A Romance of Possession* (2011) the Comte de Saint-Germain seeks Dupin's help with a puzzling legacy including a Guadagnini cello and an exotic box; the unraveling of the mystery results in Reynolds' possession by the vampiric spirit of an egregore, which enables him to play the magical instrument at a garden party hosted by the magnetizer Baron Du Potet, where potentially-alarming consequences are averted in the nick of time.

In *The Cthulhu Encryption, A Romance of Piracy* (2011), Dupin is consulted by Pierre Chapelain and the director of Bicêtre Hospital, with regard to a mysterious patient who has a cryptogram magically engraved in her flesh. Also interested in the patient, Ysolde Leonys, is a magician who styles himself Oberon Breisz, although he also claims to be a notorious pirate named Edward England and a reincarnation of John Dee's one-time associate Edward Kelley. The adventure culminates in a confrontation in Bretagne in which Dupin and his fearsome concierge, Madame Lacuzon, Reynolds, Chapelain and Saint-Germain are menaced by shoggoths, monstrous agents of the "encrypted" Cthulhu, and are briefly aided by Ysolde's long-dead father, Jack Taylor, now a member of the crew of a ghost ship captained by a Maratha warlord called Angria, whose long struggle against the British was guided and aided by the magician who incorporated the cryptogram into Ysolde's flesh, who calls himself the Mahatma.

In *Journey to the Core of Creation, A Romance of Evolution* (2011) Dupin and Reynolds travel to Mont Dragon in the Ardèche, where a college friend of Dupin's, the paleontologist Claude Guérande, has discovered relics of prehistoric humanity in a deep cave. The entrance to the subterranean location in question is on land whose ownership is disputed, and is of interest to various other parties, partly because it provides difficult access to a strange Underworld inhabited by life-forms produced by an evolutionary sequence other than the one that produced life on Earth's surface.

In *Yesterday Never Dies, A Romance of Metempsychosis* (2012), Reynolds encounters the ghost of the statistician Blaise Thibodeaux, whose theories of temporal resonance once intrigued Dupin. Before dying, Thibodeaux instructed Dupin, along with the Prefect of Police, Lucien Groix, to be sure to attend an 1847 performance of the opera *Robert le Diable*, but Dupin is unable to comply because Madame Lacuzon is very ill and he is attempting to save her life, basing his treatment on a theory recently developed by François Raspail, which attributes diseases to microbes invisible to the naked eye. As a result of Reynolds' meeting with the ghost, however, he, Dupin and Groix set forth with Saint-Germain—currently the custodian of Thibodeaux's manuscripts and other effects—the ballet dancer Marie Taglioni, and Pierre Chapelain, now working in association with Jana Valdemar, for the forest of Fontainebleau, where they encounter a much more substantial temporal echo, also anticipated and apparently orchestrated by Saint-Germain's coachman, Anton. In the course of the vision Reynolds has another conversation with Thibodeaux's ghost, and then attempts unsuccessfully to save Jana Valdemar from drowning in the Seine, catching a severe chill in the process.

In addition to the novels in the series, which terminated prematurely when their publisher, the pseudonymous Robert Reginald of Borgo Press, died suddenly, there is a related work sharing the same metaphysical backcloth, self-published via Amazon in a Kindle edition, *Echoes of Eternity* (2016). It features Blaise Thibodeaux as a character, who assembles a group of interested parties in the cathedral of Notre-Dame in 1830 in the hope of hearing a temporal echo of the so-called Quasimodo peal, which used to be rung on the Sunday in question before all but one of the cathedral's bells were melted down to make cannons in the Revolution. The group includes Victor Hugo, his friend Paul Lacroix, also known as "the Bibliophile Jacob," and a theater musician who calls himself Doctor Prospero, and who is searching avidly for any relics of the music of Erich Zann—a quest in which Lacroix cannot help him and Auguste Dupin refuses to do so.

The series and its addendum sold miserably in the original editions, but selected volumes published in French translations by Catherine Rabier have done considerably better in France in recent years. I hesitated for a long time over the possibility of producing the long-projected final volume, in spite of the nagging dissatisfaction of its incompletion, but, still having to fill in time after my supposed retirement from writing, occasioned by old age and ill-health, I finally decided to make the attempt. The race against dementia and death was a close-run affair, and the margin of victory not much more than a short head, but I limped to the finish line, sustained by bloody-mindedness and the closeness of the *Necronomicon* to my stubborn heart . . . and if I have contrived to persuade someone to publish it posthumously, here it is.

THE CTHULHU
PALIMPSEST

I

THE PONT DE LA TOURNELLE

BY the time I had recovered from the influenza that I had contracted following our hallucinatory expedition to the outskirts of the forest of Fontainebleau on the Day of the Dead in 1847, winter was unleashed on Paris in its full force, and it was bad. Food prices had rocketed because of the second bad harvest in a row, deaths from cholera were multiplying, and morale was very low among the city's legendary street-sweepers. Their efforts to keep the streets navigable by carriages and pedestrians were a trifle short of heroic. In retrospect, it seems to me that the street-sweepers' negligence probably did more to slow down the Campagne des Banquets—the gatherings in cafés that defied the ban on political meetings—than any edict issued in the name of Louis-Philippe or any action on the part of the police. No matter how radical a Republican might be, he was not going to relish trudging to a conspiratorial conclave through snow and ice that could cause problems for the sturdiest boots. Doubtless the historians of the future will have a dozen good explanations for the fact that Revolution did not erupt in Paris until the last week of February 1848, but I was there and if anyone asks me I always tell them that it was entirely a matter of the impossibility of starting before then because the would-be revolutionaries' feet were too cold and the business of moving around too difficult and treacherous.

I am, of course, being glib and over-simplistic. Future historians will probably not pay much heed either to the predictions of the statistician Blaise Thibodeaux, whose papers were by then in the custody of the Société Harmonique de Paris and a subject of intense interest for its president, Laurent Falleroux, alias the Comte de Saint-Germain, but Thibodeaux had identified February 1848 as the date of the next Revolution as long ago as the mid-1830s, using some arcane mathematical formula derived from his theories of transtemporal resonance. Having conversed with Thibodeaux's ghost—another effect of transtemporal resonance, if what the ghost told me could be believed—in the forest on the Day of the Dead, I suppose that I should give his thesis more credit than my own, which is certainly ridiculous by comparison with the sublimity of his, but I am essentially a down-to-earth person, all the more so when the ground in question is soggy and does not provide secure footing. I am certainly in no position to deny the effects of the supernatural in human affairs, but I feel bound to assert that even people with their heads in the clouds—or far beyond—ought not to forget the condition of their feet.

It was not, strictly speaking, impossible to go out during the three months that followed the Day of the Dead, and those of us who had been caught up in Thibodeaux's strange hallucinatory time bomb mostly managed to pay our obligatory visits to one another once we were able to get out of bed, before the heavy snow set in. By mid-December, however, it was definitely a time for "hunkering down." as we Americans put it—which gave us time to reflect on our experience and ask ourselves, in a reasonably disciplined fashion, whether we had gone mad . . . or, more accurately, exactly how mad we had gone.

The Fontainebleau vision was not the first I had experienced, of course, nor even the first that had been shared by other people, following not very distantly on the heels of our confrontation with the minions of Cthulhu in Bretagne. Once again, however, it raised acutely the question of the exact extent to which the collective experience had been objective rather than purely subjective: a question complicated by the fact that only part of the vision had been shared, my conversation with Thibodeaux's ghost—or temporally displaced image—being puzzlingly private. Unsurprisingly, given that I do not possess Auguste Dupin's titanic intellect, my initial attempts to grapple with that problem did not lead me to any form of comforting conclusion.

I urged Auguste Dupin to move back into my town house from his apartment in the Rue Dunot, where I had no confidence in his ability to keep warm and feed himself adequately. He eventually agreed to do so, as a temporary measure, but only, he assured me, because he was worried about the health of his concierge and housekeeper, Madame Lacuzon, who had also been caught up in the influenza epidemic, not long after suffering a bout of serious illness through which he had nursed her with a quasi-filial devotion, and only on the condition that my handyman, Bihan could help him to transport his "essential luggage"—which is to say, his recently-acquired books. Many of his not-so-recently acquired books were already becalmed on my shelves, and I could have sworn that there was no means of fitting more in, but Dupin, a past master of rearrangement, not only managed to accommodate them in my study but also to keep them in some sort of order.

Not by coincidence, Bihan's wife, my own housekeeper, was Madame Lacuzon's cousin, and one of the few people not terrified by her, so she had no difficulty in allowing the supposed witch to take up temporary residence alongside her kitchen stove, where the old woman could not only keep warm but also help to ensure, to the best of her ability, that Dupin and I were sufficiently well-nourished and protected. Madame Bihan had not needed any arcane predictions to lay in what supplies she could for the winter siege, but Paris is the heart of world civilization, and its markets never close entirely, so poor Bihan was dispatched every day, in spite of his cold wet feet, to fetch fresh bread and whatever comestibles could still be bought locally. I will not say that the five of us were comfortable, but we were better off than nine-tenths of the city's population.

We did not see many people during December and January. Lucien Groix was no longer in Paris, having vacated his position as Prefect of Police before he had recovered from a bout of influenza as bad as mine, and having apparently left the city as soon as he was able to travel—perhaps wisely, as he would have been an obvious target for the Revolutionaries when the barricades went up, being the notional head of the not-so-secret political police. Pierre Chapelain had been keeping his distance even before the fiasco at Fontainebleau, and he had to suspect that I blamed him for Jana Valdemar's death by drowning, which was a forceful deterrent to continued association. Even Saint-Germain seemed satisfied with the conviction that the Harmonic Society's library would act as a magnet infallibly drawing Dupin to his headquarters once conditions eased, and he seemed, in any case, to be fully occupied with internecine battles within the society, which, although theoretically apolitical, was apparently being ripped asunder by the same ideological conflicts that were dragging the city and the nation into confusion.

Dupin, naturally, wanted to stay out of the political conflict, and I, as an American in temporary exile, was supposedly uninvolved. However, because of Dupin's friendships with François Raspail and Paul Lacroix—occasioned by the former's medical theories and the latter's bibliophilia, not their politics—it was often assumed by the uninformed that he was a staunch Republican, and because the United States is a Republic, some Parisians unacquainted with the intricacies of Boston society naturally assumed that I must be one too. On the other hand, Dupin's simultaneous friendship with Lucien Groix, whom he had known long before Groix became the Prefect of Police, made him deeply suspect to those

Republicans who did not know him as well as Raspail and Lacroix, and the automatic false assumption made by many uneducated Parisians that "American" was synonymous with "rich" made me equally suspect. Incentives for people who were not close friends to socialize with us in tense times were therefore minimal.

Dupin, who posed as a cynic, in the true tradition of Diogenes, made a fetish out of not caring about that hint of ostracism, and I did my best to imitate him, as I had in the early days of our friendship, of which I could not help think as the Golden Age of the murders in the Rue Morgue, in spite of the gross distortions incorporated into the story when Edgar Poe reconfigured the account I mailed him for his own literary purposes. But for a series of extraordinary encounters, culminating in the hallucinatory episode at Fontainebleau, I would have had no difficulty at all in doing that, having prided myself in those days with a perverse fondness for darkness and reclusion, but there is nothing like frequent contact with the supernatural to cultivate a fierce appetite for conventional normality. I had been badly shaken by the various exotic adventures with which my association with Dupin had involved me, and if the affair of Erich Zann's violin and its opening of a window to the Crawling Chaos had not resulted in an immediate conversion, it had certainly laid the foundation for a drastic reconfiguration of attitude, completed by my brief but profound conversation with Blaise Thibodeaux's ghost at Fontainebleau.

After that, believe me, no one would have been the same person they had been back home in Boston, or in the blissfully affected early days of my sojourn in Paris, and I was no exception. I no longer knew precisely who or what I was, or who or what I might become when—or if—the present turmoil settled again into some kind of routine. There seemed to be no prospect of that in February 1848—and, indeed, the disruption that was in preparation was more profound than any of the contending parties could have imagined.

I never believed, even for a moment, while we were hunkering down in December and January, that the icebound pause was anything but a brief hiatus. How could I? I couldn't even begin to understand the fine detail of Blaise Thibodeaux's theories of temporal recurrence and infection, but precisely because of that, I had no way to dismiss them. On the other hand, I knew full well that once a man has become a seer, he can no longer refuse to see—or, more pertinently, to hear. Once the defensive walls of stern consciousness have been breached, the gap is available to all manner of things from outside, and even if he can prevent the walls from collapsing entirely, scrupulously maintaining his artificial sanity, he cannot recover his former state of protective innocence. I felt it in my bones, as February began to bring changes, that it was not only political revolution that was going to trouble my imminent future in the City of Light, and that, as soon as it was possible to walk the streets again without freezing my feet or breaking a leg by slipping on the ice, there would be worse impediments to progress for me to fear than mere bullets and barricades.

It was, therefore, with a nagging sense of trepidation that I set forth with Dupin one night in February for the Faubourg Saint-Victor—a district that had not featured large in our itinerary in the days of our nocturnal wanderings. The partially-melted and refrozen snow had been gathered into brown piles of slushy ice, leaving passages clear for vehicles and pedestrians, which were negotiable without too much difficulty in boots with soles adapted for walking on an icy surface, with which we were both equipped. We were also wearing quilted jackets under our overcoats, recently supplied by an expert Breton seamstress recommended to us by Madame Bihan—in my case replacing the jacket I had ruined by jumping into the Seine. They did not quite live up to their advertisement, but they really were a good deal warmer than those marketed for winter usage by the native tailors of Paris, who do not like to add stodgy bulk to their garments in case it injures the harmony of their lines—something that did not concern Dupin or me.

As usual, Dupin was cautiously uncommunicative; when he was on the track of the unusual he did not like to prejudice my expectations, and he had been even more taciturn than was his wont since his meditations on Blaise Thibodeaux's pseudoscience of temporal tides had taken control of his obsession. He always said that his reluctance to explain what he was thinking when he was on the trail of a mystery was a matter of enabling me to function as an unprejudiced witness for his consultation, but my opinion was and still is that he was simply cursed with an instinctive secrecy.

"Where are we going?" I asked him, as we went along the left bank of the black and sluggish Seine. Although the weather was relatively clear, the mist gathered over the water limited visibility on the quais and obscured the right bank completely.

"The Quai de la Tournelle," he said, curtly.

"Why?"

For once, it appeared that someone was playing him at his own game. "Because it has been suggested to me, mysteriously," he replied, "that if I am on the quai in question immediately after midnight, I might hear something that will interest me."

I knew that he had received a letter that morning from Paul Lacroix. "Are we meeting the Bibliophile Jacob?" I asked him. Lacroix had long had a habit of signing much of his published work with that pseudonym.

"Afterwards, perhaps. I shall certainly see him tomorrow, at the Louvre; he was most insistent about that, but he says that I might be in a better position to understand what he has to show me if I am on the Quai de la Tournelle at midnight. He can be infuriating at times, with his teasing."

The words "pot" and kettle" came to mind, in the context of comparative blackness, but I refrained from making the comment. Instead, I asked: "Why the Louvre—that isn't his usual stamping-ground?"

"Nor is the Faubourg Saint-Victor, but there is apparently a literary café there from the window of which one can see the old witch-house in what's left of the petty Rue de l'Hirondelle—not the one that was once dependent on Saint-Germain-de-Prés but the one that has already been partly demolished and is due to disappear completely, along with its duplicated name, in the near future. Someone at one of his cenacles has told him that strange lights and eerie music have recently been seen and heard in the house, which has supposedly been deserted since the last Revolution but one, so he went to keep vigil there two nights ago. Whether he saw any specters I don't know, but he certainly seems to have heard something that gave him pause for thought and speculation."

"So why are we going to the quai rather than the café?"

"Because whatever Lacroix heard didn't appear to be coming from inside, or at least wasn't confined to, the old witch-house. He evidently has some reason to think that it might be more clearly audible from the quai—or, at least, he wants to ascertain whether it is audible from there."

"And he wants you to hear it before you go to see him tomorrow at the Louvre?"

"Apparently."

Evasive as Lacroix was evidently being, there were no prizes for guessing why he might have wanted to call upon the evidence of Dupin's ear in a matter of perhaps-supernatural audition. For nearly twenty years, Lacroix had been . . . let us say "preoccupied" rather than obsessed, in order to avoid undue exaggeration . . . with one of the notorious "forbidden texts" of the Parisian occult tradition, *Les Harmonies de l'enfer*, signed by the presumably-pseudonymous "Abbé Apollonius," which was even more celebrated in Parisian bibliophilic circles than the legendary *Necronomicon*, the name of which had been whispered in awe by the supposed Hermetic cognoscenti of my native Boston. Lacroix and Dupin had both had the opportunity to inspect copies of the *Harmonies* at their leisure, although it would be an exaggeration to say that they or anyone else could read its arcane musical notation reliably, and it had been something of a bone of scholarly contention between them.

Lacroix knew that Dupin had been acquainted more than twenty years ago with the eccentric musician and composer Erich Zann, and that something had happened more recently, when Zann's violin had resurfaced briefly, but Dupin, who had made promises of confidentiality, had refused to give him the details. Lacroix had even attempted to get information out of me behind Dupin's back, but I had naturally refused to give him any, mostly out of loyalty to Dupin, but partly because I had vague plans to write a narrative version of the episode, taking inspiration from the way that Edgar Poe had exploited the Rue Morgue affair and a number of other anecdotes I had relayed to him in the course of our correspondence.

"So the Bibliophile thinks that someone in one of the houses on the Quai de la Tournelle, or at least audible from there, has taken to playing music that might be taken from the *Harmonies de l'Enfer?*" I suggested to Dupin, proud of my facility in deduction.

"I don't know," he replied, with a touch of asperity, "but as Lacroix has never managed to decode with certainty the system of notation employed in the *Harmonies*, he cannot possibly have recognized any snatch of music he heard from the Rue de l'Hirondelle as having that origin. It would not be the first time, I fear, that the poor Bibliophile has jumped to the conclusion that something overheard might belong to that phantom tradition, but on the previous occasions that he has referred them to me, I have been able to prove otherwise. He must think that the present challenge, if that is what it is, is more likely to succeed, but he has always had an unfortunate tendency to optimism, which I do not share."

I didn't have to ask him why. Most of the bibliophiles avid to track down copies of the elusive volume in question were equally avid to play the "harmonies" that it contained, but none, so far as I knew, had ever succeeded, not only because the esoteric notation of the music was difficult to decipher but because the instruments for which the music had been scored were obsolete and long superseded. Erich Zann had been a modern composer, who had destined his original music to be played on a violin; it might conceivably have had some analogy with the music that the fictitious Abbé Apollonius had had in mind, but that was a matter of pure conjecture. The piece that Dupin had played on that fatal night in the Rue d'Auseuil might well have been diabolical, but it had not been derived from the legendary text in question, or any other work of neo-Pythagorean mysticism.

"And what has the Louvre got to do with it?" I asked. "Why does Lacroix want you to meet him there?"

"Again, he's concealing his hand for the moment," Dupin told me, with a hint of chagrin, "but he wants me to meet him in the study of one of the curators of modern art, so I assume that it's a matter of a painting . . . or something found in a painting."

"*In* a painting?" I queried. The curator in question, I assumed, might have consulted Lacroix with regard to the image in a painting by one of the numerous artists with whom he had been acquainted in the heyday of Romanticism, but it was far more likely, given the Bibliophile's reputation, that it was a matter of a manuscript. It was not unknown—indeed, it was a game that had enjoyed a certain popularity in the last quarter of the previous century—for artists to secrete pieces of paper or parchment in a gap between the inverse of their canvas and a backing board nailed to the rectangular frame on which the canvas had been stretched. The curators at the

Louvre frequently removed such boards in order to reframe pictures, but most of the scribbled documents that they found were of no interest, and most of the rest were so transparent in their import that there was no need to consult an expert as to their significance.

"That's what his letter said," was Dupin's only reply. He sounded slightly irritated, as was understandable given that the weather was still cold and the night very dark—not an ideal night for chasing wild geese—but he was also resigned, having been unable to resist the bait that Lacroix had cunningly laid down. It seemed to me that Dupin and I were being given the worse part of the vigil, if Lacroix was going to keep his in a warm café in the Rue de l'Hirondelle, one of the back streets running parallel to the quay on the far side of the opulent town houses that lined it. The tangle of those streets was already partly demolished, and was surely scheduled to disappear as the city's slow but drastic modernization continued.

We had reached the quay, and I looked across the river in the direction of the Île Saint-Louis, whose aligned town-houses were even more pretentious, although they too formed a façade of sort, behind which were similar labyrinths of back-streets, similarly colonized by shabbier constructions and poorer folk, but currently undergoing a similar slow transfiguration in the direction of greater prosperity and respectability. The upper stories of the houses were visible above the low-lying mist accumulated over the river-water, but there were only occasional lighted windows, and the general impression was a trifle ghostly. There were lights on the river itself, of course, carried by the multitudinous barges moored at the various docking-stations along the watercourse, but they were mere dots in the fog, many of them blood-red, which made them seem sinister and predatory.

We took up a position near the middle of the quay, not far from the entrance to the Pont de la Tournelle, presumably north-east of what was left of the Rue de l'Hirondelle, the huddled houses of which were completely hidden by the much finer edifices whose facades were facing the quay.

Dupin took out his watch. "A few minutes to midnight," he said. "Lacroix's phenomenon, whatever it is, had better not be late. I'm not going to hang around for very long in this weather. On reflection, I shouldn't have dragged you out with me. I'm not convinced that you've completely recovered from the chill you caught in November. Such things tend to linger in winter."

"You caught it too," I pointed out. "I can't be at any more risk than you are."

"You were much worse," Dupin said, truthfully. "I didn't get wet, but you nearly drowned. If Lucien hadn't pulled you out of the river . . ."

Technically, I knew, it was Dupin and Chapelain who had pulled both of us out of the Seine, with the aid of a rope, while Lucien Groix had merely kept my head above the water, but I wasn't about to quibble. I was still deeply ashamed of the fact that I hadn't been able to save Jana Valdemar, who, I was firmly convinced, had gone into the river under some kind of hypnotic compulsion, and had not intended to drown herself, in spite of being pregnant and unwed—a combination of circumstances responsible for a good many Parisian suicides. I was still haunted by the recurrent thought that if I had only reached her two seconds earlier, or had been just a fraction stronger . . .

"It seems to me," I said, in order to change the subject, "that if Lacroix's informant heard whatever he heard in a café in the Rue de l'Hirondelle, our chances of hearing it from here aren't very strong. It's a crisp, clear night, but the sound waves would have to get through the houses on the Quai. Even if an instrument were being played in a room at the rear of one of those houses, we probably wouldn't be able to hear it from where we're standing."

"True," Dupin admitted, his eyes going to the roofs of the houses, some of which were mansards probably enclosing lofts that extended from the front of the building to the back with no substantial partition. Perhaps he was trying to calculate whether someone playing a violin in one of those attics, even with the skylights open, might be simultaneously audible in the Rue de l'Hirondelle and on the quay. It seemed unlikely, although not impossible. But why would anyone be playing a violin in a mansard in the Faubourg Saint-Victor, with the windows open, after midnight in February?

Church bells began to chime midnight, audible enough even though at least a dozen of them were much further away than the Rue de l'Hirondelle. The thought immediately occurred to me that I might have been stupid in automatically linking Lacroix's note with his curiosity about Abbé Apollonius and Erich Zann—but it seemed unlikely that it was the bells that we were expected to hear, given that they chimed every night, and had done so for years, similarly since the last Revolution but one had silenced the greater number of the church bells of Paris and transfigured the undisciplined cacophony of the remainder.

Dupin was listening to the bells too, but it was too dark for me to see whether the expression on his face might reveal a reaction. The moon was better than a sliver, the stars were visible through the usual atmospheric haze and the Quai was equipped with street-lamps, but the light was by no means good. The quay was deserted, and the Île Saint-Louis so seemingly dead that the Pont de la Tournelle gave the impression of a bridge over the Styx that ought to bear a Dantean warning notifying anyone reckless enough to set foot on it to abandon hope.

When the last stroke of midnight died away in the churches, it seemed to leave the air full of vibrations, inaudible by dint of being pitched too low for human hearing but nevertheless capable of stirring vibrations in the pulmonary cavity, seemingly surrounding the heart. I was straining my ears as intently as I could, but I couldn't hear anything else . . . even when Dupin suddenly gasped, grabbed my arm and pulled me along the quay.

We only went ten meters, but those ten meters made a considerable difference to the sonic ambience. Suddenly, I could hear something: the strains of a musical instrument of some kind. I realized that we were now stationed opposite a narrow gap between two of the large houses on the quay, and that the sound was coming through that gap, facilitated and focused by it. The gap itself was pitch black, with no hint of light beyond it, but I calculated that it might very well be extrapolated all the way to the topmost story at the rear of the houses on the Rue de l'Hirondelle, and that it was at least conceivable that the sounds might be coming from the house that Dupin called "the old witch-house," in which Paul Lacroix's informant had observed an unexpected presence two nights before.

"What is that instrum . . . ?" I started to ask, but Dupin motioned me urgently to silence.

"Listen!" he commanded.

I obeyed—and immediately wished that I hadn't. It wasn't the first time, by any means, that I had heard magical music; indeed, in recent months I appeared to have become something of a magnet for it. When I had heard Dupin play the music of Erich Zann in the Rue d'Auseuil, I had certainly been affected by it, but I had assumed thereafter that the effect had only lasted for as long as the diabolical violin was being played. Even the bizarre event in Baron Du Potet's garden, when I had actually played diabolical music myself on a haunted cello—or had been played *by* the entity possessing the cello—had not immediately changed my presumption. But when the pseudonymous Anton had played Blaise Thibodeaux's "gypsy fiddle" at the dance of the ghostly fays in the forest of Fontainebleau, and Thibodeaux's ghost had lectured me on the subject of temporal resonance and infection, I had begun to see things differently.

I wish I could say that I had *immediately* begun to see things differently, but that had not been possible. I could still remember a great deal of what Thibodeaux's ghost had said to me, as if it were engraved in the deep strata of my memory, but I had hardly begun to make sense of it.

"Time is not really a river," he had said, "and does not flow . . . but that is the way that we are bound to perceive it, as figments of consciousness, all the more so as figments of flesh. We have no manner of speaking about the eternals, except to call them eternal, and cannot understand how they have always been in existence, at least sporadically, and have always been active in our lives, at least sporadically, when they will not be born for billions of years, after an exceedingly long and difficult engineering of their own evolution. Timebound as we are, we can only take refuge in the illusions of coherency and fate . . . but we can take some comfort from the fact that the ultimate descendants of matter and life will be able to swim upstream, even if they are not directly descended from our own flesh and blood. They are interested in us nevertheless . . . they might in themselves be so tiny as to be beyond the range of our microscopes, but we have a role to play in their story . . . we have a resonance in their souls."

My unplanned dip in the Seine and the fever that I had developed subsequently had clouded my mind so drastically that weeks had passed before I was able to begin interrogating myself as to the significance of those gnomic utterances, and to imagine thematic connections between my various recent adventures with the exotic music underlying magic. I had not yet managed to bring any order into those thought-processes—not to the extent, at any rate, that I felt able to present my ideas to Dupin for discussion—but the moment I heard the notes of the stringed instrument washing over the Quai de la Tournelle from the direction of the Rue de l'Hirondelle, my instant reaction was that the music was intensely and dangerously magical, and that the magic in question was finding a strange resonance in me: a resonance that did not call forth any recognition or understanding, but was nevertheless profound . . . going to the deepest roots of my identity.

"Dupin . . ." I began, but he interrupted me with an atypical sharpness that suggested to me that he too must be sensing a resonance, and that it was an ominously disturbing resonance within his soul too.

"Listen, damn it!" he snapped.

I thought for a moment that he must want me to try to memorize the piece of music that was being played, but then he gestured with his hand in the direction of the Île Saint-Louis, and I realized that he wanted to draw my attention to the fact that a second instrument was being played, almost, but not quite, in unison with the first, the sound of which was coming from the other side of the river—not the other side of the Seine considered in its entirety, but the other side of the arm separating the Faubourg Saint-Victor from the island.

Again, I obeyed, and tried hard to remember what Erich Zann's music had sounded like when Dupin had played it. Were the unknown instrumentalists—if there were, in fact, two of them, and the second was not a literal echo of the first—playing the lost music of Erich Zann? I could not tell, but I dared not draw any conclusion from my incapacity.

On the other hand, it seemed to me to be quite plausible that the echo the music was producing in my own soul might well have something in common with the entity that Zann's music had seemed—if only in a hallucination—to be summoning from the atmosphere beyond the window of the mansard in the house in the Rue d'Auseuil: the entity that Dupin had named, albeit tentatively, as Nyarlathotep, the Crawling Chaos.

I listened, intently, trying in vain to make some sense of the spectral music, while possessed by an odd prickling sensation in my skin, akin to the one that people sometimes describe as "someone walking over my grave," and a far deeper sensation, spatially located somewhere in the vicinity of my heart . . . but not within my body, if that makes any sense. I was hearing the music with my ears and my brain, but I was feeling it in a part of myself that was unconfined by my flesh . . . a part of myself accessible to echoes from recent and remote time, mingling and overlapping in quest of a harmony that was not accessible . . . yet.

I could not determine whether that inaccessibility was due to faults in my organization or faults in the configuration of time itself . . . but in either case, I sensed that perception of the harmony was possible, if only my mind, or something else to which my mind was accessible, could reach out and grasp it.

I dared not make any further appeal to Dupin until I had something to communicate to him other than utter incomprehension and inexplicable anxiety. But I wanted to talk to him about it. I wanted to explain myself, if only I could make myself explicable . . . but as yet, I couldn't.

No more than twenty seconds went by before Dupin, who seemed suddenly agitated, squeezed my arm again, although the interval seemed much longer . . . and, if the phrase makes sense, much *deeper*.

"Reynolds," he said, in his most urgent tone. "I must head for the Rue de l'Hirondelle to try to pinpoint the apparent location of the first instrument. You must cross the Pont de la Tournelle, and try to pinpoint the location of the other, if there is time to do so."

I wanted to ask questions then, the door having apparently been opened to inquisition, but he did not give me the time. He literally shoved me in the direction of the bridge. I already knew that he felt a sense of unusual urgency, or he would not have used the word *must*, but he had only ever shoved me before when he believed someone's life to be in danger. I did not even think of hesitating to obey his order.

I set off at a rapid walk—I dared not run in such treacherous conditions—for the entrance to the bridge, with every intention of carrying out his instruction to the letter: which is to say, of crossing to the island, and then following the sound of the uncanny tune being played on the mysterious stringed instrument, and carefully taking note of the address from which the sound was coming, so that further investigation would become possible.

If only it had been that simple!

II

THE BRIDGE OF DARKNESS

ALL the bridges in Paris have street-lamps nowadays. In 1848, nearly twenty years after the first gas lamps had been established in the Place du Carrousel, the old Argand burners had been replaced throughout the principal thoroughfares of the more prosperous quarters. The Pont de la Tournelle was not supposed to be dark at midnight, and had there been an accidental failure of the gas supply, oil lamps should have been placed without delay to make up the deficit. But that night, by virtue of some simultaneous dereliction of equipment and duty, there was no light in the middle of the bridge. Both ends were illuminated, but the center of the span was pure shadow, darker even than the mist-shrouded water flowing beneath it, which was catching fugitive glimmers of light from the quays and the stars, as well as the lanterns of the moored boats.

I did not hesitate, of course, but I did slow down even further, knowing as I did that a collision with the stone parapet of the bridge—all too easily contrived in the darkness by a slight deviation in my stride—would be painful, and might occasion a fall. I avoided any such false step, but by the time I was at the mid-point of the span my stride, although not exactly querulous, was not as bold as I could have wished. I had begun to feel that the bridge was, indeed, a bridge of darkness, that it was not merely separating two quarters of Paris but two worlds. Naturally, I told myself sternly that it was a silly illusion, and that I had merely been spooked by the strange music, which was still audible, albeit very faintly . . . but I did not believe my attempted self-reassurance.

The river, inevitably, tends to channel any air current that might be blowing, however slight, and hence carries an extra chill of its own, so I was not unduly surprised when I suddenly felt an icy gust on the right side of my face. I looked along the stream, reflexively, and had the illusion that a big ship was making slow progress upriver, shrouded by the mist—but I told myself that it had to be an illusion, because no ship of that size would be able to come so far up the river until the much-discussed canal permitting the construction of the "Paris Seaport" was dug, even allowing for the fact that objects perceived in mist often seem magnified, and because any real ship would have been displaying the obligatory beacon light, whereas this one was dark except for a central splash of yellow light shaped like a crucifix.

I believed that dismissal by defensive consciousness, but alarm grabbed me nevertheless, and horribly, a mere second later, when the literal chill of the slight breeze was direly confused with a metaphorical one, and I saw the ghost.

It was by no means the first ghost I had seen, but when I had seen the others I had not been in any position to give any deep or complicated attention to the metaphysical implications of the existence and nature of ghosts of different kinds, including the cruel question of whether they have any objective existence at all, or whether they are entirely a product of the mind—deluded, bewitched or merely dreaming—of the beholder. This time, inevitably, it was different.

The first thing of which I took clinical note was that, however paradoxical it might seem, I really could see her. She wasn't glowing, so she wasn't emitting a light of her own, and she didn't seem to be reflecting the starlight from the sky and the gaslight of the city, as the river mist was, albeit feebly; nevertheless, I could see her. I told myself that it must be with my mind's eye rather than my physical eyes that I was seeing her, but I still couldn't convince myself. The normal discriminations of my consciousness seemed suddenly to have broken down . . . something terrifying in itself, implying a commencement—or an intensification—of insanity. But however it was occurring, I could see her, and I recognized her instantly as Jana Valdemar.

Absurdly, all I could think of to say, as I stopped dead, was: "You have no reason to haunt me. I tried to save you."

"I know," the ghost replied.

"I did everything I could," I said. "I'm truly sorry that it wasn't good enough."

"I know," she said.

Apparently, I thought, absurdly, *rumor can be trusted and the dead do know everything—or think they do.* "Then why haunt me?" I demanded.

"Wrong question," she said, tersely.

She was right, of course. I knew that, really, but it had been pointed out to me before, and not just by Dupin, that I am sometimes a little slow to get a secure mental grip even on things that are not unprecedented. I knew that I ought to be asking her the kind of questions that Dupin would have asked her, in order to prompt some valuable revelation, but my mind was utterly confused. Even so, I tried to collect myself.

The right question, I thought—unsure whether it was absurd or not—was not why she was haunting me, because it was surely not a matter of desire or decision on her part, but *why was I seeing her?* Guilt, my earlier questions suggest-ed—except that I wasn't really guilty of anything. I really had tried to save her, and I really had done my best. Nobody else present had even seemed to realize that she was in danger in time to do as much. But that explanation was superficial, a matter of psychology, a hook on which the apparition could hang itself. The fact that I was dreaming while awake—hallucinating, in the modern jargon—was easily accountable in those terms. The real enigma was metaphysical; how could another individual, a dead individual, be manifesting herself within my dream?

Having no bodies, their material dust having returned to dust, the only existence the dead can retain is a dream identity; that is the only stuff of which they can be made. Within that strange existence, however, discontinuous in time and space, consciousness apparently remains potentially possible, if only parasitically. Jana Valdemar was, in a perfectly literal sense, all in my mind, visible and audible only because she could draw vampirically in the resources of my imagination, contained within my blood and brain. And yet, like Blaise Thibodeaux at Fontainebleau, she did exist; in collaboration with a seer—or, in the terms of another jargon, in *resonance* with a seer—she remained an entity of sorts, capable of action and purpose.

But what purpose? And with what motivation?

"You've come to warn me," I guessed. "Something terrible is going to happen."

"Not necessarily," she told me—logically enough, as the whole point of a warning, if in fact she had come to issue one, is to try to avert terrible things that might happen. On the other hand, the phraseology strongly suggested that something terrible might indeed be about to happen, and that the odds were against my being able to prevent it.

"What do I need to do?" I asked, swiftly.

"Be careful," she advised, unhelpfully.

"Of what?" I countered, as we seemed to be embracing terseness.

"Of the music. Of your state of mind. Of the Dwellers of the Threshold. Of the book, especially. Most of all, of the dreamer of R'lyaieh. Remember what you have seen and done, and try to make use of what you have learned."

If the dead did know everything, I thought, then she might well be thinking about what I had seen and learned in the forest of Fontainebleau, but that was by no means the only extraordinary thing I had seen in recent months, and given that it was her who came to give me the warning it was possible that she had in mind something I had once seen, or thought I had seen, in her presence. She had referred back to that particular hallucination before, insistently, not long before her drowning. She had looked to me for support in regard to the memory of the confidence trick she had tried to play, which had backfired. She had seen, or believed she had seen, an entity she called the Dweller with the Eyes of Fire, which allegedly lurks on the threshold of space, lying in wait for those who aspire to transcend its limits. She was convinced that I had seen it too—as, in fact, I had, although I had previously been convinced that what I saw was nothing more than a product of my own deluded imagination, deliberately provoked by her. Since then, I had learned that the distinction between reality and hallucination is not nearly as clear as we could wish—as further evidenced by the fact that I was standing in the middle of the Pont de la Tournelle conversing with a ghost that I could see in the dark, grappling fervently with the metaphysical enigma of its existence.

"I'm imagining this," I told her, positively, although I did not reach out, as I could have done, to test her apparent materiality. "Is it an effect of the music?" Again, it was the wrong question, but this time, she didn't pause to point it out.

"Of course it is," she said instead. "Did you think you could hear Dupin play the music of Erich Zann in the Rue d'Auseuil, and look into the Crawling Chaos, without something of Nyarlathotep infecting your soul permanently? How else would you have been able to thwart the egregore in Du Potet's garden? The stars are wrong, alas, and, vast as the Ocean is, currents travel through the earth, as well as through time, by strangely sinuous paths. Time and space are one, and resonance is ubiquitous, here as in R'lyaieh. You are an instrument, who can and must be played—but you have free will, unlike a passive dulcimer. You can suppress, deflect or pervert the resonance, if you are clever enough and strong enough."

My instant reaction, of course, was to wonder whether I could possibly be clever enough or strong enough; it was not simple modesty that made my frightened mind howl reflexively that the answer was negative.

I had never seen the copy of the *Harmonies de l'enfer* that Dupin had once possessed, but I had tried very conscientiously to read his copy of Blaise Thibodeaux's *Resonances du temps*, and to understand the brief commentary on the text that Dupin had offered at Fontainebleau. I had also read the copy of *The Mad Trist* that Saint-Germain had once asked me to give to Dupin, and which Dupin had refused to accept, giving it instead to Stephen Coningsby, a bibliophile even more avid than himself and Paul Lacroix. I had even encountered agents of "the dreamer in R'lyaieh" and had almost come into contact with the copy of the *Necronomicon* owned by the Breton sorcerer who called himself Oberon Breisz. In consequence, I was by no means unacquainted with forbidden and forbidding texts, and I knew full well that I was not clever enough even to begin to make any sense of them. As for strength, my contribution to the crisis that our little company had experienced when we confronted shoggoths in the stone circle near Oberon Breisz's house, and the near-disaster that had overtaken another party in the bowels of Mont Dragon, had been negligible. I could not recall a single instance in which my wit or my muscles had prevailed over hostile forces. My qualifications as a hero seemed conspicuously lacking. Fate seemed to have cast me in the role of the eternal bystander, always present but never in control.

While that discomfiting thought was flashing through my mind I also remembered something else that Jana Valdemar had told me during the long day of All Hallows' Eve: that reading *The Mad Trist*, in defiance of Stephen Coningsby's urgent advice, had put a curse on me without my being consciously aware of it. Was it possible, I wondered, that Blaise Thibodeaux's book had also infiltrated some sort of awareness or sensibility into my unconscious mind even while the text was boring and bewildering my consciousness half to death? Was that curse now operating upon me, producing or shaping this bizarre encounter?

That seemed only too probable, in the light of the thesis likening supposed magic to François Raspail's theory of infection, which Dupin had seemed to endorse at Fontainebleau. Although I might have recovered completely, or very nearly, from my influenza, I certainly had not recovered from all the other infections of my mind and soul I had encountered on that and other recent occasions.

I shuddered at the reckless phraseology of my internal monologue, thinking that I must, indeed, be in the preliminary throes of insanity, in the dangerous borderland between the comfortable citadel of consciousness and the awful wilderness of the dream-dimensions. I deliberately turned my gaze away from the ghost, but that did not help; there was far too much mist in the vicinity, and the glimpse that I caught of a distant beacon shaped like a crucifix provided no reassurance at all.

I pulled myself together, making every effort to assert the authority of my rationality. It worked—or seemed to.

"Are you going to haunt me routinely from now on?" I said to the ghost, not entirely sure whether I was really asking myself whether I was going to imagine myself being haunted by her from now on. "Are we bound together now because I tried to save your life?"

"Who can tell?" she said.

Obviously, I thought, *either the dead don't know everything, or they sometimes delight in provocative teasing.* The latter possibility seemed all too plausible to me.

"Can't you?" I riposted.

"Wrong question," she said, again, regretfully rather than teasingly, and disappeared, leaving me in total darkness, save for a few stars, a sprinkling of moonlight and the gas-lamp at the far end of the bridge, which suddenly seemed to be another ardent but deceptive beacon in a vast murky abyss.

The music was no longer audible, even faintly.

Was it possible, I wondered, that the whole and only purpose of the hallucinatory encounter had been to interrupt my attempt to carry out Dupin's instruction and pinpoint the source of the mysterious nocturne? If so, whose purpose could it be? The musician's? The dead Jana Valdemar's? It seemed far more likely that my own treacherous unconscious mind was playing tricks on me.

My attempted reasoning was, of course, polluted by my conviction, firm by then, that any man who has once been touched by the Crawling Chaos carries an infection that ought to prevent him ever from trusting himself again. Otherwise, I might have been able to find better questions and better answers. As things were, my ability to think was being severely hampered by the fact that my feet were exceedingly cold. Standing still was not doing them any good; I needed to move. Quilted jackets can only preserve body heat if one takes care to generate it, metabolically rather than diabolically.

I turned round promptly and headed back toward the left bank, which also had an ardent but possibly-deceptive beacon, as swiftly as I dared. I cursed myself as I went, but I wasn't at all sure why. What had I done wrong, if anything? What else could I possibly have done, in the circumstances? Dupin, I felt sure, would probably be able to think of something, but Dupin always could—after the fact, at least.

I turned right on to the quay and then left into the first side-street leading south-west, hoping that it might bring me to the western end of the Rue de l'Hirondelle, and that I would be able to identify it if it did. There were street-lamps there, but not many, and it was unfamiliar territory. I assumed that the café where Lacroix was probably keeping vigil would be illuminated, but I could not take that for granted; nor could I assume that I would be able to find a junction from which it would be visible.

Because of that uncertainty, I was rather relieved at first when I saw someone coming along the street toward me, although that is not the usual emotional response to seeing a tall, burly, black-clad, long-striding stranger approaching at half past midnight, even in a quarter of Paris that is not Montmartre or Belleville. In spite of the gloom I could see that he seemed to be strangely but not poorly dressed, wearing a capacious loose black cloak, a wide-brimmed hat and sturdy boots of the kind necessary to keep one safe when the footing is treacherous.

His gait gave the impression of what Parisian slang calls a "matamore"—literally, a Moor-slayer in the legendary mold of the old crusaders, but metaphorically, a strutting aristocratic swashbuckler of a type obsolete since the abdication of Charles X—but he did not seem to be wearing a sword beneath his cloak. As he approached, though, I realized that I could see his eyes, which I should not have been able to do, given that they were shadowed by his hat. There was something about them reminiscent of the eyes of nocturnal animals that collect poor light with extraordinary facility and glow in consequence.

Given my state of mind, it was only natural that my first thought was that he might be another ghost, but I could hear the muted clicking of his heels as they struck the icy ground, which seemed to indicate that he was possessed of solidity. I made a movement toward him, intending to invite him respectfully to pause in order that I could ask him for directions, but when our gazes met momentarily I changed my mind instantly, and instead of trying to make him pause I veered sideways in order to give him plenty of room to pass by—which he did, although his swirling cloak brushed the edge of my overcoat very lightly. Not a word was exchanged, and our reciprocal glance was very swift, but still I felt intimidated by the glimpse, suddenly glad that I had not engaged him in conversation.

I paused in my stride momentarily, a trifle dazed, and I saw that the matamore was not the only pedestrian in the street; there was another shadow on the far side, going in the same direction as the man with the strange gaze, perhaps following him at a respectful distance. I could not make out any details of his appearance, but I judged by his furtive gait that it could not be Dupin or Lacroix.

That all happened in a matter of a few seconds. At the time, my reaction was automatic and irreflective; it was only a little while later, attempting to analyze what had happened, that it seemed to me that when our eyes had met, the big man's uncanny gaze had seemed to look *into* me, commandingly rather than inquiringly, exerting a mesmeric power.

In juxtaposition with what Jana Valdemar's ghost had said, that gaze reminded me, inevitably, of the Dweller with the Eyes of Fire, and I could not help wondering, in consequence, whether the Pont de la Tournelle had brought me far too close to the strange borderland separating our world from the dream-dimensions, and whether I had returned completely to the world that ever-anxious human consciousness is pleased to define as "real."

I continued on my way, though, and from the next corner, I saw the reassuringly ordinary vision of the illuminated windows of a café, for which I immediately headed, almost at a run in spite of the difficulty and the danger posed by such recklessness.

III

THE BIBLIOPHILE'S STORY

DUPIN and Lacroix were inside the café, with a table all to themselves. The only other customers in what passed for the narrow "hall" of the establishment were three men, sitting at a table next to one of the windows with a dark-haired young woman, who glanced at me briefly, perhaps with a momentary glimmer of optimism, before seeing me exchange familiar gestures with Lacroix and Dupin and turning back to her companions, who did not appear to be paying any heed to me. My gaze did not linger on her once my mind had categorized her as a common prostitute, a certain reflexive prudery forcing me to look away and refusing to find her truly attractive, in spite of her youth, her seemingly flawless complexion, her dark eyes and her lush black hair.

I joined Dupin and Lacroix, after opening my mouth to ask the old woman at the counter for a cup of hot mulled wine—which she poured immediately from a saucepan, clearly having anticipated the order, presumably having been informed of my imminent advent by Dupin.

"Well?" said Dupin. I could tell from his tone that he was not expectant.

"I wasn't able to identify the precise source of the music," I told him, simply. I didn't mention having seen a ghost, partly because I was embarrassed by the interpretation that Dupin might put on my being haunted by Jana Valdemar, and partly because I had been warned to be careful; although Lacroix was a good friend of Dupin's, his keen interest in infernal harmonies had always made him slightly suspect in my eyes. All bibliomaniacs have a hint of danger about them, and it was not unknown for the booksellers of Paris to bracket Lacroix—and Dupin himself, for that matter—with the likes of Stephen Coningsby and Oberon Breisz, with whom my brief contacts had been greatly conducive to mistrust.

"Nor was I," said Dupin, gruffly. "Did you cross the path of the man who came out of the witch-house? He turned in your direction."

"I crossed the path of a man," I admitted. "I had no way of knowing where he had come from. His eyes caught a stray gleam of light which made them seem oddly feline as well as mesmeric, although he walked like an old-fashioned bravo. I gave him a wide berth. Who was he?"

"I have no idea," Dupin said.

"Nor I," Lacroix put in.

"Did you speak to him?" I asked

"No," said Dupin. "I tried, but . . . well, to say that he cut me dead would be an oversimplification. I only caught the merest glimpse of his face, almost as if he were hiding it from me, and I did not see his eyes."

"I thought he was a ghost, at first," Lacroix said, "clicking Spanish heels and all."

"He seemed solid enough to me," I told him, a trifle uneasily. I made a more concerted attempt to recall exactly what had transpired during the glance we had exchanged, which had somehow forbidden me to speak, or even to think, but nothing else sprang to mind, except for one peripheral datum, which I felt obliged to report to Dupin. "Somebody appeared to be following him, though."

"I saw that," said Dupin. "And I'm sure that the fellow with the big hat was no ghost, in spite of his furtive manner and old-fashioned attire. I rather suspect, in fact, that he might have been here for the same reason as us—as a phantom-hunter. He evidently has ordinary access to the witch-house, as he locked the door with a key when he came out, but I doubt that he was the person playing the viol."

"Are you sure, Dupin, that it was a viol?" Lacroix asked. Obviously, I had arrived before they had had time for an elaborate comparison of impressions, and I presumed that Dupin had not yet confirmed Lacroix's suspicion that the music was supernatural—if, indeed, he had drawn that conclusion from what we had heard—or embarked upon any elaborate discussion as to what that conclusion might imply.

"Not entirely," said Dupin, "but it was not a mere gypsy fiddle operated by some idle dilettante. What alternative can you suggest?"

"A rebec," said Lacroix.

"Have you ever seen a rebec or heard one played?" Dupin asked him, skeptically.

"No," Lacroix admitted, "but someone who claimed to be an expert once told me that the fragments of the *Harmonies de l'enfer* that he had learned to play on a violin must have been scored originally for a rebec . . . not implausibly, given the antiquity of the volume in question."

"And who was this supposed expert?" asked Dupin, with the same hint of conscientious skepticism. I concluded that he was trying to draw Lacroix out without giving anything away himself, with his customary parsimony.

"I don't know his real name," Lacroix said, "but he called himself Doctor Prospero. He played in theater orchestras in the Boulevard du Temple back in 1830, immediately prior to the July Revolution. He nearly lost his violin in a fire at the old Moineaux because he was helping Blaise Thibodeaux to get out—Thibodeaux had arthritis even then, and the Moineaux's staircase was rickety—but it was saved, and he played it for me."

Dupin frowned. "I once met the man in question," he said. "He struck me as a charlatan of much the same breed as Saint-Germain, but the judgment might have been hasty. He came to see me asking questions about Erich Zann, looking for samples of his music."

"Which you didn't give him," Lacroix suggested, accusingly.

"Which I didn't have," Dupin said. "All of Zann's handwritten scores were destroyed, before or after his death."

"That's not what rumor says, and not what Prospero believed," said the Bibliophile, provocatively.

"Rumor is a notorious liar," Dupin said, equably.

"Is it also a liar when it says that you played Zann's music on his own violin in the house at the top of the Rue Auseuil on the night when it collapsed?" Lacroix said, combatively. "From memory, no doubt, if it's true that no written scores survived?"

"That's not exactly what happened," said Dupin, evasively. "Suffice it to say that Zann's violin went the same way as his sheet music. It no longer exists, and couldn't be the instrument that we heard tonight."

"Much like a Neapolitan cello that some unknown person played at one of Du Potet's soirées on the night someone died there? I presume that that wasn't Erich Zann's composition, though, any more than what we just heard?" Lacroix continued, still playing the game of provocation aggressively. "Come on, Dupin, I've always known that you know far more about the harmonies of Hell than you pretend. It's time to come clean, now that I have a *quid pro quo* to offer you for the information."

"A few snatches of a tune played on a stringed instrument, the origin of which, in spite of both our efforts, we have been unable to locate, or even identify, and which we have no reason to suspect to be connected with *Les Harmonies de l'enfer*?"

"More than that, as you'll see at the Louvre tomorrow. I couldn't bring the parchment away, obviously—I'm lucky that Fernichat permitted me to see it—but it's very old, and although he couldn't make head nor tail of what appears to have been written on the palimpsest before it was overwritten, any more than he could understand what was inscribed on it after the erasure, I believe that I've seen that notation before. I recognized it for what it was, because I have a sample of something similar, copied by my own hand."

"From the *Harmonies de l'enfer*?" Dupin queried, skeptically.

"Of a similar ilk. It's something I copied from a manuscript fragment of Prospero's back in 1830—something he claimed to be the authentic tune of the *danse macabre*. I was writing my novel about it at the time, if you remember."

"I remember," said Dupin. "Not your best work, in my opinion. Did Prospero share your theory that the *danse macabre* was a real dance, composed by a traveling player named, or nicknamed, Macabre?"

"He was evasive—almost as evasive as you—but yes, he was certainly prepared take it seriously, although he de-Frenchified the name and proposed that the player in question might have been an Englishman like himself, nicknamed Will Maccabee, *maccabee* being a slang term for a cadaver."

"But what you heard tonight, and the night before last, wasn't Prospero's supposed *danse macabre*?"

"No, it wasn't. I'm certain that my memory can be trusted to that extent."

"Which is why you fell back on your second-best flight of fancy, the *Harmonies* of Apollonius?"

"Very well," Lacroix conceded, "let's call it a flight of fancy. But the music is real: you heard it, and so did Reynolds. And the palimpsest is real too, as you'll see tomorrow. Whether there's any connection between the two, I don't know, but I knew Blaise Thibodeaux well enough, in his final years, always to be looking for connections in coincidence. You know, I suppose, that he singled out 1848 as a potentially important and eventful year some fifteen years ago?"

"Yes," said Dupin. "And you doubtless had an opportunity to see and discuss the notes he made for the unfinished second volume of the *Resonances du temps* even before they ended up stuffed in a cupboard in the vaults of the Harmonic Society, so you probably know more about his ultimate ideas than the little he communicated to me—but tell me honestly, do you really take his theories entirely seriously?"

"Not entirely," Lacroix admitted. "There's far too much crammed into his notes, too many trivia obfuscating the kernel of significant truth—but I don't dismiss the basic thesis as nonsense. Do you?"

"No," Dupin admitted, unable to say anything different after the Day of the Dead, even though, so far as I knew, I was the only one who had seen Thibodeaux's ghost, while he had simply listened to Saint-Germain's flights of fancy and the gypsy fiddle played by the Comte's mysterious coachman, "but the trouble with theories like his is that they can be stretched to encompass almost everything. It's too generous in admitting possibilities and making dubious connections."

"Perhaps—but something strange is definitely going on. One mysterious instrument playing in the vicinity of the old witch-house is peculiar; another instrument, similar if not identical, echoing it on the Île Saint-Louis is positively sinister."

"Playing *in the vicinity* of the witch-house, you say?" I queried.

"Yes," Lacroix replied. "My informant told me that it was coming from the house, but when I heard it the night before last, my impression was that it wasn't coming from the skylights of the uppermost floor, but from somewhere beyond the house. That's why I told Dupin to go to the Quai de la Tournelle while I came back here . . . but he followed its apparent origin here, and when the music stopped, we saw the man come out of the witch-house. I'm no longer sure where the instrument was being played." Addressing Dupin, he added: "We ought to have followed the man who came out of the witch-house, even if it meant abandoning Reynolds."

"Perhaps so," said Dupin, "but he seemed very disinclined to speak to us, and he could have given us the slip easily enough on a night like this, even if he had no particularly expertise in evasion. I suspect that the man who left the café in order to follow him won't find it easy to track him. Did you see which way they went, Reynolds?"

"Not exactly, but the burly fellow seemed to be heading for the river."

"For the Pont de la Tournelle?"

"Possibly. How do I know? What is this so-called witch-house to which he has a key?"

Dupin looked at the Bibliophile, leaving it to his expertise to provide the answer. "One of the many supposedly haunted houses of Old Paris," Lacroix said. "Rumor had it that a beautiful female vampire was resident there for a while at the beginning of the last century, during the Regency, who lured young men to their doom. There were the usual tales of secret underground passages beneath the cellars, but the historical records I've consulted show that the house was raided and searched by the Duc d'Orléans' police, who found no sign of any diabolical or murderous activity, and asserted that the cellar floors were absolutely solid. The alleged lamia had vanished or fled, as such creatures invariably do when identified—so legend has it."

"Is there anything in the documents relating to the house about strange music?" Dupin asked.

"Yes. The vampire allegedly employed diabolical music as an aid to luring her victims—but that's standard siren lore, associated since time immemorial with such myths . . . as you know very well, if you and Reynolds really did encounter a siren of sorts at Du Potet's garden party."

We did know it very well, and we had every reason to take it seriously, especially after our bizarre experience in the

Ardèche, when we had heard the very different but possibly kindred siren song of the Flameflower. That, Dupin was convinced, had been an entirely natural phenomenon . . . but Dupin was fond of saying that everything that happened, no matter how strange, had to be reckoned natural, and had to be explicable in rational terms. Personally, I thought that if the assertion were to be sustained, it required the definition of the words "natural" and "explicable" to be twisted out of all recognition.

Again, Dupin ignored the invitation that Lacroix had offered him to tell him the truth about what had happened in Du Potet's garden, so far as he knew it. "Is there any indication in the documents of where the alleged lamia might have come from, or where she went?" he asked, instead.

"Not in the contemporary documents," Lacroix said, with a slight sigh, "but you know full well that the episode in question wasn't the first such report to reach the files of the Sûreté, nor the last. The most recent local panic was during the Consulate, and was said to have been hushed up by one of Lucien Groix's predecessors. I asked him about it once, but he dismissed it as nonsense—although he might give you a different story."

"I doubt it," said Dupin. "In any case, Lucien is apparently no longer in Paris, and unlikely to return any time soon—officially, at least. He's an assiduous policeman, so it wouldn't be at all surprising if he were involved in some clandestine operation, given the current turbulent political climate, possibly keeping the upstart Bonaparte under surveillance while he's relentlessly scheming, but I really have no idea where he is. In any case, what we heard didn't seem to me to be a siren song intended to lure anyone, and surely didn't last long enough to have any such effect."

"I don't know about that," I put in, uneasily. "Merely the rumor of it lured us, didn't it?"

"A lamia specializing in luring antiquarians and scholars would be unusual," Lacroix observed, with a smile that seemed oddly sinister in the candlelight. He looked around, his gaze passing over the proprietress sitting behind the counter sipping a cup of her own mulled wine—a perfect personification of boredom—and inevitably settling, albeit briefly, on the black-haired young woman drinking with three taciturn men who seemed to me to resemble Montmartrean Apaches strayed from their home turf. They appeared to be paying no attention to us, but I knew better than to trust that appearance, especially given Dupin's remark that a fourth man had left the café to follow the man with the broad-brimmed hat, and the fact that their table by the window gave them a clear view of the so-called witch-house.

"But you told me in your letter that this is a literary café," Dupin remarked. "Although there seems to be a conspicuous dearth of poets here tonight, surely they have always been numbered among the favorite victims of supernatural seduction, at least in their own mythology."

"This isn't the kind of place where Gautier, Esquiros or Alphonse Karr would hang out nowadays," Lacroix said. "Things have gone a long way downhill since the old days. The Romanticism of the cenacles isn't dead, but it's certainly going hungry at present. Even Dumas is complaining of being desperately hard-up—although he always does, if only as an excuse for short-changing poor devils like me who draft the work he signs. But you're right about the unusual lack of custom . . . although it is late and the nights have been bitter recently. I'm sorry to have dragged you out for such thin pickings, Dupin—I hope to make up for it tomorrow. The manuscript will certainly interest you, even if you can't make any more sense of its various scripts than I can. With luck, Fernichat will have been able to make a clean copy of the overwritten script by now, even though he can't understand it."

"What is the painting in which it was found?" I put in, curiously.

"Much more recent than the palimpsest," the Bibliophile judged, "definitely late eighteenth century, painted not long prior to the 1789 Revolution, during the aftermath of which it appears to have been seized or looted by robbers posing as Revolutionaries, probably part of Hoche's rabble, and subsequently deposited in the Louvre as part of a consignment of art-works recovered by what passed for police under the Directoire. The batch included a couple of Fragonards—but it's definitely not his, or Chardin's; it's a dilettante effort, in my judgment: a picture of a nondescript house in a nondescript landscape, probably Breton—there are megaliths in the background. Unusual in being nocturnal—the sky is moonless, but dotted with stars. I can't recognize the constellations, if they're nor merely random dots, but you might, Dupin. Look, I'm sorry to have brought you out on a wild goose chase, but I have to get back. I'll see you tomorrow. Give my apologies to the dragon for keeping you out so late in such filthy weather. I can do without her casting spells on me—she's never liked me, you know." He meant Madame Lacuzon.

"She's never liked anyone except Dupin," I observed. "She barely tolerates me, even though she's living in my house for the time being."

"Rather you than me," said Lacroix. "You didn't invite her to take up residence last time Dupin was staying with you, as I recall?"

"She's been ill," I said. "A severe dose of sickness from which she was very fortunate to recover, and then a touch of the influenza that Dupin and I contracted at the end of October. Dupin didn't feel that we could leave her alone in her lodge in the Rue Dunot. People call her a witch and a dragon, but she's simply old, and lucky to be alive after what she's been through. I'm not sure that her spell-casting days are over, but I doubt that she'd waste any such effort on the likes of you or me."

"You might yet have cause to be glad that she's in the house," Dupin observed, ominously, "if things go from bad to worse, as they seem to be doing. She's old, but she's a woman of great resource, and she has knowledge handed down from her forebears that hasn't yet crept into the most esoteric of scholarly texts."

I had never understood Dupin's peculiar relationship with his concierge, which seemed far more intimate than their apparent association warranted. My own housekeeper was allegedly her cousin, but she had never given me any indication that she knew why Madame Lacuzon was so fiercely protective of Dupin.

Lacroix had stood up and extended his hand to be shaken. We took it, in turn, and bid him good night, separating from him at the door of the café. I glanced back at the establishment's other patrons, and saw the presumed prostitute, idle for the time being, make a swift gesture with her right hand, elevating the index-finger and the little finger to make the sign of "the devil's horns." I couldn't be certain whether it was aimed at Dupin or me, but I had my suspicions. I had seen it leveled at Madame Lacuzon more than once, and it would not have been in the least surprising if some of her reputation had rubbed off on her protégée. But how could the clientele of a small establishment in the Faubourg Saint-Victor know who any of us was?

Dupin seemed determined to be his usual taciturn self as we set forth to walk home—usual, that is, when he had no relevant erudition to display—but I soon risked a prompt. "That music was definitely unearthly," I said to him. "Lacroix thought so too, obviously, even though he was being a trifle cagey."

"Obviously," Dupin agreed, but he didn't seem to be in a mood to elaborate. That annoyed me somewhat, and didn't incline me to be any more forthcoming myself. Two I thought, could play at that game—three if we included Lacroix. I was also reluctant to admit that it had frightened me, doubly so since I had so recently accused myself of neither being clever nor brave, and was reluctant to confirm the judgment.

"If you don't think that the man you saw coming out of the witch-house was the person playing the music we heard," I said, cautiously, "what do you suppose he was doing there? How could he have a key to the house?"

"I wish I knew," was Dupin's only reply. "I'm sure that I've never seen him before, and so was Lacroix, but that's not surprising, as his clothing and his manner suggest strongly that he's no Parisian, without offering any clues to a specific origin. What you said about his eyes, on the other hand . . ." He broke off, but only momentarily. "Lacroix says that he didn't notice anything in Thibodeaux's notes relating to the Rue de l'Hirondelle in connection with the year 1848, but I doubt that he looked very attentively and it was a long time ago. I might have to visit the Harmonic Society's archives, in spite of the risk of being mistaken by the police for a conspirator in league with Lamartine. Lacroix is under surveillance, as you know, and since his abrupt resignation, Lucien can't be in any position to shield me from his over-zealous colleagues."

A thought occurred to me. "Is it possible," I asked him, "that the three men at the other table in the café were police spies?"

Dupin sniffed. "Proverbial wisdom has it that whenever three men sit down in a Parisian café nowadays, two are police spies and the third a fool. One or more of those at the window might have been honest, but I've seen one of them before, and you probably noticed the signal the woman gave me as we left. That's one of Lucien's tricks, but I have no way of knowing whether his successor has inherited its use, or whether the young woman knows what Lucien's present situation is, relative to the labyrinthine disorganization of the Sûreté."

"But either way, you think agents of the police are watching the witch-house?"

"I can't even be absolutely certain about that. They might have followed Lacroix there on his first visit and lain in wait for him—but he's a very minor cog in the Republican machine, and sending a whole pack of bloodhounds after him seems like ludicrous overkill. The likelihood is that they were, indeed, posted there to watch the house. They were playing the part of layabouts, but the young woman seemed less than half-hearted in playing her role as a whore in quest of custom. The probability that they're police agents, and not very well-disguised, would explain the conspicuous absence tonight of the café's usual clientele."

I didn't have to ask why agents of the political police might be watching the mysterious house, allegedly haunted houses always being a popular meeting-place for political conspirators. In any case, Lamartine and Lacroix were far from being the only Romantic poets up to their necks in Republican conspiracies, and the vicinity of a literary café might have attracted attention even without Lacroix's visit.

"Why did you ask Lacroix about spectral music?" I queried, instead. "Do you think the viol, or rebec, or whatever, was being played by a ghost?"

"No," he said. "I'm prepared to assume that it was being played by a human hand—but I'm not entirely convinced that it was being played in the present, let alone inside the so-called witch-house. In view of our recent experiences, I can't rule out the possibility that what we heard might have been what Thibodeaux calls a transtemporal echo—or perhaps two transtemporal echoes. Thibodeaux seems to have been expecting a convergence of such echoes this year, and his record as a prophet can't be reckoned negligible, given what happened on the Day of the Dead. I'll have to consult his notes at the Harmonic Society myself, given that Lacroix doesn't know what we know."

"You could tell him," I pointed out.

"True," Dupin agreed, in a tone that suggested that he had no intention of doing any such thing, unless necessity gave him a shove.

I could have told him about my encounter on the Pont de la Tournelle, and I even thought that I ought to do so, but I was still hesitant and couldn't yet feel the imperative impulsion of necessity. Instead, I started thinking privately about the thesis to which Dupin had just draw attention.

Evidently, I could hardly dismiss that thesis out of hand, having been in conversation with a ghostly echo only an hour before, and having been present at an extravagant ghostly dance only a few months ago. And had not Jana Valdemar's ghost, which had no reason at all to wish me ill, been very careful to tell me to beware of resonance, while apparently delaying me in my mission to identify the source of one of the alleged transtemporal echoes? Perhaps it was better to wait until I had had an opportunity to think about what had happened at leisure.

The chance, as they say, would have been a fine thing.

IV

THREE VISITORS

BY the time I got home I was exhausted, and the chill of the night seemed to have seeped into the marrow of my bones; evidently, the aftermath of my influenza had left me weak, and lack of exercise while I had been virtually confined to the house for two months had not helped my muscles to recover their elasticity. I wanted to think seriously about ghosts and temporal resonance, and their possible relevance to the music that was haunting the witch-house, but I was literally incapable of doing so. I simply went to bed, huddled as warmly as I could contrive to do in my blankets, and soon fell unconscious—I do not say "asleep" because I am certain that, in spite of all the provocations my mind had received, I did not dream. It was almost as if my consciousness went to hiding, hunkering down more fearfully than it had done by day under the threat of Revolution. If the crawling chaos that had infected my being was about to make itself felt, my mind seemed to be all set to make an attempt to withstand the siege.

In the morning, not unnaturally, I slept late, and Madame Bihan brought me coffee in bed, accompanied by what was passing for bread at the time, although it was more like "prison bread" in my opinion. The post-Revolutionary reform of the legal Code intended to protect the poor from hunger fixed the price of bread and specified the weight of loaves, but the unintended consequence of that mathematical regulation had been that when times were hard and wheat flour was in short supply, the bakers of Paris employed all manner of substitutes to stretch it—imaginative improvisations that began with barley- and rye-flour and sometimes went as far as sawdust. The poorer faubourgs had seen more than one recent outbreak of ergot poisoning, with the attendant hallucinatory symptoms of "Saint Anthony's Fire," which had previously been thought to be almost extinct for more than a century, since the bizarre episode of the Convulsionnaires of Saint-Médard and the Apocalyptic prophecies of the Abbé Vaillant in the 1730s.

In spite of the poor quality of my daily bread, however, I eventually felt well enough to get out of bed, get dressed— carefully putting on my quilted jacket—and go downstairs to the study. I hoped to find Dupin there, feeling that I was finally in a condition to interrogate him seriously regarding our experience in the Faubourg Saint-Victor, but he had already left for the Louvre. I was slightly annoyed that he had not invited me to accompany him, but not unduly surprised, and not ungrateful, given that the weather, although clear, was still exceedingly cold. It seemed to be a very good day for sitting by the fire with a book—perhaps even the *Resonances du temps*, with the excuse that it would constitute relevant research. I suspected that Dupin would rather have joined me, under normal circumstance, but he could hardly have refused Lacroix's request that he look at the mysterious palimpsest even without the sharp spur of curiosity to urge him on.

In consequence, I went to the shelves and took a book off the shelves; I even reached for the *Resonances du temps* before thinking that something more relaxing might be in order and selected one next to it instead, which had no title on its spine, although its thinness and its cheap binding suggested that it was unlikely to be one of the forbidden, or even the forbidding, sort. I went to sit down in my favorite armchair but had not even opened the volume when the doorbell rang.

I cursed, and slipped the book, almost unthinkingly, into the capacious inside pocket of my jacket, where it fit very snuggly next to my heart.

Having answered the summons, Madame Bihan came in immediately to tell me that Dupin had a visitor, who, having been told that he was absent, was asking to speak to me in his stead. The manner in which she made the announcement made it perfectly clear that she did not approve of the visitor in question and would be pleased were I to forbid him entry.

"Who is it?" I asked.

"The man who calls himself the Comte de Saint-Germain," she replied, her tone making it obvious that she did not believe for an instant that the young man in question really was the legendary magician's legitimate heir, but merely an impostor of a similar ilk.

I sighed theatrically, "I suppose I'd better find out what he wants," I said. "Please send him in, Madame Bihan."

The fake comte came into the study with his usual swagger. He was not tall enough or grizzled enough to qualify as a matamore, and did not give the impression of a man who could handle a military saber with any degree of expertise—although I had once seen him make very clever use of a slender sword-stick similar to the one he was presently swinging—but that did not prevent him from exhibiting himself with a certain prideful strut.

"Where's Dupin?" he demanded, unceremoniously. "I must see him, on a matter of the utmost urgency."

"I'll be glad to tell him that you called," I told him, "but I'm not expecting him to return imminently—perhaps not until this evening."

"Where is he?" Saint-Germain said, bluntly.

I hesitated, but eventually decided that there was no harm in telling him. "The Louvre Museum," I said.

"The Louvre! What on earth is he doing there?"

"I don't think that he would consider that to be any of your business," I retorted, stiffly. "Can I give him a message when he does return?"

"I suppose so," he said. "Tell him that I have information—sound information, I believe—that one of the Nine Immortals is in Paris, and I need his help in locating him and arranging a meeting. He ought to be as enthusiastic as I am to achieve that—it's the kind of opportunity that only comes along once in an ordinary lifetime."

"Who the hell are the Nine Immortals?" I asked, suppressing an urge to laugh.

The Comte raised his eyes to the ceiling. "Even in American occult circles," he said, "I would have thought that everyone had heard of the Nine Immortals."

"I didn't move in so-called occult circles when I lived in Boston," I informed him. "The common interests that I have with Dupin are fundamentally literary in nature, as you know."

"Oh, yes," he said. "You're acquainted with that poseur Poe, who has used Dupin as a character in his newspaper stories—doubtless using details supplied by you. Lamartine is quite an admirer of his work, I believe. I wish he'd stick to his literary interests, instead of using the Society's headquarters as a convenient meeting-place and bringing the police knocking at my door in search of conspirators. In any case, it's not important for you to know. Just give the message to Dupin when he returns. He knows where to contact me."

"All Paris knows where to contact you," I muttered.

"You really must get over this bout of sullen hostility, Mr. Reynolds," Saint-Germain said. "We were getting along quite famously before the Day of the Dead. What happened in the forest of Fontainebleau was not my fault, and I really can't imagine why you care so much, given that the chit was no friend of yours. You do know, don't you, that it wasn't my child that she was allegedly carrying?"

"I know that it could have been," I retorted, tight-lipped.

"Well, it wasn't—it was Chapelain's, if it was anybody's. And it's all water under the bridge now anyway."

The turn of phrase struck me as particularly unfortunate, in more ways than one, but all I said was: "Was there anything else, Monsieur Falleroux?" I knew that would annoy him.

"No," he said. "I'll bid you *au . . .*"

The doorbell rang again before he could add *revoir*. "Is that Dupin?" he said.

"Dupin doesn't ring the bell," I said—although it was not unknown for him to do so.

Saint-Germain waited anyway. Madame Bihan came in again.

"It's another gentleman asking to see Monsieur Dupin," she said. "He's a seaman, to judge by his clothing. He has a child with him. When I told him that the Chevalier was not at home, I told him that you were here, and he immediately asked to see you. He recognized your name, sir."

"My name?" I said, slightly startled, although there was no real reason to be. "Well, then, I suppose you'd better show him in as you show the Comte out."

Saint-Germain, however, made no move to follow her as she returned to the front door. Curiosity was probably not the worst of his many faults, but it was one of the most conspicuous.

The newcomer was, indeed, every inch the seaman—what conventional parlance calls an "old sea-dog"—and he gave the impression of having not long disembarked, even though Paris is a long way from Le Havre and the roads were terrible at present. It had probably been a wise move for him to retain his seaman's jersey and thick jacket, adapted to preserve him from all kinds of weather. The little girl accompanying him also had a naval pea-jacket of sorts, but it was several sizes too big for her, and left her thin legs vulnerable to the cold, being only covered by light woolen socks.

The seaman barely glanced at Saint-Germain before dismissing him as a person of no apparent interest, but he seemed to have no difficulty in recognizing me, although I was sure that I had never seen him before in my life. He strode toward me and extended his hand.

"Do I have the honor, sir," he said, "of addressing the famous Jeremiah N. Reynolds?" he said. He had obviously drawn the wrong conclusion from Madame Bihan's statement that "Monsieur Reynolds" was at home.

I sighed. "Actually, no," I said. "I'm Samuel Reynolds. Jeremiah is a relative, but I hail from a more obscure branch of the family." *A more respectable branch*, I had been tempted to say, but it would have been unworthy of me. I had nothing against my cousin, who had become respectably famous as one of the first men to set foot in the Antarctic continent and had renewed that fame by means of his account of *Mocha Dick, the White Whale of the Pacific*, after blotting his reputation in scientific circles by teaming up with the younger John Cleve Symmes to help him popularize his lunatic thesis of the Hollow Earth.

"I do apologize, Mr. Reynolds," said the seaman. "Your housekeeper only mentioned your surname, and I jumped to the wrong conclusion. I am mistaken, then, in thinking that we might have a mutual acquaintance in Edgar Poe?"

"No," I said; "I do, indeed know Poe, perhaps better than my namesake does, who is known to him mainly by reputation."

"Ah!" said the seaman, seemingly slightly confused. "No matter. I too have a cousin and namesake known to Mr. Poe primarily by reputation. My name is Jacob Pym—Captain Pym of the South Seas merchanter *Excelsior*. You've certainly heard of my relative, Arthur Pym. You probably have the rather fanciful book that Mr. Poe wrote about his supposed adventures on your shelves."

"Arthur Gordon Pym?" I queried, astonished. "You're a relative of Arthur Gordon Pym? But I know him—the real

Arthur Pym, I mean, not the fanciful one featured in Poe's story. I'm the man who introduced him to Poe."

"He is, indeed, my cousin," said the captain. "A small world, isn't it? I suspected, of course, that in coming in search of Monsieur Dupin I might encounter a friend of Mr. Poe's, but I naturally expected it to be your cousin, whose adventures Mr. Poe plundered in concocting his imaginary account of Arthur's. But no matter, as I said. Well met, sir, well met indeed."

Overcome by astonishment, I was speechless—which gave an unwanted opportunity to my other visitor. The fake Comte stepped forward and bowed.

"Le Comte de Saint-Germain," he said. "I'm very glad to meet you, Captain Pym. I'm the President of the Harmonic Society of Paris, a great admirer of Mr. Poe's work, and a great friend of Monsieur Dupin. If I can help you in any way, please don't hesitate to ask. And who is this, might I ask?" With an elegant gesture of his excessively delicate hand, he indicated the child who had come into the room behind the seaman, and who was now looking around with confused amazement. At first glance—and I had barely granted her that—she resembled an ordinary Parisian waif, less chlorotic than most, black-haired and dark-eyed, but no less thin and poorly clad than an average street-urchin. She seemed to me to be about ten years old.

Captain Pym did not seem free of amazement himself as he contemplated the charlatan. After a momentary hesitation, he said: "I can't introduce you, milord, I'm afraid. I don't know the little girl's name . . . she can speak well enough, but the language she speaks, if it is a language, is unknown to me, and she doesn't seem to be able to respond coherently to any language spoken aboard my ship—which are quite a few, I can assure you—although some of my crewmen claim to recognize some of the strange words that she speaks . . ."

I found my voice. "I think we're getting a little ahead of ourselves, Captain," I said. "You've evidently been traveling, in this direly cold weather, and the little girl must be chilled to the bone in spite of the naval jacket you've wrapped her in. Will you please take her into the kitchen, Madame Bihan, and give her something to eat while she warms herself beside the stove? And would you make some hot coffee for the Captain? I have some rum to put in it, Captain, if you wish, or whisky, if you prefer. But do sit down, please."

I was about to add that Saint-Germain was just leaving but I was too late. He had already sat down, and clearly had every intention of listening to what Captain Pym had to say.

Madame Bihan did as she was requested and went back to the kitchen with the little girl, who went with her very meekly, without saying a word.

"Monsieur Dupin might be absent for some time," Saint-Germain said, smoothly, "but Mr. Reynolds will be happy to convey a message to him on your behalf—unless, of course, you'd be willing to explain the reason for your visit to him. He is, after all, Jeremiah Reynolds' cousin."

I could not tell whether Saint-Germain was familiar with my cousin's name, which had never come up in conversation between us, although I assumed that he must have heard of John Cleve Symmes junior, as an animal of a similar stripe to himself.

"Oh, there's nothing confidential about what I have to ask of Monsieur Dupin," the seaman said, blithely. "His name was given to me by an acquaintance in Le Havre—a Breton sailor, and a veteran, like Arthur and myself, of the South Seas. He only knew Monsieur Dupin by name, but the Chevalier has quite a reputation in the Breton region—his homeland, I believe—as a great scholar of strange and mysterious lore. I hoped that he might be able to succeed where I failed in communicating with the little girl we picked up on Booby Island, or at least in recognizing some of the strange names she pronounces. Have you, by any chance, Mr. Reynolds, ever heard the name Cthulhu?"

I was not the only person who suddenly sat bolt upright. I had, indeed, heard the name of the "dreamer of R'lyaieh," far too frequently for my liking—and so had Saint-Germain.

"That little girl knows the name of Cthulhu?" I queried, hardly able to credit it.

"Indeed," said Captain Pym. "It's not particularly astonishing, I suppose—it's a name often whispered in the region, in association with various mysteries, and she might easily have heard it aboard whatever ship it was that dropped her off on Booby Island, if—as I strongly suspect—it was a pirate vessel. Most of the local pirates are Malays or Kanaks, of course, and they're all direly superstitious. Some of them even swear by Cthulhu, as we would swear by the Devil, in spite of—or perhaps because of—the difficulty of the name's pronunciation."

"Forgive me, Captain," Saint-Germain put in, smoothly, "but where is Booby Island, if you please?"

"You don't know of it?" said the Captain. "Well, I suppose there's no reason that a Parisian gentleman would. It's an island in the Torres Strait, ten or twelve leagues north-west of Cape York in Queensland. It was named by Captain Cook. The surrounding sea is full of dangerous reefs, and the waters are exceedingly dangerous, even in good weather, for vessels traveling between Sydney or Brisbane and Batavia—traffic that has increased dramatically in recent years since the English colony of New South Wales has become a thriving enterprise. So many ships have been lost there and so many castaways became stranded on the island that a permanent provision was established there of supplies to aid victims of shipwreck. It has become a kind of letter drop, where passing ships leave messages and warnings for one another. It's also host to some remarkable rock art of unknown antiquity, much of it overwritten by modern graffiti but still decipherable, including depictions of strange sea-creatures or demons—which some people claim to include images of a monster named Cthulhu, marking a secret portal to the demon's lair, or tomb, which can only be opened by magic."

"And the little girl was marooned there?" I said. "But she's surely no Kanak—she has the appearance of a European, albeit a pauper. She's a victim of pirates, you think?"

"I don't know that for sure," Pym admitted. "There was no indication at the letter-drop of whatever ship had abandoned her, but it's not unknown for pirates to do that. They have the reputation of being bloodthirsty murderers who slaughter everyone aboard the ships they attack and plunder, but they're human, like you or me. They're often reluctant to kill innocents, especially little children—not that there are many children aboard ships in the region, which don't often have families among their passengers, as you can imagine. She can't have been there long when my men collected her, as the supplies on which she'd been living weren't significantly depleted."

"And you brought her all the way back to France?" Saint-Germain queried. "That must have taken months. Why France?"

"Well, milord, as I said, no one aboard *Excelsior* was able to communicate with her, but two of my crewmen are Bretons, and they claimed that some of the words she used, including *Breizh*, which is the Breton word for Brittany, proved that, unlikely as it might seem, she might hail from there. I could have left her in Sydney, or another port on my route—but I didn't have any scheduled ports of call and you can probably understand that colonial merchant ports aren't exactly hospitable places in which an orphan girl can be left to the mercy of charity. I thought she'd be safer with me, in spite of superstitions that declare it bad luck to keep a so-called Child of Ocean aboard ship. I don't believe that, obviously; this is the nineteenth century, after all—and I fly the American flag, proudly, so I have no truck with popular tales of demons and exotic sirens. In fact, we had a surprisingly trouble-free journey, in spite of the superstitious mutterings, faster than any I've achieved before."

I wanted to ask him what he meant by exotic sirens, but I was too slow, and Saint-Germain was quick to pick up on what might well have been the more important datum in Pym's speech.

"Are you sure that the word she used was just the Breton word for Bretagne?" he asked, curiously. "It couldn't, by any chance, have been part of a name . . . or, strictly speaking, a pseudonym: Oberon Breisz?"

"That's the phrase," said Captain Pym. "It's a name, you say? That would be Oberon as in Shakespeare, I suppose? I thought it was probably two mangled French words: *au berne,* or something similar. The Breton lads couldn't make sense of it, though. If you can, perhaps you might be able to talk to the girl . . . ?"

"Absolutely," said Saint-German, without hesitation. "Don't get up. Reynolds—I'll go and fetch her from the kitchen."

"Better watch out," I counseled, controlling my vexation. "Madame Lacuzon is there, and she likes you even less than Paul Lacroix does."

Saint-Germain was already on his feet. "Lacroix?" he said, pausing. "What has Lacroix got to do with this?"

I was saved the trouble of declining to explain because the doorbell rang yet again.

"That must surely be Dupin," said the fake Comte, although it was still early. He cut off his expedition to the kitchen, however, and waited for Madame Bihan to answer the door, while exchanging a glance with me that he probably intended to be conspiratorial, reminding me that, before the fiasco at Fontainebleau, he and I had once stood shoulder to shoulder in Saint-Sulpice against Cthulhu's minions. He had asserted more than once that he had saved my life that day and that I owed him a debt, whereas I was perfectly certain that it was the pseudonymous Oberon Breisz who had saved us both, for his own nefarious reasons.

This time, Madame Bihan did not come in to inform me that there was yet another visitor who wanted to speak to Monsieur Dupin; the visitor came in himself, apparently not being a man to observe conventional etiquette.

I was rising to my feet, but I stopped, absurdly, before reaching an upright position. Saint-Germain started like a scalded cat—although, so far as I knew, he had less reason to recognize the newcomer than I had. I had seen him only a few hours before, in the vicinity of the Rue de l'Hirondelle, and although it had been dark then and his eyes no longer had that peculiar feline glow in the daylight, I was in no doubt that he was my mysterious matamore.

His eyes, although no longer gleaming so eerily, were still possessed of a remarkably intimidating gaze. His stare passed over Saint-Germain without any evident flicker of interest, lingered a little longer on me, with evident curiosity, presumably recognizing me, but soon moved on to the old sea-dog, who had been the last of us to struggle to his feet.

"Captain Pym of the *Excelsior*, I believe?" he said, in a silky baritone voice. "I could not intercept you in Le Havre, I fear, but I suspected strongly that you might be intending to visit the Chevalier Dupin. He is not here, I understand? I'm fortunate to have found you, then. Tell me, please, where is the Child of Ocean whom you brought here from the austral seas?"

It was impossible to calculate the sum of our amazement as Saint-Germain, Pym and I all stared at the newcomer, who stood there with perfect equanimity, as if his question were perfectly natural. His wide-brimmed hat was still perched on his head and his capacious cloak was still wrapped around him, but that garb did not seem inapt even for a comfortable study. He gave the paradoxical impression of having stepped out of a dream, or another world, although he was evidently quite solid and seemed perfectly at home in this one.

For once, I seized the privilege of breaking the silence; we were, after all, in my house.

"Just a second," I said. "You burst into my study, without being announced . . ."

"Oh, shut up, Reynolds!" Saint-Germain interrupted. "Do you not realize to whom you are talking? I do beg your pardon, Magister, on behalf of my friend Mr. Reynolds—he is, alas, an American, like Captain Pym. Might I introduce myself: Le Comte de Saint-Germain, President of the Societé Harmonique Philosophique de Paris. We are extremely honored by your visit, and . . . ."

The intruder silenced him with a peremptory gesture, and returned his attention to me.

"Jeremiah Reynolds?" he inquired, curiously.

"I'm afraid not," I said. "Samuel Reynolds. Jeremiah is a distant cousin, but . . ."

The stranger nodded. "I apologize," he said. "Finding you in the company of Captain Pym, I assumed . . . but no matter. Please forgive my intrusion, Mr. Reynolds, but the matter is urgent. Is the Child of Ocean here?"

Again, Saint-Germain interrupted. "She's in the kitchen, Magister, warming up beside the stove," he said. "I was just about to fetch her . . . ."

He took a step in that direction, but another imperious gesture on the part of the matamore stopped him in his tracks. "I have met the Comte de Saint-Germain," he said, bluntly. "You, Monsieur, do not resemble him. In any case, you have no business with the child. I advise you strongly to keep away from her."

Saint-Germain's eyes widened at the insult, or perhaps at the assertion that the newcomer knew the original Comte de Saint-Germain, who had not been seen in Paris since his supposed death in 1784, and whose reincarnation or perpetuation Falleroux claimed to be—falsely, I had always assumed. He was obviously intimidated by the unexpected visitor, but he was not without a certain reckless courage.

"On the contrary, Magister," he retorted. "I believe that I have every right—even a responsibility—to interest myself in the child. I was present when Oberon Breisz died, and I helped to counter his black magic. I heard the Chevalier Dupin recite the incantation designed to repel the agents of Cthulhu, which quieted the shoggoth-infested storm that Breisz had provoked. I remember it quite clearly."

I made no attempt to enumerate the lies and distortions contained in that brief speech; it did not seem to be a good time to start issuing corrections.

The stranger was unimpressed. "The Societé Harmonique evidently has not improved since the dire days of Cagliostro," he said. "Please sit down and be quiet, Monsieur Saint-Germain. Monsieur Reynolds, would you be so kind as to ask your housekeeper to bring the Child of Ocean here, so that I might have a word with her, if possible. I assure you that I mean no harm to her or anyone else here, but I have reason to believe that her presence here might be a threat to the safety of the inhabitants of Paris."

Saint-Germain did not sit down. "You're here to protect Paris by preventing the impending revolution?" he queried, although I could not see how or why he had jumped to that conclusion. "According to the late Blaise Thibodeaux's calculations, that is impossible."

"Sit down, Monsieur," the stranger repeated, in an imperative voice. This time, Saint-Germain obeyed, meekly.

I did not wait for a further instruction, having an intuition that I would be unable to disobey it even if I wanted to. I left the room and went to the kitchen.

Madame Bihan was alone there, placidly warming her hands in front of the stove.

"Where is the little girl?" I asked her.

"Amélie took her away," Madame Bihan reported, tranquilly. "She told me that it was necessary."

"Madame Lacuzon thought it necessary to take the child away!" I said, utterly flabbergasted. "Why? And where to?"

"She did not confide either of those things to me," said Madame Bihan, still perfectly calm. "You know her well enough, Mr. Reynolds. She's not one for explaining herself. Amélie has always had hidden depths, which she takes great care to keep hidden."

Defeated, and perhaps numb with shock, I returned to the study.

"It seems that the child is no longer in the house," I reported, matter-of-factly. "Madame Lacuzon apparently thought it appropriate to remove her, without asking permission or informing anyone of the reason, and left by the back door."

If the stranger was surprised or disconcerted, he was careful not to show it. "Would the Madame Lacuzon to whom you refer be Amélie Lacuzon of Morbihan, by any chance?" he asked. The question seemed no less astonishing to me than everything else about his uncanny person

"Amélie is certainly her given name," I confirmed, "and she lived in Brittany for many years before she followed Monsieur Dupin to Paris, in order to serve as his concierge. Do you know her?"

Did the remarkable eyes show a hint of amusement? I could not be sure. "Concierge?" he queried. "An interesting description. Is it hers?"

"Yes," I said, "but it has always been evident to me that their relationship is much closer than that of employer and employee. He trusts her implicitly. If she has judged it necessary or desirable to take the child away, Dupin will not contradict her, however puzzled he might be."

Still the matamore did not give any outward sign of annoyance. "Amélie Lascuzon said that it was *necessary* for her to take the child away?" he queried.

"So Madame Bihan says," I confirmed. "By what entitlement, I have no idea, but Dupin might. I believe that

Madame Lacuzon was once a tenant of land owned by the Chevalier's father, and he appears to have known her since he was a child."

Saint-Germain laughed. "He hasn't told you any more than that?" he remarked.

"No," I confirmed, far less shy about showing my own annoyance, "and I cannot believe that he has told you any more."

"He hasn't," Saint-Germain agreed, "but I have my sources, even in Brittany. The Harmonic Society is a broad church."

"Excuse me," Captain Pym put in, "but are you telling me that the child I placed in your safe keeping has been abducted? Abducted by someone known to this gentleman, whose interest in the child seems utterly mysterious to me? She has been in my care for three months, now; as the man who collected her from Booby Island, I have responsibilities toward her. I must insist that the child is returned to my custody—and that you give me an explanation of what is going on here."

He was looking at the stranger, as I was myself. I had only had the child in my own custody for a minute or two, but I felt that I too had a certain responsibility, given that she had been taken from my kitchen by the cousin of my housekeeper.

The stranger was shaking his head, slowly, seemingly lost in thought.

"Since your uninvited guest is in no hurry to introduce himself," Saint-Germain interjected, "allow me to take the first step. Unless I am greatly mistaken, Mr. Reynolds, this is the person I came to inquire about—the person I hoped that Dupin might aid me in locating and questioning. I cannot tell you his name, but allow me to introduce to you one of the Nine Immortals. Your house is greatly honored by his presence here, as mine will be, if he cares to accept my invitation to visit the Society, which has half a hundred members who would be very glad indeed to meet him. Naturally, if we can be of any assistance to him in fulfilling the mission that has brought him to Paris, after what appears to have been a long absence, we will be only too glad to help."

Having reached the culmination of his cogitation, the stranger looked at me." I need to see Monsieur Dupin, urgently," he said. "Can you tell me where I can find him?"

I didn't even think of refusing. "He's visiting the Louvre," I said. "Paul Lacroix asked him to go in order to examine a manuscript discovered between the canvas and the backboard of an eighteenth-century painting, in the custody of a curator named Fernichat."

The stranger nodded his head in polite acknowledgement. "Thank you, Mr. Reynolds," he said. "I will go to the Louvre in the hope of catching up with him there. In the meantime, if Madame Lacuzon should return, please tell her that it is absolutely imperative that I see the child. She might think that she knows what she is dealing with, but she is adept enough to know her limitations. She does not know me by name, but if you describe me and tell her what Monsieur de Saint-Germain has just said, she will understand better than he does who I am."

"Where shall I tell her to contact you?" I asked, adding, in a spirit of perversity: "The house in the Rue de l'Hirondelle where spectral harmonies of hell were played last night?"

"No," said the stranger. "It would be wise to keep her away from there, if you can, and wise to stay away from it yourself, especially if you believe that you heard the music in question. It can be dangerous to those who hear it."

"You're not the first person to give me that warning," I observed, and I added, provocatively: "but the other was a ghost, and might not have had any existence outside my imagination. Would you care to tell me where the danger in question originates? From Cthulhu, or the Dweller with the Eyes of Fire?"

I had hoped to startle him, but I was disappointed.

"The Dwellers will not harm you if you do not trespass on their terrain, Mr. Reynolds," the alleged Immortal replied, still utterly unmoved by any and all attempted provocations, and giving me the impression of being slightly amused by my doubtless-naïve question. He continued: "Nor is Cthulhu hostile, no matter what superstitious souls believe, but it has its existential imperatives, like any living being, and they can have dangerous side-effects, so it is far better left alone, and even dissuaded from its attempts to manipulate our intelligence. There is no active evil, Mr. Reynolds, not even in the Crawling Chaos, but since you know the names of Cthulhu and the Dweller with the Eyes of Fire, you must have realized by now how inconsequential you are as a bystander in the struggles in which such beings are engaged. If you want to live long enough to grow old, you would do well to curb your curiosity. The lust for knowledge is a dangerous vice."

"Is that really the advice of one whose esoteric knowledge has enabled him to live for thousands of years?" Saint-Germain put in, seemingly more than a trifle resentful at the casual fashion in which the burly man was treating him.

"It is the advice of every being whose knowledge has facilitated that burden," answered the stranger, "save for those who want to exploit human curiosity for their own ends. But that is enough idle chatter; I must find Dupin, in order to find Amélie Lacuzon and the child. If he returns before I find him, please ask him to wait here for me, and please say the same to Madame Lacuzon if she should reappear. I shall return."

And with that, he left the room. A moment later, I heard the click of the door latch. I breathed out then, although I had not realized until I did that I had been holding my breath.

V

THE DREAMER OF R'LYAEIH

I turned to Saint-Germain and said: "What the hell is going on, Saint-Germain?"

"I was just about to ask you the same question," Saint-Germain retorted, with equal impatience. "What's this about the harmonies of hell being played in a house in the Rue de l'Hirondelle, where you apparently saw the Immortal last night? Was Dupin with you?"

"I really feel, gentlemen," Captain Pym put in, "that I am the one entitled to an explanation. May I remind you that a young girl who was in my charge has been taken away without my permission, by someone about whom everyone seems to know a great deal more than I do? Who on earth was that bizarre man, who looks like a fairground pugilist and talks like a charlatan?"

"A good question," I said. "Would you care to answer it, Saint-Germain?"

"I'll answer your questions if you'll answer mine," the fake comte retorted. "That way, we'll all end up wiser."

"Fair enough," I said. "You first. Who are the Nine Immortals?"

"That's only one of the names by which they're known in the occult tradition," Saint-Germain reported, after a moment's hesitation. "Nobody knows whether the number is really accurate, and the most reliable sources assert that they might not know how many they are themselves. Some sources allege that they originated in India, as the most knowledgeable and powerful of the ancient yogis; others associate them with the nomadic Hescheboix, but that is pure speculation. What is certain, to the extent that anything can be certain in the realm of legend, is they have been alive for a very long time, and that they know the secret of how that extreme longevity can be obtained and secured, which they guard very jealously. You've just heard that one assert that the reason for their jealousy is that they deem their immortality, and the knowledge that they have acquired over the millennia, to be a burden, but many seekers consider that to be a mere pretence, and that their pose as protectors of humankind is simply a sham. It's said that they only visit cities occasionally, preferring remote solitude most of the time, but that when they do put in an appearance, it's by virtue of something they've learned with the aid of prophetic powers that make calculations like Blaise Thibodeaux's and fantasies like Abbé Vaillant's seem like child's play. Your turn, Reynolds. What were you doing in the Rue de l'Hirondelle last night?"

"Not yet," I countered. "How did you recognize the supposed Immortal, if you've never met him before?"

"Silly question," Saint-Germain countered. "In spite of his casual dismissal, I really am who I say I am, and I *have* seen him before, albeit fleetingly, It's only to be expected, I suppose, that the occasion left a deeper imprint on my memory than on his, but I must admit to feeling a trifle wounded by his blunt accusation that I am an impostor. And even if I had not seen him before, I would have been able to recognize him for what he is, as any skilled magician or mesmerist would."

I was not about to acknowledge that his part of our bargain could be fulfilled by such blatant persiflage, but I suspected that there was no point in pursuing the matter and switched tactics. "What do you know about Dupin's relationship with Madame Lacuzon that I don't?" I demanded, instead.

"Oh, that's simple enough," he said, dismissively. "She's his foster-mother."

"What! So far as I know, Dupin's mother has been dead for some time, but he certainly wasn't orphaned at birth."

"No, he wasn't," Saint-Germain agreed, tiredly, "but you've been in Paris long enough to know how things work here. Parisian aristocrats routinely send new-borns to the country to be nursed by peasant women, and those children often develop long-lasting affectionate relationships with the mother-substitutes who nurse them."

"But Dupin's parents aren't Parisian. He was born in Brittany, where customs are quite different."

"True," said Saint-Germain, "and my informant says that Dupin's mother had every intention of nursing him herself—but something was wrong with her and she couldn't feed him. No provision had been made in advance for that possibility, and Dupin's father had to cast about urgently for a wet-nurse. His only tenant who had recently given birth wasn't really a tenant at all, but a pauper whom he'd allowed to live in an abandoned cottage after she had apparently been expelled from her village, accused of witchcraft—a charge that, as an enlightened man, he thought nonsensical. He gave his son to the woman to nurse, which she did all the more ardently because her own child—a girl—soon died. Dupin became very fond of her, and remained so after he was weaned. It's a common enough story, except for the involvement of witch-craft—which I've always been prepared to take seriously, even before discovering that her name is known somehow to one of the Nine Immortals. Now, please, what occurred in the Rue de l'Hirondelle last night?"

"Dupin and I went there to meet Paul Lacroix," I told him, a trifle reluctantly, but obliged to fulfill the bargain I had made. "He had been informed by a colleague that strange music had been heard coming from a so-called witch-house, supposedly deserted for more than a century save for occasional phantom visitations. It isn't empty any more—Lacroix and Dupin saw that man coming out of it, locking the door behind him with a key. As regards the music, Dupin and I heard it being played from the Quai de la Tournelle, but whether or not it has anything to do with *Les Harmonies de l'enfar*, I have no idea. Lacroix leapt to that conclusion, but you know him via your society—you're familiar with the bees in his bonnet."

"That's true," Saint-Germain admitted. "But he's a mere antiquarian, not a serious occultist—just an obsessive hunter of trivia, like his old friend Thibodeaux . . . and Dupin, alas, who seems ever more determined to disown his true identity. If only he'd work with me instead of holding my past against me, we might achieve great things. But you're not being straight with me, Reynolds. What ghost gave you the warning that the Immortal just repeated to you? Was that last night as well?"

"It was a hallucination," I said, evasively. "I haven't entirely recovered from the fever I caught on the Day of the Dead, and hearing mysterious music played on a stringed instrument reminded me of the violin played by your former coachman Anton, just as infallibly as it put Lacroix in mind of the fabled harmonies of hell."

"The two might not be very different," Saint-Germain muttered, with a troubled expression that made me wonder exactly how much he remembered of the collective hallucination we had experienced while entranced that night, and how different it might be from what I remembered. In a louder voice, he said: "You mean the fever you contracted when you jumped into the Seine trying to stop Jana from killing herself?"

"When I jumped into the Seine trying to stop Mademoiselle Valdemar from following a murderous hypnotic compulsion," I corrected him.

Saint-Germain raised his eyebrows. "Is *that* what you thought?" he said. "And you jumped to the conclusion that it was me who had mesmerized her? Nothing could be further from the truth. It was Chapelain's spell she was under, re-member, or Anton's . . . and it was surely Chapelain's child she was carrying, if the allegation that she was pregnant is true."

"Chapelain is not a killer," I said, flatly. "I know him; he would never have done that."

"But you think I might? How little you know me, Reynolds. Had I realized what was happening, I would have jumped into the river myself to try to pull her out, even though she betrayed me, more than once."

"I don't believe you," I said, flatly.

Saint-Germain sighed. "Not does the Immortal, apparent-ly," he said. "It's my fate in life to be forever misunderstood."

"Excuse me, gentlemen," Captain Pym interrupted, with a certain asperity, "but we're straying from the point, are we not? None of this is helping us to find the little girl. So, which of you would care to tell me who or what this Cthulhu is, since you both seem to know far more about it than the ig-norant dolts who pronounce the name in hushed whispers all over the Southern Seas?"

"I'm very confused regarding that matter myself," I con-fessed, "in spite of having had some direly uncomfortable close encounters with its minions. Dupin is the only one of us who really seems to understand what happened when we went in search of Oberon Breisz and unleashed a storm of hallucination. And there's no point asking Saint-Germain, who merely tagged along."

"*Tagged along!*" repeated Saint-Germain, hotly. "I saved you from the shoggoths, remember, risking my life to get Levasseur's medallion to Dupin. And I was in the stone circle to help the old witch pull you out of the jolly-boat in the hallucinatory bog, although she's never shown me the slightest gratitude for my help. And thanks to the Society's archives, I know far more about Cthulhu and his ilk than Dupin, and probably more than any man in Paris, except perhaps . . . *him*."

"In that case, Monsieur Saint-Germain," Pym snapped, "I'd be very grateful if you'd tell me." I noticed that he had stopped addressing the supposed comte as "milord."

"Of course, Captain," Saint-Germain said. "In brief, Cthulhu is an entity that apparently arrived in our world a very long time ago, before humans existed, presumably traveling from one of the many dimensions that exist in parallel with our own, normally separated from it but occasionally permitting glimpses and incursions. The literature often calls them the dream-dimensions, but they're perfectly real. Cthulhu was not the only such entity to reach the Earth in the days before the advent of humankind, but along with numerous others it was apparently imprisoned . . . *encrypted*, Dupin would say . . . by other beings with which it was in conflict, which some documents call angels, assuming Cthulhu to be a kind of devil. Other documents refer collectively to all such beings as Great Old Ones.

"Opinions vary as to exactly what kind of entity Cthulhu might be, but the phrase *dead but dreaming* often crops up in the literature, and what is suspected about it is allegedly summarized in a text called the *Necronomicon*, which I do not have the privilege of ever having seen, although Dupin is undoubtedly far more familiar with it than he is willing to admit. The *Necronomicon* is said to contain incantations capable of establishing links between human minds and Cthulhu's mysterious posthumous dreams, which are extremely dangerous, sometimes driving their would-be users mad, and even capable of disintegrating their flesh by means of a strange whistling sound, and reducing it to a repulsive sticky substance.

"Cthulhu is said to be imprisoned in a place called R'lyaieh, the portal to which is somewhere in the South Seas, where it is dormant, albeit dreaming. The intermittent dreams that echo in receptive human minds—which are rare but supposedly educable—are said to be contagious and dangerous, at least at certain propitious times. The portal is said to be guarded, as all such portals are, by mysterious dwellers between the dimensions. Because of the contagion of dreams provoked by Cthulhu and other Old Ones, inevitably experienced as obsessive delusions, some people in the past have worshiped Cthulhu as a god, or have attempted to exploit its power by means of incantations akin to those used to entomb it . . . or, as Dupin would have it, to encrypt it.

"Opinions differ as to whether the power contained in such incantations is musical or mathematical, or both, and on the occasions when Mr. Reynolds and I have encountered shoggoths, which are dangerous fragments of Cthulhu's being, in addition to seeming loathsomely monstrous, their hallucination—for they are hallucinatory, although no less deadly for that—seemed to have both sonic and mathematical components. There are numerous documents containing incantations or musical scores supposedly capable of invoking the magical power of various encrypted beings, but when they work—which is very rarely—they tend to do so only partially or perversely. Among the most celebrated, at least in Paris, are the aforementioned *Necronomicon* and *Les Harmonies de l'enfer*, but the formulae contained in the former generally defy attempts to represent them phonetically by means of human tongues and vocal cords, and the airs mysteriously annotated in the latter defeat attempts to play them on familiar musical instruments. Skeptics, of course, consider all that to be pure fantasy—but Mr. Reynolds and I cannot. We have experienced relevant hallucinations all too acutely."

Pym looked at me for a reaction. "Very succinctly put," I admitted. "All of that conforms with what I have experienced and what Dupin has told me."

"And what has this to do with my castaway—my Child of Ocean?" the Captain demanded.

"I haven't the faintest idea," I admitted. Saint-Germain said nothing.

"And this Oberon Breisz," Pym persisted. "Who is he?"

"A would-be magician who died in Brittany a little while ago," I supplied, "after attempting to make use of incantations apparently engraved in flesh and in wood by magicians in India, at the behest of an eighteenth-century warlord of whom you might well have heard, named Angria."

"The pirate?" Pym said. "The one who is said to sail a ghost ship in the Indian Ocean bearing the Flaming Cross of Goa nailed to its mast."

"That's the one," I confirmed, without adding any further comment on my brief encounter with the ghost ship in question.

"As to what this might have to do with your castaway," Saint-Germain supplied, "does she, by any chance have any tattoos on her body?"

"Not that I have seen," said the Captain. "Why?"

"Because Breisz kept a girl not much older than yours captive for some years," Saint-German replied, "attempting to use her as what he called a skryer. She had been tattooed with an inscription at Angria's request, with the same intention."

"It wasn't a tattoo," I put in, by way of correction, "and it only became visible intermittently, in exceptional circumstances."

"Are you suggesting," Pym asked, looking at Saint-Germain and myself as if we were mad, "That my castaway was abandoned on Booby Island by a ghost ship—Angria's ghost ship?"

"No," I was quick to say. "We have no reason to think that . . . but if the girl were marked in some way . . . some way invisible to you but perhaps not invisible to Madame Lacuzon, that might be a first step in helping to understand why she linked the name of Cthulhu with that of Oberon Breisz. But what I can't understand is why Madame Lacuzon took her away immediately, without waiting to consult Dupin."

"What I can't understand," Saint-Germain interjected, "is why the Immortal is interested in her, and how he even knows that she exists, let alone how he knew that she would come to Paris."

"I made no secret of the fact that I had picked her up, and I reported it in the Booby Island letter-drop" Pym said, reflectively, "but our crossing was uncommonly rapid, and I don't see how the news could possibly have outpaced us. The grapevine of seamen's gossip is astonishingly fast and far-reaching, but not *that* fast. English ships sometimes race between Sydney and London, and all tea-clippers, British and American, are always trying to break records coming and going from the Indies, but *Excelsior* can hold her own easily in that company. I can't see how the news of my bringing the girl here could possibly have got here ahead of me, unless you believe in the kind of long-distance thought-transmission of which the yogis of India and Tibet are said to be capable."

"And the Nine Immortals," Saint-Germain put in, thoughtfully,

I was still busy wondering whether I ought to mention that Oberon Breisz had claimed to be an English pirate, and a reincarnation of a notorious charlatan named Edward Kelley, a skryer who communicated with angels. I decided against it; the affair was already complicated enough. Breisz had also suggested that Angria, in spite of his legendary captaincy of a ghost ship, might still be alive, in spite of his great antiquity, and still actively engaged in occult research involving the portal to R'lyaieh with a mysterious associate, whose victim had referred to him as the Mahatma. Once, I would have dismissed any such suggestion as nonsense, as Captain Pym presumably still would, but I knew better now; even so, I held my tongue.

Saint-Germain, not normally one for bringing discussions down to earth, picked up on the more rational aspect of what Pym had just said. "But it's not impossible," he said, "even if it's unlikely, that someone with an interest in the girl might have been able to anticipate her arrival, at least in Le Havre, without any supernatural aid?" he queried.

"I suppose it's possible," Pym conceded, reluctantly, "but I don't believe it—and who, in any case, could possibly have an interest in her . . . except for her parents? Is it conceivable that the man who just left is her father?"

Saint-Germain smiled wryly. "You saw and heard him, Captain. *Is* it conceivable?"

Pym shook his head. "I suppose not," he admitted. "But I must admit that I find it equally inconceivable that he could be some ancient Immortal . . . or, come to that, that you're some kind of immortal yourself."

"It is hard to believe," Saint-Germain conceded. "I've had my own doubts . . . and such proofs as I have are not of a nature to convince anyone determined not to believe me. What about you, Reynolds? Do you find it inconceivable that your recent visitor is . . . more than human?"

"Not inconceivable," I admitted, "but also not proven. I won't know what to think until I've consulted Dupin."

"The story of your life, in a nutshell," Saint-German said, with a hint of a sneer.

"It's always a wise precaution, in my experience," I countered.

"Whoever that man was," Pym observed, "he recognized the name of your Madame . . . Lacuzon, and he didn't seem unduly astonished to think that she might have taken my castaway away. Do you have any explanation for that, Mr. Reynolds?"

"None," I said, "but it seems that Saint-Germain knows more about Madame Lacuzon than I do, having taken the trouble to seek information about her. What more do you know, Saint-Germain?"

"Very little, beyond the obvious," Saint-Germain said, cagily. "She evidently thinks of herself as Dupin's guardian, and must have served, to some extent, as his mentor. Until a few moments ago, I thought the fact that she had fostered him in infancy was sufficient explanation of that fact, but Captain Pym is right—the fact that her name is known to one of the Nine Immortals might put an entirely different complexion on the matter, perhaps implying that she's more than a common-or-garden Breton hedge-witch. I think we need to interrogate Madame Bihan, don't you, Reynolds?"

I agreed, in theory, but the prospect of interrogating my housekeeper in Dupin's absence, on matters that concerned him intimately, was one that intimidated me considerably.

"She won't tell you anything," I said. "She doesn't like you any more than her cousin does. She won't tell me anything either, even though she's in my employ—a position that she owes to Madame Lacuzon's suggestion. But you and I already know, Saint-Germain, that Madame Lacuzon took a fervent interest in the Oberon Breisz affair. She accompanied us to Brittany in order to confront him."

"Dupin insisted on giving her a share of what remained of Levasseur's treasure," Saint-German remembered, a trifle bitterly.

"You can't pretend that she didn't earn it," I countered, remembering that she had done as much as anyone else, if not more, to save us from the shoggoths in the stone circle.

"Wait a second," said Captain Pym. "Are you saying that you've found Olivier Levasseur's legendary treasure? That was one of Arthur's preoccupations—he'll be very sorry to hear that someone else got to it before him."

"As a matter of fact, we did find it," I said, "but legendary is the right word, alas—there was nothing left of the little he managed to keep for himself but a handful of gold coins and a few gems. The Flaming Cross of Goa, as you mentioned a few minutes ago, is apparently nailed to the mast of Angria's ghost-ship, and the rest of the gold was dissipated. All the manuscripts, alas, were dissolved with Breisz's house, which was situated in a borderland between dimensions that turned out to be precarious."

"I don't understand that," the sea-dog said, bluntly. "What are these dimensions where the Cthulhu-demon is supposedly imprisoned?"

"The world accessible to our senses," Saint-Germain told him, never loath to show off his erudition even when impatient to concentrate on other matters, "exists in parallel with countless others that are close at hand, but invisible and intangible, except when our minds are prey to what some of the Society's physiologists call altered states of consciousness and the vulgar call dreams. Apparently, there are boundaries between the dimensions allegedly policed by entities that are similarly invisible and intangible under normal circumstances, but which become murderous if provoked—you'll recall that the Immortal told Reynolds that the Dwellers won't harm him unless he trespasses in their domain, when he asked whether it was the so-called Dweller with the Eyes of Fire of whom he ought to beware."

"And who posted these supposed police agents to protect the borders between dimensions?" said Pym, skeptically. "God?"

"The more religiously-inclined members of the Society certainly believe that," Saint-Germain said, "but those of us who doubt the existence—or at least the nature—of God are perennially in search of other explanations . . . which is why the religious often consider us, falsely, to be diabolists and why the Church has persecuted our predecessors relentlessly for hundreds of years. That is one of the matters that I am very enthusiastic to discuss with one of the Nine Immortals—who, if legend can be trusted, also like to conceive of themselves as police of a sort . . . guardians of the peace, as modern jargon puts it. It is not unknown for members of the Harmonic Society to represent themselves in the same light, or at least to credit other magi with such a role . . . even common-or-garden magicians like Madame Lacuzon. The likelihood is, I believe, that she simply appointed herself as Dupin's bodyguard, and that the fact that our recent visitor seemed to be interested in her implies no more than the old adage that birds of a feather tend to flock together . . . but it is not impossible that both of them are agents of something, as I put it a few moments ago, *more than human*. Mr. Reynolds has his own theories, I believe, as to what the nature of those agents might be."

In fact, I had, and although they were largely borrowed from the ghost of Blaise Thibodeaux, which had gone to some trouble to explain them to me at Fontainebleau, I had made considerable additions to his ideas in recent weeks as well as adding in the imaginative fruits of my previous encounter with the Flameflower in the bowels of Mont Dragon. I was not about to delve into them in Dupin's absence, however.

Instead, I said: "The Comte knows very well that the borderlands between the dimensions are patrolled, and not merely by would-be angels. They are where ghost-ships sail, while they are roaming the high seas, and pirates might well outnumber police forces there. But as you have remarked yourself, Captain, even pirates are not unalloyed agents of evil. Jack Taylor was undoubtedly a bad man, as Ysolde Leonys kept repeating insistently, but he was not essentially evil, and although I only caught a fleeting glimpse of him and his associate Angria, it was in the course of what was, essentially, a mission of mercy. Angria was, in any case, only deemed a pirate by the British, whose projects of colonization and plunder he opposed, and his apparent investigations of Cthulhu remain cloaked in mystery. You heard the man Saint-Germain calls an Immortal say that Cthulhu is not essentially evil either, but merely a being in pursuit of its own existential imperatives. Dupin would agree, being convinced that everything existent must be reckoned natural, and capable of rational explanation."

"Reynolds is being a trifle disingenuous, Captain Pym," Saint-Germain countered. "His friend does not appear to have confided in him to any considerable degree, but Dupin must know as well as I do that some esoteric scholars assert that Cthulhu and other Old Ones provoked the evolution of the human race as an instrument in their own ambitions, and that they intend to destroy it as soon as it has fulfilled its purpose. Some would say that that is as good a definition of essential evil as any."

"You are using the term 'scholar' very loosely, Comte," I pointed out. "But you consider yourself to be a great scholar, do you not?"

"*Miaow*," said Saint-Germain. "Yes, Mr. Reynolds, I do consider myself to be an exceptional scholar, just as Dupin does; but at least I am humble enough to know that he and I would both be greater scholars by far were we able to combine our knowledge and our efforts—something that esoteric scholars are, unfortunately, rarely inclined to do. Neither of us is numbered among the legendary Nine Immortals, who are rumored to constitute the most exclusive of secret societies, but we are both immortals of a sort, and if we pooled our knowledge and joined forces, we would surely be far better able to cultivate our immortality and our true identities. Dupin is insistent in denying who and what he is, and maintaining a pathological secrecy regarding his more esoteric knowledge, but I am now inclined to suspect that his chief collaborator knows very well what he is."

"I know nothing of the sort," I asserted, unthinkingly.

"Of course not." Saint-German retorted. "I was referring to Madame Lacuzon—his wet-nurse, his guardian and, it appears, the only member of his intimate circle who was capable, instantly, of recognizing Captain Pym's Child of Ocean for what she really is . . . whatever that might be. Unlike you, Reynolds, who hesitate to take a breath without consulting Dupin, she evidently has sufficient confidence in herself to act independently, without waiting to obtain instructions from him . . . although I dare say that she will hasten to do so as soon as she can, if, in fact, she did not take the child directly to the Louvre."

"Do you think that is what she did?" Pym was quick to ask.

"How would I know?" Saint-Germain retorted. "Do you have a better hypothesis to offer, Reynolds?"

I had not. I was completely out of my depth. All I could think of to say was: "If that is what she did, then our mysterious visitor will surely catch up with her. He has a much longer and more purposeful stride—although he will need to be careful of his footing, even wearing those winter boots."

"I suspect that she is too resourceful simply to be overtaken by a long stride," Saint-Germain said, "And if he knows her, at least by name, she probably knows him, at least by reputation. We really should interrogate Madame Bihan, at least to discover exactly when her cousin left the house—it was not necessarily before the visitor who came looking for Captain Pym arrived, and if it was afterwards, Madame Lacuzon might well have been prompted to depart by a glimpse of him obtained through the kitchen door, which she probably opened slightly for precisely that purpose. Surely she can have no objection to telling you that?"

That seemed reasonable enough. I left the room and went to the kitchen.

Madame Bihan was no longer there—but Auguste Dupin was, having apparently entered the house without ringing the bell, presumably via the back door.

As I opened my mouth to exclaim, he put a finger over his lips to command me to keep silent. Then be drew me to the back door and took me through it, into the alleyway at the back of the house. The narrow sliver of sky visible between the roofs of the houses was filled with bright stars—unusually, given that the air above Paris is normally murky—but the visibility at ground level was nevertheless poor. I had plenty of questions queued up for asking, but as usual, I was not quick enough in selecting and framing one of them.

"Who is the man who was sitting in the study with you and Saint-Germain?" Dupin demanded, as soon as he was certain that he could not be overheard.

"A sea-captain named Pym," I said "He . . ."

"Arthur Gordon Pym?" he interrupted.

"His cousin, apparently," I said. "He . . ."

"He brought me a child?" Dupin said, interrupting again. "A so-called Child of Ocean . . . an alleged castaway."

"Yes," I said "He . . ."

"He might be who he claims to be," Dupin said, cutting me off yet again, "but he might not. Saint-Germain's interference is pestiferous, as usual. This matter must be far more serious than I thought, though. Amélie might be in danger. I've sent Madame Bihan away, for safety's sake, but I need you. Can you get rid of Saint-Germain and the Captain? I'd rather talk to you in the comfort of the library than out here in the freezing cold and near-darkness."

"I think so," I said. "Who . . . ?"

"No time," he said. "Go tell them that Madame Bihan has decamped, probably to look for me at the Louvre. Get them to follow her there, if you can. I'll slip back inside as soon as I'm sure that you're alone. This is a deep affair, Reynolds—very deep indeed—and something is trying to make pawns of us. I don't like that, on principle, but it might also place us in dire peril."

"What kind of peril?" I queried.

"No time," he repeated "Go."

I went. I certainly didn't want to hang about in that dark alley—my feet were freezing already.

VI

The Secret of the Painting

I told my two remaining visitors that Madame Bihan had gone out, probably to the Louvre, following in the likely footsteps of her cousin—although the mere fact that Dupin had made that suggestion prompted me to assume that it was false—and I suggested to them that if they wanted any further answers they ought to head for the Louvre in the hope of intercepting Dupin, or perhaps picking up the trail of the mysterious Immortal. Saint-Germain evidently accepted that his time might be more profitably spent in that way than in further verbal sparring with me, and Captain Pym accepted his invitation to accompany him.

A few minutes after they had gone, presumably having ascertained that they really were going away, Dupin slipped into the house through the back door and settled down in the study after pulling his armchair closer to the fire and feeding a few more logs to it.

I still had a thousand questions to ask, but so did he, and he always took priority in an annoyingly casual fashion.

"Is that seaman really a cousin of Arthur Pym?" he demanded.

"I saw no reason to doubt his word," I told him, "but how can I possibly tell?"

"Well," said Dupin, peevishly, "tell me everything that he said—and everything your other visitor said—word for word, if you can remember it."

Saint-Germain, I knew, would have answered that demand by proposing an exchange of information, but I knew better than to bargain with Dupin in that tawdry fashion. I did as I was asked and related the conversations that had taken place in my study, verbatim, or as nearly as I could.

"Hum!" mused Dupin, when I had finished. "Even if he is Arthur Pym's cousin, it proves nothing. And if he really found the girl abandoned on Booby Island and decided to bring her all the way to Paris, that proves nothing either, except that he has an uncommonly fast ship."

"Have you seen Madame Lacuzon?" I said, finally overcome by impatience.

"No," he replied, tersely. "Madame Bihan brought me up to date swiftly, as best she could. The other man who came looking for me didn't give you his name?"

"No, but he's definitely the man whose path I crossed last night on the way from the Quai de la Tournelle—the one you saw coming out of the witch-house. As I told you, Saint-Germain says that he's one of the Nine Immortals, but I have no idea what he meant by that."

Dupin had raised his eyebrows when I first mentioned that datum, although he could not have been overly surprised by my ignorance, and he still did not appear to be in any hurry to explain.

"And he definitely recognized Madame Lacuzon's name," I added. "Perhaps that doesn't seem surprising, since he knew yours, but it astonishes me that he knew her forename as well as her surname, and referred to her as Amélie Lacuzon of Morbihan. What the hell is going on, Dupin?"

"I wish I knew," he said. "I had always considered the Nine Immortals to be a myth, or a mere company of impostors and fantasists akin to the Rosicrucians, but if they're after Cthulhu's child . . ."

"Cthulhu's child!" I exclaimed.

"Not literally, I presume—and I can't be absolutely certain that she's the same child as the one to which the document found in the painting refers, but I no longer believe in fortuitous coincidences . . . I do believe in hoaxes, but Lacroix is honest, and although I don't know Fernichat personally, his reputation is unsullied. If the document is a fake, neither of them can be the faker . . . but if it really was secreted in the painting before the '89 Revolution, and the painting was then stolen, preventing the message from reaching its intended recipient . . . but no, I really can't believe . . ."

His confusion was extremely atypical of his extraordinarily logical mind. I found that rather disturbing.

"You're not making any sense, Dupin. Perhaps you could bring me up to date, swiftly. What happened during your meeting with Lacroix at the Louvre?"

Dupin hesitated momentarily, but then seemed to decide that he had no more profitable way of spending his time, for the moment, than to answer my request.

"As he told us last night," he commenced, "Lacroix wanted me to look at a manuscript found between the canvas and backboard of a painting apparently dating from the late eighteenth century. Seemingly, it had been looted from some Vendean château by Lazare Hoche's forces in the early days of the disorderly suppression of the Chouannerie, as part of a collection of minor works of art, including a few Fragonards and Bouchers, and had eventually been stowed away with them in the Louvre's over-full vaults when the loot was eventually recovered by agents of the Directoire. It appeared to be of little intrinsic interest by comparison with the company it was keeping: Lacroix identified it correctly as a nocturnal image of a cottage, with a starry sky in which the constellations were unrecognizable to him. I realized immediately that his failure to recognize them was because the star-pattern—quite meticulously reproduced, in spite of the poor quality of the painting—would only be visible from the southern hemisphere."

"But you said that the cottage was in Brittany."

"Lacroix said that, because of the megaliths in the background, but Brittany isn't the only part of the world in which there are mysterious megaliths—although, in fairness, it would be extremely unlikely to find the megaliths of the South Seas in the background of a cottage more typical of my homeland. If the cottage was Breton, the stars were definitely wrong . . . but significantly wrong. In any case, it seems likely that the painting was merely an envelope for the palimpsest, and the picture merely a subscription enabling it to be identified by the intended recipient.

"Fernichat says that he took the backboard off the picture because he hoped to find some clue inside as to the painting's origin or its author. He found the manuscript, saw instantly that the original inscriptions had been erased and overwritten by more recent ones that were utterly incomprehensible to him, and, being as curious as any curator, immediately tried to decipher the erased script using the lighting techniques that have recently been applied so successfully in the Vatican. Unable to make anything of the erased inscription either, he decided to consult Lacroix—who, as he told us last night, believed that he recognized in the recovered inscription symbols similar to those employed by the antiquarian would-be disciple of Erich Zann who called himself Prospero.

"I am in no position to challenge that assertion, but my own attention was immediately caught by one of the more recent inscriptions: an array of forty-nine symbols that I had seen before, quite recently, engraved in the flesh of the woman who called herself Ysolde Leonys, allegedly placed there by a magician in the temporary employ of the Maratha warlord Kanhoje Angre, known to the English naval commanders against whom he fought as Angria. History records that Angre was killed in 1729, after which the remainder of his fleet was soon defeated by the English navy, but after our strange encounter in Brittany, you and I have some reason to think differently."

"You think that he really might be still alive, even though I think I saw him on the deck of a ghost ship?"

"That I don't know, but it's possible that, knowing that further armed resistance to the British was impracticable, he might well have joined one of the secret societies of India engaged in active resistance against the East India Company by subtler and more insidious means, to which the person Mademoiselle Leonys called the Mahatma probably belonged. The British called them Thugs, and naturally condemned them as an association of murderers and gangsters, but they did not succeed in penetrating to the occult heart of the cult, an ancient society of yogis notionally affiliated to the god Shiva."

"British ethnographers have recently published a great deal concerning the alleged magical feats of yogis and what they call fakirs," I put in.

"Indeed," said Dupin, "and French ethnographers and occultists have joined in with great avidity. Most of their reportage is fakery and charlatanry—but the British did succeed in driving the cult of Thuggee further and further underground, and forcing its members to make use of cryptological methods of transmitting their messages. Some of that correspondence was exchanged with foreign allies, including Frenchmen who had been expelled from India by the British and the Dutch, being less expert in the business of brutal colonization than their rivals, although they had often arrived in various parts of India ahead of them. If it is genuine, the version of the Cthulhu cryptogram added to the manuscript presumably dates from the 1770s, before the British suppression of the Thugs, while the cult was still moderately active and powerful. Whether it was written by someone who knew of the version that Angria's so-called Mahatma, who was evidently a knowledgeable yogi, engraved in Ysolde Leonys' flesh, or someone else who had seen the original from which that was copied, I cannot tell, but . . .

"But you suspect the involvement of Edward England," I suggested, eager to show off my own powers of creative speculation, "who called himself Oberon Breisz when he settled in Bretagne, usurping a misspelling of the Breton word for Breton in much the same spirit as when he had earlier adopted the pseudonym England. He didn't have Levasseur's medallion in his possession in 1770, on which an inscription of the same kind was engraved, because—if Saint-Germain can be believed—it was in the possession of the Harmonic Society, but he certainly knew of its existence and its origin."

"I have an open mind on that matter," Dupin said, scrupulously, "but the possibility certainly occurred to me that England, or Breisz, might have been the intended recipient of the manuscript and the message, if it is genuine. The erasure of the original script was not intended to render it unreadable, any more than the encoding of the more recent message accompanying the Cthulhu cryptogram was intended to be impenetrable."

"What message?" I asked.

"One thing at a time," Dupin retorted, slightly annoyed by what he considered to be another unnecessary interruption. "The original manuscript, written on a kind of parchment that I could not identify, is harder to date. The incompletely-erased script is not Sanskrit and has few analogies with it. If, as Lacroix suspects, it is actually a system of musical notation, it bears little resemblance to modern systems, but Lacroix insists that it is reminiscent of a system discovered by the antiquarian musician who called himself Prospero. The connection between the music, if it really is music, and the Cthulhu cryptogram, is not immediately obvious, but there must surely be one. You have heard the syllables of the cryptogram recited, to the best of my ability, and you have seen the effect that the recitation in question had; you have also seen me play an excerpt from the music of Eric Zann, and saw what effect that had . . . .and more recently, you saw the Flameflower in the bowels of Mont Dragon and experienced the effect of the dance performed on the Day of the Dead, in accordance with Thibodeaux's anticipations of a particular temporal resonance, apparently masterminded by another mysterious individual employing the pseudonym Oberon."

"And played by the Harmonic Society's former coachman, a former associate of Blaise Thibodeaux," I put in.

"Precisely. But you and I knew even before then, from experience, that the walls separating the dimensions are sensitive to vibrations and to music played in the right place at the right time; such music can stimulate remarkable hallucinations, both individual and collective, by means of resonances allegedly connected with various temporal rhythms or tides. Thibodeaux identified 1848 as a year of political upheavals all over Europe, a year of potential catastrophes . . . catastrophes that some occult entities and organizations might have a perceived interest in precipitating, and others a perceived interest in preventing."

"What you're suggesting," I inferred, "is that the music, if it is music, contained in the original manuscript, might . . . must . . . have some relevance to the Cthulhu cryptogram— perhaps even a means of securing a partial or complete release of the entity from it entombment . . . it's encryption . . . if played at a particular point in time and space? But what can Pym's castaway possibly have to do with it?"

"The Cthulhu cryptogram was not the only recent addition to the original manuscript, apparently added in the 1770s," Dupin said. "The other was a message disguised by a simple letter-substitution code that was child's play to crack. If my clarification is correct, it reads: *Cthulhu's child release from Rlyaieh Toussaint 1847. Transport to Paris, house of Addhema.*

Four symphony players denoted, American required. Beware the Nine."

"Who or what is Addhema?" I asked.

"According to Lacroix, it is one of the names attached to or employed by the lamia that was manifest in Paris during the Regency established while Louis XV was still a child, and again under the Consulate. The reference is, therefore, presumably to the so-called witch-house. The rest of the instructions are not as clear."

"They seem clearer to me," I objected.

"They are not," said Dupin. "The terms *symphony* and *American* are both ambiguous."

"*Symphony* just means musicians or instruments playing together," I said. "*American* seems plain enough."

"Symphony has been used in several different ways," Dupin said, "including references to particular musical instruments, most frequently a dulcimer. The modern dulcimer, however, is a recent American invention improvised by allegedly Gaelic immigrants. The juxtaposition of the two words might be coincidental, but it might not . . . with the slight objection that the modern American dulcimer probably had not been invented in 1770. On the other hand, if the manuscript is genuine and it really has been contained within the painting for more than seventy years, the message clearly refers to a date well in advance of that time of writing . . . a date that has a particular significance for us, in the context of the most recent of Thibodeaux's hypothetical temporal nodes. We have not even made a detailed comparison of the hallucinations that you and I experienced, let alone attempting to induce Saint-Germain and Lucien Groix to tell us exactly what they saw, but there can be no doubt that we all witnessed some truly remarkable phenomena, just as you and I did in the underworld beneath Mont Dragon."

"And you think that our experience in the Ardèche is connected with this mystery?" I hazarded. "You think that the entity that the local people of that region called the Flameflower is an entity of the same kind as Cthulhu?"

"Not the same," Dupin said, "and perhaps not even similar—except that it too can infect people with hallucinations, employing music of a sort to do so . . . and let us not forget that the music in question was more easily audible to the sensitive ears of children than to adults, who tend to lose auditory sensitivity as they grow older. Let us not forget, either, that the inscription that Angria's Mahatma incorporated into Ysolde Leonys' flesh was implanted there while she was a child, under some kind of hypnotic compulsion, probably in order to enhance her abilities as what Oberon Breisz called a skryer."

"And Jana Valdemar was murdered by a mysterious hypnotic compulsion," I could not help adding, while also remembering, silently, that Jana Valdemar's ghost had mentioned a dulcimer—an instrument unfamiliar to me even in its American version.

"So you have always alleged," Dupin agreed, but with an audible gloss of skepticism.

"I saw her ghost last night," I told him, belatedly, "while the spectral music was being played."

"What?" said Dupin. "Where?"

"On the Pont de la Tournelle. It was a hallucination, of course—but she told me to beware."

"Of what?"

"She was frustratingly vague on that point, albeit generous in her enumeration. She might have given me more detailed information, I suppose, had the music not stopped, causing her to vanish."

"Why didn't you mention it last night?"

I hesitated, but then said: "I thought you would be bound to put a psychological interpretation on it, regarding it as a reflection of my . . . feelings."

Dupin did not assure me that I had no reason to feel guilty about having failed to rescue Jana Valdemar from drowning. He knew that that was not what I meant. Nor did he bother to assure me that it was perfectly natural for a man, even of my age, to be sexually attracted to young women . . . including, and perhaps especially, young women they could not help seeing as tragic victims of misfortune. Nor did he attempt, for the moment, to follow up the possible implications of his observation that children apparently have a greater range of auditory perception than adults. Instead, presumably following his own labyrinthine train of thought, he simply said: "Do you know when Captain Pym picked up his castaway on Booby Island?"

"Not exactly," I said, "but he used the phrase *three months*, and he boasted that his ship had an unusually rapid and smooth journey; it might conceivably have been the first or second of November . . . he was, at any rate, insistent that news of his castaway could not possibly have reached Paris before him by ordinary means."

"That would, in fact, be remarkable, if the news traveled by mundane channels," Dupin agreed, pensively, "but we have evidence, it seems, that it might have been anticipated some eighty years ago by occult means, and perhaps long before then."

"By someone who took the trouble to warn the intended recipient of the message to beware of the Nine," I agreed. "Which means, I assume, the legendary Nine Immortals . . . whose representative does not seem to have crossed your path as you returned from the Louvre, where he had gone to look for you. As I said, Saint-Germain claims to have seen him before . . . quite likely in the 1770s. I had assumed that it was mere bluster, and can surely be confirmed in that opinion by the fact that the supposed Immortal declined to recognize him and implied that he is an impostor."

"I made a note of that," Dupin confirmed. "It's an interesting point."

"Is it? Haven't you always assumed that the self-styled Comte is, in fact, an impostor?"

"I have—a supposition licensed, if not proven, by his apparent youth and the fact that he bears little resemblance to portraits of the notorious Comte de Saint-Germain who was active in the Bourbon court—but he has excuses to explain those facts, and if the model of immortality that he proposed to us on All Hallows can be taken seriously, it would be impossible to rule out the possibility that the person baptized Laurent Falleroux really did become a reincarnation of sorts of the individual previously incarnated as the notorious fraudster."

My memory of the speech that Saint-Germain had made that night was a little hazy—we had all been in an altered state of consciousness—but the gist of it was quite simple. According to him, metempsychosis does not work in accordance with the crude model suggesting that the soul of a dead individual migrates into the body of a new-born child or animal. Instead, the soul of the dead person is capable of gradual integration with the mind of a much more mature individual, who comes to "remember," by degrees, having lived a previous existence . . . or, in very exceptional circumstances, a whole series of previous existences, those memories slowly superseding, erasing and overwriting the memories accumulated by the host in his or her own lifetime, thus constituting a kind of psychic palimpsest. I remembered that Jana Valdemar, who had experience in excavating supposed memories of anterior lives by means of hypnosis, had issued a significant challenge to Saint-Germain's assumption that the relevant process of metamorphosis was accomplished by the will-power of the immortal soul in quest of reincarnation rather than by virtue of what Blaise Thibodeaux called temporal resonance. Thibodeaux's ghost had offered a different account, suggesting that all living beings harbor fugitive memories inherited from previous organic existences, extending all the way back to the first evolution of mind—and also the paradoxical capability of "echoing" future existences.

"So you think our Comte de Saint-Germain might, indeed, remember having been the eighteenth century Comte de Saint-Germain . . . or, at least, is convinced that he remembers it?" I suggested, sticking to the matter at hand.

"It's possible," was all that Dupin would concede.

"And is that the kind of immortality that the legendary Nine Immortals are supposed to have—serial reincarnation with a memory of past incarnations?"

"Not according to legend," Dupin said. "According to legend they really do possess the secret of extreme longevity and immunity to aging . . . a secret that they keep very religiously. Legend asserts that numerous attempts have been made to force one or other of them to reveal it, but that such attempts always fail. Their mesmeric power is allegedly sufficient to deter any attempt to harm them, and they are said to be immune to fatal accidents . . . but legend is not a reliable witness, and is heavily polluted by invention. Skeptics claim that if the Nine Immortals have any actual existence at all, they are simply a society like the legendary Rosicrucians or the actual Académie Française, which has a numerically-fixed membership, renewed by substitution whenever a member dies."

"Saint-Germain said that some so-called authorities link them to ancient yogis, and others to the Hescheboix nomads . . . the so-called Thierachians who visit Mont Dragon on a regular basis. I wonder whether Saint-Germain's Immortal might be able to cast further light on those suggestions."

"So do I," said Dupin, "but the legendary Immortals are said to be extremely parsimonious with information and easily capable of deflecting interrogation.

Just like you, I thought—but all I said aloud was: "Saint-Germain suggested that they might conceive of themselves as guardians or policemen of a sort, akin to the Dwellers in the borderlands between dimensions, and he made the same suggestion about Madame Lacuzon."

Dupin permitted himself a small laugh. "Amélie certainly sees herself as my protector, but she is definitely not one of the Nine Immortals, or akin to the legendary Dwellers, although she considers herself to be an associate of a loosely-knit community of Breton witches. You have seen for yourself that she has ordinary mortal frailties, and the abilities that she and others consider to be magical owe nothing to yogis or the Hescheboix, being purely Breton in descent. As for her self-assigned role as my guardian, she is simply . . . affectionate."

"Because she nursed you as a child?"

Dupin frowned. "Did Saint-Germain tell you that? Yes, it's true. She regards me, I suppose, perhaps subconsciously, as her own child, because unfortunate circumstance dictated that I replaced the child to whom she actually gave birth. She would never say as much in so many words, and it is not a topic that I would ever broach with her, but I suspect that she has always regarded my mother's inability to produce milk as an intervention of destiny rather than a mere physical ailment, with the intention of placing me in her care . . . an obligation that, in her eyes, did not end when I was weaned, and has not ended yet. She is certainly not wicked, or inclined to violence, whatever malevolent tongues might allege, but I suspect that she would be easily capable of murder if she thought that I was threatened with harm. Does that satisfy your curiosity?"

"Not even nearly," I said. "Where has she taken Pym's castaway, and why?"

"I don't know," Dupin said, although something in his tone suggested to me that he might not be being entirely honest, "but I have learned over the course of a lifetime to trust her judgment. If she thought it necessary to remove the child from your house, urgently, then she had a reason that she thought imperative, probably that she did not want her to fall into the custody of the supposed Immortal mesmerist. Whether she thinks that the child is under an imminent threat, or whether she thinks that she might pose a threat to me, I cannot tell, but I presume that she will let me know as soon as she thinks it wise or safe to do so."

"How did the alleged Immortal know her name?"

"Your guess is as good as mine—but if he obtained information somehow that Captain Pym had set forth from Le Havre in search of me, he would probably have made haste to obtain whatever information he could about me. My association with Amélie is well-known in Paris as well as certain places in Brittany, and is subject to all kinds of fanciful interpretation on the part of the ignorantly superstitious. I cannot believe that his knowledge of her name is eloquent testimony to any occult power, or any prior acquaintance, although he might have intended you to take that implication, in the interests of supporting his imposture."

"Fair enough," I said. "In any case, the real mystery is the message you deciphered. If it really does date from 1770, it certainly gives evidence of some occult power of anticipation—and if it does not, what can its purpose possibly be? If it is a hoax, as you put it, then the intended target of the hoax can only be you. Who would perpetrate such a hoax, and why?"

"I don't know," he said. "It's surely far too complicated to have been contrived by Saint-Germain as an element of his relentless quest to involve me in his fanciful research into the supposed secrets of immortality, and it seems to me that, although he is certainly very enthusiastic to become a player in the game into which he has drawn us, he was only a pawn in the affair at Fontainebleau, manipulated by the mysterious Anton."

"Alias Oberon the Fay," I supplied.

"That is your interpretation," Dupin said, "conceived in a state of hallucination . . . but that doesn't necessarily mean that it's incorrect. And the other potential candidate as a perpetrator, if this were a hoax, seems even more implausible, at least superficially . . . unless, of course, she is not actually dead."

"Jana Valdemar?" I queried, astonished. "Impossible!"

"Is it?" Dupin countered. "If Saint-Germain and Chapelain can be believed, she is a mesmerist of unusual ability, superior to theirs in some ways, and she certainly tried to dupe us once by convoluted means. The evidence of her death relates to a body initially classified as one of the Seine's many unknown victims, and subsequently identified by Chapelain. So far as I know, Lucien never saw it, and neither did you or I."

"I've seen her ghost!" I objected.

"Indeed—having previously jumped into the Seine, very foolishly, to try to save her life. You have asserted ever since that she was acting under some mysterious hypnotic compulsion, but I have sometimes wondered whether the person who was actually acting under a hypnotic compulsion was you."

"Me! That's ludicrous!" Even as I said it, though, I realized that the denial must ring rather hollow, especially as Dupin knew that I had spent some considerable time alone with Jana Valdemar on the afternoon prior to our expedition to Fontainebleau. I immediately changed tack: "What motive could she possibly have?"

"That," said Dupin, "is a very good question. What motive, in fact, could anyone have for concocting a hoax as elaborate as this one must be, if it is, in fact, a hoax? But if we accept that it is not, that the document contained in the painting is authentic, and has indeed been concealed there since the 1770s, the question still remains: what possible motive can the instigator of the mystery have? The invocation of the name and power of Cthulhu cannot set aside the necessity of finding an answer to that question, at least hypothetically. In fact . . ."

He was interrupted, as my informants that day seemed doomed to be, by the sound of my doorbell. Knowing that Madame Bihan and her husband were not in the house, and being very wary of simply going to open the front door, I moved to the one position in the study from which the area outside the front door was obliquely visible.

"It can't be Amélie," Dupin judged, correctly. "Is it your mysterious Immortal?"

"No," I reported. "It's two men clad as seamen, who give the impression of having recently disembarked without taking the trouble, or without having had the time, to change into Parisian costume. One, if I'm not mistaken, is Arthur Pym, and the other, I believe, is my cousin Jeremiah."

VII

THE SECRETS OF THE DEEP

I answered the door to my two new visitors myself, there being no one else to do it. It was Arthur Pym who stepped forward, holding out his hand to be shaken, apparently glad to see me.

"Mr. Reynolds!" he said. "It's been a long time, But I hope that you recognize me—Arthur Pym."

"I do indeed, Arthur," I said. "And it has been even longer since I saw you, Jeremiah, although I naturally recognize you, as the most famous member of my family." Having received Arthur Pym's handshake I naturally grasped my cousin's hand—a trifle distractedly, admittedly, immediately switching my attention back to his companion in order to add: "If you're looking for your cousin, Arthur, you've just missed him."

I had evidently jumped to the wrong conclusion—not for the first time.

"Cousin?" queried Arthur Pym, evidently having no idea what I was talking about. "What cousin?"

I remembered then what Dupin had said about Jacob Pym perhaps not being who he claimed to be.

"A seaman who named himself as Jacob Pym came to see me this morning," I told him. "He introduced himself as your cousin."

"Jacob?" said Arthur Pym, still astonished. "But . . . surely the *Excelsior's* in the South Seas. The last news I had of him was that he was busy trading between Batavia and the burgeoning Australian colonies."

"He's evidently in Paris now," I replied, "and he seems to believe that you're somewhere in the South Seas. He seemed to think the same about you, Jeremiah, although the last news I had of you was that you were attempting to raise money in America to mount a new expedition to the Antarctic, looking for evidence in support of the theory of the Hollow Earth proposed by the late Mr. Symmes of New Jersey. But let's not stand on the doorstep exchanging misconceptions. Do come in, and I'll introduce you to my friend Auguste Dupin."

I expected some reaction to Dupin's name, and I was not disappointed. There was an evident satisfaction in their expressions, which led me to think that it might well be Dupin, rather than me, that they had really come to see.

"My housekeeper and her husband are not here, I'm afraid," I explained, as I led them into the study, "but I'd be very glad to make us all a pot of coffee—you must be very cold, in spite of those thick seamen's coats." Then I made the necessary introductions and invited everyone to sit down near the fire, which I stimulated vigorously with the poker.

"A pot of coffee would be very welcome, Sam," said Jeremiah, using my forename quite naturally, even though he hadn't clapped eyes on me for nearly twenty years, not long after his first return from the Antarctic and some years before his account of the history of Mocha Dick had redeemed his popular reputation somewhat, although his standing in the scientific community had been spoiled by his heretical adherence to the Symmes theory. He had always considered himself to be a serious and committed scientist, even though others regarded him as a mere journalist . . . or even a crank.

I had no alternative but to disappear in order to prepare the promised hot beverage, and by the time I came back with the tray, my two new visitors had already embarked on an earnest conversation with Dupin, evidently on the subject of the Hollow Earth.

"Symmes changed his mind more than once," Jeremiah was saying, "and he was not the obsessive eccentric that the newspapers represented him to be, any more than I am. He modified his initial notion that the Earth consisted of five concentric spheres with gaps in between, to propose instead that there might be a vast hollow core within the crust, but he was never entirely unsympathetic to the notion that the truth was far more complicated, and that there might well be a whole series of such lacunae—hollows in the plural rather than a single hollow—and that his hypothetical Antarctic entrance might not be the only means of access to such underworlds from the Earth's surface. There is, of course, a rich legendry of supposedly bottomless pits, and any number of tales associated with the chimneys of extinct volcanoes. Numerous descents have been attempted in various parts of Europe—including, I believe, one that you and Sam undertook yourself."

Evidently, rumor had reached him concerning our expedition to Mont Dragon. I had not published any account of it, and nor had Dupin or Guérande, but I had mentioned it in letters to family members, and it was presumably by means of that grapevine that the rumor had reached Jeremiah in New York, where he was nowadays based between his exploratory missions—missions that were sometimes veiled with secrecy, because, so the same family grapevine alleged, they were partly financed by the US government in the interests of espionage.

Dupin did not seem delighted that news of his adventure had become public knowledge, probably because he was not entirely sure what had happened in the bowels of the mountain, even though he had not merely heard the flameflower sing but had joined in. Dupin loved a mystery—but he loved it far more once he had found a satisfactory explanation for it. Mysteries had arrived thick and fast in recent months, but complete solutions to the puzzles they posed had been in conspicuously short supply.

"We did," Dupin confirmed, and left it at that.

Not unnaturally, Jeremiah was not satisfied with the evasion. He switched his gaze to me: "And you found evidence of exotic life down there, I believe," he said. "You saw and heard the entities that the people of the region call flameflowers."

"I believe so," I admitted, "but I am not sure of the extent to which the phenomena were merely hallucinatory."

"*Merely* hallucinatory?" Arthur Pym queried. "We are both friends of Edgar Poe, Sam, are we not . . . and therefore familiar with the notion that the boundary between the real and the . . . seemingly supernatural . . . is far more blurred and confused than is assumed and asserted by the followers of your Monsieur Comte, who have made a religion out of his stern positivism."

"It certainly is," I was content to agree, still uncertain as to where my visitors were going and what the purpose of their visit might be. It seemed unlikely that their materialization today, of all days, could be attributed to pure chance.

"Good," said Jeremiah. "You will be prepared to accept, then, that even if what you experienced in the underworld that you accessed via the caves of Mont Dragon was partly hallucinatory, that does not make it any less significant or interesting. I do understand your reluctance to talk about the matter, having long suffered the problems associated with too great a liberality in the expression of unfashionable ideas. Perhaps you would be more comfortable telling me why Captain Pym's cousin came to see you today. Our arrival on the same day would be a remarkable coincidence, don't you think . . . if, it were, in fact, a mere coincidence." He emphasized the word *mere* slightly, reminding me of the probable impropriety of my use of its adverb a few moments before.

"He came in search of Monsieur Dupin," I said, "who was unfortunately absent at the time. He had a little girl with him—a castaway the *Excelsior* had picked up—whose speech he could not understand. He hoped that Monsieur Dupin might be able to help him communicate with the girl."

That information seemed to electrify both of them. "A castaway!" blurted Jeremiah. "A girl! You mean a so-called Child of Ocean?"

"That is a term that was used in her description," I admitted, "but not by Captain Pym. Someone else arrived shortly after the captain, looking for the girl . . . but he did not give me his name."

"Did he take her away?" Jeremiah demanded, urgently.

"No," I said. "She had already left; Monsieur Dupin's concierge had taken her—to Dupin, I assumed, who was at the Louvre at the time. Captain Pym—Jacob Pym, that is—set off for the Louvre too, but seems to have crossed paths with Monsieur Dupin without seeing him, as the other man who was looking for the little girl also must have done."

"We seem to be talking slightly at cross purposes, Monsieur Reynolds," Dupin interjected, mildly. "If the two of you came here go ask us about our expedition to Mont Dragon, why has the fact that your visit was preceded by that of a Child of Ocean startled you so much? I presume that it is not a matter of what my friend carelessly calls *mere* coincidence?"

"Indeed not," said Reynolds. "Arthur and I have sailed extensively in the South Seas, and, for slightly different but connected reasons, we have both taken an intense interest in the folklore of the region, particularly that of the islanders who are, unfortunately, in the process of being corrupted—or, to put it more brutally, exterminated—by waves of European colonists. Was the castaway that Jacob collected found on Booby Island, by any chance?"

"She was," I confirmed.

"And did she, by any chance, in the course of her incomprehensible speech mention the name Cthulhu, or *the dreamer of R'lyaeih?*"

I exchanged a long glance with Dupin instead of replying immediately, but he seemed to be waiting, just as the two newcomers were. Eventually, I said: "Yes, she did. Why do you ask?"

"Because there is nothing *mere* about this coincidence, Sam," Cousin Jeremiah retorted, "and if I'm not mistaken, you must know that very well. The name of Cthulhu is not unfamiliar to you?"

"No," I admitted. "In fact, I believe that I have encountered the entity in question, albeit in a hallucinatory fashion. I was almost killed by a shoggoth not long ago. I was testing the water, trying to figure out how extensive Cousin Jeremiah's knowledge of the Great Old One in question might be."

His only reaction, for the moment, was "Damn! Thibodeaux was right! The nexus *is* in Paris, not in the South Seas at all. We've been dragging our feet, Arthur—but we're all prisoners of the resonance, it seems, even the Nine. We're here now, though. If we're to play a part in this, we need to act quickly. We need to find that girl."

"Let's not go overboard, Jeremiah," Arthur Pym replied mildly. "We don't *know* anything at all. We've been chasing ghosts for years without ever grasping anything but mist, in the Austral seas or in America. You know perfectly well how easy it is to spin the raw thread of rumor and dreams into fantastic cloth, and how hard it is to locate any kernel of truth that might be lurking within the embroidery. If Symmes didn't give you pause enough to realize that, the search for Mocha Dick surely did . . . and at least there really was a white whale. We can't be sure yet about the reality of flameflowers, although Sam and Monsieur Dupin might be able to help us with that, let alone the reality of sirens and ghost ships. We have to be careful that the abandonment of skepticism doesn't lead us to utter credulity." He turned back to me. "It appears that you know far more about this than we had any right to expect when we decided to pay you a visit, Sam. Like Jeremiah, I understand perfectly why you might be reluctant to talk about it, but you must have realized by now that we aren't going to laugh at you or think that you're insane. Jacob, I assume, has no idea of what he's got himself into . . . but you must have suspicions akin to ours?"

I glanced at Dupin, but he was impassive, giving no indication that he might step in.

"Not really," I said. "I was told, although not by Jacob, that the other man who came looking for the girl was one of the Nine Immortals, but I'd never heard of them before the name was mentioned. For what it might be worth, though, I have encountered both sirens and a ghost ship, which were undoubtedly hallucinatory but no less dangerous for that. So, like you, I'm not going to laugh at anything you care to tell me, or dismiss it as insane . . . although, to tell you the truth, I've certainly begun to entertain severe doubts about my own sanity."

Jeremiah intervened again. "What ghost ship have you encountered, Sam?" he asked. "And where? Not in Paris, I assume."

"No," I said, evenly. "It was in Brittany, but still inland, however nonsensical that might seem. It was manned by a pirate named Jack Taylor and a Maratha warlord known to the British East India Company as Angria."

"Double damn!" said Jeremiah, seemingly greatly impressed. "When you say *encountered*, what do you mean, exactly?"

"I mean that that it came to my rescue while I was adrift in a chaotic mire in the vicinity of a circle of megaliths, which was then besieged by shoggoths," I told him. "One of its crewmen pulled me out of the mire—but whether that was at Angria's behest or Jack Taylor's, I don't know. I wasn't aboard for very long—a matter of minutes—and I was somewhat dazed at the time, not in any condition to make disciplined observations or to take any action."

Cast by fate as the eternal bystander, I recalled

"Double damn!" said Cousin Jeremiah, repetitively. "Did you see the other little girl . . . the one with the inscription tattooed on her back?"

"Yes," I said, surprised by the fact that Jeremiah must have heard mention of Ysolde Leonys as well as Jack Taylor's ghostly piracy. "But it wasn't a tattoo—it was encrypted in her flesh. And she was no longer a little girl; she'd grown up. Where and when did you encounter the ghost ship, Jeremiah?"

"A long time ago," said Jeremiah, "north-east of what is nowadays called Queensland. But we only passed in the night, and I was assured that I'd had a hallucination. It wasn't until recently, when I was able to compare notes with Arthur, that either of us became half-convinced that we really had seen something—we were both able to identify it by the golden cross nailed to its mast."

"The Flaming Cross of Goa," I said. "I mentioned it to Jacob—he said that you'd be very disappointed, Arthur, that Dupin and I had found what little was left of Olivier Levasseur's treasure."

"What!" Arthur Pym did, indeed, seem profoundly shocked and disappointed to hear that. "How?"

"The young woman with the inscription in her flesh showed us where it was buried, just before she died. She was very ill . . . there was nothing we could do."

"Damn!" said Jeremiah, yet again.

Dupin finally intervened. "We seem to be proceeding in a rather haphazard fashion, gentlemen. Perhaps, Mr. Reynolds, you wouldn't mind beginning to clarify matters by telling us what you know about Cthulhu, since that entity seems to be at the very heart of this affair."

"To say that we *know* anything might be an overstatement," Jeremiah said. "The name, of course, has been bandied about the South Seas for many years, as an element of Kanak superstition, dismissed by almost all Westerners either as pure nonsense or as garbled accounts of creatures living in the deeps of the sea: *giant squid* is the term recently used. Opinions similarly vary as to whether the monsters depicted in antique rock art on several islands are exotic products of natural history or imaginary demons. For myself, as a scientist, I incline to the hypothesis that there are, indeed, strange creatures dwelling in the utmost depths of the sea, and also in lacunae beneath the Earth's crust—vast cave systems connected to the surface by tortuous tunnels, most of which, but not all, are wholly or partially filled with water.

"Symmes believed that those lacunae were illuminated by reflected sunlight, but I never agreed with him. I suspect that the energy sustaining life in those underworlds is heat energy coming from the molten core of the planet—what fashionable jargon often calls the Central Fire—although I suspect that the entities occasionally glimpsed by humans and mistaken for flames are actually living creatures: flameflowers, in one popular terminology. In my view, they are not products of the same evolutionary sequence that produced the light-fueled living organisms of the surface, and I suspect that they must be much older—millions of years older, perhaps billions. You are undoubtedly aware that my opinion is not merely seen as heretical by Christian Churches, which are still very reluctant to admit the evidence of evolution and the true age of the Earth, but also by the contemporary scientific community.

"I think it highly probable that the living organisms of the deep sea bed and the various underworlds beneath the Earth's crust are as various and as complex as the organisms of the surface, although the fact that surface-dwellers only catch rare and fugitive glimpses of them—almost always dismissed by their fellows as delusory—prevents us from appreciating their true variety and complexity. It is not impossible that some resemble vertebrate animals, even human beings, but I think that a remote possibility. Most of them, I assume, must be vermiform or insectile . . . .but that does not rule out the possibility that some of them are possessed of a kind of consciousness and a degree of intelligence. None, I assume, have eyes, but all of them presumably make use of other senses, including hearing. I believe that they make a wide range of sounds, including sounds imperceptible to the human ear, and that they make use of those sounds in communication.

"The legend of Cthulhu, I believe, is at least partly, and perhaps principally, based on accounts and mistaken interpretations of creatures that evolved, like those called flameflowers, in the underworlds within the Earth, and the means that they employ to communicate with one another, primarily through sound but perhaps . . . probably . . . via other vibrations. I am convinced that human beings have a usually-latent capacity to perceive vibrations of which the familiar sensations of sight, hearing, touch, taste and smell do not normally take account, although you are doubtless familiar with the notion that we actually have at least one extra sense, from which we do not normally extract information for want of comprehending the signals that we receive. Such signals can, however, stimulate nerve-cells in the brain, especially when the neurons are temporarily idle, producing dreams and other pseudosensory phenomena that human consciousness generally learns to ignore or screen out, as a defense mechanism protecting the orderly organization of rational thought and calculation.

"For that reason, I believe, Cthulhu and other entities of a broadly similar kind seem to enjoy a strange semi-existence on the margins of the world that our brain selects from our sensory input as 'reality.' It is almost as if they inhabit another dimension, parallel to ours and problematic in its overlaps with ours—and that is precisely the manner in which some occult philosophers like to represent it, including Arthur, who has been collecting items of legend concerning Cthulhu for some time, including the prediction that some kind of awakening of the dreamer is imminent, and that it will be provoked by a Child of Ocean possessed by a witch in thrall to the Great Old One. I cannot take that entirely seriously myself, but I am familiar with Blaise Thibodeaux's *Resonances du temps*, and I have encountered scholars in America who claim that his discoveries are recapitulating methods of anticipation long known to the society of magicians known as the Nine Immortals—although that is not the name they employ themselves.

"It might all be a tissue of illusions, but it would be a serious matter even if it is simply a matter of false belief. Arthur and I both believe it to be more than that: that the entity called Cthulhu not only exists but is capable of limited and indirect interference in human affairs . . . and that its influence on human dreams does indeed allow it, at least occasionally, to hold people in thrall. What purpose it has in so doing, if it has a conscious purpose, in this or any other instance, we cannot tell, but the tales told in the South Seas of its manifestations, directly or via Shoggoths, almost always involve death and destruction.

"I do not know what Cthulhu and other entities of the underworlds think of us, if they do think and reason as we do, but I am sure that they are aware of us, and almost certain that some of them, at least, make occasional attempts to communicate with us, in spite of all the difficulties that must involve. Sometimes, I think—perhaps often—such attempts do have harmful consequences, even though the entities are probably not malevolent and do not mean to cause harm. Indeed, I suspect they have occasionally made what attempts they could to assist the development of our brains, by means that are necessarily indirect but not ineffective, usually involving sound signals that we inevitably construe as strange music, and the stimulation of mental images that we necessarily construe as hallucinations.

"I ought to emphasize, of course, that this is a personal interpretation—the detail of which is, to some extent, idiosyncratic to myself. Other people, including Arthur, put different interpretations on the few facts available to us—which do, in fact, lend themselves to many different interpretations, but that is how I see the situation myself. Does that answer your question adequately, Monsieur Dupin?"

"Indeed," said Dupin. "I will even go so far as to say that I am delighted by your explanation—which, although hypothetical, is very close to the interpretation I have recently begun to put on the evidence available to me. But it is only a commencement, is it not? You have mentioned Blaise Thibodeaux, and seem to place some trust in his prophetic artistry. You also appear to take very seriously the legend of the so-called Nine Immortals, as well as that of the ghost ship created and perhaps controlled, if I'm not mistaken, by an individual who once called himself—probably among other names—the Mahatma. If those really are all parts of the same metaphysical jigsaw as your account of the Cthulhu entity, I must admit to having some difficulty in fitting them all together."

"That isn't surprising," said Cousin Jeremiah. "I have made a life's work of it, and the process of slotting the pieces of the puzzle together has been exceedingly difficult. I believe that I now have an idea of what the ensemble might look like, but I suspect that getting a clear and detailed view of the picture would take far more than one lifetime . . . even, perhaps the kind of protracted lifetime allegedly possessed by the so-called Nine. They are, I believe, what legend represents them to be: human beings who do not automatically die of so-called 'natural causes' because their bodies, once they reach a certain maturity, seem to be almost immune to the ageing process. That seems magical and mysterious, but if you look at the situation from a different angle, the real mystery might not be why they do not waste away and die after the pro-verbial three-score-years-and-ten, but why almost everyone else does. I doubt that their biological science is capable of providing an answer to that enigma any more than ours is. They undoubtedly have knowledge that we children of the so-called Enlightenment do not, and abilities that we do not, but I suspect that they are not as far in advance of us as they would like to think.

"Such individuals are not, of course, literally immortal, and there must certainly be more than nine of them. There are any number of ways in which such individuals could be violently slain, and any who have already survived for a thousand years and more have undoubtedly had to be very fortunate as well as very careful. They tend to shun the danger of sustained intercourse with other human beings, even—and perhaps especially—their own kind. With the aid of powers nowadays known as mesmeric or hypnotic they have developed intimidatory methods of self-defense, and they are, indeed very defensive and very secretive. Like short-lived individuals, the long-lived have to find reasons for living—ambitions and purposes—which tend eventually to turn into obsessions. Alienists would undoubtedly consider them to be monomaniacs of a kind—but not all of the same kind. Few of them like to work in association, at least for any considerable length of time, but one such long-lasting association undoubtedly gave rise to the legend of the Nine. Whether Angria's Mahatma is one of the Nine I do not know, but I strongly suspect that he is an Immortal, as Angria might well be himself . . . but the indications that Arthur and I have gleaned from the burgeoning folklore of seamen recently operating in the South Seas suggest that Angria possesses a different kind of longevity. There are, I believe, several. In some, the price of longevity involves periods of stasis, or suspended animation. Others are even more complicated, involving a process of apparent reincarnation."

"*Apparent* reincarnation?" I queried, unable to resist the temptation to interrupt, in spite of Dupin's evident disapproval, expressed by one of his intemperate frowns.

"The difference between the real and the apparent, in this respect as in many others," Jeremiah opined, "is much less clear-cut than people think."

"Indeed," Dupin agreed, swiftly reclaiming the prerogative of guiding the interrogation, "and we should not forget ghosts, should we, which can be viewed as another species of reincarnated beings?"

He did not so much as spare me a sideways glance, or even prolong his frown of annoyance, although I was certain that he must now be thinking about my encounters—real or hallucinatory—with Blaise Thibodeaux and Jana Valdemar, just as he must have been thinking a few minutes before about Lucien Falleroux, alias the Comte de Saint-Germain, and the strange child who had coerced him into playing the music of Erich Zann on Zann's own violin, in order to open a door to chaos.

"No, Cousin," Jeremiah agreed, "we must not forget ghosts. Might I enquire, Monsieur Dupin, as to how well you knew Blaise Thibodeaux?"

"Not very well, I fear—my friend Paul Lacroix knew him better. How well did you know him?"

"I only met him once, and briefly. He was old and crippled at the time—far from immortal, alas, in the literal sense—but a great man nevertheless. Given more time, I believe that he would have made vast progress in sorting out the philosophical wheat from the chaff of his statistical analyses. It is not given detailed consideration in his book, although I believe that he intended to put it in a second volume that he never completed, but he was perfectly certain, toward the end of his life, that 1848 would be a year of revolutions, not merely in France but all over Europe . . . and perhaps of a catastrophe far greater than any mere political upheaval."

"Involving Cthulhu" Dupin prompted.

"In my interpretation, yes. Thibodeaux knew the name, of course, but little more than that, categorized in his thinking as fanciful folklore, just as he was familiar with the myth of the *Necronomicon* and other fake grimoires . . . but yes; in my opinion, Cthulhu is crucial to an understanding of the potential catastrophe."

"And the child?" I put in, thinking that to be a more fruitful topic of immediate investigation than a discussion as to whether or not the fabled *Necronomicon*, nowadays only existent in corrupt translations, really was entirely fake.

"*A* child, at least," Jeremiah confirmed. "Children, you see, have sharper senses than adults, especially in terms of hearing. As we grow older, our evolving consciousness builds defenses against stimuli that we do not want to hear, or do not want to understand: stimuli that are potentially understandable either as language or music, but which can be dangerous. Children differ, of course, just as adults do, in the degree of their sensitivity to exotic neural stimuli, and just as there are rare mathematical geniuses among young adults, there are rare visionary geniuses among children, very precious to those interested in such exotic matters. The languages we speak and understand, like the various kinds of music that we value, are carefully filtered and diluted by ordinary people, and almost all adult brains become unconsciously expert at screening out or dismissing unwanted materials that do not fit into their constructions of belief or pleasure . . . but we remain vulnerable, in spite of all that defensive consciousness can contrive, to certain kinds of gibberish and cacophony, as well as to seductive rhetoric and siren songs. No matter how determined we are to be good positivists, the seemingly supernatural, or the unaccountable, is always close at hand, lurking in the borderlands of perception."

"Gibberish that includes the alleged dead names of the *Necronomicon* and siren songs that include the infernal jigs of *Les Harmoines de l'enfer*," I supplied, ignoring Dupin's censorious frown yet again.

"Among others," my cousin agreed.

"So you think that Jacob Pym's Child of Ocean might be capable of hearing notes in a musical composition to which adult ears would be deaf, as well as capable of understanding and pronouncing a language that none of his versatile crewmen could comprehend?" I said, stubbornly persisting in pursuit of my own train of thought.

"Probably. She might also be capable of singing in the mysterious language . . . and, which is probably more important, of a limited understanding of the songs she can sing . . . not necessarily on a conscious level, but in a manner capable of giving them a contagious effect . . ."

"But probably not singing *a cappella*," I persisted.

"Perhaps," Jeremiah agreed. "If my interpretation of seamen's folklore can be trusted, she might well need the collaboration of an instrument, perhaps more than one—and Arthur agrees, I think."

Pym nodded, apparently perfectly content, for the time being, to let Jeremiah provide all the explanations, even though my cousin punctuated his account, scrupulously with occasional suggestions that his friend did not agree entirely with his inferences.

"A quintet," Dupin said, as if thinking aloud—or perhaps trying to prompt some further suggestion from one or other of our interlocutors.

"Perhaps," said Jeremiah, obligingly but unhelpfully.

I knew why Dupin had chosen that particular term, and I guessed that the hypothetical quintet he had in mind might involve one or more dulcimers as well as or instead of viols or rebecs. For myself, though, I wondered whether it might not be over-thinking the matter to construe the reference in the overwritten palimpsest to an "American" as a reference to an American dulcimer. *Sometimes*, I thought, *an American is just an American, like cousin Jeremiah . . . or Arthur or Jacob Pym . . . or even me.*

At one time, I would not have added my own name to the mental list, because I could not play an instrument . . . but I was acutely aware that I *had* played an instrument in the not too distant past . . . or, more accurately, I had *been* played, along with the instrument in question. I had not only heard siren music, but had been press-ganged into serving as a siren. It seemed perfectly possible that it might happen again—and that, in spite of Jana Valdemar's warning, there might be nothing I could do to prevent it . . . .unless I could discover more cleverness and bravery than I had exhibited thus far in my dealings with the dream-dimensions

We were swimming now in deep conceptual waters, I knew; perhaps too deep for my poor beleaguered consciousness . . . and conceptual waters, I knew, had metaphorical monsters of their own, which might well be delusory, and not even actively hostile, but which could nevertheless do great harm, especially to poor swimmers.

I still had a thousand questions to voice, and I dare say that Dupin, Arthur and Cousin Jeremiah had almost as many, but the accursed doorbell rang yet again before any of us could frame one.

I ran to the spot from which the ringer could be seen.

I could not help groaning. The man on the doorstep, using the end of his sword-stick to yank the metal ring at the end of the bell-cord, was the Comte de Saint-Germain.

I answered the door.

"Dupin's here now," I admitted, without giving him time to voice the question that I assumed to be inevitable, and added, albeit very reluctantly: "I suppose you'd better come in."

"On the contrary," he said, continuing the trend that had filled the day with surprises. "You and he had better come out, and very urgently. There's been . . . an accident."

The way he pronounced the last word made it obvious that he considered whatever had happened to be anything but a mere accident . . . but he was looking over my shoulder, and he could not only see Dupin, who had come into the doorway of the study, but also that the Chevalier was not alone. He evidently intended the details of his mission for our ears only.

VIII

Return to the Witch-House

SAINT-GERMAIN had a carriage waiting, but it was not the giant that he had employed to conduct us to the forest of Fontainebleau, and as soon as he realized that Dupin's companions intended to accompany him he was quick to say: "There's no room for your friends, I fear, Dupin. I can't take them with me."

Dupin, who had not yet introduced Arthur Pym and Jeremiah Reynolds to the newcomer, was not to be put off so easily. "Nonsense, Saint-Germain," he said. "It will accommodate four inside, and one on the seat beside the coachman. We all have an interest in this matter." As he spoke his gaze slipped sideways, looking along the street. He could not resist the temptation to add: "And your horses cannot be very fast, else they would have been able to outpace the fellow following you, who does not seem conspicuously out of breath."

Saint-Germain followed Dupin's gaze. "Damnation!" he said, although he must surely have known that he was under police surveillance. "They're going to think . . ." But he shut his mouth abruptly, unwilling to tell us what "they" were going to think. Instead, he said: "I need to speak with you in private, Dupin, where no one can hear us."

I realized that not only did I recognize the man who had apparently been following Saint-Germain's vehicle, but that he evidently knew me by sight, or at least that he knew Dupin, because he made the same swift hand signal as the young woman in the café across the street from the witch-house. He was not only a police agent, but one familiar with Lucien Groix's secret sign language. I had no doubt that Dupin had seen the signal too, but he was careful to give no evidence of the fact.

"Do you intend to take us to the witch-house?" Dupin demanded of the fake comte, abruptly.

Saint-Germain knew Dupin well enough not to be astonished by that deduction. "Yes," he said, "but you don't understand . . ."

Dupin ignored the objection. "I intended to head there imminently myself," he said, "and to take these two gentlemen with me. You can save Reynolds a cab fare."

"You don't understand . . ." Saint-Germain began, for a second time, but Dupin interrupted him again unwilling to let go of the reins of the conversation now that he was holding them firmly again.

"I'm forgetting my manners," he said. "May I introduce Reynolds' celebrated cousin Jeremiah, and Arthur Gordon Pym, who are certainly known to you by reputation, if not by sight. Gentlemen, this is the Comte de Saint-Germain, President of the Parisian Harmonic Society. He has knowledge and associates that will be invaluable to us if we are to solve this puzzle, and our meeting is very fortuitous."

If the names that Dupin had cited startled Saint-Germain, the assertion that his knowledge and associates might be invaluable to them startled him even more—but he still seemed direly anxious about something. For a moment, he was atypically speechless, not knowing what to do or say.

Dupin took the decision out of his hands. "Captain Pym," he said, "Would you mind very much taking the seat beside the coachman? I would ask Reynolds to do it, but he has lately been ill."

Given that he had recently dragged me to the Faubourg Saint-Victor on foot in the dead of night, that excuse rang as hollow in my ears as John Symmes' Earth, but I was not about to contradict him. In spite of the quilted jacket I was wearing under my overcoat I could not imagine that I would be very comfortable riding on the seat of a slow carriage in air whose temperature had to be below the freezing point of water. On the other hand, even though Arthur Pym was wrapped up as he would have been on the deck of the ship in an Antarctic tempest, I could not imagine that he would enjoy such a journey either. He was evidently made of sterner stuff than me, however, because he was quick to reply to Dupin by saying: "Yes, of course," presumably being anxious that Saint-Germain might deny him the requested permission if he hesitated. He matched his affirmation with action, already climbing up as Dupin stepped forward and opened the carriage door in order to invite Cousin Jeremiah to precede him into the interior.

Saint-Germain accepted defeat, perhaps not graciously but with evident resignation. He gave the coachman the order to take us to the Rue de l'Hirondelle. As we pulled away he looked out of the portière at the police agent, who did not seem at all delighted at having to resume his pursuit, even though running would undoubtedly be healthier than standing still in the ambient conditions.

"Damnation," he repeated. "Where on earth did I pick up that fellow? He wasn't with me when I called at your house earlier, or at the Louvre."

"He probably followed you from the Rue de l'Hirondelle," Dupin said, equably. "Lucien's successor apparently has a whole squad stationed in the café there, although I must admit that it seems excessive, if it is only to maintain surveillance on the house of a vampire unseen for almost half a century . . . unless, of course, she has been seen again more recently, and mistaken for a dangerous Republican. The opposite mistake might have been made before, I suspect, given that it is statistically more likely that dangerous Republicans have been mistaken for supernatural beings, perhaps having represented themselves as such in order to deter surveillance."

It seemed plausible to me that some such imposture had been suspected when mysterious lights had been seen in the witch-house, although the music I had heard at midnight certainly inclined me to the presumption that something uncanny really had occurred there, and I assumed that Dupin was being disingenuous in offering his hypothesis.

"Damnation!" said Saint-Germain again, becoming almost as repetitive as Cousin Jeremiah. I knew that he could not be worried about the mere possibility of being mistaken for a Republican himself, in spite of Lamartine's alleged misappropriation of the premises of the Harmonic Society to hold discussions with fellow liberal intellectuals. Whatever was troubling him was more serious than that.

Purely in the interests of mischief, I said: "Don't feel persecuted, Saint-Germain. The secret police also set out to follow the man with the big hat when he left Addhema's house last night. Perhaps I ought to have a word with the fellow following us, in case he can tell us where the supposed Immortal went after crossing my path."

Saint-Germain laughed briefly, although I couldn't see that I'd said anything humorous."

"Don't do that, Reynolds," said Dupin. "I don't know why, or on whose behalf, he gave us the signal, but it's surely wiser to be discreet, for the time being."

"Signal!" Saint-Germain exclaimed. "You mean that you're still in cahoots with Groix, and that he hasn't left Paris at all?"

"I wish I knew," Dupin said. "The arcane politics of the Prefecture are beyond my understanding; it might be that I am under suspicion of being, as you put it, in cahoots with him, and perhaps that traps are being set for him as well as me. He has definitely moved his family out of Paris, as a precaution, but whether he has gone with them, I really don't know. He has cut off all communication since our expedition to Fontainebleau, for reasons unknown to me. But that is irrelevant to our present concerns. Mr. Reynolds came to see his cousin about an unrelated matter, but it turns out that he has information and insights very relevant to the mystery of the witch-house, to which you might be able to add useful supplements, Saint-Germain, especially in regard to your mysterious Immortal, about whom I need to know everything that you can tell me."

Saint-Germain laughed again, humorlessly. "I can tell you that he's no immortal," he said.

"What do you mean?" Dupin asked.

"I mean that as we speak, he's lying dead in the drawing room of the witch-house, where I found his cadaver less than an hour ago—and from which, you've just assured me, a whole gang of police agents saw me emerge."

I realized that the reason Saint-Germain was so agitated was that he thought he would be under suspicion of murder . . . the murder of a man he had unhesitatingly identified, even before clapping eyes of him, as one of the legendary Nine Immortals, hundreds, if not thousands, of years old . . . not to mention that the fellow was built like a pugilist, seemingly capable of breaking any ordinary assailant in two, even without the aid of his mysterious magnetic eyes."

"Are you certain that he's dead?" Dupin asked, in a tone of concern rather than amazement.

"Quite certain," the fake comte replied." I can tell when a man is no longer alive, even when he doesn't have a crossbow bolt piercing his heart."

"A crossbow bolt?" I exclaimed, astonished.

"Fired from where?" Dupin wanted to know.

"Not from this world, if I'm any judge," said Saint-Germain. "It must have hit him full in the chest as he came through the doorway, fired from the direction of the fireplace—except that it couldn't have come from the hearth, as the angle of impact seemed to be downwards. Unless his stance was very peculiar, though, there's nothing in the direction from which it seemed to have come but the chimney-breast. There might have been a clock there when the house was inhabited, or perhaps a portrait on the wall, but there's nothing there now but dusty plaster covering a brick wall. If the bowman was sitting on the mantelpiece, though, I have no idea where he could have gone after launching the fatal bolt. I searched the house and found no one upstairs or in the cellar, and when I got there the door was locked, the pretended Immortal apparently having locked it again when he came in, and put the key in his pocket."

"How did you get in, then?" I asked.

"I used what modern argot calls a *monseigneur*, although it used to be known as a *roi David* or a *Davyol*." He meant a lockpick.

"That won't help you persuade the police agents of your innocence," I observed.

"The fact that I wasn't carrying a crossbow should," replied Saint-Germain, hotly, "and would, if any French policeman, including your dull-witted friend Groix, had the imagination to believe in a shot fired from another dimension. Not to mention the fact that I had absolutely no motive for killing a man with whom I was extremely enthusiastic to have a conversation. If he hadn't been so rude this morning I'd have offered there and then to roll out a red carpet for him at the Society headquarters."

"Where the rumor had doubtless run already around like wildfire that he had been seen and recognized," Dupin deduced. "Spread by whom, might I ask?"

Saint-Germain only hesitated momentarily over reservations of confidentiality. "Alphonse Constant," he said.

I was surprised, knowing that Constant was something of an intellectual butterfly, having not long deserted Fourierism for an extreme socialism that had landed him in prison; he had only recently been released, in response to the pleas of his pregnant wife, apparently having sworn—falsely, I assumed—to steer clear of his Montagnard friends.

"Where had Constant seen him, and how did he recognize him?" Dupin demanded.

"At the Baron Du Potet's house. Constant has recently been studying mesmerism and magic, intensively, under Du Potet's tutelage. Apparently, the supposed Immortal called on Du Potet in search of information about contemporary Paris . . . including information about you, Dupin. All of this is highly confidential by the way. He didn't introduce himself by name to Du Potet, let alone to Constant, but they only had to look at him to guess what he was. Du Potet told Constant afterwards that only one of the Nine Immortals could be possessed of that much mesmeric power."

"And Du Potet—or Du Potet's judgment, reported second-hand by a clown like Constant—is your idea of a reliable witness?" Dupin said, skeptically. "Especially given that your so-called Immortal is apparently lying dead."

"Du Potet is a genius," said Saint-Germain, "albeit misunderstood, as geniuses tend to be." I had no need to ask which other misunderstood genius he had in mind.

The carriage lurched as it turned on to the quays, where it would have a relatively clear run to the Quai de la Tournelle. As I glanced out of the window reflexively, scanning the bouquinistes' stalls, I spotted Paul Lacroix walking in the same direction as the carriage. I was tempted momentarily to hail him, or at least to mention his presence to Dupin, but we had no space left to offer him a lift, and Dupin seemed to be engrossed in his interrogation of Saint-Germain, so I kept silent.

"And what did Du Potet tell the mysterious mesmerist about me?" Dupin asked Saint-Germain, a trifle testily, "apart from the fact that I have a fearsome concierge named Amélie Lacuzon, originally from Morbihan?"

"I don't know—but he's bound to have told him what happened at his garden party, when you or Reynolds played an enchanted cello and someone got blown to bits by an exotic gun."

"Du Potet wasn't present in the arbor where the incident in question occurred," said Dupin, grimly. "Nor was anyone capable of giving him an accurate account of what transpired—including Reynolds, even though he was the one vibrating the strings. No wonder the so-called Immortal came knocking at your door, Reynolds, when he heard that Captain Pym was bringing the girl to me in the hope that I might be able to identify her exotic language. Who else was present, Saint-Germain, when Constant passed that item of gossip on to you?"

"A couple of the elders, and a fellow I don't know personally, although he claims to have been a member back in the old days, and his papers were in order when checked. He uses a different pseudonym now, but that's not uncommon— Constant's own membership is inscribed under the fanciful soubriquet of Éliphas Lévi."

"What pseudonym?" Dupin demanded, curtly.

"Will Maccabee, now, although he was Prospero back in 1829. Maccabee is Cockney slang for a corpse, I believe. I only caught a glimpse of him, but he seems harmless enough to me, albeit not long for this world—hence the ironic *nom de guerre*, I assume."

"Paul Lacroix wasn't present when those names were voiced, I assume?"

"No, I haven't seen him for days—although I understand that he was with you last night at the witch-house. He's involved in this affair, then?"

"He is," Dupin confirmed, tersely. "Since you're such a good judge of exotic individuals, can you tell me whether there's any possibility that this Will Maccabee might be some kind of immortal . . . and, for that matter, whether he's the kind of man who might have experience wielding a crossbow?"

Saint-Germain tried to laugh, but thought better of it. Eventually, he said: "If he's an immortal, he certainly hasn't worn very well; he looks to be seventy years old, if he's a day, almost at death's door, and his hands are severely arthritic, which would surely make it impossible for him to use a crossbow."

"Or play a violin?" I put in, feeling that I ought to make a contribution.

"I'd be amazed if he could," said Saint-Germain. "On the other hand, amazement is very much the order of the day, isn't it? He did seem very interested in Constant's anecdote, though—especially the brief mention of the enchanted cello. He might have buttonholed Constant after I left, and I wouldn't be at all surprised if he comes looking for you, Dupin, to get your version of the story."

"Nor would I," said Dupin. "I'm surprised that he hasn't already joined the queue that has been forming all day at Reynolds' door—but perhaps he had other fish to fry."

"You know him, then?" Saint-Germain's interest in the decrepit member in question seemed to have increased by an order of magnitude.

"We've met," Dupin confirmed. "Lacroix knew him better than I did, when he was last in Paris, and he heard him play the violin . . . on the Île Saint Louis. I suppose that he would probably have given us that item of information more emphasis last night, if he hadn't got it into his head that I was hiding information from him and wanted to play tit-for-tat."

"Which, of course, you would never do . . . conceal information, that is?" Saint-Germain said, his voice dripping with sarcasm.

"It's a contagious habit," was all that Dupin said in reply, before turning to Cousin Jeremiah. "Is any of this making sense to you, Mr. Reynolds?" he asked.

"Very little," my cousin admitted. "I know of Baron Du Potet's reputation as a mesmerist, of course, and his interest in the occult, but I only know him by name. I never heard of this Will Maccabee, or Prospero . . . or Alphonse Constant, for that matter. I would like to hear the tale of the enchanted cello, though, just as I'd like to hear your account of the flameflower . . . and any other sirens you might have encountered. I'll show you mine if you'll show me yours, as we say in America . . . and in the South Seas, for that matter."

I suppose there was a slim possibility that Dupin might have obliged him, had the carriage not pulled up in the Rue de l'Hirondelle at that moment. Arthur Pym was already jumping down to the icy ground, and I opened the door beside me, but I sat back politely in order to allow Cousin Jeremiah to precede me, while Saint-Germain got down on the other side.

Dupin grabbed my arm and whispered in my ear: "Go to the café. You know the sign. Find out what you can, but don't give too much away. I need to know whether Lucien's signal is being used treacherously. Be extremely discreet."

It was an order, not a suggestion, and the way it was given, although quiet, was imperative. I gritted my teeth slightly, having been very curious to see the cadaver of the supposed Immortal slain by a crossbow, but I did as I was told, meekly. While the others went into the house, once Saint-Germain had plied his "monseigneur" with a suspicious expertise, I crossed the road diagonally and went into the café where we had met Lacroix the previous evening.

It was now mid-afternoon, but the place was almost as deserted as it had been at midnight. The young woman who had made the sign of the devil's horns at us when we left was sitting in the same seat at the same table, with two men. Whether or not they were two of the men who had accompanied her the previous night, I wasn't sure, but I thought not.

I ignored the old woman at the counter and walked straight up to the table by the window. "Excuse me, Mademoiselle," I said, "but I'd like a word with you, if that's possible?"

Dupin was right; her pretence of being a hooker waiting patiently for custom was not entirely convincing. Nevertheless, the black-haired woman simply looked me up and down with her slightly-unsettling dark eyes, and said, smoothly: "Of course, Monsieur. Would you like to come upstairs with me?"

"I would," I said, unsure whether my own pretence was any more convincing than hers, given that it was not the kind of encounter in which I had much experience to draw. She stood up and moved toward the stairway to the upper floor, moving in an oddly serpentine fashion that I assumed to be practiced.

She led me through the curtain that screened the entrance to the steep staircase and took me up to a small room whose dirty window overlooked the street. The witch-house was clearly visible from that position, but I could understand why the police spies were not using it as a vantage point; the room was freezing, it reeked unpleasantly, and it was filthy—especially the bed. I could not imagine that she would have obtained much custom if she had been a real whore—which was, I suspected, partly the point.

As I peered through the murky window, however, I could not help remembering the window in the garret in the Rue d'Auseuil, through which I had seen the edge of chaos beyond the borders of our own dimension, and I felt a strange twinge in my chest-cavity. Suddenly, I wondered whether the fake prostitute might not be a police agent after all, but something far stranger, and whether her inept disguise might be a trick, intended to cover a much more effective disguise. I pulled myself together, however, and instructed myself sternly not to add further imaginary complications to an affair that was already far too complicated.

She closed the door, and immediately said: "Why didn't Dupin come himself? Monsieur Groix wants to deal with the organ-grinder, not the monkey."

"Really?" I said. "Is Lucien here?"

"No," she said "What is Dupin doing in that house?"

I didn't like her attitude. Dupin had instructed me not to "give too much away," but I thought I could use my own judgment as to how much might be enough.

"He's inspecting the crime scene," I said, "exactly as Monsieur Groix would want him to do."

"Crime scene?" she said. "What crime?"

I contrived a laugh. "Some police spy you are," I said. "You've been sat downstairs watching the house since last night, and you don't know what's happened inside? Tell me, apart from the man whose carriage just brought us, who has gone into that house this morning?"

She scowled. "That's not your business," she said. "I make my reports to the head of the Sûreté."

I took note of the fact that she had not said "the Prefect of Police." I did not even know the name of the present head of the Sûreté.

"Of course you do," I said. "And it seems that you have nothing to report. He'll doubtless be very pleased with you. But you took the trouble to signal us last night, and so did the fellow who followed the coach just now, so you obviously wanted to make contact with us. So make it. What do you want with Dupin? I can assure you that I have his complete confidence."

She hesitated, but eventually said: "Tell him that Addhema is back."

"A lamia last reportedly seen under the Directoire, who bears no resemblance to the strapping fellow who was in the house last night and who has obviously returned in the interim? That's not going to impress Dupin, or me. Where did the man your associate followed last night go?"

She scowled again. She wasn't pretty enough for the scowl to make her look more attractive, but she was evidently intelligent enough to know that if she simply told me that it was none of my business, it would be counter-productive. Her attitude shifted.

"I don't know," she admitted. "We lost him. Who is he?"

"You don't know?"

"Only that he's presumably an accomplice of the supposed vampire. Those glowing eyes are a neat trick, but not enough to fool us. I doubt that he's a run-of-the-mill Republican conspirator, but who can tell, these days?"

"Not me," I admitted. "Does your uncertainty mean that no one else has been to visit him, except us?"

"Not that we could see," she confirmed, her phraseology suggesting that she wasn't prepared to express a firm opinion regarding unseen beings—perhaps wisely."

"Was it him who was playing the viol last night?" I asked her.

"No," she said. "We've searched the house and there's no musical instrument in there. We think the music must come from the far side of the block . . . or above it."

"Above it? You mean from mid-air?"

"That's what it sounded like to me—but what do I know? I've never had dealings with vampires before, real or fake. One of the fellows I was with last night, who recognized your Monsieur Dupin, reckons that he has had dealings of that sort—and when we made our report this morning, the boss agreed, and told us to find out more if we could. So—what was Dupin doing here last night and what is he doing here now? If there really has been a crime, the boss will need to know and quickly. If you don't tell me, we'll have to take another look for ourselves, and if we do that we might have to arrest the lot of you and take you to the depot for questioning . . . and you probably know how long that will take."

That didn't leave me much choice. "The man with the intimidating eyes has been murdered," I told her. "Monsieur Dupin would doubtless be obliged if you give him time to gather evidence himself before your men burst in. He will, as always, be glad to make the Sûreté party to his findings, as a matter of urgency, but I doubt that it will be easy to identify the murderer, if you haven't seen anyone entering the house except Saint-Germain."

"Saint-Germain? The fellow with the carriage is the Comte de Saint-Germain? The crook who runs the Harmonic Society?"

"He didn't do it," I said, wondering uncomfortably whether I'd just said far too much. "As you'll see soon enough, the man with the weird eyes was shot with a crossbow. Have you seen anyone in the vicinity with a crossbow?"

"Don't be ridiculous," she said. "This isn't the Middle Ages, and if we'd seen anyone wandering the streets with a crossbow, the way things are at present, he'd have been in Saint-Pélagie before you could count to ten. A crossbow! Having all the blood drained out of him through a bite in the neck I might be able to believe, but a crossbow . . ."

"Have you actually seen the alleged vampire?" I asked her.

"Not in the flesh, if she has flesh. We've seen strange lights in the house, though, when there was supposed to be no one in it—and there was no one to be found when we investigated, although no one came out. It's definitely haunted . . . again."

Presumably, Paul Lacroix was not the only one who had consulted the old records concerning the house, going all the way back to the reports made during the Regency of Philippe d'Orléans.

"And what message do you want me to give Dupin?" I asked.

"Tell him to contact the Head of the Sûreté as soon as possible . . . and as discreetly as possible . . . although I assume that the boss is only going to ask him to do what he's already doing, and it'll all come out, if someone has been murdered there. Do you know the foreigner's name?"

"No. He came to see me this morning, but he failed conspicuously to have himself announced." I assumed that it would be better to admit that he had come to see me than to be thought to have been covering the fact up if it came to light subsequently.

"He came to see you?" the female agent said. "What did he want?"

"What everyone wants—to see Dupin. Unfortunately, Dupin wasn't there. The bruiser said he'd come back, but it seems that he won't have the chance to tell us what else he wanted.

The young woman frowned. "He must have recognized Dupin when he passed him in the street last night," she said, apparently playing the recently fashionable game of logical deduction. "Look," she added, "when I tell the lads downstairs that there's a dead man in the house, they won't waste any time before going to take a look. If I give you five minutes, you might be wise to tell your friends to pile into the carriage and make yourselves scarce. Saint-Germain might call himself a comte, but the general opinion at the Sûreté is that he's a pretentious crook, and even though the old Prefect has disappeared, there's no shortage of people there who'd like an excuse to lock him up, even for a little while."

"Lucien Groix has disappeared?" I queried. "But you're using his signal, and you said earlier that he'd sent you."

"The sign is common property now," she said, "but I thought it best to drop his name. The lads think that Groix piled up too many grudges, as many among the Reds as the Blues, and figured that he ought to leave Paris without waiting to see who comes out on top in the power struggle. He wouldn't be the only one, by any means—a lot of rats are leaving the sinking ship, sick of bad bread and scared of cholera. The old hands say that he's no Fouché, for guts or for intelligence, although not one of them was alive back then . . . but this is Paris, and you can't throw a stone into a crowd without hitting some old fool who swears he once fought side by side with Bonaparte—the real one, not the upstart. Your five minutes starts now, by the way. When you go back downstairs, try to look as if you've had a good time."

"You've been very helpful," I assured her, "and I'll give Dupin the message. Tell your boss that he can rely on his complete cooperation, as always, and that when he figures out who killed the foreigner, the Head of the Sûrete will be the first to know, able to claim all the credit . . . just as you'll be able to claim the credit for discovering the body when you make your report, skipping over the interval of time during which you were apparently blissfully unaware that anything untoward had occurred and the fact that you let four gentlemen and a cheap crook make themselves scarce."

"We'll look after ourselves," the young woman assured me.

I believed her—at least, I believed that she would try.

I went downstairs, without bothering to pretend that I had had a good time, and was about to open the door and cross the road again when I saw that Paul Lacroix was now sitting at one of the other tables, making urgent covert signals to me—although he must have known that the woman, who had come downstairs behind me, would recognize him and would see the signals. She only hesitated for a moment, though, before going discreetly to sit with her cronies. I went over and sat down at Lacroix's table while the woman regained her own station.

"What the hell are you doing here, Reynolds?" he asked.

"Following Dupin's orders," I said. "Why did you follow Saint-Germain's carriage along the quays?"

"Because I saw you through the window, guessed that Dupin must be inside with Saint-Germain, and wondered why he didn't stop. I thought you must be on your way to the Pont de la Tournelle in order to cross to the Île Saint-Louis to pick up on last night's unfinished business, so I followed you. I wasn't the only one, so I thought I'd better be discreet . . . although it's hardly surprising that Saint-Germain is under close surveillance."

Unable to resist the temptation to show off, I said: "You were doubtless going to the Île to take a look at the house where you met Prospero, alias Will Maccabee, back in 1830," I said.

Instead of expressing amazement at the uncanny extent of my deductive acumen, the Bibliophile demanded: "What do you mean, *alias Will Maccabee?*"

I hesitated momentarily, but then decided that I was committed—and also that I was at risk of being late in delivering the female agent's ultimatum.

"No time to explain," I said. "The police are going to raid the witch-house in less than five minutes, and I have to give Dupin and my cousin the chance to get out." I stood up as I spoke and headed rapidly for the door. The police agents followed me with their gazes, the woman a trifle impatiently, having not expected me to dilly-dally.

IX

MORE HASTE BUT LESS SPEED

L ACROIX followed me across the street.
I knocked on the door of the witch-house, although I didn't suppose that it was locked. Cousin Jeremiah let me in, seemingly just as impatient as the black-haired agent, and I looked swiftly into the room that opened on the right to the corridor of the stairwell, where Dupin, Arthur Pym and Saint-Germain were standing around a supine body only a couple of strides from the doorway, the head almost on the threshold. The bulky body did indeed have a crossbow bolt sticking out of its chest at an odd angle. The room was bare, and showed no obvious sign of recent habitation. I would have liked to take a closer look at the cadaver of the supposed Immortal, whose mortality was now all too obvious, but it didn't seem to be the right moment.

"No time," I said, again, in response to Dupin's interrogative glance. "The police are coming. They've given us a few minutes' grace to clear out, so they can pretend to have discovered the body themselves."

"Idiot," said Dupin—unfairly, I thought. "I told you not to give too much away."

"No time," I repeated, yet again. "Lacroix's outside, on his way to the Île Saint-Louis. We can't all fit into the carriage—do you want me to go with him?" At least, I thought, it would give poor Arthur Pym a chance to sit inside instead of exposing himself to the chilly wind on the seat.

"Things are moving far too rapidly for my liking," Dupin muttered—but he was not slow to make decisions when it was necessary. "No, I need a word with Lacroix too. Can you take Reynolds' cousin and Arthur Pym back to Reynolds' house, Saint-Germain, and wait for me there? I'll join you as soon as I can."

Nobody seemed to like that suggestion. Arthur Pym got his objection in first. "I'd like to see Jacob, if I can," he said.

"So would I," said Jeremiah. "Perhaps we could bring him to your house, Sam, so that we can all put our heads together, as it were?"

Saint-Germain opened his mouth, but shut it again as Dupin cut him off.

"Good idea," he said, tersely. "But let's get out of here. If we don't want to be embroiled in tortuous interrogations by the local commissaire and the dolts of the Sûreté, we'd better take the opportunity they've given us to make ourselves scarce."

"Especially you, Saint-Germain," I put in. "The agents watching for conspirators and vampires seem to be under the impression that you're a crook, and are rather eager to try out the thumbscrews on you."

"Delusions of competence," snapped Saint-Germain. "But I don't want to be tied up for hours while the wheels of influence turn in their annoyingly slow fashion. We really do need to get away, if that's all right with you, Monsieur Reynolds and Monsieur Pym. Believe me, American gentlemen in Paris aren't as untouchable as they used to be. No one's safe in a Revolution, and a Revolution is what we have. The paving-stones will surely be torn up by the end of the week, used to make barricades."

"We've seen all that we need to see here," Dupin declared, hastily. "Do you know where to find Jacob Pym, Saint-Germain? You went to the Louvre with him, I believe."

"I do," said Saint-Germain. "I did my duty as a considerate host and escorted him to the Society's headquarters, asking him to wait for me there while I made enquiries about the likely whereabouts of Madame Lacuzon, assuring him that I had an infinitely better chance of finding his protégée than he did."

I was tempted to ask whether the mysterious Will Maccabee had been present in the said headquarters while Saint-Germain made those assurances, but there was no time. While we were speaking, we had left the house and Saint-Germain was already giving an order to the coachman to proceed to the Society's headquarters, while Arthur Pym climbed into the carriage, understandably glad that he had not been requested to sit outside again.

"But we don't actually have any encouraging information to give Jacob Pym," I pointed out to Dupin, "unless you've had an inspiration as to where Madame Lacuzon might have taken the girl . . . and why."

"No, I don't have the slightest idea," said Dupin, unconvincingly, moving off along the street on foot, presumably heading for the Pont de la Tournelle; Paul Lacroix followed him, and I had to move quickly in order to catch up with them. I didn't have the slightest idea myself as to whether or not Dupin was telling the truth about not having the slightest idea about where his concierge might be, but my suspicions inclined strongly in the direction of mendacity.

"The pugilist swore that he didn't mean the girl any harm," I commented, "But I suppose we can't believe that, given that he seems to have convinced Baron Du Potet that he was one of the Nine Immortals . . . falsely, we must presume."

The carriage had moved off as well, going in the same direction for the moment. Cousin Jeremiah stuck his head out of the portière, obviously having heard what I'd said. "Actually," he put in, confirming the impression I'd earlier formed that he was even more of a know-it-all than Dupin, and almost as keen to show off his pedantry, "I'm not sure that we can presume that. The Nine Immortals, if they exist, can't be immune to violent death, even if they don't age. That's presumably one reason why such individuals are said to live very discreetly, rarely risking themselves abroad in society. The fact that this one has done so implies that he had a powerful motive for coming out of hiding."

"Or that he was simply a charlatan," I suggested.

"Don't be ridiculous," said Saint-Germain, who had taken the seat opposite Jeremiah, and was as keen as ever to stick his oar in. "You saw him, as I did . . . and Du Potet, for that matter. That man had a mesmeric power greater than any I've ever encountered. It was almost tangible. The most remarkable thing about his murder isn't the fact that the shot was fired from another dimension, but that it took him completely by surprise."

We turned the corner heading for the quays then, but the coachman had plied his whip and the carriage drew ahead on the downward slope, putting too great a distance between us for the conversation through the vehicle's windows to continue comfortably.

"I agree that it must have taken him by surprise," said Dupin, although I didn't think that Saint-Germain could still hear him, "but I disagree that the shot must necessarily have been fired from another dimension."

"Where did the bolt come from, then?" I asked, taking up where Saint-Germain had been forced to leave off. Lacroix opened his mouth to ask a question, but thought better of it, and allowed Dupin to talk—always a wise decision.

"Exactly where it appeared to come from," Dupin said. "The chimney-breast, or perhaps inside it. If the latter, that is presumably the route by which the murderer is likely to have made his escape. The plaster covering the brickwork over the fireplace is by no means seamless, and although I did not have time to search for a panel of some kind, its apparent solidity might be deceptive. You will recall, Reynolds, what Lacroix has told us about the search of the house carried out by the Duc d'Orléans' agents at the beginning of the last century. They discovered that the cellar floor was perfectly solid, and therefore concluded that there could not be another lacuna beneath it—but they did not investigate the possibility that there might be another vertical shaft behind the flue of the fireplace in the drawing room. I cannot be certain without taking much more careful measurements, but it seems to me to be possible that there is a narrow shaft between the so-called witch-house and the house next door, which might extend all the way up to the roof and all the way down to a space far beneath the cellar that is accessible from the ground floor. That might be what the mysterious murder victim was searching for, and could be the means by which the viol-player was able to hide, thus giving the illusion that he was playing from above or beyond the house."

"And why would anyone want to do that?" I asked.

"I don't know—but two possibilities come to mind. The first is that the music was a secret signal of some kind. You and I know from experience that the sound of the viol was audible on the quay, and perhaps all the way across the nearer arm of the river, on the Île Saint-Louis, from which a reply of sorts came."

"And the other possibility?" I asked.

"That it was a test, to see whether the viol was able to harmonize with another instrument, or more than one—perhaps including some that could not mingle their vibrations from street level, but needed to be higher up."

"We only heard one other viol," I pointed out.

"It is not logically necessary that the other instruments would all have to be stringed instruments of some kind," Dupin said. "We did hear other sonic vibrations, if you recall."

"The church bells," I said, immediately catching on.

"Indeed, including the bells of Saint-Médard and Notre-Dame, about both of which legends exist, well known to Blaise Thibodeaux and, at least in the latter case, to you, Paul. You and he were actually in Notre Dame, I believe, immediately prior to the July Revolution of 1830—in the company of the musician who gave his name to you and to me as Prospero, but who now appears to be calling himself Will Maccabee, the name he attributed then to the inventor of the *danse macabre*. You were there hoping to hear an echo of the so-called Quasimodo peal, even though most of the bronze bells that once produced that carillon had been melted down after the Revolution in order to forge cannons. Is that correct?"

"Perfectly," Lacroix agreed.

"And did you hear the phantom peal?" I asked, curiously.

"Perhaps. Our experience was, however, far from uniform. I felt no conspicuous effect, and Victor Hugo, who was also present, only had a brief hallucination which he dismissed as an understandable product of his own imagination . . . but the priest who was on duty in the cathedral that night died there the next day, with no detectable cause. The whole experience was the stuff of which legends are made . . . ambiguously, as ever."

"Indeed," agreed Dupin. "Quite possibly a tissue of illusions—but illusions can sometimes be fatal, and can also provide motives for murder and massacre. Chaos is always closer at hand than we believe, alas."

"And sometimes it crawls," I supplied, uneasily, "especially when stimulated by vibrations that our poor ears cannot help but understand, crudely, as music or incantation. And sometimes, what we can easily mistake for chaos is not really chaos at all, but merely an order of things we cannot comprehend . . . an encrypted order."

I was proud of that speech, thinking that it demonstrated my capacity not only to take part in the scholarly discussion but also go make a useful contribution to it.

146

"True," said Dupin, and added, atypically: "Very true." Then he reverted to type as we turned again on to the quay, in the direction of the Pont de la Tournelle. Saint-Germain's carriage was some distance away by now. "Tell me more about this Prospero fellow," he said to the Bibliophile, abruptly.

"You met him yourself," Lacroix retorted, typically. "What did you think of him? And shouldn't we consult Saint-Germain, who seems to have met him more recently, if I took the right inference from what Reynolds was stubbornly refusing to tell me a few minutes ago. It seems that he's back in Paris, calling himself by the name of the supposed inventor of the *danse macabre?*"

"I didn't have time to tell you," I protested, lamely.

"Yes, he's back," Dupin confirmed, uninterested in any apologies I might make to Lacroix, "and he has been to the Harmonic Society, presumably in search of information for much the same reason that our murder victim consulted Du Potet, more discreetly. Saint-Germain poured cold water on the notion that he too might be an immortal of sorts, or even that he could play a musical instrument with his arthritic fingers, but I've never been convinced that Saint-Germain's judgment is sound, even if he really is who he says he is . . . especially if he is who he thinks he is, in fact."

"What?" queried Lacroix. "He's a charlatan. I've heard you say so yourself."

"A pretentious crook, according to the police," I put in.

"The distinction between charlatans and honest men might not be as clear as some people think," said Dupin, and then repeated: "What was your impression of Prospero, Lacroix?"

"That he was an antiquarian with a bee in his bonnet about Erich Zann, and also about Goliards, on which subject he challenged me; but I think my scholarship matched his esoteric knowledge very well. He could certainly play the violin with considerable expertise and artistry, though—he was wasted in the pit of the cheap theaters of the Boulevard du Temple. Not that you'd admit to knowing anything about that kind of expertise, would you, Dupin, in spite of what rumor alleges? And there's no possibility, is there, that you might be one of the musicians mentioned in the secret message hidden in the painting, ready to play the music of the palimpsest when the time is right?"

"No possibility at all," said Dupin, unconvincingly, "and I still think it more likely that the reference to an American is to a dulcimer, not to our good friend Reynolds . . . or to either of our more recent visitors, although they are both intriguing individuals, and I would be interested to know whether either of them has any musical expertise."

Cousin Jeremiah evidently had some knowledge of acoustic science, but that did not mean that he could play an instrument. In any case, I was still privately convinced that if my experience in the arbor in Du Potet's garden was anything to go by, none of us would require any previous expertise, if we really were to be summoned by demonic possession to play in the mysterious symphony accompanying the Child of Ocean in her evocation of Cthulhu . . . if that was, indeed, why she had been shipped to Paris from an alleged portal to R'lyaeih, knowingly or unknowingly, by Jacob Pym.

We had just reached the mid-point of the Pont de la Tournelle and I inspected the gas lamp—still unlit at the present hour of the afternoon even in February, but showing no external evidence of damage. I said nothing, though, waiting for Lacroix to carry forward the spiky exchange.

"You do believe, then, Dupin," said the Bibliophile, "that I'm correct in my conviction that the original script on the palimpsest is a kind of musical score . . . specifically, a score that has something in common with one that Prospero claimed to have discovered?"

"I'm certainly prepared to take the hypothesis very seriously," Dupin agreed, cautiously.

"And that it might, if played at the right time, in the right place, by the right combination of musicians, be capable of evoking the entity named Cthulhu?" Lacroix continued, in a tone that suggested to me that he did not know himself whether or not he was being sarcastic.

"That too," Dupin said, quietly. "At the very least, it seems that someone does believe that, and that someone appears to have believed it eighty years ago, taking the prophetic information seriously enough to try and make some preparation for it, in conspiracy with at least one other party . . . preparations that must now be nearing completion, if the hectic pace of recent events is a reliable indication. Evidently, the individuals making the preparations were not unopposed, but if the fellow murdered by the crossbow bolt really was one of the Nine of whom the intended recipient of the message hidden in the stolen painting was told to beware, it appears that the people intent on thwarting the plan do not have the upper hand, for the moment."

I was astonished, and completely out of my depth. "Do you have any idea who might have fired the bolt?" I asked.

"I have three admittedly-unlikely suspects in mind," Dupin said, "but there might well be more candidates still veiled from my sight. I might know more when I have spoken to Prospero and Jacob Pym. I thought at first that it was more imperative to speak to the Captain, but I changed my mind, which is why Lacroix is kindly leading us to the house to which the mysterious violinist took him eighteen years ago, in order to show him the example of the musical notation that he rediscovered in the palimpsest, and to play him his version of the piece."

"But he's at the Harmonic Society's headquarters," I objected. "That's where Jacob Pym is, and where Saint-Germain and the others are headed."

"He *was* there," Dupin agreed, "but I strongly suspect that the information he obtained there will have dissuaded him from spending too long on the premises. Even if he is merely a curious antiquarian no longer capable of playing the violin—which I beg leave to doubt—he will probably have moved on. If he was not the person playing the viol on the Île Saint-Louis at midnight, he would surely have been curious to investigate the rumor himself, and he probably set forth before Saint-Germain. Either way, he is almost certainly on the Île, quite probably in the house where he was lodging in 1830."

"All this is completely bewildering," I observed,

"For once," said Lacroix, "I'm compelled to agree with Reynolds. It's far too complicated for my liking."

"The world," said Dupin, dryly, "is far too complicated for anyone's liking. Unfortunately, it's the one we have to live in, and even the most ingenious human consciousness—although I probably ought to say *especially* the most ingenious human consciousness—cannot screen out all the things that it would prefer to ignore for the sake of the artificial simplicity that the majority of men call sanity. What did you learn from the fake whore, Reynolds, while you were carelessly spilling information you'd have done better to keep to yourself?"

That hurt, but I decided to overlook it. "She claims to have no idea where Lucien Groix is; allegedly, his signal is now in common use among the agents of the Sûreté. She told me to tell you that Addhema is back, but I'm not sure she really believes that the lamia exists. She told me that lights had been seen in the witch-house but seemed unsure that they were really supernatural, and although she couldn't find any kind of musical instrument when she and her fellows searched the house, she seemed reluctant to accept that the music they heard was supernatural."

"That's understandable," said Lacroix. "This is 1848; I can't believe that any agents of the Sûreté take tales of vampirism seriously nowadays, no matter what their remote predecessors might have thought and recorded. On the other hand, it's equally understandable that they want you to clear the matter

150

up for them, given all that you did to help Lucien Groix with the Rue Morgue affair and doubtless others that nobody will tell me about."

"The Head of the Sûreté wants to see you, in secret, as soon as possible," I put in.

Dupin sighed. "The Parisian police have always been addicted to concealment and deception," he said, "even when they would be far wiser to act openly. Nor are they the only ones—and to spare you the trouble of further sniping, Paul, I admit that I've long acquired the habit of secrecy myself. The many occult societies of the last century had the same obsessive addiction, and have undoubtedly passed it on to many present members of the Harmonic Society, in addition to Saint-Germain. His former coachman was surely not the only member jealously keeping arcane secrets before Saint-Germain's election as the society's public figurehead. Whether the notorious eighteenth-century Comte de Saint-Germain has been resurrected or not, the spirit of his enterprises is still thriving in those hallowed halls . . . and I'm not referring to Alphonse de Lamartine's political dabbling, Chapelain's experiments in therapeutic magnetism and Alphonse Constant's eagerness to pass himself off as a mage now that he's failed to advance quickly enough in Fourierist circles or to make his mark as a poet. Where else would real magicians find it convenient to hide while carrying on their clandestine exploits, knowing that vulgar positivists, seeing them in such company, would automatically assume that they were cranks or charlatans?"

"There was nothing very secretive about the fellow slain by the crossbow," I observed. "His eyes were virtually an advertisement—last night, at least. They didn't shine like a tiger's eyes when he called on me this morning, but his presence was still . . . commanding. Saint-Germain had no hesitation in identifying him as one of the legendary Nine, and Du Potet apparently leapt to the same conclusion."

"If he really was a powerful magus exhibiting his abilities brazenly," Dupin opined, "he must have had a good reason or an unusual sense of urgency. Legend affirms that such individuals usually wear careful camouflage, like the fellow who called himself Anton and volunteered so obligingly to drive Saint-Germain's lumbering carriage while carrying forward his own clandestine research."

It would have been ironic, I thought, if Saint-Germain, who was so excited about the prospect of encountering one of the Nine, had had one under his nose for years without suspecting it. It occurred to me, however, that if Anton had been a member of that legendary group, perhaps there had been more than one in the Society's membership, given that it really had been the foremost occult society in the world in Cagliostro's day, whether or not Cagliostro had been a charlatan himself. Dupin was surely correct to suggest that it much have been an attractive refuge for the secretive, as well as flamboyant characters like Mesmer

"Surely, in that case, it's more likely that the dead man's appearance *was* his camouflage," I suggested, "and he was only masquerading as an Immortal. If he sought out Du Potet on arrival in Paris, he is probably a Mesmeric healer himself, probably from Heidelberg or Vienna, where that art is said to be even further advanced than it is in Paris or London."

"That," said Dupin, "is certainly a possibility, although the peculiar manner in which he appears to have been killed raises further questions."

"A crossbow is certainly an odd choice of weapon in nineteenth-century Paris," I admitted.

"Not if one wanted to perforate a heart with a wooden shaft," Lacroix interjected. "For that, it would surely be ideal."

"You think the fellow was a vampire?" I said, skeptically.

"It would only have been necessary," the Bibliophile pointed out, "for the person who fired the shot to believe— or at least to suppose—that he was slaying a vampire . . .

and, of course, for him to believe folkoristic accounts of the manner in which that feat could be achieved. That has been common knowledge in France, of course, ever since my late mentor Nodier edited his anthology of *Fantasmagorie*, riding on the coat-tails of a sensational melodrama produced at the Porte-Saint-Martin and likewise plundering Dom Augustine Calmet's treatise on vampires, but it had long been an item of popular belief in Eastern Europe."

Dupin shook his head. "The murder appears to have been committed surreptitiously," he said, "and mysteriously. I do not say that vampire-hunters would never operate in that way, although the literary and theatrical mythology usually features wooden stakes driven in with hammers, but the present affair is far more peculiar. I wish I had had more time to examine the body. Signs of life were certainly absent, and the bolt appeared to have skewered the heart, so those observations caused me to deflect my attention immediately to the chimney-breast and the puzzle of what had become of the weapon. I wish, now, that I had interrogated the young woman myself rather than sending you, Reynolds, and then allowing her to send us on our way in haste. But there is little time, alas, to investigate this matter in a calm and methodical manner . . . especially if the magical echoes are to be audible again tonight. We must hope that Doctor Prospero, alias Will Maccabee, who appears to have had some foreknowledge of this occurrence, will be able to offer us a further dose of enlightenment. Are you sure that you can find the house where you visited him before, Paul?"

"Certainly," said Lacroix, who had paused, and was looking round in order to get his bearings in the maze of streets at the south-eastern end of the Île. "We're nearly there. But it would surely be extraordinary if it had remained empty since 1830, awaiting his return. By the way, Reynolds, that was another question you avoided answering. Why did you refer to Will Maccabee as his alias?" he set off walking again as he spoke, picking his way between piles of frozen snow that had been set away from doorsteps and treading gingerly where the cobblestones were covered with treacherous ice.

"Because that is the name under which he reintroduced himself to the Harmonic Society," Dupin interjected, saving me the trouble of replying. "Although he had to reveal his previous pseudonym, in order that his membership could be ascertained. It is probable that he abandoned the Prospero pseudonym when he left Paris in the 1830s and took the name of the suppose composer of the Dance of the Dead as a theatrical device for employment in Germany, England or elsewhere."

"What employment?" I asked.

"The theaters of the Boulevard du Temple are a symptom of the times," Lacroix supplied. "We are living in an epoch of theatrical melodrama. The present Revolution is not only an aspect of political progress but the accelerating tempo of human intellect and emotion. Popular theaters have been teaching people how to think and feel for centuries, evolving all the while, and music has always been an invaluable complement to the words of the scripts. A good fiddler need never lack employment anywhere in Europe, even where he cannot speak the local language." He raised his arm to point at the block of houses on the other side of the street into which we had just turned. "And that, I believe, is the house where Prospero entertained me eighteen years ago with the alleged harmonies of Hell—although they did me no harm."

"Apparently not," Duopin agreed. "But it is one of the properties of the education that you have just described, is it not, that its effects pass largely unheeded by consciousness? Who can tell what you might have become had you never heard those harmonies, and what effect their resonance might still be having in your inner being?"

"True," Lacroix agreed, equably. "But if I have been possessed these last twenty years by some subtle imp of Satan or

Cthulhu, I have been comfortable in his company. Have the two of you not been equally comfortable with your imps . . . or infections, as Raspail would undoubtedly term them?"

Dupin made no reply, his attention already focused on the house that Lacroix had indicated to him, where one of the windows on the upper storey was already illuminated by lamplight, the narrow street already being very gloomy in the cloudy twilight. Neither did I, but I could not help being reminded of one of Raspail's ideas, as reported to me by Dupin.

Raspail's medical research was directed toward the possibility of finding curses for diseases—primarily cholera—which he believed to be caused by tiny organisms invisible to the naked eye, akin to those that could be glimpsed by the best microscopes. Such microbes, Raspail believed, must be multitudinous, but the vast majority must be harmless, because their own existence must be dependent on the life of their hosts. The ones that caused deadly diseases, he believed, must be aberrant, operating against their own essential interests. The most efficient of all, he proposed would be those that not only did no harm to their hosts but actually increased their hosts' wellbeing, thus creating the possibility of a better future for their own offspring as well as their hosts'.

Dupin liked that idea, while maintaining his customary agnosticism as to its likelihood, but I knew that Blaise Thibodeaux had liked it too, because his ghost had told me so . . . and although I had never met him when he was alive, I knew that he had been a man ever ready to throw intellectual caution to the winds. He, I felt sure, would have been prepared to follow the train of thought wherever it led, as far as he could possibly take it. He had been a true hero.

I would have like to be able to imitate him, but I knew my limitations. Even so, I felt that I ought not to be content to be a mere bystander even in that arcane and challenging arena of thought and action.

X

DOCTOR PROSPERO

W E had arrived outside a nondescript house in what seemed to me to be one of the artisanal districts of the Île. The street was quiet, by Parisian standards, but by no means silent; there was a muffled purr of industry, and lamplight was now burning in more than half of the buildings. The smoke seeping from the chimneys and spreading out as it cooled was adding an extra layer of gray to the wintry cloud accumulated over the city, but it did not seem unduly hostile, the atmosphere at street level being permeated by cooking smells, even though it was not yet late and darkness was only beginning its slow fall.

"This is definitely the place," said Lacroix. "Prospero's residence was on the first floor, up that shabby external staircase, which looked rickety even in 1830. Shall we make enquiries?"

Dupin looked back the way we had come. I had no difficulty picking out the lurking policeman who probably imagined, mistakenly, that we had been blissfully unaware that he had followed us from the Rue de l'Hirondelle. Dupin barely spared him a glance before stepping on to the staircase, which did not seem to be in danger of imminent collapse. He went up to the first floor, and knocked on the door, which was not equipped with a bell. Lacroix and I had followed him.

I had never entirely lost the queasiness that had afflicted me when I crossed the Pont de la Tournelle and saw the ghost, and this staircase too took on a suggestion, in my overworked imagination, of a transition between worlds, even though there did not seem to be anything unusual or alarming about it.

The door opened almost immediately, while I was still instructing myself sternly not to let my imagination run away with me, and to continue to be brave—but I had to suppress a gasp of mistaken astonishment. For a moment, I thought that the woman who opened the door was my own housekeeper, Madame Bihan, but after a second or two I realized that the resemblance, although marked, was not so very exact.

"Come in, Messieurs," she said. "The master is expecting you." She appeared to be looking past Dupin at Lacroix.

I was not sure that the Bibliophile was the specific individual that her master had been expecting, but he certainly took that inference. "Bonjour, Meg," he said. "I'm surprised that you remember me; it's nearly eighteen years since I came here with Blaise Thibodeaux to hear Doctor Prospero play . . . and we only met briefly then, on the second occasion."

"I remember you perfectly, Monsieur Lacroix," the old woman assured him. "The doctor played you the harmonies of hell—but you did not hear them, any more than I did. Even so, the music must have entered into your soul, and helped to bring you here today."

If Lacroix was surprised by that speech, he did not show it. "This is the Chevalier Auguste Dupin, Meg," he said, "and his American friend Mr. Samuel Reynolds,"

"I know," said Meg, as she showed us into the drawing room . . . or, given its furniture, what might more aptly have been called the music room. Lacroix drew in his breath as we entered, and then muttered uneasily, to explain his surprise: "It's like stepping back in time. It's exactly as it was in 1830."

The phrase was conventional enough, but his tone had a certain edge to it, as if he were not entirely certain that he was not speaking literally.

Dupin's eyes were fixed on the old woman, curiously, and I wondered whether she reminded him of Madame Bihan too, or perhaps of Madame Bihan's cousin—but perhaps he was only speculating as to how she could possibly claim to know him, given that he evidently had not met her when Prospero had called on him in the late 1820s.

An old man came into the music room then, from what was presumably his bedroom. As Saint-Germain had said, rather cruelly, he appeared to be within easy stepping distance of death's door, extensively withered by various kinds of physical deterioration. His hair and beard were white and his face furrowed by multitudinous wrinkles, but his eyes were bright and alert, and his thin lips were curved into a smile that could have been construed as benevolent. He might not have been any older, chronologically speaking, than his housekeeper, who seemed to have been respected more generously by the passage of time, but he had not worn well, even for a common mortal

"Monsieur Dupin," he said. "It's been a long time. And Monsieur Reynolds too—I'm honored. How goes the quest for arcane knowledge, Monsieur Lacroix?"

"Neverending, Doctor Prospero," Lacroix replied, "but I believe that I have carved out my little niche in the annals of historical research. Did you ever manage to locate copies of the music of Eric Zann? Or any more harmonies of hell?"

"The written records of the music of Erich Zann were all destroyed," Doctor Prospero replied, "in an act of vandalism of which Monsieur Dupin ought to be ashamed, although I cannot deny that the documents in question were probably . . . a trifle hazardous. As for the harmonies of hell . . . I believe that I have been more successful in that regard. Do you have your copy of the Cthulhu palimpsest about your person, Monsieur

Lacroix? I need to see it, desperately . . . but in my haste, I'm being impolite. Fetch us a bottle of wine, will you, Meg."

It was only then that I noticed that four armchairs had been set around a small table by a window looking out in the direction of the left bank of the Seine—a window sufficiently highly placed that it might be possible to hear from there music played on the bank in question, even from behind, or above, the houses on the quay. There was an imposing violin on the music stand placed in front of the opposite wall of the room, but when I looked at Prospero's gnarled hands I could not believe that the left was any longer capable of picking out the notes on the strings, and I was not even sure that the right would be able to manipulate a bow. There were other cases on the shelves designed to contain and carry musical instruments, some of unfamiliar shapes.

In response to Prospero's invitation, the three of us took our seats. Lacroix had made no move to reach into his clothing in search of any copy he might have made of the palimpsest found in the painting, although I knew his reputation well enough to be certain that he would not have left the Louvre that afternoon without having made one, whether Fernichat had succeeded in making his own clean copy or not. Our host had obviously made the same assumption. I also suspected that Lacroix would have kept the document on his person, tucked into the inside pocket of his jacket next to his heart— but Prospero did not pursue the matter, for the time being, in spite of his declared desperation.

"Do you know where my housekeeper might have taken Captain Pym's Child of Ocean, Doctor Prospero?" Dupin asked the ex-musician, abruptly.

If he had hoped to elicit surprise with the reference to such a Child, or the revelation that she had been taken away, he was disappointed—although, I thought, the absence of such surprise might well be reckoned an interesting and informative datum in itself.

"Alas," said the old man. "I have no knowledge of any child, or any Captain Pym."

He seemed sincere.

"You have not returned to Paris, then, in anticipation of the fulfillment of Abbé Vaillant's prophecy regarding the advent of a miraculous child?" said Lacroix.

"I am aware of the alleged prophecy to which you refer," Prospero replied, "but I could never take the Convulsionnaires seriously, and I only heard the rumor of their recent reappearance today. The newspapers are attributing the scandal to bad bread, I believe . . . but there are the usual murmurs about witchcraft among the elders of the Harmonic Society. Returning to those hallowed halls was like stepping back in time, although Puységur's absence leaves a big hole, which the present president seems to me to be inadequate to fill."

"The child in question was a castaway brought back from the South Seas," said Dupin, who evidently knew what Lacroix was talking about, as our host seemed to do, although I only had the vaguest inkling. "I am rather worried by having lost track of her. My housekeeper is a very trustworthy person, in spite of her reputation as a witch, but she is old and frail, and I am anxious about her too."

"My own housekeeper has a similar reputation," Prospero commented. "It follows us everywhere, I fear, and even the Societé Harmonique was not a safe refuge when I was last resident in Paris. Its members were unjustly contemptuous of the Sorority back then. The young man who has assumed the presidency seems to be cast in the same mold, alas . . . unsurprisingly, if he really is possessed by the spirit of old Saint-Germain, who never had an atom of understanding of the powers he was playing with. It's a great shame that the members of the Societé only had Blaise Thibodeaux in their company for a brief while, and that only a handful had the wisdom to take him seriously . . . or me, for that matter . . .

not that I was entitled to be taken very seriously in those days myself. I've learned a great deal in the interim."

"But you already knew how to play the harmonies of hell—or believed that you did," Dupin observed, in a neutral tone.

"Some of them—but you really ought not to condemn me for that, Monsieur Dupin. I'm a scholar, like you and Thibodeaux, not a diabolist. And rumor has it that you've played the music of Erich Zann yourself, from memory, and that the infection is still within you, so I am surely more entitled to be suspicious of you than you evidently are of me."

"You seem very well informed for a man who has not been in Paris for nearly twenty years," Dupin observed, while Prospero's housekeeper uncorked the bottle of wine that she had brought and began pouring it into the four glasses that she had brought in on the same tray, which she had placed in the center of the table.

"I have not been idle," Prospero said, "and I have always had an exceptionally keen ear for rumors concerning the music of Erich Zann. But please don't worry—as I say, I am simply a scholar, like you and Baron Du Potet. I am not involved in any conspiracy, for or against the fulfillment of any so-called prophecy. Please, Monsieur Lacroix, may I see your copy of the music annotated on the manuscript found in the painting that Hoche's men stole? I can assure you that you have no chance of decrypting it without my help, and I assume that is why you have come in search of me, before I had the opportunity to go in search of you."

"Do you believe that you might be able to play it?" Lacroix asked, his gaze fixed on Prospero's hands, as he reached forward to pick up the glass of wine that had been poured for him. I hesitated before doing likewise. Dupin did not even reach out.

Prospero sighed slightly. "It's just wine, Messieurs," he said, "with nothing diabolical about it. He took his own glass, by way of example and took a substantial draught from it. "And no, Monsieur Lacroix, I have no delusions about being able to play that music, or any other, with these arthritic hands."

"So it wasn't you who was playing hereabouts at midnight last night, in response to the music played in the Rue de l'Hirondelle?" Lacroix followed up, still making no move to explore his pockets for a piece of paper.

"It was not. I was very busy yesterday hunting for information on my own account, and I was delayed at the Harmonic Society until after midnight. I fear that I left poor Meg to make all the arrangements for our accommodation by herself—but she has done a fine job, as you can see. Meg was here, and heard an instrument playing, but she has long grown used to ignoring my music, so she was unable to reproduce what she heard. She told me that it appeared to be coming from the direction of the quay, but could not add anything more. May I see your copy of the text erased from the palimpsest, Monsieur Lacroix?"

"Of course," said Lacroix, taking another sip from his glass. "But first, do you know who the intended recipient of the overwritten message might have been?"

Prospero sighed when Lacroix failed to match his promise with any immediate action. "Not for certain," he said, "but the likeliest contender is the Comte de Saint-Germain, who was addicted to such games . . . and who was also under constant observation by the Duc de Richelieu's police, the agents of which might well have intercepted the painting not long before the death of Louis XV. If so, Richelieu's agents probably found the palimpsest and consulted someone in the Societé Harmonique, in quest of an explanation. It was presumably sealed up again even before Richelieu was banished from the court and his organization disintegrated, and sent to Morbihan for safe keeping . . . which turned out, alas, to be anything but safe after the Revolution, when Hoche's looters were sent to put down the Vendean counter-revolution and punish its supporters, if Monsieur Fernichat's deductions are accurate. My inclination is to trust his judgment.

"You know him of old, then?" Lacroix queried.

"Yes, indeed. It has been a great pleasure to renew our acquaintance—but he only gave me a second-hand account of the parchment, and could not give me an appointment to see it because he had already made a second one with you and Monsieur Dupin. He advised me to seek you out in order to consult the copy that he intended to give you belated permission to make once he had completed his own. Like all curators, he is dutifully parsimonious with his treasures, but as you say, we had known one another for a long time. What he told me about it implies strongly that someone read it back in the last century who wanted to thwart the prophecy or plan to which the supplementary note referred—hence, perhaps, the rumored reappearance in the Rue de l'Hirondelle of the supposed vampire Addhema. We can, I think, take it for granted that yours is not the only copy that has ever been made of the original text and the overwritten text, Monsieur Lacroix . . . and we can also assume that, although I cannot play the music, there are numerous musicians in Paris who can . . . or think they can. Once again, may I see the copy of the score that you undoubtedly made this morning in the Louvre?"

I thought immediately of the mysterious Anton, wondering whether he might be one of the other people who had seen a copy of the palimpsest, and who might be able to play the music mapped therein. Meanwhile, Lacroix reached into the inside pocket of his jacket and took out a folded piece of paper. He handed it over very grudgingly, but I assumed that his reluctance was mere bibliophilic jealousy.

Prospero accepted it in his crippled right hand, and began to scan it earnestly. As he did so, he talked.

"It is possible, of course, that someone really was standing on the quay last night, playing a rebec—but I doubt it. I suspect that it was not being played in the present at all. I know that you're familiar with Thibodeaux's theory of temporal resonance, Monsieur Dupin, and you know full well that there are echoes in time emerging from the past, and even from the future, into the fleeting present moment. That emergence seems to have been unusually abundant of late, and any belated followers of Abbé Vaillant who still exist in Paris would undoubtedly have interpreted that as a sign of the impending End of the World, but I tend to agree with the skeptics that his grossly mistaken predication of the date of that catastrophe—not to mention his conviction that he was a reincarnation of the Biblical prophet Elijah—casts his entire prophecy into absurdity. Where and when the instrument that Meg heard was actually being played, I cannot say, any more than I can say where and when the dulcimer was being played that was allegedly audible in the Rue de l'Hirondelle, but I would certainly be very interested to know."

"The music was certainly audible," Lacroix put in. "Dupin and I were both there and we both heard it—and Dupin and Reynolds both heard the music emanating from the Île—but none of us recognized the instruments."

"Can you tell me more about the prophecy to which you refer," Dupin interjected. "I've read what Thibodeaux wrote about the Convulsionnaires of Saint-Médard, and I've seen them mentioned in other documents, but I've never investigated the recorded texts of Abbé Vaillant's preachings."

"Very wise," opined Prospero. "A fine farrago of nonsense, far worse than anything attributed to the actual Prophet Elijah. The few fanatical followers remaining after Vaillant's death continued to believe he had been genuinely inspired, at least some of the time, and some paid particular attention to a prediction he made in 1730 or thereabouts, of the advent in the year 1847 of a female Messiah born from the Pacific Sea, who would speak the language of the angels and renew or loosen the binding of the Devil in Pandemonium. Later, he claimed that a premature Day of Judgment prompted by the agents of the Devil might prevent his prophecy from being fulfilled by ending the world in 1733, and he was apparently exceedingly glad that he lived until 1761 before dying in prison, raving all the while about an ongoing battle between evil forces continuing to try to prevent the fulfillment of his prophecy, including a conspiracy he called the Nine, generally believed to refer to the ancient legend of the Nine Immortals, although that is pure speculation. While he was in prison, the Abbé had apparently met, and might have recruited to his own company of followers, a man who had caught a necklace that a pirate named Levasseur had thrown into the crowd when he was about to be hanged on the island of Réunion in 1730 and subsequently brought it to Paris . . . what's the matter?"

The last remark was addressed to me, because Dupin, with his usual self-control had not started at that item of information, although he knew as well as I did that Saint-Germain had claimed to be the person who had taken possession of Levasseur's necklace, or at least a medallion therefrom—in his previous incarnation, of course—and had given me the medallion in question, containing the encrypted incantation that Dupin had used to dispel the shoggoths in the stone circle in Brittany.

"Nothing," I said to Prospero. "Just a twinge of residual fever. Do go on."

"There's not much more to tell," said Prospero. "The heir to Levasseur's necklace apparently told Vaillant things that the mad abbé incorporated into his prophecies, but by then, hardly anyone could take him seriously and when 1733 rolled around and the world didn't show any sign of ending, he was almost universally considered to be a lunatic. His prophecy regarding the female messiah was maintained and transformed by a few of the convulsionnaires, though, who had had to go into hiding because the persecution of the cult was then reaching its culmination. Even now, the sect still has a few secret adherents, further divided by schisms, and one reinterpretation of the original prophecy apparently substitutes Cthulhu for the Devil and a female antichrist-figure for the messiah, perhaps in accordance with what Levasseur's heir told Vaillant. I don't know how many versions of the story exist now, but one of them, at least, substitutes a group of stringed instruments for the traditional Last Trump, including a rebec and a dulcimer, both of those instruments having been mentioned by Vaillant . . . but Meg isn't competent to judge whether what she heard last night might have been one of those instruments. Are you?"

I certainly wasn't. I looked at Dupin, who was frowning deeply, but he made no immediate reply except for a cursory shake of the head. The fact that he had construed the reference in the 1770 cryptogram to a "symphony" as a possible reference to a dulcimer suddenly seemed, however, to make more sense, especially given that he now seemed prepared to entertain the hypothesis that the eighteenth-century Comte de Saint-Germain really had been the intended recipient of the message and really had been reincarnated, one way or another, as the present president of the Harmonic Society.

My knowledge of the visionaries who had grouped around the grave of François Paris, the philanthropic dean of Saint-Médard, in 1727 and had been dubbed *convulsionnaires* was hazy, but I had always accepted the medical opinion that they had been poisoned by ergot in bad bread. They had all belonged to the Jansenist sect that was in the process of being suppressed by the Church as a heresy, with an altogether unwonted ruthlessness, and were therefore already being forced underground, thus lending their story to entanglement with all manner of legends and conspiracy theories.

"Did you find a musical instrument when you searched the house?" Prospero asked, evidently making the assumption that Dupin must have undertaken such a search after hearing the mysterious music played there.

"No," said Dupin, but added, provocatively: "When Saint-Germain went to mount his own search this morning, however, he found the body of a man who had been shot with a crossbow bolt."

That did appear to be news to Prospero, and he interrupted his continuing scrupulous study of the palimpsest in order to react. "Did you really?" he said. "Who was he—and who shot him?"

"We were rather hoping that you could tell us, since you seem to know so much that we do not," Dupin commented.

"Alas, no," said Prospero. "Some other curious individual in search of the vampire Addhema, I assume, who doubtless could not find her. She's very elusive, alas. I never managed to catch a glimpse of her back in the 1820s. Was the dead man a policeman?"

"No," said Dupin. "According to Saint-Germain, he was one of the so-called Nine Immortals."

"Really? That might make sense, I suppose, given the confusion of the Vaillant prophecy with the legend of Cthulhu. The Nine Immortals are said by the elders of the Harmonic Society to have been investigating that entity for hundreds of years, trying in the meantime to destroy all the printed copies of John Dee's mangled version of the text he called the *Necronomicon*. I suppose they might be anticipating the attempted evocation, with or without the aid of their own copy of the palimpsest, and naturally want to put a stop to it, whether or not they take Vaillant seriously. Vandals, Monsieur Dupin . . . but you probably sympathize with them."

"You don't?" Dupin said, seemingly a trifle surprised.

"Not in the least. I have a very powerful curiosity, as any true scholar must. The idea that Cthulhu's minions might be assembling an orchestra to accompany the song of a miraculous child, in response to an ancient instruction, is . . . very intriguing. But I can understand why the Sorority might want to prevent them from doing so, and why your housekeeper might have thought it necessary to spirit a child away, if she thought she might be the child of the prophecy. Meg would have done exactly the same thing, and I would not be able to find it in my heart to hold it against her. She is very protective of me, and who could resent her for that?"

"Meg is a member of the Sorority too?" Dupin queried, seemingly familiar with the term, although I had only heard vague mention of it in passing, and I thought that his query might be a feint.

"Yes, of course."

I was glad when Lacroix chipped in with: "What is the Sorority?" although Dupin frowned intensely, the Bibliophile's gaze having been directed at him.

He need not have worried; Prospero did not wait for him to improvise an answer. There was obviously a hint of Cousin Jeremiah about him. "A loosely-knit company of female magicians," said the musician. "Not an organization—they have no membership lists or pretentious rules of procedure, like the Rosicrucians or the Freemasons; that's a very masculine thing—but they share a common heritage of traditional wisdom. They can recognize one another and they help one another if required, unlike the members of the Harmonic Society . . . or the Nine Immortals, if rumor can be trusted.

"Is Addhema a member?" I put in, curiously.

"Certainly not," said Prospero. "The undead Addhema, if she exists, is hardly even human—she is probably a predator of the dream-dimensions, a so-called Dweller on the Threshold, although other Dwellers might well be her enemies. The members of the Sorority, by contrast, are entirely human, and reputedly conscientiously benevolent."

"Might Addhema have killed the member of the Nine who was investigating her house, then?" I hazarded.

"You say that he was killed with a crossbow?" Prospero queried, rhetorically. "Not really her choice of weapon, more likely one intended for use against her . . . but who can tell? Was he drained of blood?"

"No," said Dupin, when I looked at him inquiringly.

"Probably not, then," Prospero supplied. "Nor could it have been a shoggoth—they don't use crossbows either, even when circumstances permit them to achieve a measure of solidity . . . and the members of the Nine, if they really are powerful magicians, surely have means of warding off shoggoths. But Cthulhu has been worming its way into human dreams for millennia; it doubtless has a few human minions, and might well have rallied them to defend the evocation, if it is really capable of conscious scheming and purposive action. Can you exonerate the Child of Ocean of the murder, Monsieur Dupin?"

"I'd like to think so," Dupin replied, "but if she's given Amélie the slip, or harmed her, I can't rule it out. Amélie could probably ward off a shoggoth too, but if she were taken by surprise . . . she might not have realized quite how dangerous the child might be when she decided to take her away."

That reminded me of what he had said earlier about having three suspects for the murder in the witch-house. Subtracting Addhema and the Child of Ocean, I wondered who the third might be. "Who else came to your mind as a potential assassin," I said, figuring that he would be able to follow my train of thought easily enough.

"The police agent who signaled to us in the café last night," he said, readily enough. "She evidently wanted us to return, and might have wanted us to discover the body. That's partly why I wanted to find out whether it was Lucien who had sent her to make contact with us. I was rather hoping that it was."

"She didn't seem like a murderess to me," I put in.

"Nor did Jana Valdemar," said Dupin—and I realized that my arithmetic might have been faulty, even in counting up to three. "With all due respect, Reynolds, your judgment can't always be trusted when it comes to young women."

That stung. "Mademoiselle Valdemar is dead," I said, simply.

"Dead, but apparently dreaming," Dupin observed, "unless you only imagined that you saw her on the Pont de la Tournelle last night."

"I'm not a fool." I retorted, although I was far from confident in the assertion, "and she's a murder victim, not a murderess. She walked into the Seine under a hypnotic compulsion, and you can't convince me otherwise."

"I can't," Dupin admitted, "but she might have been able to. Lucien seemed to be convinced that she was dead too, last time I saw him, but his disappearance is a worrying incident. If he found out that she wasn't dead, he might have become an inconvenience."

"She was a ghost last night," I insisted. "I'm certain of it." Even as I said it, though, I knew that there could not be any certainty about my experience, which might have been all in my mind—and, if so, might have been planted there mesmerically. But why?

Prospero set down the piece of paper that Lacroix had given him on the table. "Very interesting," he said.

"Can you read it?" Lacroix wanted to know.

"I believe so."

"Does it come from *Les Harmonies de l'enfer?*" Dupin asked.

"No," said Prospero. "It's much older than that. I could be wrong but it seems to me to be a composition by the same hand that wrote down the music that I identified as the dance of the dead, the fellow whose pseudonym I have recently adopted in preference to the old one that you are still using—Will Maccabee, that is."

"The supposed Goliard?" Lacroix put in.

"The hand that wrote it down might well have been one of the so-called Goliards associated with Peter Abelard," Prospero said, "but I suspect that the song itself is much older than that . . . as you must suspect yourself, Monsieur Dupin, if you

170

really believe it to be the accompaniment to an incantation capable of unlocking a portal to R'lyaeih."

"It's not a matter for belief," Dupin replied, typically—but added: "Not my belief, at any rate. I must confess, though, Doctor, that I'm not sorry that you're incapable of playing the notes, if they really do have the power to open the crypt of R'lyaieh."

"If they aren't played as prescribed, we'll never know, will we?" Prospero retorted. "But what kind of scholar would refuse to make the experiment? We're not superstitious fools, are we? We don't believe that Cthulhu is the devil incarnate, intent on destroying or ruling the world?"

"Have you ever encountered a shoggoth, Doctor Prospero?" I enquired. "It seems to me that any scholar who had would be exactly the kind of scholar who would refuse to make the experiment of allowing such creatures a greater liberation in the human world."

"Creatures of nightmare are simply that," opined the ex-musician. "The rational way to deal with them is to face them, to comprehend and dispel them, not to surrender to the mere fear of them. Isn't that your opinion, Dupin?"

"In a broad sense, yes," Dupin told him. "But that doesn't alter the fact that some experiments are direly dangerous. One can understand why pioneering chemists like La Follie were enthusiastic to explore the properties of powerful acids and explosive substances, but while admiring his enterprise, let's not forget that the poor fellow blew himself up in his laboratory."

"And let's not forget either that powerful acids and explosives have thousands of virtuous technological applications as well as providing men with new ways of killing one another," said Prospero. "Knowledge is what enables such things to be exploited; the things are not hostile in themselves. Nor, I believe, is Cthulhu. It isn't satanic, in my opinion, merely an alien creature."

"Like Nyarlathotep?" Dupin queried.

"I don't know," Prospero replied. "Aren't you supposed to be the expert on that subject, as the sole remaining custodian of the music of Eric Zann, if only in the coverts of your memory, and probably the only man alive who has played it . . . apparently having suffered no lasting damage from so doing?"

"I might be the only man still alive," Dupin observed, "because all the others died trying."

"But you survived, because you're a serious philosopher and not a superstitious fool," Prospero countered, "just as you and I—and Lacroix, and many others—would survive the awakening of Cthulhu, no matter how many others might be driven mad."

I didn't know whether or not to be offended by his omission of my name from his list . . . but I took what comfort I could from the presumption that I might be included in the category of "many others."

"Perhaps," said Dupin, shaking his head. "Is that what you imagine would happen if that piece of music you're holding were played?"

"How can I know?" Prospero countered. "But I would certainly be interested to try, if I were still capable."

"Even at the risk of bringing about the end of the world?" I queried.

"I do not know what such music might be capable of achieving in the minds and souls of men," Prospero said, "but I certainly do not believe that it could bring down a rain of fire and brimstone from Heaven, and if it could bring about an upheaval of stagnant ideas . . . well, is that not exactly what your Republicans are endeavoring to bring about, with every apparent chance of success in Paris within a matter of days. The world as men conceive it is always ending, Mr. Reynolds, and necessarily so, in order to make way for new and better ones. What reason for existence do we have, otherwise?"

He fell silent then, giving me a chance to ask one of the thousand questions haunting my troubled mind. "When you had dealings with the Societé Harmonique twenty years ago, Doctor Prospero," I asked, "did you make the acquaintance of the member of the society who inherited Blaise Thibodeaux's violin—a man who has recently been going by the name of Anton and serving as the President's coachman, although I doubt that was his real name?"

"I don't recognize that name," Prospero replied, "but the members of the society often used pseudonyms and some-times changed them, so I might well have run across the man unknowingly. Thibodeaux did mention to me that he was thinking of taking up the violin again, but I don't know what progress he made after I left Paris. There were numer-ous members of the society who, like me, had an interest in musical magic, but we all tended to be a trifle jealous of our arcane knowledge, and I was by no means the only one sailing under a false flag. It's also typical of scholars of magic to hide their real names—call it a superstition or an affectation, if you wish, but the practice is respectably ancient."

"He might also have used the name Oberon," I suggested.

"He wouldn't have been the first to do that, by any means, or the last. I'm a Shakespearean myself . . . but I presume that your Frenchman borrowed the name from *Huon of Bordeaux*?"

"Probably," I agreed. "But whoever he really was, he played the violin very cleverly on last All Hallows, and either called forth or responded to what Thibodeaux called *temporal reso-nances* of a phantasmagorical variety. Thibodeaux's ghost was present, and suggested to me that the ultimate source of the echoes was the far future."

"Did you believe him?" Prospero enquired, interestedly.

"Dupin would undoubtedly say that it isn't a matter for belief," I countered, "but if I were looking for someone to play an instrument in the strange symphony of which the music in Lacroix's palimpsest appears to be a part, I'd certainly be prepared to give Anton an audition . . . if I could find him. He disappeared after his performance at Fontainebleau."

"There was mention of something like that at the Society," Prospero said. "The elders are terrible gossips, in spite of their passion for secrecy—but it was represented as one of the President's escapades. There was also mention of a Guadagnini cello and an explosion in Baron Du Potet's garden, but it all seemed rather confused. I planned to make further enquiries if and when I could, but the matter of the palimpsest seemed far more urgent."

"Good luck with those further enquiries," said Lacroix, dryly. "You could start now, but Dupin will only tell you that he doesn't have time."

"I can understand that," said Prospero. He tapped the piece of paper. "May I ask Meg to make a copy of this document for my own study?" he asked. "Her handwriting is much more assured than mine, and very meticulous."

"I suppose so," said Lacroix, grudgingly. "It will save you a trip to the Louvre—unless, of course, you want to check the accuracy of my draughtsmanship."

Prospero made no reply to that suggestion. Instead, after ringing for his maidservant, he said: "I do hope that you'll all stay for dinner. There are a great many topics of common interest that we might discuss, Monsieur Dupin, as well as what happened in Du Potet's garden."

"I'm afraid I can't," said Dupin, unembarrassed by having to fulfill Lacroix's prediction. "A gentleman came to my house this morning asking to see me, and I really must oblige him as soon as possible. In fact, I really shouldn't have allowed Monsieur Lacroix to sidetrack me, although I was exceedingly curious to meet you again, Doctor Prospero. I'll take my leave now, if I may . . . there's no need for Meg to show me out."

"What!" said Lacroix. "You'll wait until Meg has copied the palimpsest script for Prospero, won't you?"

"I can't, I'm afraid," said Dupin, "but I'm sure that you can catch up with us at the Harmonic Society. I expect that we'll be there for some time."

Lacroix's expression was thunderous. "This is too much, Dupin," he said. "I was the one who brought you into this affair, remember. You can't simply throw me out of it."

"I'm not," said Dupin, curtly, "but time is of the essence, I fear, and I need to question Jacob Pym regarding the castaway."

And with that, he made his exit, hardly seeming to care whether I followed him or not. Evidently, he had obtained all that he wanted from Doctor Prospero, at least for the time being. I still had my thousand questions, but as usual, Dupin was not paying any attention to what I, the eternal bystander, might want.

*

XI

MORE GHOSTS

WHEN we reached the bottom of the wooden staircase, which seemed a little less steady going down than it had while we were going up, Dupin immediately made the sign of the devil's horns to the police agent lurking on the other side of the street and then beckoned to him. The agent looked confused, and worried, but he responded to the summons.

"Will you please give a message to the head of the Sûreté for me?" Dupin said. "Tell him that I haven't yet managed to discover the identity of the man who was posing as a vampire in the house in the Rue de l'Hirondelle, or the reason for his imposture. Until I do, it will be difficult for me to identify his murderer. You're very welcome to continue following me if you wish, or if you think your orders require it, but if it's of any assistance, I'm going to take a cab to the headquarters of the Societé Harmonique, and I expect to be there for some time. The man who was following Saint-Germain's carriage is presumably still there, and can keep an eye out for both of us. And if you should happen to see Lucien Groix at the Prefecture, please give him my best wishes."

"He's not there," said the agent, with suspicious swiftness. Dupin was already striding away toward the river, seemingly careless of whether anyone followed him or not. I had some difficulty catching up with him.

"That was a trifle rude" I suggested. "I don't mean giving orders to the agent, but dumping poor Lacroix."

"Yes, it was," Dupin admitted, "but he'll be of more use interrogating his old friend Prospero than he would be tagging along with us. He'll understand that when he's had time to think about it. And it really is imperative that I discover what Jacob Pym knows about his Child of Ocean—although, if I judge your cousin Jeremiah correctly, he'll have been subjected to a thorough interrogation by the time we reach the society's headquarters. Hail that fiacre, would you?"

I did as I was told, as usual, and the horses set off at a veritable trot, perhaps eager to keep as warm as they could now that dusk had fallen and the wind was becoming even sharper.

As we rattled over the Pont de la Tournelle I checked the gas-lamp in the middle of the span again, but it was still unlit and the evening mist that was forming over the river, as usual, made to difficult to discern whether the apparatus was capable of functioning or not. Looking along the river, though, I could see, vaguely, that the lanterns on the next bridge along were illuminated. The lanterns of stationary barges and lighters tinted the mist with various colors, creating a rather charming effect, but there were no illusory ships visible in the current, going upstream or down.

"It's going to be terribly cold again tonight," I commented.

"Good," said Dupin.

"Why?"

"Because it will help to postpone the Revolution for a few more days. We don't want barricades going up while we might need to be flitting back and forth. There are more important things at stake than Louis-Philippe's impending abdication and the Bonapartists' ambition to bring back the latest imaginary version of the good old days."

"Prospero doesn't seem to be alarmed about the possibility of the supposed evocation going ahead . . . and I got the impression that cousin Jeremiah might agree with him. You don't really think that it could destroy the world, do you?"

"It depends what you mean by 'destroy' and 'the world'," said Dupin. "Perhaps stimulating the dreamer of R'lyaeih can't do much more than spread a few nightmares . . . but you and I have experienced an incursion of shoggoths, and we know perfectly well how much damage such waves of hallucination can do . . . and also what power incantations have to precipitate or halt them. Amélie was there too, and it must have frightened her badly, although she'd never consent to show it; hopefully, it was just anxiety that led her to take the little girl away from your kitchen, and perhaps needless anxiety—but there are much more worrying possibilities."

"Such as?" I queried.

"Such as the possibility that it wasn't Amélie who took the little girl away, but *vice versa*."

"Do you think that's likely?"

"How can I tell? There are too many unknowns in this bizarre equation . . . far too many. But if Prospero's hypothesis regarding the intended recipient of the message overwriting the palimpsest is correct, it might put a great many things into a different and worrying light."

"You mean the suggestion that the intended recipient of the message was the original Comte de Saint-Germain?"

"Yes."

"But surely he was a charlatan, just like the present one? He wasn't really a great magician, just a great liar?"

"That has always seemed to be highly likely—but the highly likely is not always correct, and when one is assessing a liar, it is always difficult to determine exactly where the lies stop, and what the truth is that they are shielding. If the original text of the palimpsest is Medieval and the overwriting eighty years old, the possibilities opened up by them certainly pose a stern challenge to conventional wisdom. Lacroix knows that, and that is why his interrogation of Prospero might be invaluable."

The streets were not busy and the fiacre reached the Rue Vivienne in very good time, in spite of the gathering fog. We got down at the corner of the short impasse at the end of which the doors of the Harmonic Society headquarters were situated, and Dupin, still in a hurry, rushed off without a word while I was still fumbling in my pockets for the coins I required to pay the cab-driver. I could not find the exact sum, and had to give him a louis—which meant that I had to wait for change, being unprepared to give him a tip larger than the fare. By the time he had counted out the sous, with a conspicuous slowness, Dupin had disappeared inside the building and the ever-cautious concierge had closed the door, although he must have seen me beside the fiacre, even in the misty gloom.

As the cab moved away, a man materialized out of the mist of the Rue Vivienne impasse and collided with me. The fog was not nearly thick enough or the gaslight faint enough for him to have been unable to see me, and I cursed his clumsiness—before realizing that clumsiness had had nothing to do with it, when the fellow stuck the barrel of a pistol in my ribs, painfully, and snarled: "Curse away, Monsieur Dupin, but don't make any other sign of alarm. Walk with me, please."

So saying, he grasped my arm and began to pull me along the Rue Vivienne at a brisk pace.

My first thought was to tell the oaf that he had made a mistake and that I was not Dupin. He obviously did not know Dupin, or he would have known that I was not him on seeing me pay the cab fare. My second thought was to look around in search of a policeman, but there was no sign of the one who had been following us on the Île Saint-Louis, or the one that must have followed Saint-Germain's carriage; the fog and the darkness, alas, made it all too easy for them to make themselves unobtrusive in between the street-lights, and their first instinct, on seeing me abducted—if, in fact, they even realized that they were witnessing an abduction—would have been to follow rather than intervene. My third thought was that, on the balance of probabilities, my abductor might well be a policeman, and my fourth was that, even if he was not, the sensible thing for me to do was to let him take me wherever he wanted to take me, in order to find out who had sent him and what they wanted. Evidently, the man with the pistol did not have murder in mind, or he could simply have fired the gun and made his escape in the gathering gloom.

My captor led me along the recently urbanized upper part of the Rue Vivienne and then into the recently renovated Passage des Panoramas, densely packed by small shops of various kinds. The passage had always seemed claustrophobic to me because of its roof, and although the fog had not crept into it to any great extent, it had a conspicuous lack of illuminated gas jets. In spite of the many lighted windows, and the fact that many of the shops were still open for business, the passageway was very dark in places.

My abductor rapped on the door of one of the unlit shops with his knuckles, and it opened immediately. It appeared to be a minuscule art dealership of sorts, but I had no time to inspect the stock.

"Guard the door," said my captor to someone invisible in the darkness, "but don't do anything foolish. The police and other bloodhounds are watching." I found that observation reassuring, although the fact that my abductor evidently regarded the police as adversaries probably ought not to have had that effect.

I tried to penetrate the darkness with my gaze, in order to find out how many people might be lurking there and to estimate what manner of men they might be, but it was impossible. I was taken to a room behind the counter before being bundled down a wrought-iron spiral staircase that evidently led to a basement. I went as slowly as I could, not wanting to stumble and fall, even though the barrel of the gun was being applied to the nape of my neck. Initially, I attributed the lurching sensation in my gut to the fear of taking a tumble, but my fear increased in intensity so rapidly that before I reached the bottom I had become convinced that the "basement" into which I was being shoved was no mere storeroom, but a genuine Underworld beyond the border of our own.

That impression was confirmed when the man with the gun stopped dead on the bottom step of the stairway rather than stepping down on to the basement floor.

"Go on," he said, but without emphasizing the command with a prod of the gun barrel.

The basement was almost pitch dark, but not quite. A small hooded lantern was placed in the center of a rather capacious table, on the near side of which a single chair was positioned. The light of the lantern was orientated in that direction, and it was impossible to make out anything beyond the other edge of the tabletop, except that there appeared to be three human shadows there, sitting in a row like the judges of a tribunal. That could well have been a melodramatic contrivance of a sort routinely contrived by conspirators and secret tribunals of various sorts, but I did not think, even for an instant, that it was mere theatricality and I suspected the shadows of lacking solidity.

Until that moment I had not been unduly frightened. I had understood that the gun pointed at me was merely a punctuation mark in the rhetoric of my abductor's action, and that he could not have any intention to fire the weapon. Its vulgar solidity was, in its way, rather reassuring. The figures lurking in the shadow were something else entirely. Their shape was human, but not for an instant did I imagine that it they were *merely* human. I cannot explain exactly how I knew, but I *knew* that I was confronted by something uncanny, something not really alive and not even material.

In the past, I had even confronted ghosts without being terrified: ghosts that had somehow carried with them an appearance of familiarity, not just in the trivial sense that they were known to me but in the sense that they still belonged to the world of which I was a contented component. These ghosts, I thought, did *not* belong. The shadows did not make any hostile movement, but they contained, somehow, an element of the alien and the inimical.

I knew that I had to be brave. I did not want to let Dupin down. I forced myself to sit down in the chair opposite the central figure of the three.

Being forewarned, I was not unduly surprised when the shadow in question uttered a curse, but what it said after the oath seemed bizarrely bathetic.

"Idiot," he said, pronouncing the word in the English fashion, although my abductor was certainly French. "This is Reynolds, not Dupin." He seemed to me to be a vulgar Englishman, not an American—or, at least, to have been one in a more-or-less distant past, while he was alive.

"How was I to know?" my abductor complained. "They only split up for a moment. I grabbed the only one I could, as quickly as I could. Does it really matter, since they're as thick as thieves and probably have no secrets from one another?"

How little you know! I thought, still attempting an appropriate bravado.

"If you want me to take a message to Dupin," I said, in English, trying to sound perfectly calm, "I'll be glad to do it. You only had to ask—there was no need for the pistol."

"I apologize for that," said the ghost in the center of the trio, in the same language, who seemed to me to be exerting every fiber of his non-being to be amiable, and who had evidently been appointed as their spokesman, "but it seemed safest for our friend to insist rather than risk an argument that might have attracted inconvenient attention from any of the fellows dogging your footsteps or watching the Harmonic

Society. Hopefully, the numbskull assigned to track you from Prospero's den will have been content to follow you here and will wait patiently in the passage, even if he saw the gun. We mean you no harm, Mr. Reynolds. You're perfectly safe."

"I'm glad to hear it," I said, sincerely without being entirely convinced. "You can hardly blame me for being nervous, though, with a gun in my back, confronted by three ghosts, while a man lies murdered in the Rue de l'Hirondelle."

"That wasn't us," said my invisible interlocutor, without bothering to deny that he was a ghost.

"Oh," I said, still contriving to keep tremors out of my voice. "Who was it, then?"

"Addhema, I presume. The house is a sensitive location, as you're undoubtedly aware—but we needn't concern ourselves with that. Our immediate concern is to recover our property, urgently."

"And what property would that be?" I asked employing curiosity to fight the insistent thrill of fear.

"The little girl that Jacob Pym brought to Paris. We need to know, urgently, where Dupin's concierge has taken her."

"So do we," I retorted. "On what grounds do you describe her as your property?" I thought that asking the question was a genuine act of heroism, in the circumstances.

"We were supposed to bring her from Booby Island, but that imbecile Pym blundered in and took her away. He's thrown the whole timetable out of kilter. We had the devil of a job chasing him—either that ship of his sprouted wings, or there's magic at work. He's probably an innocent, though, and surely no magician, so we don't mean him any harm either, as long as we can recover the child. We're not so sure about your cousin Jeremiah, though."

I tried to laugh, but my unease betrayed me. "Jeremiah's certainly no magician," I said. "I can vouch for that."

"You'd probably say the same about Dupin . . . but you're something of a magician yourself, and not such a fool as you pretend to be. And you've just been hobnobbing with Prospero, who isn't as much of a magician as he thinks he is, but isn't exactly a layman, and asks far too many questions for his own good. Can you arrange a meeting with Dupin for us, right away? We'd like a serious word with him, even if he really doesn't know where the girl is. We've checked the lodge in the Rue Dunot, obviously, but she's not there. Dupin must be able to tell us where else to look, unless his reputation is greatly inflated—which it didn't seem to be, last time we met."

I ignored the insulting accusation that I posed as a fool. "I hardly think he'll want to come, when he hears about my abduction at gunpoint," I said.

"You think not? If that idiot on the staircase hadn't snatched the wrong man, don't you think that Dupin would have reacted exactly as you did, and come along in the hope of finding out something that would interest him. And haven't you found out something that interests you . . . enough to whet the appetite, at any rate?"

"No," I said, bluntly. My eyes were peering into the darkness, trying to make out the shadow's features, but it was a purely physical instinct; I really wasn't sure that I actually wanted to see my interlocutor, because my conscious mind was more inclined to flee—but I suppressed my impulsive terror and tried to focus my sense of duty. "Nor will I discover anything of interest," I went on, "while you and your two associates stay so resolutely in the shadows to which you belong, unless you care to tell me something much more useful than the fact that you think you have some claim to the ownership of the little girl. What claim?"

"We're not slave traders," said the shadow-man. "We don't mean to harm her—but we need her, as you must know very well."

"In fact, I don't," I said, "Is she carrying some kind of message."

"You don't have to play the fool with us," the other said. "You know who and what she is . . . at least, the old Breton witch must."

"If she's carrying the same kind of inscription that the Mahatma engraved in the flesh of Ysolde Leonys," I said, still using the fascination of the argument to suppress the urge to get up and run away, gun or no gun, "you have a very strange notion of meaning her no harm."

"That certainly wasn't my fault," said the other, with a certain asperity. "That swine England stole her to pay back a grudge. Believe me, I'd have done anything in the world to prevent that, and I certainly don't want anything similar to happen again, especially at the last moment."

It was at that point that I realized, belatedly, that however alien he seemed, the ghost *was* actually familiar, in the trivial sense that I'd met him before. Oddly enough, I wasn't particularly amazed, not merely because I'd seen a lot of ghosts lately but because the presence of this one seemed somehow apposite, like a jigsaw piece shaped to fit the puzzle. Abruptly, the presence of the seemingly-illusory sailing ship on the Seine seemed entirely understandable, and I wondered why I hadn't realized immediately what the crucifix nailed to her mainmast must be.

The knowledge that I could put a name to my interlocutor put a much more forceful damper on my terror than my curiosity or a sense of obligation, even though his presence wasn't any less menacing for it. I almost began to feel, if not genuinely brave, at least comfortable.

"I wouldn't want it to happen again either, Mr. Taylor," I said, "but you'll understand why you don't seem entirely trustworthy to me."

Jack Taylor shifted in his seat, but didn't bring his phantom face into the light.

"I saved your life, Mr. Reynolds, in Brittany," he said. As with Saint-Germain, I felt entitled to doubt the claim, but I didn't want to argue the point.

"And I was glad to see your ghost-ship looming up out of the mist," I said. "I'm truly sorry about what happened to your daughter thereafter, but there was nothing I could do. There was nothing any of us could do, at that point. You came far too late to render her any useful assistance,"

"You don't know that," the dead pirate retorted. Strictly speaking, it was true; I didn't have the slightest idea what the ghost pirates might have been capable of doing, if the poor young woman hadn't jumped ship—but I was sure that whatever it might have been, Ysolde Leonys hadn't wanted it. She had had enough, and I could hardly blame her for that.

"If you want me to arrange a meeting with Dupin," I said, boldly, "he'll want to see the organ grinder, not the monkey."

"There's no need to be rude," the pirate said, equably, "and since you know my reputation, your bravado is a trifle reckless—but don't you think that Dupin would be interested to have a conversation with a company of dead pirates? A true scholar ought to jump at the chance, don't you think?"

"Your companions do talk, then?" I said, sarcastically. "I presume one of them is Angria, and the other the Mahatma?"

Jack Taylor did not seem annoyed by my impertinence; he merely said: "Wrong on both counts. We're all lowly crewmen, but Yvon, to my right, is the man who actually pulled you out of the morass in Bretagne, and you might well have heard of the fellow to my left: Olivier Levasseur, alias La Buse. There was bad blood between us once, but we're all friends now. Death has a way of making old enmities seem irrelevant, and Olivier doesn't even want you to return what's left of his treasure. All we want is the child."

"In order to open a portal to R'lyaeih? I don't think Dupin would agree to help you to do that."

"Which is why we need to negotiate with him in person. He'll want it too, when he understands the situation more clearly, because he'll never understand what's happening otherwise."

He was probably right about Dupin being eager to meet with him—but I still thought that I might be in a position to haggle. "You have to tell me what the Mahatma intends to do with the girl," I said.

"Isn't it obvious? It will be to Dupin, and he's surely magician enough to know that we won't hurt her, unlike that thrice-damned bastard England. I can understand why the witch panicked when she realized that the girl is Cthulhu's child, but Dupin is made of far sterner stuff, by all accounts. He'll understand—and he's up to his neck in it, anyhow, whether he realizes it or not."

That seemed like overconfidence to me, but once again, I wasn't about to argue. I did know Taylor's reputation, and reckless bravado can only take a man so far. A certain amount of subtle probing seemed to be safe, though, now that I knew who I was dealing with, if not exactly what.

"Edward England," I said, "alias Oberon Breisz, claimed to be a reincarnation of Edward Kelley, and also claimed that Dupin is a reincarnation of John Dee. Is that true?"

"Edward England, alias Oberon Breisz," the pirate mimicked, "was out of his tiny mind, matey. He thought he could read the *Necronomicon*, but he didn't even know what it is. He's not the first wayward scholar to have made that mistake, though, and he won't be the last."

"And do you know what the *Necronomicon* is?" I asked.

"The dead know everything," he replied, but his spectral voice was oozing sarcasm.

I didn't want to get into a contest of repartee with a man— or ghost—who was evidently becoming impatient, so I said: "I'll pass your request for a meeting on to Dupin. When and where?"

"Bring him here," said the dead pirate, "as soon as possible. Tell him that if he really doesn't know where his Cerberus has taken the child, we can help him find her—and if he does, he'd be a fool to play games with us. We saved his life too, remember—and if he has to face shoggoths again, he might well be very grateful to be on our side . . . that goes for you too, Mr. Reynolds. The Seine may look like a mere paddling pool, but you're in treacherous waters full of reefs, and without the Mahatma, you won't have a pilot."

That made a certain sense, and I knew that Dupin would be as enthusiastic to talk to the Mahatma as the latter's phantom hirelings were to talk to him, so I was just about to conclude that, on the whole, the meeting had been very satisfactory, insofar as conversations with the dead went, when a gunshot rang out on the floor above, followed by the blast of a whistle and the sound of running feet in the passage outside the shop. They were probably the feet of tradesmen and clients panicked by the shot rather than potential combatants, but the fuss that my captors had wanted to avoid had presumably been triggered, and the possibility of their arranging a clandestine meeting with Dupin had become far less likely.

Jack Taylor cursed volubly. "Cthulhu!" he said, presumably using it as an expletive, exactly as Cousin Jeremiah used "Damn!"

I couldn't see that three ghosts had anything to fear from the hapless bloodhounds of the Sûreté, but the prospect of a raid and a round-up of their human associates evidently threw something of a spanner into the works of their scheme. They faded away into the darkness—literally, it seemed to me, although it is, I suppose, conceivable that they simply slipped away through a hidden door. By the time policemen in heavy boots clattered down the stairs carrying lanterns, however, spreading light throughout what was, indeed, a perfectly ordinary basement storeroom, I was alone there, my abductor having thrown away his gun and surrendered half way up the staircase.

I was still looking round in slight bewilderment, when a voice from the top of the stairs groaned theatrically and said:

"You idiot! That's not Dupin, it's Reynolds!"

"I distinctly heard the gunman call him Dupin!" protested a police agent, who was not clearly visible to me but was definitely not the one who had followed us from the Île Saint-Louis. "It's not my fault."

Such limited experience as I had with the agents of the Sûreté inclined me to believe that it never was their fault when things went wrong, in their own opinion, but I didn't dwell on that thought, because the voice from the darkness behind the beam of a lantern that had accused the poor agent of idiocy was only marginally less surprising, in context, than that of Jack Taylor.

"If I'm not supposed to be here, Lucien," I said to the ex-Prefect of Police, "neither are you. If you haven't really resigned, haven't you got a Revolution to repress?"

XII

MISTAKEN IDENTITY

"DAMN!" said Lucien Groix, once he had bundled me into the back of a sealed carriage and sat down opposite me. "Damn! Damn! Damn!" He was not in a good mood.

"My cousin Jeremiah couldn't put it any better," I observed. "Would you care to explain to me why you've arrested me and where you're taking me?"

"I haven't arrested you," he told me, grimly. "I'm rescuing you, and I'm taking you to a safe place. I thought I was rescuing Dupin, but it seems that there's been an awkward case of mistaken identity. If you don't mind, though, I'll ask the questions from now on."

I did mind. Since he was no longer the Prefect of Police, I didn't think he had any right to ask me any questions. For a moment, I was tempted simply to leap out of the carriage, given that it was only moving at walking pace, and make my way back to the headquarters of the Societé Harmonique to rejoin Dupin, but given the state of the road and the sidewalk, such a gymnastic feat would undoubtedly be dangerous—and in any case, I thought, Dupin would want me to find out everything I could about where Groix had been and what kind of game he was now playing. I had to stay where I was and continue going with the flow.

"I didn't need rescuing," I said, trying to make myself a little more comfortable on the hard banquette of the vehicle. "Things were actually going quite well, until you and your heavy brigade turned up. I had a grip on things."

He voiced a slight mutter of incredulity. "Where did the other people in the basement go?" he demanded, intemperately, blatantly ignoring my protest, "and how did they get out."

"I can't be absolutely sure," I told him, resentfully, "but I don't believe that they were really there in the flesh. I assume they forsook any solidity they might have had in order to cross back over the borderland between the dimensions and return to the ghost ship that brought them up the Seine all the way from Le Havre and Honfleur."

I was trying to amaze him, or at least to throw him off his stride, but in fact he merely grunted incredulously before lapsing temporarily into a sullen silence, presumably protected by his censorious consciousness from any possibility of believing what I'd said, in spite of the fact that he hadn't found anyone else in the basement and it had no other obvious exit.

It was dark inside the carriage and the scant gaslight that filtered through the shuttered windows from the street lights was insufficient to allow me to see any more of him than I had been able to see of the phantom Jack Taylor. The carriage was moving slowly because of the fog, but I had no idea where we were, or in which direction we might be traveling

"Damn!" he said again, after a pause; then he added: "Do you know who grabbed you?"

"I don't know who the fellow with the gun was," I replied, scrupulously. "But I recognized one of the ghosts as Jack Taylor. He said that the others were Olivier Levasseur and someone called Yvon. All former pirates and all long dead, I presume, but seemingly resurrected as phantoms with the aid of a magician sometimes known as the Mahatma, in order to serve under the captaincy of an Indian warlord named Angre or Angria. They're looking for a child who is supposed to play a key role in the fulfillment of some old prophecy. Apparently, that species of the not-quite-dead needs vehicles for long distance travel, just as we do. They intended to invite Dupin to step aboard the ship in order to talk to Angria or the Mahatma, but when Taylor realized that I wasn't him, they didn't bother with the invitation. I'm apparently not important enough to warrant much courtesy—an opinion that you seem to hold yourself. I'm sorry to disappoint you."

This time, I didn't even get the favor of an incredulous grunt, so I said: "Who did you think had kidnapped Dupin? The Republicans or the Royalists?"

"Don't play the fool, Reynolds," the ex-Prefect retorted, unkindly. "You know that this is more complicated than that."

"I do," I confirmed, unconvinced that he knew how complicated it might be. "Your resignation from the Prefecture was a feint, then, and you're still the secret head of the Sûreté, even though your agents have strict orders to deny it?"

"I didn't resign," he said, flatly. "I was sacked—officially, at least. And I'm not the head of the Sûreté. I had to go underground, but the police are so fragmented these days and the loyalties of the agents so divided that I was able to take an elite squad with me. They're still in the pay of the state, as I am, but we don't show up in the accounts of the Ministry of Finance. We're one of the proverbial left hands whose actions are a mystery to the government's right hand."

"How could you be sacked?" I wondered. "Weren't you directly responsible to the king?"

"There's a power at work that even the king can't dispute," Groix said, sourly, "and couldn't even if he weren't about to abdicate and go into exile. And I'm supposed to be asking the questions, remember?"

"Whose power?" I queried, ignoring his assertion of entitlement to lead the discussion.

"God's," he retorted, with a weary sigh. "Or rather, that of the Holy Office, operating in his name—notionally on behalf of the Vatican, although I don't suppose anyone has bothered to inform the Pope of the fact, or even the Archbishop of Paris. The Church has more secret organizations within it than the State, and they tend to be more efficient, having had centuries of Machiavellian practice."

"The Holy Office!" I said, astonished. "You mean the Inquisition?"

"There is no Inquisition any more," he said. "It's now the Congregation for the Doctrine of the Faith. The defense against heresy is now supposed to be purely a war of words—but black magic hasn't gone away, as you know very well, and words can occasionally be far more potent than most people are usually content to believe. The days of Black Masses are probably not yet done, and the days of demonic possession certainly aren't, so the Church continues to make war against them with all the weapons at its disposal."

Enlightenment dawned. "This has something to do with the prophecies of Abbé Vaillant, hasn't it?" I ventured. "The Church—or a faction within the Church—still takes them seriously."

"I wouldn't go that far," said Groix, "but there are certainly factions within the Church who try to keep track of Vaillant's remaining adherents, always ready to take alarm. You know, I suppose, that the Convulsionnaires have suddenly enjoyed a resurgence in Paris, even though the newspapers are simply accusing the city's bakers of adulterating their bread with polluted rye in order to make up the statutory weight. There are fashions in panic and in scapegoating, as in everything else."

"But you're not one of Vaillant's belated followers," I objected. "Why should the Holy Office want you removed from your post?"

"Not merely removed from my post but obliterated from the public record," Groix replied, bitterly. "An anathema has been cast upon me; I've been excommunicated—and not merely from the Church's communion."

"But why?"

"For participating in a Sabbat, evidently having sold my soul to the Devil."

I almost said "What Sabbat?" in a tone of utter incredulity, but enlightenment dawned again. I knew perfectly well what Sabbat, because I had been there. It hadn't been a Sabbat at all, of course, but it was very easy to see, in hindsight, how it might have been mistaken for one by an uninitiated observer.

"We were followed to Fontainebleau at All Hallows!" I deduced. "Saint-Germain was already under covert observation, by rival factions of his own society as well as your men. They mistook what happened that night for ritual diabolism, and reported it to the Holy Office, doubtless colored by all manner of embroideries!"

"They didn't need any embroideries," said Groix, with another sigh. "They only had to report what they saw. You and Dupin have been atheists since childhood, and saw everything in that light, but Chapelain and I were both brought up in the faith, and the taint of apparent diabolism was very obvious to us, no matter how scrupulously we tried to set it aside.

"The Holy Office no longer has the authority in France to arrest and imprison anyone, let alone burn them at the stake, but they're by no means impotent. Why do you think Chapelain has suddenly fallen silent, and that fellow Anton has disappeared completely? Saint-Germain was under surveillance anyway, and you can be certain that an equally close eye is now being kept on Dupin, with a view to sending both of them into exile and disgrace as soon as sufficient evidence can be accumulated and formal charges drawn up for whatever secret tribunal the Holy Office requires.

"Deporting you, of course, will be a mere formality, but Saint-Germain and Dupin have friends just as influential as mine and, however amazing it might seem, fewer enemies in the relevant high places, so I was the easiest target. It's impossible to serve as Prefect of Police without treading on political toes, alas. Even you can probably understand why our little expedition to the forest was a sharp spur. The Prefect of Police at a conventicle of devil-worshipers! That demanded action, and they took it."

Obviously, his dismissal and the ruination of his career, on the basis of a stupid mistake, rankled sorely, even though his career would have been fortunate to survive the Revolution anyway.

"While the agents of the Church have been monitoring you covertly, of course," he went on, "we've been monitoring them. They would have completed their strategy already if they hadn't been so anxious about coming too far out of hiding on the eve of an inevitable Republican victory in the Revolution—but I've suspected for some time that the gathering certainty of that outcome might lead them to take . . . unusual measures. When Dupin's abduction was reported to me—mistakenly, as it now turns out—I had no idea whether Cthulhu's crazies or the Church's were responsible, but either way, I thought my hand was being forced. He's my only chance of obtaining an accurate understanding of what's happening, and perhaps my only chance of stopping it. If the supposed magician that you call the Mahatma has brought his closest adherents to Paris, as well as a child that Vaillant's followers have mistaken for the child of his prophecy having appeared here, the matter must be . . . extremely urgent. Now, for God's sake stop pestering me with idiotic questions and let me do my job. Why has Dupin gone to the Harmonic Society's headquarters? I thought he had enough sense to avoid the place."

"He went to talk to Jacob Pym, the ship's captain who brought a young castaway to my house this morning, looking for Dupin. Unfortunately he wasn't there, and now, neither is she, having been taken away by Madame Lacuzon. Pym went with Saint-Germain to try to catch up with Dupin at the Louvre, but they missed him and Saint-Germain took

Pym to the Society's headquarters, so Dupin was going to talk to him there. Paul Lacroix has probably caught up with him at the headquarters by now, and I can't imagine that they'll linger there. There will be eavesdroppers behind every door, of course, and Saint-Germain will probably want to stick to them like a burr, but Dupin will doubtless slip away as soon as he's figured out where to look for his concierge. In the meantime, though, he'll surely be safe enough from enemy agents in such a populous building."

Groix groaned. "That's your idea of safe?" he said, sarcastically. "It's a nest of vipers. We don't know for sure which members are on which side, or how many sides there are, and Saint-Germain seems to be making it up as he goes along, not even knowing what side he wants to be on. The Rue Vivienne is probably the least safe place in Paris at present for Dupin. As for the likes of Jeremiah Reynolds, Lacroix and the rest, you and I know that they're mere curiosity-seekers with not an atom of malevolence in them, but the Holy Office only sees heresy and evil wherever it looks, and the mere fact that they've been asking questions about Cthulhu is enough to brand them as instruments of Satan so far as the righteous are concerned, as well as making them a target for the crazies. I doubt that the Thugs have anything against them, but that won't save them from being strangled if they get in the way of the mad Mahatma's scheming."

Evidently, he knew more about the Mahatma than I had assumed. I reminded myself that he had been the head of an organization of spies for some time, and that the Mahatma had been scheming for more than a hundred years—perhaps far longer.

"The Thugs?" I queried, once again ignoring the injunction to let him ask the questions. "You mean worshipers of Shiva intend on driving the British out of India?"

"Yes—but that tide was always against them, and the cult splintered long ago. In the 1720s, one faction was said by spies inserted into the British East India Company to have been run by a mystic who claimed to be able to exploit the power of deities known by various names, translatable as *the Great Old Ones* . . . particularly one worshiped in parts of Asia and Oceania under the name Cthulhu. The British have always considered his followers to be a minor nuisance, having defeated his only ally of any political importance, the Maratha admiral Kanhoji Angre, whose fleet incorporated numerous European mercenaries. The East India Company's ships reduced his navy to near-impotence, but the Thugs weren't as easy to crush.

"Angre's magician has been presumed dead by the British for more than a century, although his title—the Mahatma— continues to be used by various plotters and troublemakers, who invariably claim that the original Mahatma is still alive and is planning some great coup. Some diplomats serving under Louis XV, presumably controlled by the Duc de Richelieu— who was always trying to match the reputation for scheming obtained by his namesake, the Red Cardinal—established clandestine contact with the Mahatma and lent him sup- port for political reasons before 1730. They maintained that contact subsequently with his successors, but Richelieu's fall from grace should have put an end to all that long before the Revolution. It didn't, quite, and clandestine communications of some sort with descendants of Angre and his mercenaries have always been maintained by at least one of the supposedly secret societies working under the cover of the Harmonic Society, in spite of all the political difficulties. The Thugs still maintain the myth of the survival of their magical master- mind. Recently, that communication increased to the point of attracting my attention, but my attempts to investigate it hadn't got very far when the Holy Office put their spoke in my wheel, and I hadn't had a chance to consult Dupin about it before the fiasco at Fontainebleau. Now, events have over- taken us. There are Thugs in Paris, and according to you, the most recent incarnation of the Mahatma is here too, with a gang of supposedly ghostly pirates."

"They're not *supposedly* ghostly pirates," I told him, flatly. "They're actual ghostly pirates, probably including Angre, or Angria, no matter how hard you find that to believe."

"Not as hard as you might imagine," Groix retorted, gruffly. "Especially given that the communication Angre or his descendants have maintained with the successors of Richelieu's old agents has been channeled through the Harmonic Society rather than the new ministries—a nest of vipers, as I said."

I was thinking hard, or trying to. "Have you ever heard of the Nine Immortals?" I asked, suddenly.

"Of course," he said. "Everyone knows the legend—but we don't record alleged sightings of them any more. The files of the Sûreté are periodically weeded of their more fanciful insertions, but they don't get thrown away, merely relegated to something like the Bibliothèque Nationale's *enfer* . . . Dupin loves rooting around in there, but I've always kept Lacroix out, much to his chagrin. Why do you ask? No, on second thoughts, I don't care. Do you have any idea where Madame Lacuzon might have taken the supposedly-miraculous child?"

"No, I don't," I said. "Nor does Dupin."

"I beg leave to doubt that," said Groix, "just as everyone else must, which is why he's in greater peril that he probably suspects. The likelihood is that the only reason that he's still walking around is because Vaillant's believers and the Thugs are hoping that he'll lead them to the child, or that Madame Lacuzon will bring the child to him. If I know Dupin, he'll do everything he can to avoid tipping them off as to the old witch's whereabouts . . . but she might not be wise enough to keep away from him. In any case, when their patience runs out, the crazies will do exactly what I suspected them of doing an hour ago and they'll grab Dupin and try to force him to talk. It's possible, though, that he really doesn't know where she is. The dragon has always been a law unto herself, ever since she adopted Dupin."

198

"You know about that?" I queried. "About Madame Lacuzon being Dupin's foster-mother, I mean?" I was annoyed that everyone seemed to know Dupin's personal history better than I did.

"I'm the commander of the most efficient limb of the secret police," he said, "even though I don't officially exist any longer. Most of what can be known, I know—but unlike that weasel Saint-Germain, I don't brag about what I know, and I'm a lot more careful in maintaining my skepticism in regard to what I'm told. But yes, I've known for some time about the dragon having nursed the infant Dupin in the days of the Chouannerie, just as I knew that the fellow you and he visited with Lacroix this afternoon had returned to Paris as soon as he and his aged mistress got off the train. They're under observation, but they seem to be harmless."

"Dupin thinks that the weasel Saint-Germain might not be the mere charlatan that everyone assumes," I told him. "Since All Hallows, we've had every reason to take theories of reincarnation seriously, and I, for one, can no longer doubt the reality of ghosts. My only problem is figuring out exactly what they are and what the limitations of their manifestations are. It's a great pity that the Mahatma only sent his hirelings to grab me; I'd really like to interrogate him personally on the subject."

"That's because you're one of those proverbial fools who never fail to rush in where angels fear to tread," Groix observed, unkindly. "If you had an atom of common sense you'd take the first ship back to America . . . in fact, you'd have done that before you stated playing silly games with hellish harmonies in Du Potet's garden."

"I wasn't playing silly games," I couldn't resist saying. "I was playing the cello—and rather well, if I say so myself, until blood and entrails were splashed all over the strings."

"In a pig's eye," he retorted, still in the clutches of his bad mood.

If Lucien Groix hadn't notionally saved my life by pulling me out of the Seine in the forest of Fontainebleau I could probably have taken a serious dislike to the secret policeman, but I felt that I owed him a certain tolerance, and I decided to forgive him his gibe about proverbial fools. I returned to my own train of thought. "I doubt that Jack Taylor has any real understanding of what he is," I went on, pensively, "but his puppet-master must. Jana Valdemar might, but I have no idea how to evoke her phantom, if it can be evoked . . . assuming, of course, that she really is dead."

"She's dead, Mr. Reynolds," said Lucien, flatly. "It wasn't my fault—if I could have saved both of you, I would have." I thought I detected residual traces of guilt in his brusquerie.

"I know you would," I said, generously, "and I don't suppose that the dead know everything, any more than we do—perhaps they know even less—but some of them, at least, must try hard to interrogate their own existential situation, and if anyone has the intelligence and knowledge necessary to do that, she probably has. Did you ever figure out who murdered her?"

"Murdered her?" Groix queried. "She walked into the river because she was pregnant and Chapelain had refused to marry her."

"Not so," I said, positively. "She walked into the river under a powerful mesmeric compulsion—more powerful, I suspect, than Chapelain could have contrived, although I can't believe that he would ever have tried. I don't know about Saint-Germain, and I'm certainly not prepared simply to trust his word that he didn't do it, but I can't see that he had a plausible motive for murder. What have your bloodhounds found out about Anton the fiddler?"

"Not much. He'd been living at the Harmonic Society's headquarters for a long time, serving as a general factotum, ever since Puységur was the president—like Dupin, he's older than he looks. His real name isn't recorded in the Society's records, but that's not unusual. My men couldn't find any evidence of criminal behavior on his part, although he was said to have been studying conjuration and to have dabbled in magic. Again, that's far from unusual in the Society, where everyone not ambitious to be a real magus or magnetizer is ambitious to be a convincing fake. My lads couldn't find any evidence of a link with the Thugs, but that doesn't mean that he's not in their camp . . . just as the original Comte de Saint-Germain probably was, if only as a diplomatic game."

That was a slightly disturbing thought, if our Saint-Germain really did remember being the other in a previous life. "What about the dead man in the witch-house?" I asked. "Do you have any idea who he is . . . or was?"

"What dead man?" he asked, sharply.

"The report hasn't reached you yet?" I said, surprised by the apparent laxity of his agents. "A man with a key to the witch-house, identified by Saint-German and others as one of the mythical Nine Immortals, was killed there this morning with a crossbow, thus proving not to be immortal at all. That's why I asked you about them."

I couldn't see Lucien Groix's face, so I had to imagine his expression of astonishment and wrath at the discovery that he didn't know as much of what could be known as he thought. "By the witch-house," he said, harshly, "you mean the house in the old Rue de l'Hirondelle—the one further along the Left Bank, not the one near the Monnaie—supposedly haunted at long intervals by a seductive vampire?"

"That's right," I said. "The house you posted a squad of agents to watch, after strange lights had been seen there, and where ghostly music was played, which might or might not be part of the preparation for the impending evocation of Cthulhu by the Mahatma's miracle child."

"Damn!" said the ex-Prefect of Police again, explosively. "Have you seen the squad in question?"

"Of course, I told him. "Twice, although they seem to be working in shifts, and they weren't the same agents—except for the woman."

"They're not my men," said Groix, in the same harsh tone, "and I don't have any female agents."

"They used your secret signal, twice, to attract Dupin's attention. The young woman even implied that you'd sent her, although she withdrew that suggestion when it was questioned."

"That signal's in common usage nowadays—and not just by the police. Where do you think I borrowed it from?"

That was an easy one. The signal had, after all, long been traditionally used to ward off the spells of the Evil Demon. "You think the Holy Office is watching the witch-house for Addhema?" I said, skeptically. "You think the young woman pretending to be a whore was actually a nun in disguise?"

"Don't be ridiculous," said Groix. "Even the agents of the Holy Office wouldn't stoop that low . . . but I don't know what to think, and that's worrying. You say that a man claiming to be one of the Nine Immortals was shot there—with a crossbow?"

"He didn't *claim* to be anything," I said, "but his eyes glowed like a tiger's in the dark, and Saint-Germain wasn't the only one who said that he'd never met such a powerful mesmerist. You mean that it wasn't your men who followed Saint-Germain's coach there either."

"Damn!" said Groix, yet again. "No, it wasn't." His choice of oaths, I thought, was not a habit likely to exculpate him in the eyes of the devout from suspicions of diabolism.

Knowing Dupin's methods, I tried to apply them. "Well," I said, "even if the fake whore was lying about you, she told me to ask Dupin to report to the present Head of the Sûreté, so she's probably working for another arm of your organization, unless she was running a monumental bluff that was bound to be soon uncovered. And the man who followed Dupin, Lacroix and me to the Île Saint-Louis to visit Prospero, and then followed us to the Rue Vivienne, certainly behaved like a policeman . . . but now I think about it, he wasn't the man who misidentified me to you, who must have been posted to watch the headquarters of the Society independently. I can't make head nor tail of what that might signify, alas. We need to consult Dupin. You need to send someone to the head-quarters of the Society right away, to arrange a meeting. I'll do that for you, if you wish—he's undoubtedly worried about me, since I didn't follow him into the building. It would be only natural for me to invite him, Cousin Jeremiah and the Pym cousins back to my house, and with three lusty seamen as bodyguards we'll surely be safe from any sudden assault while we make our way there. You can join us there surrepti-tiously easily enough."

I was rather proud of that hastily-improvised plan,

"Very kind of you, I'm sure," said Groix, "but I already sent someone to take a message to Dupin while you were climb-ing into the coach, to tell him that you'd been abducted and to warn him to get away from Saint-Germain's lair. Things have undoubtedly moved on since you were first taken to the Passage des Panoramas, there and elsewhere. If you're correct in thinking that the Mahatma—or *a* Mahatma—really is in Paris, personally supervising this operation, he probably won't be pleased that his attempt to arrange a secret meeting with Dupin misfired, and he's surely likely to try again. His sense of urgency has probably been multiplied tenfold, if the scheme he and his predecessors have been hatching since God alone knows when is time-sensitive."

God, it seemed to me, was probably far from alone in knowing when this bizarre scheme had first been set in mo-tion, more than eighty years ago . . . but I, alas, was not one of those privileged to share that precise information—yet.

My invisible interlocutor pulled down the shutter of the portière, put his head out of the window and shouted: "Are we being followed, Bertrand?"

"Yes, Patron," replied the coachman, "but they're on foot and I can lose them if you wish. The horses are more sure-footed in these conditions than a runner. That's probably safer than trying to grab one or more of them for questioning, unless the fellow with you is a clever fighter."

Groix sat back in his seat. "Are you a clever fighter Mr. Reynolds?" he asked.

"Clever enough," I assured him, insincerely, "but I don't have a sword-stick with me, and we have to bear in mind that they might outnumber us . . . not to mention that they might be ghosts . . . or possessed by shoggoths. I'll risk it if you will, though. Presumably, you and your coachman are armed with pistols—you could always let me borrow one."

He barked a brief laugh, but all he said was: "Americans!"

I couldn't argue with that. "Well?" I said.

After a moment's hesitation, Groix stuck his head out of the window again. "Change of plan, Bertrand," he said. "Take us to the Rue de l'Hirondelle—the one in the Faubourg Saint-Victor."

"Yes, Patron," the reply came back. The whip cracked, and the horses immediately broke into a brisk trot that would surely have tested the pace and stamina of anyone following us on foot . . . anyone human, that is.

"That's your idea of a safe place?" I asked him.

"Of course not," he snapped, "but if the men on watch there aren't policemen, I want to know who they are and what they're doing—and if they *are* policemen, we'll be able to pit them against the fellows following us, if necessary. In any case, I want to look into this matter of a mysterious murder. Oh, why did you have to stick your oar in and bring me out of hiding, Mr. Reynolds? Things seemed so much simpler an hour ago!"

I thought about pointing out that I hadn't "stuck my oar in," and that, if I had been left to my own devices, I would presently be in Dupin's company—which seemed to me to be the safest place available, even in a nest of vipers—but I resisted that temptation in favor of the urge to exercise my philosophical wit.

"The world, Monsieur Groix," I quoted, "is not simple; it is far more complicated and more mysterious than anyone could possibly wish."

As things turned out, I was speaking even more truly than I had yet realized.

XIII

THE CAFÉ IN THE RUE DE L'HIRONDELLE

BY the time the carriage arrived at the Rue de l'Hirondelle the fog had thickened even further, and the yellow glow of the sparse street-lamps was hardly visible in the murk. As we dismounted, church bells began to chime. Automatically, I counted nine strokes, and felt oddly glad that there wasn't a tenth or an eleventh, let alone a twelfth. I thought I could make out the particular tone of Emanuel, the one bell in Notre-Dame that had survived the last two Revolutions, but my expertise was insufficient to pick out the bell of Saint-Médard, tolling over the tomb of Dean Paris, long sealed off from the few fugitive heretics who still came to pray there in quest of prophetic visions.

"Take a look around, Bertrand," Groix said to his coach-man—optimistically, I thought, the fog being thick enough to conceal anyone intent on remaining unobtrusive.

"Yes, Patron," the agent replied, dutifully, although far from enthusiastically.

The witch-house was invisible, having no lighted windows and being—for the moment, at least—devoid of supernatural fire follets. The parsimonious hall of the café was displaying a ruddy light through its uncurtained windows, though. I went in ahead of Lucien Groix.

The old woman was at her counter, optimistically warming her saucepan of mulled wine on a small stove—optimistically because she only had a single customer, for the moment: the young woman, still seated idly by the window, without her escort of bravos. Although a cup of hot wine would have been very welcome, after the journey through the icy night in the pitch dark of the carriage, I went straight to the young woman.

"You lied to me," I said, accusingly.

"Of course I did, Monsieur Reynolds," she said, insouciantly. "You're a little early, but that's probably a good thing. Doctor Prospero isn't here yet, and nor is Monsieur Dupin, but they'll surely be on their way soon. Do sit down and have a drink—and you too, Monsieur Groix. Primitive though it is, we'll be more comfortable here while we wait than in the house across the street."

Lucien Groix had stepped forward, and he was peering intently at the seemingly-young woman—who signaled to the old lady, with a gesture that was not that of the symbolic devil's horns.

"I don't know you," said the ex-Prefect bluntly. "Who posted you here?"

The woman laughed, briefly. "Not one of your colleagues," she said, with a hint of contempt in her voice. "Several agents of the Sûreté have been haunting the establishment for days, but I didn't need them any longer, so I sent them all packing, along with the Church spies. They might have got in our way . . . but I was careful not to hurt them. We want everything to be . . . harmonious."

"Who are you?" Groix demanded, while moving aside to let the old woman pass me and place a tray on the table, containing four cups and the fuming saucepan. I caught a whiff of the fumes in question, and wasn't in the least surprised to find them aromatic—but I immediately conceived dire suspicions as to what kind of spices might be producing the odor.

The younger woman must have noticed my apprehension, because instead of answering Groix's question right away she merely said: "It's just warm wine, Mr. Reynolds, with a little flavoring. Sit down and take some—you must be chilled to the bone in spite of the protective jacket beneath your overcoat, and you must be glad to be indoors. I assure you that I mean you no harm—in fact, I've taken care of the man who might have done, if the dolt had realized what you have in your pocket. Oh, don't just stand there like a fool, Monsieur Groix; go to the door and summon your coachman. The poor fellow must be even colder than Monsieur Reynolds. He won't see anything out there. Have no fear—the stranglers won't touch either of you, if you're reasonable. All is harmony, believe me."

There was too much in that remarkable series of statements for my confused mind to grasp it all at once, so it seized upon the item that seemed to be the most remarkable. I raised my right hand reflexively to pat my overcoat above my left breast. Inside the overcoat was my recently-tailored quilted jacket, and in the inside pocket of that jacket was the book that I had carelessly slipped into it that morning when the doorbell interrupted me—the book that had nothing printed on its binding, and which I had not had time to open.

Suddenly, I felt a thrill in the marrow of my bones that had nothing in common with the chill of the Arctic cold. I had paid no heed all day to the presence of the book next to my heart, but having become aware of it, I suddenly felt the significance of that proximity, with a curious mixture of emotions. I had a fugitive feeling that I ought to be direly alarmed, but it was so fleeting that it was almost immediately drowned by a kind of fascination—a literal fascination, of the kind that one faction in the Harmonic Society still calls "animal magnetism." I had been magnetized before, by Pierre Chapelain and other physicians employing the method curatively, but that influence had been superficial by comparison with the grip that the book now seemed to have extended into my flesh.

Presumably in much the same fashion that Saint-Germain had known, as soon as he was in the presence of the bravo from the witch house, that he was confronted by a powerful mesmerist, I knew, although I had only just brought the knowledge to the level of consciousness, that I was in the presence of a powerful magnetic force, which I had casually placed next to my heart. And I thought I knew, too, what book it had to be—not just in the sense that I guessed its near-meaningless title, but by means of some deeper and more intimate awareness, which I could not yet describe.

Perhaps I should have been terrified, but I wasn't. I was . . . amused.

Strange music had just become audible, apparently played on a stringed instrument of some kind. It was impossible to tell where it came from, except that it seemed to be coming from somewhere above street level. Reflexively, I looked up at the ceiling of the room, but I knew that it wasn't coming from the fake whore's den. It was coming from outside.

When I lowered my gaze again, I met the young woman's squarely. She was staring at me with a mixture of curiosity and challenge.

"Do you recognize it, Monsieur Reynolds?" she asked.

"The instrument or the tune?" I parried.

She laughed, falsely, and answered her own question. "Of course you do," she said. "How could you help it? It's merely a prelude, of course, and a very distant echo—but if all goes well, you'll be able to join in before long."

"And if all doesn't go well?" I queried.

"You ought to hope with all the fervor you can muster that it does, Mr. Reynolds," she said. "It might be your only hope of coming through this alive, with your soul intact."

Might be? I thought. *She really doesn't know. Perhaps all she has is a fervent hope—but for what can a creature like her hope?*

"What is this?" Groix put in, with a certain asperity and more than a hint of impatience. "*Do* you know that music, Reynolds? Who's playing it, and where?"

"I can't put a name to it," I told him, "but I've heard its like before. It's anyone's guess as to who might be playing it, and when."

That was true, although I now had an inkling as to where the insidious echo was reverberating. I didn't feel the slightest temptation to reach into my clothing in order to extract the slim volume that I had carelessly inserted into it. Instead, I meekly did what had been suggested to me, sat down, and took a sip of warm wine—which felt extremely welcome on my tongue and in my throat, even though I was almost prepared to believe that there was no magic in it. The dangerous contagion of the magic, I thought, was not in the wine at all, but in the book and in my blood.

But how the hell did it get into my library? I thought. I wondered, furiously, who had placed it there, next to the copy of Blaise Thibodeaux's *Resonances du temps?* Dupin? It must, I supposed, have been with the volumes that Bihan had helped him transfer from the Rue Dunot. But if Dupin had acquired such a volume, why had he not told me that he had it?

That was a foolish question, of course. He was Auguste Dupin, addicted to secrecy whenever he did not want to show off. I could not believe for an instant that its positioning on my shelves or my removal of it therefrom had been a coincidence. In fact, I did not believe that any of the events of the previous twenty-four hours had been coincidental.

Had I really been mistaken for Dupin by the hirelings of the ghost pirates? Perhaps not. Perhaps the whole purpose of the maneuver had been to deceive Lucien Groix, lure him out of hiding and incite him to transmit a message that would bring Dupin out of the headquarters of the Harmonic Society? And what if that were so? If the ghost pirates could capture Dupin, it seemed to me, then Madame Lacuzon would probably feel forced to come out of hiding herself, in order to go to his defense . . . And then . . .

Once again, I patted my overcoat above the place where the book was nestled, doubtless able to communicate the curse that it was carrying—its infection—even unopened and unread. But whose curse? And with what purpose?

There was no way for me to be sure even as to who might have been responsible for planting the book in my library, given that I had no idea how long it had been there—hidden there in plain view but nevertheless invisible, until the time came for it to be taken down. I couldn't help wondering, though, whether I had really been the one intended to take it down and put it in my pocket. Perhaps, like *The Mad Trist*, it had been intended for Dupin . . . and perhaps it, too, had been a summons to a mad trist, into which I had blundered in his stead . . .

Oddly enough, and doubtless foolishly, that seemed to be a more attractive thought than the idea that it really had been intended for me, and that I was playing my allotted role in this convoluted plot without missing a single line of the script.

But now I know, I thought, *and I still have free will*. I also knew, though, that the art of the greatest magnetizers consists not of forcing people to act against their will but in luring or coercing the will itself, and I remembered, uneasily, that Jana Valdemar, supposedly a better mesmerist when alive than Pierre Chapelain, had looked at me with glowing eyes on the Pont de la Tournelle.

Lucien Groix also did as he was told, although I assumed that he had nothing so treacherous in his pocket. He went to the door and whistled softly—another signal, I assumed. Bertrand the coachman could not have been far away, because he responded with a grateful alacrity.

While the agent and his commander were taking their seats, I studied the woman who had made the suggestions that we were following so obediently. As I had observed before, she was not particularly beautiful, although it struck me suddenly that the ceruse and crimson make-up she was wearing might as easily be concealing a greater beauty than trying unavailingly to conceal the absence of one. Absurd as it might seem, I actually had to ask myself whether I found her sexually attractive or not . . . and the fact that I didn't know seemed strangely significant . . . as did the fact that she was still smiling, ironically if not entirely confidently.

The music did not grow any louder, but it sounded more obtrusive, inducing a slow thrill within my flesh that made me think of the music employed by snake-charmers to hold cobras in thrall.

I was trying to think, furiously. Dupin, I am certain, would have reached conclusions much more rapidly and much more certainly, and I was well aware that I had no entitlement to be considered his equal, but my mind was working nevertheless, at its own pace, and not ineffectively.

While it was working, the not-so-young woman—the mesmerist, the psyll, the siren—continued watching me, with the same wry smile. Her eyes were not glowing—she was not advertising her power—but I had no doubt that she was following the progress of my thought, to the extent that it was detectable. She knew that I was under her spell, or that of the book, and that I was not even trying to escape.

I had a thousand questions, but no matter how complex and convoluted time is, in the reality underlying the uniformity that our consciousness imposes upon it, questions can only be voiced one at a time.

"Did you really fire the crossbow from inside the chimney breast?" was the question my befuddled brain selected, perhaps without any particular reason.

The lamia Addhema smiled. "Of course not," she said. "The foolish Immortal brought the crossbow under his capacious cloak, in order to fire a bolt at me, in the superstitious belief that a wooden bolt through the heart is the one sure method of destroying a vampire. The bolt was carefully blessed—or, to put it another way, enchanted—in order to enhance its effect, but such spells are always vulnerable to redirection, and, contrary to the proverbial assumption, arrows do not always fly straight. The poor fool took aim at me, while I was seated on the mantelpiece, and shot himself."

"Why were you seated on the mantelpiece?" I asked, although it was probably the least of the questions swirling in my head.

"Because there was nowhere else to sit," she replied, bathetically.

"Who was he," I demanded, "since he was evidently not one of the Nine Immortals?"

"Oh, but he was," she told me. "All immortality is conditional, however. The Nine are wiser when they remain hidden, sheltered behind the myth of their invulnerability—the world is a dangerous place, even for such as them. I took him by surprise—perhaps because he, like you, paused to wonder why I was sitting on the mantelpiece—but it was his own murderous intention that killed him, not mine. All I did was remove the weapon afterwards, in order to deeper the mystery for its discoverer. That was a wise move, I think, although it confronted Monsieur Dupin with a puzzle that distracted him from making contact with his concierge . . . but I was able to suggest to you that you get him out of the house immediately, in order to bring his attention back to the more important issue. Then, alas, the curiosity-seeker turned up and deflected him again."

"You took the weapon away without being seen by the agents posted in the café?" I queried.

"Of course," she said. "With all due respect to the perspicacity of the Sûreté's agents, Monsieur Groix, a herd of elephants could have charged down the street without their seeing them while they were under my magnetic influence—but I did them no harm, believe me. All is harmony, for the moment, as I say . . . and I do not mean the supposed harmonies of hell that the imbecile who signed himself Apollonius devised. Like

Zann a few centuries later, he mastered the technique, but not the art. True sensitivities rarely develop by chance, and their possessors always lack the necessary education if they cannot be taken through a portal while the fruit is still unripe. But the human mind has only existed for a fraction of a million years, and has only been capable of transcending the primitive limits of consciousness for a few hundred. Miracles are not made overnight."

"Who the devil are you, woman?" Groix asked again, interrupting rudely and once again electing to use an oath that would not do his reputation for sanctity any good.

She took a sip of wine, deliberately, evidently amused by her teasing. "Won't you introduce me to your friend, Monsieur Reynolds?" she said.

"I wish I could," I said, "but I only know one of your many pseudonyms, and I assume that, like everyone else involved in the game in which we all seem to be mere pawns, you take great care not to allow your real name ever to be pronounced . . . if, in fact, it is pronounceable. But for the sake of convenience . . ." I paused for dramatic effect before continuing: "Lucien, this is the entity recorded in your files as the vampire Addhema. Being only a layman in these matters, I have only the vaguest idea of what kind of being it is when not in human disguise, and what kind of immortality it has, but if I am reading the situation accurately, it intends that the evocation specified in the Cthulhu palimpsest should go ahead tonight. May I ask, Madame—I assume you prefer that title to Mademoiselle—whether you are the actual author of the score inscribed in the parchment?"

The lamia laughed. "You may," she said, "and the answer is no."

"Cthulhu, then?" I guessed. "Not with its own hand, if it has any, but a hand inspired by a dream dispatched from R'lyaieh?"

She laughed, as if in mockery—but it seemed to me that she dared not simply say yes, because she did not know for sure.

After a moment's hesitation, I decided to hazard a guess: "Cthulhu has many instruments, but all of them are possessed of free will, and magnetic power can only operate mysteriously, even on the most primitive and stubborn brains. Common people can be induced to do what superior minds desire, but they have to be persuaded to want it, and to act of their own volition. That is often simple, human minds being so easy to manipulate, but not always—and the situation becomes extremely confused when there are more than one, and especially when there are more than two, superior minds attempting to exercise their influence. Chaos can ensue very easily . . . and almost invariably does. Is that a fair summary of the situation, Madame?"

She frowned slightly, as if resentful of my attempt to claim the prerogative of explanation, even though I was clearly rushing in where any angel would have feared to tread. Her reply, however, was interesting.

"There is no more delicate art in the universe, my dear," she said, "than the manipulation of coincidence."

She did not say *my dear* contemptuously, or even ironically, so far as I could judge. She had a kind of innate coquetry not ill-befitting a siren. It worried me that I had no difficulty imagining that she might drink the blood of lovers she seduced, literally rather than metaphorically, assuring them while she did so that all was harmony. For the moment, though, she did not seem to have vulgar predation in mind. Indeed, she seemed exceedingly anxious to impress upon me that she meant no one any immediate harm, and that all was, indeed, harmony—for now.

The music, still faint but insistent, was saying the same thing. It was a true siren song—for now. It was not being played in the witch-house, or any nearby mansard, It was coming through a portal from elsewhere or elsewhen, brought by an eddy in the tides of time, a whirlpool in the fabric of reality.

I still had a thousand questions, at least, but I could still only voice one at a time, and time was evidently of the essence. I had to be terse.

"How many Great Old Ones are there?" I asked, bluntly.

"A great many," Addhema replied, "but don't assume that any of the others will take the trouble to interfere with Cthulhu's release, or that any of the Dwellers can prevent it. Take comfort, instead, from the knowledge that the Church's bogeyman, whom Monsieur Groix is so fond of evoking, precisely because he cannot believe in him, has nothing to do with the enterprise. There is no supreme Evil Spirit, any more than there is a supreme God. There is merely an egotistical struggle for existence between evolved beings, in which the many contestants pursue different ambitions . . . different dreams, if you prefer, or different delusions. In the fullness of time . . ."

"Just a minute . . ." Lucien Groix interrupted again, considerably to my annoyance, but understandably, given that he must have had a thousand question of his own and every reason, in his own estimation, to claim the prerogative of posing at least a few. I had no special entitlement to retain the privilege of interrogation, of course, but I wasn't about to give way while I was rushing in at such a hectic and enthusiastic pace into regions where mere angels would undoubtedly have been exceedingly fearful to tread.

"We don't have a minute, Lucien," I said, harshly. "She's only filling in time by giving us a few vague answers because she knows that there isn't that much time to be filled. She's teasing us. But among the countless things I don't understand, Addhema, is what's in this for you? I can understand why and how the Mahatma might have recruited Angria and assembled a crew of ex-mercenaries to further his plotting, but you're surely a different order of being. Presumably, you used to be an honest vampire, putting on flesh occasionally in order to feed on luscious blood, in order to preserve your mysterious intermittent undeath. Why on earth would you consent to be an instrument of this ridiculous scheme?"

"You do realize, do you not, Monsieur Reynolds," she said, hissing like a viper, "that you're completely in my power at present, and that even if Monsieur Groix were to succeed in drawing and firing his harmonica gun, the bullets could not harm me?"

Jack Taylor, I remembered, had been similarly quick to remind me of his fearsome reputation, precisely because he knew that circumstance had reduced him to a status of a mere scarecrow. For the moment, at least, I seemed to be taboo; they were under orders not to hurt me. But I had an uneasy suspicion as to what the answer to the question I had posed must be: the incentive driving Addhema was the conviction that if the evocation of Cthulhu succeeded, it would lead to a rich harvest of drinkable blood.

But for the moment, perhaps foolishly, I was less concerned with myself than with the general principle; I really did want to understand what Addhema's purpose was, not just in helping to obtain the fulfillment of the Mad Mahatma's scheme, but within the greater scheme of things.

"What possible interest could you have in the destruction, or even the serious disruption, of the human world?" I asked her. "I have no idea how long you've existed, although I strongly suspect that you've only had flesh and blood for a brief interval once in every century, if that, and I don't know how much intellect you have, although I strongly suspect that it's less than mine, but you must be aware that it's a very imprudent parasite that kills its host and a lunatic predator that slaughters its prey indiscriminately—so whatever you expect from Cthulhu's liberation, it can't be the annihilation of the humankind to which your fate is clearly attached. So I repeat: *what's in it for you?*"

The ploy didn't work. Perhaps I had been foolish to think that it might. After all, it was obvious, in the context of my own argument, that it wasn't in a vampire's interest to be understood by her prey. Teasing her potential victims was one thing, perhaps a quasi-feline addiction, but retaining her essential mystery was something else.

"If my intellect were as meager as yours, Monsieur Reynolds," she said, silkily. "I wouldn't boast about it. But you're right—we're only filling in time, and it's running out. The prelude is almost complete. But I'll answer your question, out of sheer generosity. You have no idea, believe me, what it is to be a vampire, no concept of the magnetism and symbolism of blood, the quality of various kinds of blood, or the potential of various kinds of blood. All you see in your mind's eye when you think of me is gluttony, but if you could hear the music of the heart . . . well. perhaps you can, now, if you listen very carefully. Perhaps, with the aid of the book, you will . . . if only for a moment. Do try. Even if it's the last thing you do, it might be worth the effort. But now, I think, it's probably time to move on."

Her gaze released mine and went to the door, as if she expected it open at any second, and let the next actor on to the stage.

"Wait," I said, although I didn't suppose for a second that she was in command of the timing of the piece; "there's one thing I really do want to know, for my own satisfaction. *Who made Jana Valdemar walk into the Seine?*"

It did seem, then, that the siren's eyes lit up momentarily—not, it seemed to me, with anger, or scorn, or the force of intimidation and command, but with something akin to pity.

"Oh, Mr. Reynolds," the lamia said, "there really are questions that it is better not to ask of yourself, lest you understand the answer. You did."

Unfortunately—or so I thought at the time—I did not have the time even to begin to try to understand that horribly unexpected answer, because, exactly as she had prophesied, the door of the café opened then, and someone came in.

We had already been told to expect Prospero and Dupin, but I was not unduly surprised to see that the person who came in was neither of those. It was, in fact, the man who had posed as a coachman in order to convey the Comte de Saint-Germain and his strange magic wand to the pseudo-Sabbat in the forest of Fontainebleau—although, strictly speaking, he was not posing, since he really was employed by the charlatan as a coachman, in addition to harboring his own agenda and his own secret identity. He was carrying a violin in his right hand, which did not seem to me to be the one he had played on All Hallows, but a much finer instrument—perhaps even a Stradivarius, or a Guarneri . . . a fine enough instrument, at any rate, to warrant a protective case, which it did not have.

The newcomer's gaze scanned the hall, inspecting the dim-ly lamplit faces of the five people assembled there. His own eyes gave no evidence of surprise, but perhaps a slight hint of anxiety.

"The others are not here?" he asked, when his gaze settled on Addhema.

"They will be," she replied—but it seemed to me that her confidence was slightly forced, as befit a conspirator who was aware that her instruments had free will, and therefore could not be trusted entirely to follow the script laid down for them hundreds of years before, with all the hasty amendments and adjustments made to it in the last few days and hours.

Temptation is a terrible thing. I yielded to it, and said: "They might not. The Nine Immortals and the Holy Office might have failed to put a spoke in your wheel, my dear Addhema, but you still have Dupin and Amélie Lacuzon to reckon with. I might be a fool, but Dupin certainly isn't . . . and he isn't under the spell of the book."

Was I still trying to provoke an argument, or simply to stimulate apprehension? I honestly don't know now, any more than I knew then. I wasn't playing for time, because I knew full well that there was no time left to play for, certainly not time enough to ask the tiniest fraction of the million questions that were now queuing up in my mind.

"Salutations, Monsieur Reynolds," said Anton. "It's good to see you again—and you too, Monsieur Groix. I was sorry to hear about your misfortune, and I apologize for the part I played, unwittingly, in precipitating it."

"This man is wanted by the police, Bertrand," was Lucien's only reply. "Please place him under arrest."

Bertrand made a move to obey, purposefully if not entirely confidently, but had not completed a second stride when Addhema's oblique stare stopped him dead. "There's no hurry, Sergeant," she said. "I can assure you that Anton won't run away. He's been waiting all his life to play in this symphony; you mustn't deny him the opportunity."

She spoke quietly, but it was a command. Bertrand looked at Lucien, but his fearful gaze said clearly enough that a counter-command from the ex-Prefect would not be welcome, and might not be obeyed.

"It's all right, Bertrand," Lucien said. "Wait, for now." He emphasized the syllables sufficiently to make it hear that he was, indeed, only giving his man permission to wait, for a critical moment that was sure to arrive.

And, in fact, I had no time even to frame a further thought before the door that Anton had just closed opened again.

For a horrid split second I thought that Dupin was going to walk through it and prove me a hundred times a fool, with fate's customary malicious irony, but in fact it wasn't him who appeared in the frame.

First of all, it was Meg, Prospero's housekeeper and alleged mistress, but she was rapidly followed by her master. He too was carrying a violin, while she was carrying a longer and more cumbersome stringed instrument. I did not recall ever having seen its like before, but that did not prevent me from guessing that some people might call it a dulcimer and others a symphony. Like people and other entities, musical instruments can have many names, although I suspected that none of them were recorded, unpronounceably, in the book that I had been unwittingly carrying next to my heart all day long.

"Monsieur Reynolds!" exclaimed Prospero, having scanned the room in much the same fashion as Anton. "I'm delighted to see you again. Is Monsieur Dupin here?"

Another fool rushing in gladly, I thought, *without an inkling that he is here by anything other than his own free will, in pursuit of any goal but his own long-cherished dreams.*

"He isn't coming," I said, defiantly. "We shall have to form a makeshift quintet without him—not that it will do any good without the songbird. And who knows how long it will be before the tidal ebb and flow of time allow the summons to be tried again? Centuries, perhaps."

Nobody laughed. Nobody suggested that I was talking nonsense because I didn't understand. Nobody even expressed amazement at my temerity in issuing such a venturesome prophecy, although there was puzzlement in more than one expression.

"Monsieur Reynolds is confused," Addhema said to Prospero. "He is subject to a wayward magnetism that has upset the balance of his mind—but have no fear. He will play his part, as we all will. Thank you for bringing the instruments. I know how hard it is for you to part with them, even for a little while. I'm truly sorry that you cannot participate in our ceremony, but you can bear witness, and you are perhaps the only person present who will be able to appreciate fully the piece that we are about to play. Do sit down—and you too, Meg."

Meg took immediate advantage of the invitation, doubtless glad to take the weight of her cold and rather poorly-shod feet, but her master remained standing, proudly.

I did not have to ask Prospero why he was cooperating

with the agents of Cthulhu. He was not only a scholar but an obsessive scholar, who had been pursuing the harmonies of hell all his life, even though he believed that they really were infernal, and his own playing had only ever worked a very modest magic. Was he mad? Many people, I knew, would have thought so, but not Dupin. Unlike the many people who believe that there is no genius without a hunt of madness, Dupin's opinion was that genius is an infallible badge of sanity. Although he had been sufficiently pragmatic to commit what Prospero deemed to be an act of atrocious vandalism in burning the music of Eric Zann, he was not unsympathetic to the judgment.

Even so, I said: "You don't know what you're doing, Prospero. These people intend to precipitate a catastrophe, if they can."

"Oh, I know *that*," the old man replied. "And the fact that I don't know what the result of the catastrophe will be makes it all the more exciting. Can you hear that ghostly music? Of course you can . . . that's what brought you to my door this morning. I'm sorry that I hadn't heard it myself, but I'll surely make up for that shortly. How can you believe that a transformation of human being wrought by music like that could be anything but benign? And although my name was Prospero twenty years ago, it's Will Maccabee now, in honor of the composer and choreographer of the dance of the dead. The dead *can* dance, you know . . . but of course you do, Mr. Reynolds—you're a seer if ever I saw one."

I could not bring myself to believe, at that moment, that I was speaking to a genius, and I was sure that Paul Lacroix would have agreed with me . . . and Blaise Thibodeaux too, no matter how confused he might be by his own spectral status.

At Prospero's invitation I had focused my attention in the spectral instrument's seductive prelude again, but no sooner had I done so than church bells began to chime again. This time, I knew, the count would be eleven.

There was still an hour to go to the critical moment, but the authority of the distant chimes was effective nevertheless. There was an expectant pause, while everyone waited for a further appearance or manifestation. And the flow of events did not let us down, although the gazes that were directed at the door were disappointed. It was not from that direction that the apparition came.

XIV

THE MAHATMA

TO satisfy the principles of melodrama—specifically, the rhetorical rule of three—the door ought to have opened again to let in another instrumentalist, but we had all been absorbed by a reality more complicated than the simplistic ordinances of cheap fiction. A flash of lightning and a puff of smoke might also have seemed apt enough in that context, but in fact the Mahatma had simply come downstairs quietly, having presumably been waiting in the room into which Addhema had earlier invited me, perhaps lying on the filthy bed—which, when I came to think about it, seemed just as appropriate to the employment of a Hindu ascetic as to a cheap whore.

We all had to turn our heads to look at him. I don't know what effect his appearance had on the others, but I have to admit that to me, it was a trifle disappointing.

The Mahatma was every inch the clichéd Hindu ascetic, almost a caricature: exceedingly thin and wrinkled, brown-skinned, bald and beardless, and clad only in a loincloth and thin sandals, in spite of the bitter cold. He was not shivering or giving any other sign of discomfort, His eyes seemed surprisingly free of luster, considering that he was supposed to be a great magician, equipped with magnetic power far greater than the luckless member of the Nine who had apparently tried unavailingly to anticipate and disrupt his plan, and I wondered whether he might actually be blind, in a purely physical sense, entirely dependent on the sixth sense of his strange mind. I didn't ask him, but it wasn't because I was too polite to make an attempt to hog the floor.

He wasn't alone, but nor did he have a considerable entourage. He was followed down the narrow stairway by another Hindu, equally soft-footed but much more fully dressed, sporting a brown turban. As much by virtue of his stance as his costume I inferred that he was Kanhoje Angre, alias the pirate Angria. He seemed respectably old, but by no means as ancient in appearance as his master. I could not tell, at a glance, whether he was a ghost or an Immortal, but I doubted that he would have appeared to be a mere bandit, even to a prejudiced Englishman. His belt, which looked to be sturdy deerskin, was furnished with a solid cutlass devoid of any Oriental ornamentation, and an equally utilitarian dagger. Everyone spared him a glance, but all eyes were soon riveted once again to the Mahatma.

"The carriage is on its way," the latter said, simply, in English—not, I assumed at first, for my benefit—"and the ship is in position." Then he looked directly at me, and said: "The Breton witch will come of her own volition, if she is not in the carriage."

At that moment, he still seemed very ordinary to my prejudiced eyesight: just an old man who had spent his crazy life indulging in crazy conspiracies and magical dabblings.

"No, she won't," I said, "I don't know how much she knows or doesn't know about Cthulhu and prophecies regarding its liberation, but I know how stubborn she is, If she thought it necessary to take the child away, she'll think it necessary to keep her away, at least until after midnight."

"She's just a hedge-witch," the Mahatma stated. "The powers with which she's contending are far beyond hers. She's wily, but all Paris has been searching for her—the Sorority as well as the Harmonic Society. She will not have been able to hide the child any more than the other fool who wanted to claim her from Captain Pym could have done. Nor can that jacket protect you, any more than its twin can protect Dupin. We are all instruments of Fate, which is more powerful than the feeble desires of humankind."

I assumed that he was trying to convince himself rather than me. My impression was that he really did think that Fate was on his side, but that he didn't entirely trust it. "And the feeble desires of Cthulhu as well?" I suggested. "But then, Cthulhu isn't even the most powerful of the Great Old Ones, is it? No matter how much it rails against its encryption, it can't get free without human help."

I gave myself a metaphorical pat on the back, even though I knew full well that I didn't know what I was talking about, and that it was all bluff and bluster. No matter. At least I wasn't a mere bystander any more, and I was determined to play the game.

"We shall see," said the Mahatma. "We need not wait here any longer. I suggest that we cross the road. The portal is exiguous, and it will not be practicable for the whole crowd to ascend the stairway, but there will be more than enough of you, in sufficiently close proximity, to bear witness as well as to provide the nucleus. Please hand your violin to Mr. Reynolds, Prospero."

Prospero was clearly surprised by that instruction; I inferred that he had been expecting someone else to take charge of his precious instrument. "Reynolds can't play," he said.

"That's all right," Lucien Groix put in. "I'll take charge of it, if you have no objection."

I had no objection, but Prospero, to whom the rhetorical question had been addressed, made no move to hand the instrument to the ex-Prefect.

"That will not be necessary, Monsieur Groix," said the Mahatma. "Your role here is simply to observe. You are aware,

I believe, that I am an ally of France, associated for many years with the late Duc de Richelieu, and a secret correspondent of the Comte de Saint-Germain. I do not ask you to place yourself under my orders, but I do demand your respect."

"You are speaking of people long dead," said the ex-Prefect. "I am aware that some French diplomats were once involved in secret negotiations with a person bearing the title to which you lay claim, but you cannot seriously expect me to believe that you are the same person."

"I do expect you to believe it, Monsieur," said the Hindu, "and to respect my status, as I respect yours, in spite of your religious and political excommunication. We are not enemies, Monsieur Groix, and we have no quarrel. No crime has been committed by any of my associates."

I did not know what had happened to the corpse that I had briefly seen lying in the witch-house, but it seemed that no such death had been officially reported, and no matter how absurd Addhema's story sounded, it would not be easy to prove that she was responsible—especially for someone who no longer had any official existence, let alone any official authority. Lucien hesitated, but the glance that he directed at Bertrand made it obvious that he was not content and did not consider the matter settled.

I took Prospero's violin and tried to reassure Lucien with a glance of my own that I had no intention of playing it.

"Do *you* believe that this Mahatma is the same one who controlled a sect of Thugs during the Regency?" I asked Prospero.

"I do," said Prospero. "Don't you, Mr. Reynolds?"

In spite of the rather ordinary appearance of the ascetic, I did, just as I believed that Addhema had been the vampire suspected of using the witch-house in the same period, and the Mahatma's companion of being the admiral of a fleet of ships. I believed in immortality, reincarnation and ghosts, although I still felt direly short of explanations of how such entities came to exist, and what the laws underlying their exotic existence were. I also believed that I had a copy of the most notorious of all accursed books in my pocket, that it had infected me with a curse, and that even if I could not play Prospero's violin, it could probably play me. But I still had no intention of letting that happen.

I weighed the violin and the bow in my left hand in my left hand and I met the Mahatma's colorless gaze.

"You might have organized this ridiculous conspiracy," I said to him, "and nurtured it through more than a hundred years, but you have no more idea than anyone else of exactly what will happen if you succeed in decrypting Cthulhu, do you? You don't even know for sure that it will expel the British and other exploitative colonists from India, and you have no idea what effect the decryption might have on the collective unconscious—or the collective consciousness—of humankind."

"You're wrong, Mr. Reynolds" the ascetic replied in English. "I have a very clear idea of the consequences of the liberation, and its costs; and I know that you cannot prevent it. I will not say that it is written, because that would attribute too great a power to writing, but the music of time began its composition before the idea of time entered human minds, and the culmination of that composition was inherent in it from the outset. The execution is complex, and will require effort, but you need not fear being unequal to the task. Nor is there any reason for you to be horrified by the consequences of your actions. Everyone dies, even self-styled Immortals, and in the context of eternity it matters little exactly when or how the whims of Fate determine that eventuality. What matters is that, mortal or immortal, alive or undead, we play our tiny parts in the symphony of change."

"Garbage," I said, stubbornly. "Madness masquerading as philosophy."

228

"Perhaps so," he retorted, with equanimity. "But what is philosophy, in the final analysis, but a masquerade of illusions, and what is reality but the dross of imagination? Play your part, Mr. Reynolds, and be grateful that coincidence has given you a part to play, while these"—his cursory hand gesture took in Prospero and Meg as well as Lucien Groix and Bertrand—"will only stand and wait."

Prospero seemed disappointed to be thus dismissed, and looked down at his crippled hands as if he wanted to rend the fingers with his teeth. Lucien scowled, and his lips stirred, as if to protest that the Mahatma had yet to see whether he would be content to stand and wait—but he made no sound.

"Will you lead the way please, Addhema?" the absurd old man said, evidently unintimidated by the thought of stepping outside in his state of ludicrous undress. His eyes were as dull as stagnant ditchwater, and the tone of his voice was that of a polite request rather than a command, but I doubt that anyone had any thought of not following the suggestion. Lucien and Bertrand were already on their feet, as Prospero and I were, and Meg struggled to her feet again, still grasping the eccentric stringed instrument, while Addhema went to open the door, Prospero looked at his violin, and then at me, as if he were wishing that he were a demon with the power of possession, who could usurp my fingers in order to play it.

The violin was not as luxurious an instrument as Anton's, by any means, but it was no mere gypsy fiddle. It felt oddly comfortable in my hand, and even more so when I applied it experimentally to my shoulder, not far from my heart. I knew that it did not matter that I had no expertise in playing such instruments; even though Prospero did not have the power of demonic possession, I would not be the one doing the playing, once the symphony was shaped. I would merely be another instrument. It did not matter that I did not have a copy of the unreadable score, or even that Prospero did, and thought that he could read it. Anton must know it by heart, and doubtless had the means to enable his fellow musicians to follow his lead. His true name, as inscribed in the book juxtaposed with my heart, was obviously not Anton, nor Oberon the Fay, let alone Orpheus or Apollo, but something unpronounceable. I doubted that the sensibility of my poor primitive brain could have found it harmonious, but I suspected that Addhema might have had a different opinion.

"You have no idea how I envy you," Prospero said to me, with a sigh, as he began to move toward the door.

"Because I'm supposed to play the violin that you cannot?" I asked, a trifle waspishly, making no move to follow him, "or because I have a copy of the *Necronomicon* in my breast pocket?"

He had the grace to look startled. "What!" he said.

"Really," I said, glancing briefly at Addhema, who was swaying slightly to the seductive rhythm of the invisible player, before switching my attention fully to the Mahatma again.

"Your scheme has already gone awry more than once," I said to him. "The child, I imagine, was supposed to collect the book from my house—or perhaps from Dupin. Not from me, at any rate. You can't be sure that the others will come . . . and you certainly can't be sure, even if they do, that we won't make a mess of things."

Lucian Groix and his coachman had drawn closer together, but neither of them had reached for a weapon as yet. They were biding their time. The Mahatma did not spare them a glance.

"Don't be afraid, Mr. Reynolds," the Mahatma said, still speaking English. "Trust the book; it is a far better shield than any you could have contrived for yourself or the witch could have contrived for you. There is no need for any alarm. All is harmony. The portals are already open, and you have as much interest as anyone in filtering and controlling the resonances that they permit, if you value your life and your supposed sanity. We mean no harm to anyone, for the moment, but harm will certainly befall anyone who does not follow the plan conscientiously, with all due rapidity."

He was trying to remain impassive, and he had presumably had several hundred years of practice, at least, but I thought that I detected a hint of anxiety in his gaze. I didn't believe his assertions, but I assumed that he was trusting in the presence of the book to ensure that I played my part in his scheme, given that he and his ghostly henchmen had not made any attempt to persuade me of the justice of their cause. All the evidence of legend seemed to be against them, though, and I was still determined to oppose them if I could.

Nevertheless, biding my time, as Lucien Groix was, I followed Prospero to the door. The two policemen, presumably taking their cue from me, followed too. Addhema matched strides with them but Meg and Anton lingered, apparently waiting for the Mahatma to move.

As I drew level with Prospero, he said: "Do you really have a copy of the *Necronomicon* about your person?"

"I believe so," I told him. "And if I'm not mistaken, it isn't the corrupt translation allegedly made by John Dee, but a far older version—perhaps the legendary *Al Azif* transcribed by the pseudonymous Abdul Alhazred, but more likely a version inscribed in a language known only to the Mahatma and a few other adepts . . . and even then, a mere translation of a translation of the primal dead names."

"Why you?" said Prospero, the tone of his voice conveying at least a hint of the envy he had mentioned. He meant *Why not me?* although his avidity to get his hands on that particular item of treasure could have been matched by any number of common-or-garden bibliophiles, including Paul Lacroix, Cousin Jeremiah and even Dupin. There are sirens and sirens, and such is the irony of fate that it is sometimes those least avid to hear them who are ensnared by them. I was still very far from having a complete understanding of what was happening, but I knew, at least, that I had been manipulated, not merely within the last twenty-four hours or the last three months, but ever since I had first arrived in Paris, and probably long before then, while I was still a blissful imbecile in Boston, even if I had been correct in my guess that the book had not been intended to fall into my possession rather than being collected by the waif.

In any case, thus far I had done everything of my own free will, including playing the cello in Du Potet's garden . . . just as I was apparently about to play the violin that Prospero had brought me, voluntarily, not to evoke the Crawling Chaos or even to replicate the previous Will Maccabee's dance of the dead, but to insert a metaphorical *monseigneur* into the portals of R'lyaeh, and twist it cleverly in dimensions beyond the three that stubborn human consciousness permits us to comprehend.

I had the *Necronomicon* next to my heart. I could not read it, any more than any other living human being, and I would not have been able accurately to pronounce the syllables it spelled out, any more than any other human larynx could—with one possible exception—but Jack Taylor had been right when he had told me that I did not even understand what the *Necronomicon* was, although I begged leave to doubt that he, even dead, knew any better. Ghosts of his species were, I supposed, still human, and still conscious, and just as prone to self-deception as common mortals and common immortals.

Of one thing though, I was certain: I not only had the *Necronomicon* next to my heart but I had its infection in my soul, ready to resonate to its psychic vibrations. Everyone else present had doubtless been carrying a similar infection for some time, probably just as unwittingly. The walls that consciousness raises to protect our illusions of identity are, alas, too easily breachable by sly invasions.

As Prospero and I paused in front of the door of the witch-house, Addhema overtook us, but before she could turn the perfectly ordinary key that she had just inserted into the lock, a carriage came round the corner. It was the same carriage that had brought me that morning, and I noticed with a twinge of sympathy that poor Arthur Pym had once again been relegated to the seat beside the coachman, which led me to suppose that the interior must be crowded.

That was, indeed, the case. Cousin Jeremiah got down first, and held the door open, putting out a helpful hand to assist Paul Lacroix to get down. My tainted heart only began to sink when, in his turn, Lacroix bravely offered a supportive arm to Madame Lacuzon, who was followed by the little girl I had seen in my study that morning. The child did not take up much room, so it could not have been very uncomfortable for her to squeeze in between Madame Lacuzon and Dupin, who was the last person to emerge from the interior of the vehicle.

The child seemed to be very frightened, but I did not know whether to pity her for that or to feel glad that she did not seem to be wholeheartedly committed to the Mahatma's insanity

Even though my optimistic prophecy that Madame Lacuzon would not come had been brutally and contemptuously falsified, I refused to despair. However Dupin had been lured to the fateful rendezvous, I was sure that he would have a plan, or would be in the process of making one . . . and I told myself that, however many enemies were surrounding him, at close range or hidden by the fog, he was by no means alone. Most of his would-be allies might be impotent, but he had always had faith in the capability as well as the loyalty and the stubbornness of Madame Lacuzon.

I barely had time to direct an enquiring glance at Dupin before someone else leapt down from the coachman's seat to land between us, with a balletic spring in his step. It was not the coachman who had driven us that morning, but the Comte de Saint-Germain in person, clad in an absurdly stylish crimson paletot, which could not possibly have provided adequate protection against the bitter cold without magical aid. He also had a silly green feather in his wide-brimmed hat, which he doffed and swept theatrically—not addressing the gesture to me, of course, but to the Mahatma, who had followed us out of the café, still accompanied by Meg and Anton, and who bowed rather stiffly in reply.

"The entire cargo, Magister," said Saint-Germain, in a tone of self-satisfaction. "All here of their own free will. I could not have done better in my first youth. Greetings, Addhema—and to you, my dear Anton; it has been far too long. I'm equally pleased to see you, Monsieur Groix, although, to judge by your expression, you cannot return the compliment." He barely glanced at Prospero, Meg and Lucien's coachman, who appeared to be mere spear-carriers in his reckoning, but he met my eyes squarely, with more than a hint of amusement in his own. I barely spared him a blink in reply, directing my own gaze at my friend—but Dupin could not meet my stare, being busy taking census of the assembly. I did, however, catch a glimpse of an odd gleam in Madame Lacuzon's eye, and I recalled Dupin's observation that she would be easily capable of murder if any threat were made against him. I was uncomfortably aware, though, that being capable of a murderous intention and being capable of carrying it out are two very different things. If she was here of her own free will, I thought, that will was surely modifiable instantaneously, as Dupin's must be.

"I should have had you thrown in the Conciergerie when I had the chance," Lucien Groix said to Saint-Germain, bitterly.

"Don't feel bad about it," Saint-Germain replied, ebulliently. "I'd have been out before you could say *Open sesame* or the hopeful fools of the Holy Office could mumble a *Vade retro satana*. This ceremony has evidently been fated for a long time, its seeds planted even before my previous birth. Nothing so ambitious has been attempted since the Secret College and the Great Coven of England wrecked the Spanish Armada by storm . . . and that was a petty conjuration by comparison—meaning no insult to your former incarnation, Dupin. History and the human mind have taken a great leap forward since then, and will take an even greater one tonight. If you could only imagine the wonders that the next two centuries will see, you would not have mounted such a stubborn defense against true enlightenment!"

He would probably have gone on if the Mahatma had not raised a hand to instruct him to be silent.

"Give the dulcimer to Monsieur Dupin, Meg," the ascetic said, in a calm and silky voice, switching to French for the peasant woman's benefit. Meg obeyed and Dupin accepted the slender instrument meekly.

"You still appear to be two instrumentalists short," I observed, still trying to be brave.

The Mahamta did not deign to look in my direction, let alone respond to the awkward prompt. I assumed that at least one member of the loosely-organized company was already in position on the Île Saint-Louis, perhaps equipped with a rebec, as well as the instrumentalist who was playing from elsewhere or elsewhen.

Paul Lacroix had made his way around to Lucien Groix's side. "It would be optimistic of me, I suppose, Monsieur Groix," he murmured, "to assume that you have the whole area surrounded, by good men capable of fighting off a gang of stranglers?"

"There are certainly policemen nearby," Groix told him, grimly, "but whether they will respond to my summons, I don't know."

"Now might be a good time to find out," Lacroix suggested. "I fear there might not be much time left. Perhaps I ought to have remembered, when curiosity urged me to accept Saint-Germain's invitation, that curiosity kills cats, in spite of their nine lives." He was an incorrigible wit.

Addhema disappeared into the interior of the haunted house, but even in the gloom I could see that she did not turn right into the room where the Immortal had been killed. Instead, she went along the short corridor to the internal stairway that led to the upper floors of the house. Anton followed her, and the Mahatma indicated to Dupin that he should follow Anton. He obeyed, and Madame Lacuzon automatically fell into step behind him, leading the little girl insistently by the hand.

I took a step forward to follow her, but Cousin Jeremiah suddenly interposed himself between me and the door.

"Don't go, Sam," he said. "I think we should leave, now."

Arthur Pym stepped forward to join him, and glanced to his cousin for support, but that support was not forthcoming. Instead, Jacob Pym drew a pistol from inside his pea-jacket, and said: "Stand aside, Arthur . . . and you, Reynolds." He meant the other Reynolds, not me.

Like Jack Taylor, I judged that Jacob was probably "an innocent," but he had spent a substantial part of the day in a nest of vipers in company with a skilled magnetizer. He was part of the plan now, at least for the moment,

The police agent, Bertrand, had also drawn a pistol, as if in response to Jacob's action, and it was a better machine; Jacob's gun was an old-fashioned single-shot pistol, whereas Bertrand's was a modern "harmonica gun" capable of firing three shots. Unfortunately, he seemed to be having dire difficulty deciding which way to aim it.

Lucien Groix, still standing beside Lacroix, seemed to share their uncertainty—but Lacroix, presumably certain that no one was likely to fire at him, seemed to be silently willing the sergeant to shoot *somebody*. Doctor Prospero had put his arm around Meg, protectively; his mouth was open, as if to say something, but he thought better of it.

Groix made his decision. He took a whistle from his pocket like the ones issued to policemen in some British and American cities, and blew an ear-splitting blast on it, which must have been audible all the way to the quay and some way beyond.

The Mahatma was still impassive. "I'm afraid, Monsieur Groix," he said, "that your men will not respond. In any case, you could only have endangered them had you had the effect you intended. Please do as your cousin says, Captain Pym, and you too, Monsieur Reynolds"—again, he meant the other Monsieur Reynolds, not me—"there is no need for any violence, and any attempted action on your part would be futile."

Lucien Groix evidently disagreed; his patience was worn out. "Bertrand," he said to his man, "shoot the violin that Mr. Reynolds is holding—but try not to hurt him."

Then, without further procrastination he drew a harmonica pistol of his own from his overcoat, took aim, and fired, at point-blank range, at the Mahatma.

XV

THE PORTAL TO NOWHERE

M Y ears were still ringing from the blast of the whistle
when the two pistols went off, almost simultaneously.
When Groix had given his instruction I had extended my left
arm, the hand of which was clutching the neck of the violin,
in order to get it as far away from my body as possible, although I knew as I did it that the gesture was probably point-
less. Lucien Groix might not have believed what Addhema
had said about the Immortal shooting himself, but my native
incredulity had been tested to the limit and I was no longer
capable of dismissing any statement reflexively, no matter
how absurd it might be. I did not, however, have time to be
astonished when Bertrand's bullet struck me full in the chest
and the impact knocked me flat on my back.

My head collided with the cobblestones of the Rue de l'Hirondelle painfully, but not hard enough to fracture my skull or
cause me to lose consciousness. I was dazed, though, and several
seconds passed before I struggled to a sitting position, and put
my right hand to my chest, where the fingers had no difficulty finding a bullet hole in my overcoat and stuffing that was
leaking from my quilted jacket. Of the bullet, which had struck
the *Necronomicon*, there was no trace, and not a drop of blood
had been spilled, but I had to take several deep breaths in the
attempt to fight the pain of the impact to the back of my head.

238

When my vision cleared, I saw the Mahatma standing impassively, completely unharmed, and immediately looked toward Lucien. He too was still standing, staring at the pistol in his hand, unable to believe that he could have missed such an easy target and perhaps not realizing how fortunate he was to be unharmed himself. Bertrand, by contrast, seemed horrified, certain that he had killed me, without having had the slightest intention of so doing. He leapt forward to help me to my feet.

The violin was also unharmed.

"There was no need for that, Monsieur Groix," the magician said. "You have been told that we mean you no harm, and you really ought to have some inkling of what a privilege it is for you to be here, when the world is on the brink of a great transformation."

I looked up and down the foggy street. No lights appeared in the windows of the houses, even though everyone inside them must have heard the shots and recognized them for what they were. We were on the eve of a Revolution; everyone in Paris knew that the rational reaction to such an alarm was to take cover and remain silent.

Saint-Germain laughed. "Poor Lucien," he said. "Is there no end to your humiliations?"

Lucien Groix's expression suggested that he was already regretting not having fired at the fake comte instead of the magician. Even though his gun must still contain two bullets, however, he did not attempt to rectify his error.

The Mahatma turned to me. "You are not hurt, Monsieur Reynolds?" he asked. It was probably a rhetorical question, so I did not bother to reply that I was, in fact, hurt, albeit not fatally. My head felt as if it were splitting.

Lucien answered for me. "Of course he's hurt," he said. "Bertrand, lift him into my carriage, and then take the reins. If Saint-Germain objects, shoot him."

Bertrand hesitated, looking down at the gun in his hand, which had betrayed him once. Cousin Jeremiah and Arthur Pym both took a step forward, presumably intending to help me to my feet and perhaps intending to follow Lucien's instruction, but the Mahatma raised his hand and they stopped.

"It is not necessary," the ancient said, as if to provide them with an excuse that they could offer themselves for failing to carry through their impulse.

I continued trying to struggle to my feet, but before I could do it the Mahatma was beside me, and he placed his hand on the back of my head. The pain vanished. I still felt a trifle dizzy, but it was obvious that the magician had spoken the truth. It wasn't necessary for me to be picked up and placed in Lucien's carriage—quite the contrary, in fact.

The Mahatma looked into my eyes. "Do you want to do as your cousin suggested, Mr. Reynolds," he asked, "and run away?"

I could have said yes. I was on my feet and I could have taken to my heels, run all the way to the river bank, and hurled the violin into the Seine. I could, in theory, have *wanted* to do that—but in fact, and in all honesty, I replied: "No, I don't."

"He's concussed," said Lucien Groix. "He doesn't know what he's saying." He looked around for support, but none was forthcoming. Dupin and Madame Lacuzon were inside the witch-house, swallowed up by the dark stairwell. Even Bertrand seemed helplessly confused. The fog seemed very dense. I could hardly make out the outline of Lucien's carriage in the gloom, and Saint-Germain's was only a little more distinct, although it was closer to the lonely street-lamp.

"Let it go, Lucien," I said. "I don't need rescuing. I have the situation in hand."

I didn't really mean it, of course—but I didn't want Lucien to get into more trouble than he was already in. He had, after all, once saved my life, and probably thought that he was trying to do it again, even while wondering privately whether mine was really a life worth saving.

It was not mere cowardice, or fatal curiosity, that made me capitulate with the Mahatma's plan. The simple truth was that I didn't want to run away. I didn't want to assist in opening a portal to R'lyaieh either, but I didn't want to run into the fog, having no faith that there was anything beyond it into which I could emerge, whether I went down the slope toward the river or upwards in the direction of the Val-de-Grâce. I had no plan, although I certainly hadn't let go of the hope that Dupin had one, or that—unlikely as it might seem—Madame Lacuzon had magic enough, if not to combat Addhema and the Mahatma, at least to disrupt the exotic harmony that they were intent on producing in time and space.

I moved toward the door of the house. This time, Cousin Jeremiah and Arthur Pym stood aside to let me in

"Don't worry," I said to Jeremiah, as I passed him by. "It isn't the Devil or the Crawling Chaos that's behind the portal to R'lyaieh. It won't kill me. At the worst, I'll go stark raving mad."

He didn't bother to tell me that that was what he was afraid of, and not merely for me and himself. He had surely read the newspapers while he and Arthur were waiting for Dupin in Saint-Germain's study. He knew that Convulsionnaires had already begun to reappear in Paris, along with cholera, and that there was anxiety throughout the medical profession regarding the probability of an epidemic, which the Sûreté, the King, the National Guard and all of God's angels would be impotent to prevent or inhibit.

I stepped through the doorway, and paused. Reflexively, I looked to the right, through the open doorway to the drawing room, although I knew perfectly well that there would no longer be a cadaver lying just inside the doorway, with a crossbow bolt protruding from the torso. The light was very poor, but there was enough for me to see that there was nothing there.

In fact, there was literally *nothing* there: no floorboards, no walls, merely a void, an absence not merely of objects but of space.

Automatically, without any intention or thought, I reached out with my right hand to feel the void.

I think I realized, as my hand made contact with the absence, that it had to be a portal of sorts, a borderland between our world and elsewhere—or elsewhen.

Then, the silent darkness of the other dimension, or the interval between dimensions, suddenly blazed with light: the light of two terrible eyes.

I recognized those eyes immediately, having seen them more than once. They were the eyes of the man that I had seen walking along the Rue de l'Hirondelle twenty-four hours before, but greatly magnified, not only in size but in power. They were also the eyes I had seen when Jana Valdemar had attempted to open a similar portal: those of the Dweller with the Eyes of Fire.

The eyes were terrifying, as they were doubtless intended to be—but not as terrifying as the icy grip that suddenly seized my hand, seemingly far more intense in its coldness than the frosty atmosphere outside the witch-house.

Immediately, I was pulled, and as I was pulled, the chill of that grip shot through me, seemingly turning my very soul to ice.

Then, it seemed, I fell—but not through the doorway into the room. I fell across the threshold, but not on to a floor or into the center of the planet. I fell into some strange *down* that was ungraspable by my primitive conceptual geometry.

The blazing eyes vanished.

I don't believe that I actually lost consciousness, but might have done, if my consciousness was somehow switched off and on again with no detectable transition. I did lose track of time and thought in a sudden dizzying confusion, though. I had no sensation of measurable duration, and the only awareness that I could accommodate clearly, in the suddenly-eternalized moment, was an awareness of the abrupt cessation of the insidious music. Even the cessation was devoid of measurable duration, though, and when the mental flow of time regained its orderly progression, the tune that I had heard in the café was once again reverberating within me very faintly—almost, but not quite, drowned out by another sound, rhythmic in its fashion but slow and muffled . . . or perhaps muffling. I wasn't beyond the reach of either.

But which, I wondered, idiotically, *is the music of time? And what, in either case, is the other.*

It was dark, but it was not a Stygian blackness. There was a light source somewhere above me, a kind of chink in a wall of darkness, but the thin pencil of rays projected through it was soon dissipated by molecules of murky air, unable to illuminate any nearby object. The violin and bow were still in my left hand.

I thought that my fall had ended, although I hadn't felt the shock of any impact in my numb feet. I groped with my right hand, thinking that I might find a wall—as I surely should have done, if I were still in the narrow corridor leading to the spiral stairway of the house in the Rue de l'Hirondelle. There was nothing solid within the range of my tentative hand.

Perhaps, I thought, striving to recover my presence of mind, I was no longer in the house, and perhaps no longer in Paris . . . but perhaps, on the other hand, I had not moved my position in earthly space at all, but had merely been pulled into somewhere that was at least as much a *sideways* as a *down*.

I did, however, feel that I was *far away*. Perhaps that was because the entrancing music—the siren song—was so faint . . . or perhaps because of the other sound, which resembled the susurrus of blood in the temples, and had become insistently audible once it was isolated from the other ambient sounds of the environment. But if the pulse in question really was produced by the beating of a heart, the heart was surely not mine.

Was I in the presence of Cthulhu, in its "house" at R'lyaieh?

I chided myself for being melodramatic, but the suspicion did not go away. The darkness, I thought, was *expectant*.

I could have cried out, in order to make an attempt to judge from the echoes of my voice how close I might be to a wall and in what direction, but I dared not. There was no way of knowing what kind of ears there might be in that expectant darkness, or what kind of attention any sound that I made might attract.

Perhaps I should have felt glad about the fact that I was no longer in the gloomy but solid corridor of the witch-house, presumably distanced from Addhema and the Mahatma alike, but I didn't. I couldn't. Gladness no longer seemed possible for my frozen soul or my altered consciousness. Nor was any other emotional reaction, for the moment. My body, however, had not lost its capacity for reflexive action. My lungs tried to breathe in, and my legs flexed slightly, in a belated anticipation of the shock that I ought to have felt when I reached the bottom of whatever shaft I had fallen into. My left hand contracted about the neck of the violin.

Although the environment that I was in was presumably alien, my reflexes had not betrayed me. After a painful instant when my lungs were paralyzed, I did contrive to breathe in, and the air that I drew into my lungs was not icy—in fact, it seemed unnaturally unwintry. My braced feet obtained the sensation of standing on near-solid ground, apparently having reached it at a velocity which had permitted them to absorb the shock without the slightest injury to my ankles. My feet were no longer cold; that, more than anything else, suggested to me that I was no longer in Paris . . . not, at least, in February 1848.

My left hand was sustaining the violin and bow in mid-air.

My eyes strove to adapt to the ambient light, not sufficiently to allow me to distinguish any objects clearly, but sufficiently for me to form a vague impression that there might be walls of a sort ten or twelve faces away: not constructed walls, like those of a house, but uneven rock faces, liked those of a cave; but that was probably pure illusion, synthesized by my eager brain in response to sense-data of which it could not actually make sense. Of such alienations are natural hallucinations born.

I made a half-turn, peering into the shadows that had been behind me. One of them stirred, as if reacting to my own movement. I couldn't make out anything clearly, but my mind immediately pounced on the idea that it was a ghost. As if responding to that thought, or at least to the awareness that it had been seen, if only vaguely, the shadow slowly took on a close approximation of human form, but the only thing that emerged more obviously from the darkness were its eyes: eyes that were still burning feebly, like cooling embers.

The Dweller with the Eyes of Fire, I thought. *I'm in the borderland between dimensions. But I'm not trespassing on the dwellers' domain—not deliberately at any rate. I fell . . . or was pulled.*

The rhythmic sound that was muffling the faintly audible music was now oddly reminiscent of the waves of a calm, sea striking the rocks of a shore, although I clung to my first impression that it was a heartbeat. I could have imagined that I had landed on the firm sand of a fissure in a cliff, and that the sea was now to my left, its gentle waves drifting into the cave, lapping at the shore. I could have imagined, too, that I could hear the cries of seabirds, calling as they skimmed the invisible waves—but I refused the temptation. Best not to give in, I thought, to hallucination, however comforting.

I focused my attention on the shadow with eyes, and found its shape vaguely familiar. It seemed to me that it was the bravo who had visited my house that morning, no longer dead but reduced to the marginal existence of a phantom.

"What do you want with me?" I asked him, hoarsely, not knowing whether any answer I received would be anything more than a product of my own desperate imagination, synthesizing in the absence of any tangible reality. "Why have you kidnapped me?"

"I'm not kidnapping you, I'm rescuing you," said the Dweller, speaking English, as I had, unthinkingly. "As to what I want, to begin with, a little courtesy wouldn't hurt."

I was too disorientated to be courteous. "I suppose you're going to tell me that you've saved my life," I said. "It's a claim that has been made before, more than once, but in my experience, the dead are not to be trusted.

The shadow might have laughed, but I heard no sound. Perhaps I was not quite ready to grant, as yet, that the dead have a sense of humor.

"That is not dead which can eternal lie," the entity quoted, "and the treacheries of the dead are paltry by comparison with those of the living. But no matter. No, I haven't saved your life, yet . . . but it might be possible, if you do as I say."

If ever there was a statement likely to evoke mistrust, it was that one. And the thought occurred to me that my life really had been saved, only a few minutes earlier, in terms of my mind's apprehension of time, by the book in my pocket. I knew better, though, than to attribution any intention, let alone a virtuous one, to the *Necronomicon*. If it had attracted and absorbed Bertrand's bullet, it had simply been following its own existential imperatives, unconsciously, unaware that it was only a figment of a dream and a recipe for disaster.

But the Dweller had to be more than that. In all probability, he, or it, had a consciousness, an identity, and a name. It might not understand itself any better than a human being, especially if it could take on human form when the whim took it, but it clearly had a purpose, for the moment, and the ability to take action in pursuit of that purpose.

"You can't hurt me," I said. "I have the book."

"I have no intention of hurting you," the shadow assured me—but there was asperity and annoyance in its voice, "and believe me, the book is the kind of armor that will do you far more harm than good."

That seemed plausible enough, even though the book had stopped a bullet heading for my heart. Was it the book's fault if I had fallen over and almost fractured my skull?

"You're confused," the shadow-bravo said, demonstrating a certain acumen. "You need to try to think clearly. You need to find yourself within the conflict of suggestions. If you can't, you're doomed."

I already knew that—but knowing that you're confused simply becomes part of your confusion, and knowing that you're doomed is simply an aspect of your doom. Rational consciousness is a refuge, but once its walls are breached and invaders swarm in, howling and brandishing the trenchant swords of paradox, it's the devil's own job to hold them back.

But I tried. I tried to put my hand on my heart, but all it found was the book.

"Did you have that book on your person this morning, when I came to your house?" the bravo asked, perhaps thinking that if only he had realized then what I had in my possession—joke—he might have been able to put a spoke in the inexorable wheel of fate. The banality of the question was a trifle surprising, but it went some way to persuading me that I really wasn't alone in my prison of darkness, and that the dialogue was genuine, not a product of my feverish imagination. I wondered whether the ghost still had a crossbow bolt protruding from his chest, which he was doomed to carry in the afterlife, just as certain unlucky ghosts are reputed by legend to carry their severed heads under their arms.

Probably not, I thought; *legend is such a liar.*

"Yes," I told him, seeing no point in lying, or even refusing to answer. "Couldn't you tell?"

"It hides, Mr. Reynolds," said the specter, "even from eyes such as mine, sometimes in the most unlikely places. My sight is better in the dark than in daylight—something you might have noticed in your previous encounters with specters—and the same applies to my other senses, especially those normally weak or dormant in the living. Things have not gone to plan, as you must have realized. If I had perceived that you had the book, and had been able to persuade you to give it to me, it might have been possible to improvise . . . but that's water under the bridge, and the cause isn't completely lost yet. Can you give me the book now?"

The possibilities raised by that oddly-phrased question did not help to clarify my confusion. I cursed myself for having taken the book off the shelf, thus allowing it to curse me. Apparently, Dupin, however he had acquired the book—or however he had been acquired by it—had been too wise to carry it on his person. Perhaps the child would have taken it, had she had the opportunity—why else would she have come to my house?—but Madame Lacuzon must have removed her before the book could acquire her.

Was I making any sense? I had a nagging suspicion that I might be, but I was in no condition to trust my intuition.

"No," I said, although I had forgotten what the question was.

The shadow sighed. "I thought so. But let's try to be optimistic. While you, the violin and the book are not there, it's unlikely that the incantation can be completed successfully. Unfortunately, I can't keep you here forever. The borderland is inherently unstable, and the Mahatma's world will reclaim you eventually, only having lost you for a matter of subjective minutes, or even seconds. Still, the best-laid plans of mice and men gang aft agley, as your poet has it—and that applies to their plans as well as mine. If you can recover your mental equilibrium before you fall back . . . Try to think. Did you have the slightest inkling of what you were doing when you took the book from wherever it was hidden and placed it next to your heart?"

"No," I said, quasi-automatically "it was purely a matter of chance."

"There is no such thing," he told me.

I knew that he was wrong. "Yes there is," I said, bluntly. "It might not have been purely a matter of chance that I took possession of the *Necronomicon*—or *vice versa*—but that doesn't mean that there is no such thing as chance. There has to be such a thing as chance, or the world couldn't exist . . . or couldn't progress, which comes to the same thing."

He was about to argue the point, but I interrupted him, determined to seize the initiative of the interrogation. "Where are we?" I asked.

"Nowhere," he replied, unhelpfully, "and nowhen."

"Well," I said, "at least my feet aren't cold, although you probably can't imagine what a blessing that is. We're not in R'lyaieh, then, in the bosom of Cthulhu's encryption? No, that's a silly suggestion. If it were possible to travel between Addhema's house and Booby Island in a single step, Jacob Pym wouldn't have required three months to transport the child to Paris . . ." I paused, hoping for a correction or an explanation

"Things fall down," the ghost told me. "*Up* is a much more difficult direction, even aboard a ghost ship, let alone the *Excelsior*. But no, Mr. Reynolds, we're as far from the bosom of Cthulhu as can be imagined, in spite of the dangerous presence of the book. If you value your life and soul, you'll try your utmost to get rid of it. The wisest thing would be to hand it to me, if you can."

I wasn't about to accept his judgment of wisdom, no matter who or what he was. "Who are you, in fact?" I demanded, as the thought occurred to me. "One of the Nine Immortals or the Dweller with the Eyes of Fire?"

"Names are always misleading," he told me. "We are rarely nine, and our eyes rarely burn."

"But you *are* immortal, after a fashion?" I prompted.

"Certainly. More so than many people imagine—hence Addhema's conviction that her petty magic trick could deliver me to permanent extinction, even though she knew full well that the bolt was blessed. Her posthumous existence has been too intermittent and her education too direly lacking, for her to have acquired a proper understanding of the vagaries of the superhuman world. The Mahatma is more knowledgeable, but far from infallible, as you can see. Like almost all immortals, his obsessions have absorbed him to the extent that he has become blinkered to matters beyond them."

"Almost all?" I queried.

"Not excluding myself, alas," the phantom said, "and certainly not excluding Cthulhu, which is no longer anything *but* obsession, within its encryption. But don't credit yourself with any superiority in consequence. There is no particular virtue in changeability, and none at all in the faculty of being able to pursue conflicting goals at the same time."

It would have been a step too far to think that I understood what he was saying, but I felt that I was getting there, It seemed to me that I was thinking more coherently again, pulling myself together. Stepping outside the world had not made the choice between my thousand questions any easier to make, but at least it wasn't unduly difficult to select the next one.

"What happens next?" I asked him. "Where do we go from here?"

"That depends on you," he said. "I still have a permanent immortality of sorts, and I can probably go anywhere, but you could easily be stuck—marooned, in pirate talk. For the moment, we have an absence of time in hand, as you can probably tell, but as I said, the moment of suspension can't last forever, even paradoxically, and if the symphony resumes, it will reclaim you. I might be able to take you with me before then, but only if you can consent to go. First things first, though; before anything else, you have to rid yourself of the *Necronomicon*, if you can."

"And if I can't . . . or won't?" I queried.

"You'd be very foolish to want to hold on to it, but it's a sly tome, and you certainly wouldn't be the first to want it, or to be unable to discard it. If you're wise enough and strong enough, though, you can simply take it out of your pocket and hand it to me, or throw it as far as you can into the friendly darkness."

I had no idea whether I was wise enough or strong enough to do that, but I certainly didn't want to do it. Apart from anything else, I was far from convinced that the haunted darkness was friendly. Whether it was my own stubbornness, or the fact that time was in a weird suspension, I was strongly impelled to procrastinate.

"I don't know to what extent I have solidity here," I said, "but my experience of ghosts suggests to me that they usually don't have very much, so I doubt that you could take from me by means of mere brute force."

"Perhaps that's true," he countered, noncommittally, "but the fact is that there's no good reason why you should cling on to it, given that you have at least a suspicion of how dangerous it is. You and I are on the same side, and your best chance of surviving this insane escapade is to take my advice."

"You'll have to convince me of that," I said. "I'm entitled to an explanation, I think. What do you intend to do with the *Necronomicon* if I release it?"

"Destroy it, if I can take it or reach it. I've destroyed others—many others, if you include bad translations and blatant fakes. It's a dangerous book, as you know very well."

"So it's said," I agreed, "but in fact, I don't know it very well at all. Jack Taylor told me that I don't even know what it is, and I'm inclined to believe him on that score, although I have my doubts about his other assertions. So what is it?"

Did the shade sigh? I couldn't be sure; the sound of the strange heartbeat and the sound of the distant music were too closely akin to sighs for me to make the distinction.

"It would be wiser for you to remain ignorant," the specter told me. "Knowledge is power and power corrupts. You have no idea how close you already are to knowing too much. Believe me, you really shouldn't ask questions whose answers can only harm you."

"That's what Addhema said," I recalled, "but that was because she was about to tell me a hurtful lie."

"She's a soul-drinker," the shade said. "It's best not to rise to her bait—but in this instance, the advice was good. She probably didn't have enough solidity to make the attempt simply to seize the book, and might well have thought that it was better off in your pocket than elsewhere . . . which was obviously the Mahatma's judgment. Isn't that enough to persuade you that it's too dangerous to keep?"

"Not nearly enough," I said. "In order to make a reasoned decision, I need to know what the *Necronomicon* is. I'd rather ask Dupin, but he isn't here . . . and I don't have any confidence that you'll tell me the truth, but I need to know why everyone is so much in awe of a book that no one can read."

This time, the ghost's sigh was definitely real even though it blended in so harmoniously with the repetitive refrain that seemed to be drifting into the underworld from high above.

"Because those who try to read it—or, more precisely, those who strive to understand it—are opening themselves to possession by it, " he said, "and that possession is usually fatal. What's read, even in the imagination, can't be unread, and what's pronounced can't be unpronounced. A complete lack of conscious comprehension is no guarantee of safety. Human beings—any beings, for that matter—can only obtain the slightest inkling of what music actually means, but they can be attracted to it nevertheless, possessed by it and obsessed by it. The *Necronomicon*, no matter what phonetic system it's encrypted in, is capable of taking possession of your psyche, and such possession is inevitably damaging and destructive—more so than possession by any of its lesser imitations and analogues. It's exactly what it claims to be: a book of mortal names: a lexicon of incantations for unwinding or perverting aspects of the fabric of reality . . . a lockpick, if you like, for dismantling psychic encryptions, including encryptions of what you call consciousness or identity. Even if you don't make the slightest attempt to read it, it's not a safe thing to have in your pocket, and you're already trying far too hard to understand it simply by wondering what it is. If you value the coherency of your intellect, you'll rid yourself of it . . . if you still can."

"Saying *if I can* clearly implies that you don't really believe that I can."

"I'm still prepared to hope, and to assume, that you can and might. If you can't, or if you persist in your stubborn procrastination, it's capable of assisting the Mahatma, even from here, to decrypt Cthulhu . . . and once you slip out of the borderland, believe me, you'll be utterly helpless."

I didn't believe him. Now that I was thinking coherently again—or thought I was—I wanted to argue the point.

"But you've said yourself that Cthulhu isn't inherently evil. It's not the Devil. It's probably not even alive, although that doesn't seem to prevent it from dreaming. Apparently, it can generate nightmares, and perhaps provoke insanity. Perhaps, like ergot poisoning, it can make Convulsionnaires of some of us, at least temporarily, but to me, that doesn't make it seem such a terrible threat to the existence of the whole world. Clearly, it doesn't seem to be a threat at all to the Mahatma— who might want to see every Englishman on his sacred soil strangled by Thugs, but whose ultimate goal is surely to make India, and the world, paradisal. So tell me: what's so terrible about decrypting Cthulhu, or even decrypting the whole world? Consciousness is a defense, Dupin is fond of saying, but he's always vague about what it defends us *from*, and the conviction doesn't prevent him from being avid to solve every puzzle he comes across and fully committed to the progressive transformation of his own consciousness. Isn't that a peculiar paradox? And unless I'm mistaken in what I saw before you snatched me out of the world, he's now prepared to play his part in the Mahatma's projected concert, of his own free will—so why shouldn't I? Clearly, you've tried, and are trying, to disrupt that planned concert, but I still don't know why. Nor can I imagine who planned this bizarrely elaborate scheme, when, how or why . . . *and I want to know*."

This time, the sigh was so deep that it seemed to drown out even the possibility of other sounds, and I realized that the Immortal, the Dweller with the Eyes of Fire, was admitting defeat, thinking that the meager knowledge I had already acquired had been sufficient to corrupt me irredeemably. He believed that he could not persuade me to surrender the *Necronomicon*, that I was too completely possessed. And he had no faith in my ability to intervene in the Mahatma's plan in any way.

"The Mahatma made his present plan, in the trivial sense, more than a hundred years ago," he told me, "but he believes that he's fulfilling some greater purpose, following the dictates of what he regards as Fate. He's intent on making you all dance to his tune, but it's a rare and deluded composer who believes that he's the sole creator of his own music. He believes—as I do—that the ultimate components of this scheme extend further into the past and future than paltry human minds can imagine, and he believes, as I do, that the idea of an end and beginning of time are figments of our imagination, and that the stream of eventuality actually has no beginning and no end. There: I've answered your question. Now, if you can give me the book, perhaps—just perhaps—I can take you away from here, and away from the Mahatma's symphony."

It might, I thought, be a good offer . . . but I didn't like it. In fact, it reeked of treachery.

No," I said. "I think, on due reflection, that I'll keep the book, for now. It's probably Dupin's, and if it isn't, he's the only man I'd trust to advise me what to do with it."

He didn't bother to sigh again. "Fool," he said. "Go on, then—follow your stupid heart and let the violin play! Play your tiny part, bystander. Bear witness. Help to bring down the Day of Judgment. Facilitate the overwriting of the palimpsest of human conviction. Participate in the destruction of the tatters of faith and expose the nudity of the soul. I've proven to be an ineffective scarecrow. May God forgive me."

"There is no God," I told him, confidently, "and there is nothing that has to be forgiven a mere temporal echo. And you're wrong about me, too. I'm no longer a bystander. Your part is done, but I have yet to play mine. I have the book and I have the viol. You, the Mahatma, and Cthulhu itself might think that *they* have *me*, and that they can all play me like a passive instrument, that I'm just a means of evocation, but I still have a choice, and I'm going to use it, if I can. You can see in the dark with your damnable eyes of fire, so *watch me!*"

I shouldered my instrument, or my weapon, and transferred the bow to my right hand; and then, feeling a marvelous warmth in my heart, perhaps emanating from the book I had juxtaposed with it but perhaps innate in my soul, I began to play.

XVI

THE EVOCATION

I would be lying if I said that I suddenly discovered how to play the instrument in a flash of supernatural enlightenment, or that I had the slightest idea of the music I wanted to make; I wasn't myself, any more than I was anywhere or anywhen—but that didn't mean that I was no one at all, or that I was merely a helpless puppet devoid of consciousness and conscience, moving to the tug of intangible strings.

In distant or surrounding Paris, perhaps close at hand and perhaps further away than I could imagine, all the church bells began to resonate to a strange wave spreading through time, which originated as something very tiny, hardly perceptible even in its own time, but was magnified by a chain of coincidental circumstances, growing into something huge. In itself, I presume, that resonance was capable of influencing human minds, of stimulating thoughts and feelings, both in the ways that church bells were designed and intended to do, and in ways unanticipated and unintended by their architects; but at that particular moment, the sum of the efforts of the bells of Paris harmonized with a much vaster pattern of vibrations extended in time as well as space, and forming part of a symphony in which many other instruments and instrumentalists were able to join.

Doubtless there had been and would be, many moments in history at which such resonances, mostly imperceptible to the present human ear, would not have been able to achieve any more than a small alteration in the emotions felt by bodies capable of absorbing and responding to those multiple vibrations; but there are, as Blaise Thibodeaux had theorized and calculated—and as numerous mystics before him had sensed and attempted to elaborate—complex cycles in the natural vibrations of space-time. Normally, such cycles are out of phase, tending to nullify one another rather than amplify one another, but rarely, at intervals whose pattern is so complex that they seem almost random, the cycles do coincide, at certain determined points in space-time, the seeming arbitrariness of which is also a resultant of complex patterns. At such moments of complementarity, the effects on human and other minds are potentially much greater, more dramatic and more intense.

The effects of that complementarity of subliminal vibrations on defensive consciousness are highly likely to be perceived as confusion, or delirium, easily capable of provoking hallucinations and madness, sometimes with permanent after-effects, but not necessarily. Some human minds, thanks to the general evolution of mind and various forms of mental sophistication, are capable even nowadays of grasping the potential of that complementarity, of comprehending it—or, in a different vocabulary, of decrypting it—as a kind of music or mathematics, not merely reproducible with the aid of instruments and calculable with the aid of imagination but capable of transposition and variation.

To put it crudely, such moments permit the great symphony of time to become perceptible and measurable to those who have an ears and minds capable of appreciating it, and offer an opportunity for human minds to make a contribution to it: to add their own instrumentalism, or their own creative thought, to the hymn and sum of creation, and to modify it. Such modifications are, of necessity, very tiny in the great scheme of things, as human beings are themselves very tiny within the great scheme of things, but very tiny things—analogous to the cholera microbe, on the human scale of events—are sometimes capable of effects far beyond the implication of their mere size.

One day, perhaps human minds might evolve to such an extent that the great majority of them become aware of such phenomena, in spite of the attempts of consciousness to seal itself off from such unwelcome and potentially disruptive awareness. For the time being, however, it is the prerogative of a tiny minority, many of whom are mystics, visionaries and would-be magicians, although a few become great musicians, and even fewer contrive to combine the awareness with the intellect necessary to subject the resonances within themselves to any measure of discipline and to employ their potential constructively and creatively. Perhaps, as Auguste Dupin believes, that is the optimum form of sanity presently achievable by humans, but, inevitably, those possessed of it are perceived by their insensitive fellows as being just as mad as the much greater number of sensitives who really are driven insane by their sensitivity.

I, fortunately or unfortunately, am a person of very moderate intellect, and no great musician, but I am not insensitive to the vibrations in question. I am—as I had proven in no uncertain terms since I had formed an association with Auguste Dupin—a seer of sorts. Dupin had said more than once that he found me uniquely useful among his acquaintances as a "sounding-board" for his speculations, and the metaphor had a greater analogy than he probably realized. We call a seer a seer because he or she is particularly prone to seeing ghosts and other entities normally screened out by protective consciousness, but that is only a part of a sensitive's vulnerability.

As I had amply demonstrated in recent times, I am vulnerable to possession, not only by entities capable of independent existence, like Addhema or the egregore that had employed me to play the cello in Du Potet's garden, but by vaguer and stranger entities, such as the *Necronomicon*—not the first book by which I had been possessed, by any means, although undoubtedly the most insidious and the most powerful. Defensive consciousness, of course, tends to regard possession as an exotic and bizarre circumstance, but there is, I think, a sense in which all books possess sensitive readers to a degree, at least temporarily, and that there is something inherent in the process of reading, as there is in the process of musical composition, that lends itself voluntarily to possession, usually but not always harmless.

It *is* exotic, and bizarre, to be possessed by a book that one has not even opened, and could not read if one had, but there is a magic inherent in inscription, which takes possession of the physical object of a manuscript, and gives it a power of infection independent of the actual process of reading and comprehension. Even on a vulgar level, it is easy to observe that there are books and grimoires whose ideas and imagery are familiar to countless people who have never read them or heard them read aloud.

None of that, of course, really explains how it was that when I began to play Prospero's violin, joining in concert with Anton's violin, Dupin's dulcimer and countless other instruments distributed in space and time, I began picking out the notes and plying the bow as if I knew what I was doing. Calling the phenomenon *possession* is a mere matter of labeling; but it does, I think, help to provide a sketch of the context of understanding into which the bizarre circumstance has to be fitted if it is ever to be understood. I have no conscious memory now of how to play the violin, and I am sure that my clumsy fingers have no muscular memory of that art, but the fact remains that when I began to play the enchanted violin in my little enclave outside perceptible space, I had a clear emotional perception of what I was doing, and an artful muscular memory that enabled me to do it. The perception and the memory were not *mine* in a narrow sense, and I cannot put a name to whatever entity actually possessed them, but for a moment, they were capable of resonating within me, plangently.

I recognized the music I was playing. Perhaps, if I had not, I could still have played it, mechanically, like a pianola, but I was more fully possessed than that. I had not heard the tune before, but I had heard something akin to it when Auguste Dupin had played Erich Zann's violin—or had been played by it, much as I was being played by Prospero's. At the time, Eric Zann's music had seemed weird and sinister, and I suspect that the symphony in which I was now playing would have seemed weird and sinister to many listeners, but this time, I connected with the music, which resonated within me completely. I understood it. I understood its composition. I understood what Erich Zann had been trying to achieve in composing music of the same genre, why he had not been able to achieve his goal completely, and why the pseudonymous Doctor Prospero, even if he had learned to pay the notes of Zann's music as he had learned to play Abbé Apollonius' imaginary harmonies of hell and Will Maccabee's imitative dance of the dead, could not even have duplicated their limited and ersatz effect. He had the intellect, but not the sensitivity.

And that is why I, who had the sensitivity but not the intellect, was a much better instrument than he would have been for the particular purpose of playing in Anton's ensemble.

It was not really Anton's ensemble, of course; nor was it the Mahatma's. They too were instruments, charged with assembling and leading a tiny fraction of an orchestra that extended over a great expanse distributed in space and time—much further in space than the Île Saint-Louis, the pocket of nothingness in which I was temporarily folded, and the air above the Rue de l'Hirondelle, and much further in time than the few paltry decades that separated 1848 from the points of inspiration grasped by the Mahatma and others to whom I could not put a name or attribute an identity. I could not count or estimate the number of instruments that joined in with the chords that we played, or put labels on them, but I know that the number was vast. It was not infinite, and was surely calculable if one knew the requisite formulae, but it was enormous, extending further into the past and future than I could calculate, in spite of the apparent simultaneity of the resonating notes.

The intensity of sound within a medium varies with distance in accordance with familiar law of physics, but it is amenable to distortion by ambient factors. Had I still been in the corridor of the witch-house, I would undoubtedly have heard the sounds of Anton's violin and Dupin's dulcimer loudly, and more distinctly than the millions of other instruments in harmony with which I was playing, but the quality of the sound that my ears and brain actually construed was undoubtedly affected by the strange situation that I occupied. I had been told that it was nowhere and nowhen, and my impressions had seemed in conformity with that judgment, except for a single ray of light penetrating through some kind of "hole," and the audible strains of the music that I had heard in the Rue de l'Hirondelle, which maintained a connection of sorts between my nowhere and nowhen and a where and when, albeit not a midnight in Paris; oddly enough, however, I felt much closer at hand to the instruments that Dupin and Anton were playing, which not only sounded and felt louder than they would have done in the corridor, but more meaningful.

I was not *inside* their minds as they played, but thanks to the music, I had a far greater sensitivity to what they were feeling, and perhaps what they were thinking, than human minds ordinarily have to one another, even at moments of unusual sympathy. No words were exchanged, because the symphony was as yet unaccompanied by a choir of voices, but I nevertheless heard and felt something in the chords I was playing that gave me an insight into their purpose and intentions, and what I sensed surprised me—not so much on Dupin's part, because I had been hoping all along that he could contrive a disruption of the Mahatma's plan, and hoping that he had the capability to put it into operation as soon as it was contrived, but on Anton's.

Perhaps I should not have been surprised. After all, I had glimpsed his true identity once before, at Fontainebleau. He had been resident in the Harmonic Society's headquarters since the Napoleonic era, a true magician hiding among fake and would-be magicians, before finding it diplomatic to disappear quietly, but whether he had been a member prior to the Revolution, when the Society had been temporarily disbanded, the police had been unable to ascertain, and had not tried very hard because he did not give the impression of being old enough. In fact, he had been a founder-member; he had known the Comte de Saint-Germain when the latter was in secret communication with the Mahatma and he had known about the Mahatma's schemes even before then. Those schemes really were the Mahatma's, and owed nothing to Anton, but he had taken a covert interest in them, and in the legends of Cthulhu, just as he had taken an interest in Blaise Thibodeaux's research and other projects being carried out clandestinely by the Society's various members. He had been aware of Prospero's research, and had conducted his own investigation of the music of Eric Zann alongside his research into the music of time; he had learned to play the violin, more intimately than Prospero; and he had made a more concerted effort to intercept echoes in time, not by searching for ancient manuscripts and occult texts like an orthodox scholar, but by offering himself magically to possession by such echoes.

At Fontainebleau I had glimpsed one of the results of that voluntary possession, in the evocation of an entity that he called Oberon the Fay, borrowing the name from *Huon of Bordeaux*, and imagining it as a remote reincarnation of himself—which, in a sense, it was, just as there was a sense in which Dupin was a reincarnation of John Dee, even though his consciousness refused to admit any such possibility.

Anton had offered his cooperation to the Mahatma's project, to which he must have seemed an invaluable recruit—even more valuable than Addhema and Kanhoje Angre, by virtue of the added advantage of being alive, of the same immortal ilk as the Mahatma, while never having joined the society of immortals who sometimes termed themselves the Nine, or at least allowed legend to represent them by that title. He was, however, a poseur, who had always intended to usurp the apparatus of the Mahatma's project and pervert it to his own secret purpose. Auguste Dupin did not know him, but he knew Dupin, far better than the reincarnated Comte de Saint-Germain or Edward England, alias Oberon Breisz, could. He it was who had selected Dupin to play an unwitting role in the Mahatma's plan, bringing me in tow as part of the package. At first he had thought of me merely as a convenient means of making up the requisite number of players in the witch-house, but when he discovered in the forest of Fontainebleau how sensitive I was and how susceptible to possession, he had realized that I might be more useful than that—although he had been careful to represent me to the Mahatma as an innocent, completely manipulable. I had confirmed that impression more than once, especially on the occasion of my earlier encounter with the crew of Angria's ghost ship: an occasion that had also confirmed the Mahatma's certainty of Dupin's potential utility.

The Mahatma's plot had, therefore, always had wheels within its wheels, guided from within as well as without, and Anton had always intended to play his own variation on the Mahatma's theme, hopefully in harmony with Dupin and me, if we would consent, when the moment came, to offer ourselves to the same possession as him.

That was an uncertain element in his scheme, but he never considered the possibility of simply making contact with us and explaining his intentions, partly because the Mahatma might easily have obtained occult intelligence of any such explicit conspiracy but principally because he thought such an element of uncertainty essential to it. He had not wanted, either, to make contact with the Nine and make an attempt to form any kind of alliance with them; he had had nothing to do with the move that the Dweller had made in removing me from the witch-house into the borderland between dimensions, which might have disrupted his plan as well as the Mahatma's, just as Madame Lacuzon's removal of Cthulhu's child from my house might have done.

In fact, however, it seemed to him that neither removal had proved fatal, or even seriously disruptive, to his own scheme. What the Mahatma mistook for Fate and believed to be on his side really was active—but it seemed to Anton, when he began to play, to be on his own side, not his rival's.

How do I know all that? I know it because, although I could not read Anton's thoughts, or enter into his mind, as soon as we began to play in harmony, we really were in harmony, with one another, with Dupin, and with the instrumentalist of the music of time that Anton had identified with his own reincarnation, and had dubbed, for want of a more suggestive name, Oberon the Fay.

A superstitious mind, possessed of a sensitivity similar to mine and drawn into a similar composition, might easily have assumed that he was being gifted with a Revelation sent directly or indirectly from God, or at least *a* god. I did not. Equipped with a different apparatus of thought, I work from the assumption, as I have mentioned before, that there is no God, any more than there is a supreme spirit of Evil, but only independent entities, legion in number and various in species, following their own existential imperatives. I also work from the assumption that although those multitudinous existential imperatives might often come into conflict, in the short term—by which I mean the first few trillion years of the existence of the universe—the eventual resolution of all those conflicts, the only possible resolution, if existence is not to fall back into chaos, will and must be conciliation: not merely peaceful coexistence but creative harmony, a true artistic collaboration, a genuine symphony or symbiosis.

Call me a Romantic, if you will, but not an optimist, because I also work from the assumption that the path of that progress will be exceedingly long, exceedingly bloody and, from a human point of view, exceedingly horrible. I work from the assumption that there can be no progressive evolution without death, without pain and without terror: in brief, without the perennially-renewed limited chaos from a reordering of which a better order might emerge . . . only *might*, for it is a situation that cannot contain any guarantees, even in the longest term imaginable. Order has no divine right to prevail.

Working from those assumptions, however, I was ready to play my part in Anton's ensemble. I was ready to open myself to possession by the music of time, as orchestrated, to the extent that it could be orchestrated, by one of the culminating intelligences of the Symbiotic Universe, channeled by Anton. I knew that I was a fool, rushing where all the angels in Heaven would have feared to tread, but I rushed anyway, as I had more than once before. I rushed, hoping that I would not trip and stumble. Perhaps it was a foolish hope, but is there any other kind? Perhaps hope, like faith, is a disease of rationality, a corollary of optimism, but can we truly exist without it? Poor fool that I am, I cannot.

I had to rush, because I had to set an example to Auguste Dupin, who was wiser by far than me, and, precisely for that reason, hesitant. There never was a wiser or a cleverer man, in my estimation, or a man more firmly on the side of the angels, but no one could accuse him of being quick off the mark. When he acted, he acted swiftly and precisely, but he always pondered his actions first. He was not a fool, and it is a sad fact that there are circumstances in life that require fools if they are to come out well. Life itself requires fools, just as it requires death. I doubt that there are times, as proverbial wisdom asserts, when it is folly to be wise, but I have no doubt at all that there are times when it is wise to be foolish.

As soon as I realized, with the force of revelation, that Anton did not intend to open the portals of R'lyaieh and set Cthulhu free, I was on his side. Arthur Pym, I felt sure, would have reacted just as instinctively, in the same direction, Cousin Jeremiah, on the other hand, as a true scientist and a philosopher, might have hesitated, in order to wonder whether that liberation might not be an entirely bad thing—but after a second's reflection, I believe that he would have concluded that it could not be worth the risk. Saint Germain, like his forebear, would have jumped to the opposite conclusion—and, in effect, already had.

Auguste Dupin, by contrast, instantly leapt instead to a different, and more challenging question. Given that Anton did not want to decrypt Cthulhu, *what did he want to do instead?* Given that he did not want simply to cancel the Mahatma's evocation, but rather to bring about a subtle alteration within it—perhaps at the risk of breaking the door of R'lyaieh unintentionally—what was he actually trying to achieve?

Dupin had no forewarning; he had not had any opportunity to formulate a careful plan of his own. Anton had assumed that he would cooperate, for exactly the same reason that he assumed that I would cooperate, in order to maintain Cthulhu's encryption. He had good reason to think so; after all, Dupin had done it before, in response to the threat we had faced in Oberon Breiz's house; but even then, I remembered, Dupin's reaction had not been lightning fast. A harsher critic than me might have judged that he had been perilously slow in his crucial response, leaving it to the last possible moment, weighed down by the complexities of his mental calculations.

This time, the situation was even more complicated—and if things began to go bad, it was unlikely that we could rely on Angria's ghost ship to lend us its aid. This time, there would be only three of us, in contention against the impetus of a scheme that a powerful magician had been hatching for nearly a century, backed by all the dream-power of Cthulhu and its shoggoths.

Dupin did not rush in. He started playing at the same time I did, but he did not enter into instant harmony with Anton. Instead, he sought, slowly, to improvise his own variation of the variation of the Mahatma's score that Anton was playing, in response to the echo from eternity.

I had no idea what the eventual result of that improvisation might be. Nor did Anton . . . and nor, I am convinced, did Dupin. Unlike Anton, he did not have a preconceived secret plan. He was literally making it up as he went along, feeling his way.

I had heard him improvise before, when he was commanded to play the music of Eric Zann from memory; and I had seen the results of that improvisation: a penetration of the Crawling Chaos into the atmosphere above Paris, the collapse of a house and the obliteration by crushing of Zann's possessed violin. Dupin had been very satisfied with that result, and perhaps rightly so, but I had wondered more than once since then whether it was precisely what he had intended—and, indeed, whether he was a good enough violin player and a good enough composer to have contrived it precisely. Now, I wondered that again, even as I played along, in search of a triple harmony between my instrument, his and Anton's.

And that was before Cthulhu's child began to sing, and her song changed everything.

XVII

THE KEY TO R'LYAIEH

WAS it really a song? Perhaps it would be more accurate to describe it as an incantation, but its syllables certainly had a musical character. I won't go as far as to say that they were possessed of rhyme, or even of rhythm, but they were nevertheless musical, and mathematical. They had an intrinsic order, however paradoxical that might seem, given that their purpose was to break an order, to destroy a prison.

In the same way that my entering into harmony with Anton had allowed me to perceive him more intimately, the child's song permitted me a harmony of sorts with her.

She was, of course, a victim of piracy.

Initially, the British authorities had only transported male convicts to the prison colony at Botany Bay, but the Admiralty had soon ceded to the proposition that its inmates would be less troublesome if they had female company, and a number of ships were commissioned over time to supply that presumed lack, transporting "incorrigible" prostitutes rounded up in the docklands of London. Such is the logic of the profession, however, that many of those prostitutes were the abandoned concubines of sailors, many of them of foreign origin and some hardly able to speak English, Almost all of them had children, and such is the perversity of the bureaucratic mind that although their male children were taken away from them into the custody of the State, their female children were allowed to remain with them. In practical terms, it made little difference; whether the children were sent to orphanages or allowed to remain with their mothers, the great majority of them did not survive to adulthood, and those who did carried visible or invisible stigmata that consecrated them to syphilis, the hangman's rope or Botany Bay. The ones who fell victim to piracy in the South Seas, therefore, could be reckoned fortunate, in purely statistical terms.

Angria's ghost ship did not sink the British ship carrying its cargo of female flesh. Jack Taylor and his fellows boarded her surreptitiously, and did not kill a single man or woman, although they surely frightened a few and doubtless caused a small measure of maternal grief by removing half a dozen infant children, unable as yet to talk, and taking them to the Malabar coast, where Angria delivered them to the custody of Thugs, who delivered them in their turn to the Mahatma. What happened to the others, Chulhu's child did not know and I do not care to speculate, but the favored selection was well-treated after a fashion, albeit strangely educated. If the procedures that incorporated bizarre incantations into her flesh were painful, she was not aware of it, having been magnetically anesthetized.

Ysolde Leonys had only been gifted with a single encryption, for precautionary reasons; Cthulhu's adopted child was subjected to a far more radical transformation of the flesh, albeit one that was not intended to be externally legible, and thus remained invisible to the naked eye. It was, however, intended not only to be internally "legible" but also pronounceable. The girl did not have to be taught to read, but she did have to be taught to sing if and when the ability was awakened by the appropriate music . . . not merely to recite the syllables, but to master the encrypted text's pitch and musicality. It had been necessary to transform her, by occult means, into a living text akin to the *Necronomicon*.

That had not been easy. In conventional terms, it had not even been humanly possible, but the Mahatma had not been limited to conventional human terms; he was an accomplished magician, in communication with other accomplished magicians via temporal echoes emanating from the past and the future, graspable and exploitable at particular times in particular locations. Much could be accomplished on the Malabar coast, but not everything. In order to complete the process of becoming Cthulhu's child, it was necessary for the girl to be transported to a particular proximity to the portal of R'lyaieh before being transported half way across the globe to Paris— and while she was in that proximity, she had to be left alone.

Those rules seem entirely arbitrary, as the rules of perceived magic frequently, if not invariably, do. Minds equipped with apparatus different from mine would call that a mystery, shrug their metaphorical shoulders and dismiss it, but mine cannot. I do not aspire ever to appreciate the mathematics and esthetics of the underlying formulae, but I work on the assumption that there must be such formulae—and also that they must have a dimension of uncertainty built into them, a potential for things to go awry.

As Jack Taylor had told me, Angria's ghost ship had been supposed to collect the child from Booby Island when her mysterious communion with the figurative rock art of the island—or, more precisely, with the mind of sorts that had inspired it—was complete; but the *Excelsior* had anchored off the island first, and Jacob Pym had picked up the girl.

That interruption had not been fatal to the plan, in appearance at least. The child had traveled to Paris in the company of Pym instead of Angria and Jack Taylor, but there were any number of opportunities for her to still to end up where she was supposed to be—supposed that is, by the Mahatma and by what he considered to be Fate. There had been further interference when Madame Lacuzon, sensing in the flesh of the child something akin to what she had sensed previously in the flesh of Ysolde Leonys, had thought it urgent to refer the matter to Dupin, and had immediately set forth for the Louvre in order to do so.

That interruption had not been fatal either, at least in appearance. It had certainly worried Angria, and had presumably given the Mahatma a moment of dire anxiety, but, as I had seen, the ghost pirates had not only succeeded in finding Dupin, Madame Laicuzon and the child, but had promptly sent them all to the Rue de l'Hirondelle, with the aid of the Comte de Saint-Germain, and with their evident consent.

Everything, therefore, had eventually worked out as the Mahatma had intended . . . apparently.

But still, the Mahatma must have been very anxious—and rightly so, as things turned out. In coming together, his plan was about to go awry. Anton must have been equally anxious, and rightly so. In coming together, *his* plan was also about to go awry.

Was Dupin equally anxious? Certainly—but his was a different kind of anxiety. He had not had a chance to make a plan in advance; he was improvising, and improvising while woefully short of a full knowledge of the facts—although he might perhaps have guessed one fact that Anton and the Mahatma did not know, which was to prove crucial, if he had not been so intent on thinking so furiously, trying to come up with a plan of his own.

He had not provoked that fact. He would not have done so. He would not only have hesitated to provoke or permit it, guided by his intellect and conscience alike, but he would have prevented it. He was not a fool—but Madame Lacuzon was. She was not foolish in regard to many things; indeed, she was an uncommonly wise woman, but in respect of one matter, she was a perfect fool. In respect of any perceived threat to Dupin, moved by a quasi-maternal instinct, she would not have hesitated for an instant, even to commit murder.

I was not in harmony with her, of course, in the way that I was in harmony with Anton, Dupin and—once she began to sing—with Cthulhu's child. It was only belatedly that I discovered, via the child, what the so-called witch had done. Dupin did not know because she had not told him, and the child did not know, because she did not understand what had been done or why. All I could perceive at the time, even with the aid of the *Necronomicon*, was the effect . . . and at first, I could not perceive anything but the deadly harmony.

Just as I had recognized the music that Anton, Dupin and I—or our instruments—were playing, I recognized the song that the child was singing, in a choir that was distributed in time, but in which her voice was taking the lead, while all the others were merely supportive echoes. I did not understand a word of the incantation, of course, but I recognized it. I recognized it because my flesh, like hers, had been invaded and corrupted by it. It was the *Necronomicon*—or, more accurately, the source text from which the book known as the *Necronomicon* had been crudely transcribed. It was the primal text of the musical mathematics of encryption, the key not merely to R'lyaieh but to all the magical confinements contrived by the Great Old Ones, the ultimate magicians; it was the key to constructing and binding order and, by the same token, the key to deconstructing and unbinding order, and thus releasing chaos.

It was not the Mahatma's intention, of course, to release chaos; nor was it Anton's. They were only interested in reconstructing an existing order slightly, in accordance with their own political ambitions. They knew that they were playing with a lighted fuse above a barrel of black powder, but they thought it worth the risk. People with political ambitions always do; that is inherent in the nature of political ambition, as a species of obsession. It was not Cthulhu's intention either, in seeking its own release from encryption. It, too, was merely seeking an adaptation of the binding order. Cthulhu is not

Nyarlathotep, the so-called Crawling Chaos, and I suspect strongly that even Nyarlathotep is probably misunderstood and misnamed by the ignorant.

Perhaps it is an absurdity even to try to think in terms of Cthulhu's "intentions," just as it would probably be absurd to think in terms of the intentions of the *Necronomicon*, which is only an instrument devoid of a mind of its own . . . but I am not certain about that. After all, Saint-Germain's *monseigneur*, his lockpick, was only an instrument devoid of mentality, but there was a sense in which it had a purpose and an intention built into it at the level of its design. So too did the *Necronomicon* have a design and an intention built into it, intrinsic to its nature. That was not the only factor making it so very dangerous, but it was an important one. And when I entered into a kind of harmony with it, as the child's song revealed the pronunciation of the names that it contained and embodied, I understood— genuinely comprehended—that danger.

Because I had a copy of the *Necronomicon* in my pocket, next to my heart, I understood the child's song—far better, I think, than Dupin, Anton or the Mahatma could have done. I understood it viscerally, not in the vulgar sense that I could construe the meaning of the syllables that she was singing but in the deeper sense that I perceived its esthetics, its sublimity and its authority, at least for the duration of a moment of revelation. I cannot claim to have retained that comprehension, but I know that there was a moment when it seemed to be within my grasp.

I can only explain that sensation by means of metaphor, just as speaking of what transpired as "harmony" is a metaphor. I could say, for instance, that the child's voice and the syllables that it was pronouncing—syllables that no conscious, adult human voice, could have synthesized—penetrated my soul like a dagger or a drill, but it would only be a way of speaking. Was it painful?—yes, in a way. Was it maddening?—yes, certainly. Was it horrifying?—absolutely . . . by which I mean that it seemed the very essence of cosmic horror. But was it mortal?—no.

Perhaps it could have been; perhaps it would have been, had I had intellect enough to make the effort to comprehend it intellectually as well as emotionally. I think, in retrospect, that had Anton or Dupin had the *Necronomicon* over their hearts, the recital might have killed them, or at least driven them mad, but I was a fool, too stupid to feel its import in that way, too stupid even to hesitate over that cosmic horror, to dwell upon it.

Just as I was playing, or being played by, Prospero's violin, instinctively responding to the music of time as if I knew it already, as if it were integrated into the fabric of my being . . . as, in a sense, it must have been . . . I understood the song of Cthulhu's child instinctively, as if the key of the mortal names were already encrypted in the fact of my existence . . . as, in a sense, it must have been.

I heard the variations that Anton and Dupin were striving to incorporate into the music we were playing. I will not say that I understood precisely what they were trying go achieve by means of their reconfiguration of the music, but I had an idea, They were trying, in slightly different ways, to pick the lock of the fundamental encryption of the human mind in such a way as to incline it in the direction of greater intellect and greater creativity, trying to liberate only the tiny aspect of Cthulhu that could stimulate the unconscious part of the human mind and nudge its dreams in what they considered to be a progressive direction.

Could it have worked? In theory, yes it could. Perhaps, in some small measure, it did have an effect; only time will tell. But they were only doing what they could, trying to influence the significance of the musical accompaniment; they were not having any effect on the pronunciation of the song. Had the Mahatma known that they would try to modify his score—and perhaps he did know—he would probably have been anxious, but not unduly panicked. He would have trusted in Cthulhu's child, and the incantations inscribed in her flesh, to further his own intentions regardless. He would have trusted in the *Necronomicon*, and in what he considered to be Fate. And he would probably have been right to do so, if there had not been a fly in his ointment, a spoke in his wheel, a mispronunciation in his litany.

I sensed in the syllables of the child's song everything that it might accomplish; that was the horror, the pain and the penetration; but I also sensed the wrong note, struck when the litany abruptly went awry. I don't believe that the passage, the name or the syllable that was distorted into discordance, was any more crucial than any other. The interference that caused the error was crude and brutal, unguided by any intelligence—but it worked. The song was spoiled by the note that the child's miraculous voice could not reach, the syllable that it could not pronounce—and that error disrupted the entire decryption, scrambling the underlying message.

The child did not stop singing. Dupin, Anton and I did not stop playing. I suspect that Dupin and Anton played even more fervently, trying desperately to complete their own effects . . . but the moment had passed; the harmony was broken, the spell shattered. The garment of reality was reconfigured, but the pattern was flawed. The world did not end, in a crude or in a sophisticated sense, but nor was it reconfigured in any more elegant fashion. Cthulhu remained encrypted, and so did everything else—for the time being.

The echoes through time persist, of course, still capable of disrupting worlds if seized at the right moment and deflected in the right way . . . or the wrong way.

The Mahatma, a great magician by paltry human standards, had obtained intelligence of that wave and its potential, echoing from its future, hundreds of years ago. He had tried more than once to catch it in passing within the thread of subjective time, and he had not been the only mere human to make that attempt. Nor had humans been the only beings to do so—but even entities as potentially powerful as Cthulhu are tiny by comparison with the energy of temporal cycles, tides and waves, let alone the tensile strength of the space-time manifold, and they had only ever succeeded in leeching a little of a particular wave's energy. They had never had more than infinitesimal fraction of the understanding required to achieve more. One day, however . . .

That is not dead which can eternal lie, I thought, as the violin finally completed its part in the symphony, *and with strange eons* . . .

One day, I knew, the syllables of the *Necronomicon* would be sung properly; Cthulhu would be decrypted, and the human world would be utterly transformed. And what then? When all things became possible, how would reality be reconfigured? Where would the power of creative transfiguration reside? Which eternals would seize the initiative of eternity?

More to the point, for the moment, so far as my tiny mind was concerned, what kind of echo would travel back in time from that moment of culmination, potentially graspable in the present, if only in a moment of suspension, by a willing recipient?

Not me, of course—obviously. But that didn't make me a mere bystander. Even great magicians cannot work alone, and the greatest of all are well aware of that. They require support and sustenance, and sounding-boards for their ideas. They require their own creations, as products of resonance, to generate further resonance.

When I had begun to play the violin that Prospero had handed to me so reluctantly, the book, the Mahatma and Cthulhu itself intended that I would collaborate passively in the erasure that would enable Cthulhu, probably without any conscious direction of its own, to overwrite the collective unconsciousness of humankind with its own strange existential impetus. The Mahatma probably did not know, any more than Dupin did, whether the American required by the "prophetic" prescription that he had sensed was a person or a musical instrument, so he had covered both alternatives . . . and perhaps one of the flaws in his plan lay therein.

One way or another, though, I had been a fly in their ointment, a spoke in their wheel; and no matter what lay next to my heart in the pages of the fatal book, what I already had within my heart, within my soul, was something different, something stubbornly bloody-minded.

When I played, completing the quintet not merely from outside the mansard of the witch-house in the Rue de l'Hirondelle but from outside the confines of reality, I was still capable of blundering. I was capable of harmonizing and collaborating with Anton and Dupin, but I was also capable of collaborating with the child. Alone, I would have been impotent, but I was not alone, and I was sensitive. I heard the false syllable that was intruded into the concert by her error, and by virtue of hearing it, by sympathizing with it, by feeling it, I echoed it and amplified it. Not only did I hear her, but she felt my reaction, and felt it as an amplification of her own action; there was an instant of positive feedback, felt not merely in the moment of the present, but throughout the resonances extending through space and time, up, down, sideways, forwards and backwards. Had my reaction been in tune with the Mahatma's score, it would have been lost, or at least insignificant, but it was not. It was discordant. It stuck out, as the vulgar saying has it, like a sore thumb.

I had not known that I had that faculty of amplification, that sensitivity to error. It was not a conscious ability, merely a passive reaction independent of any intention, an aspect of my sensitivity. Dupin was aware that I had it, but not so conscious of it that he understood exactly what it was or what potential it had. It was the basis of our friendship, of my unique status among his acquaintances, but if he had been asked to explain it, he would only have been able to do so in terms of feeling comfortable in my presence and in conversation with me, of sensing that I was a useful reflective "sounding-board."

Other people had sensed that too, with even less comprehension. I could cite other examples, but the only one of any real significance was the fact that Jana Valdemar, a magnetizer at the height of her own sensitivity, had made her confession to me on the eve of All Saints' Day, before our strange excursion to the forest of Fontainebleau. I had sympathized with her, to the extent of anticipating what she was going to do, and I really had trued to save her. She knew that. But my intention—my hope—had not had the effect that I would have wished. My reflective presence had, in fact, amplified her momentary obsession, intensified the determination of her despair.

There was a sense in which Addhema had not been lying when she told me that I had caused Jana Valdemar to commit suicide. Without my innocent reflection of her anxieties, perhaps Chapelain, or someone else, might have been able to soothe them. But she had not made her confession to them; she had made her confession to me, perhaps an eternal bystander but not devoid of effect in my bystanding. Had she, in fact, mesmerized herself with her own dread by virtue of sensing its reflection in me? Perhaps she had; I suspect that is something that we all do, at times, with or without the aid of a sounding-board . . . but there was also a sense in which Lucien Groix's simpler account had been perfectly correct: that she really had committed suicide, because she knew what fate awaited in Parisian society an unmarried woman who gave birth, deserted and disowned by the father of her child. In any case, the fact that she was now able to haunt me, in the sparse moments propitious for such haunting, was a lingering aftereffect of a bond that neither of us had intended or wanted to form, but which had formed anyhow.

The bond that had formed between myself and Cthulhu's child had also been unintended, by her, by me or by anyone else. It had formed of its own accord, because I was part of her accompaniment, all the more intense because it was taking effect through a portal, across the limits of the material world. The contact between us had been brief, but she had had a version of the *Necronomicon* in her flesh and I had a version of it next to my heart. Her mispronunciation of one of the syllables might have been sufficient to subvert the spell in isolation, but it was not isolated, and its echo in me, and throughout time and space, was akin to a scream.

A scream is a reflexive reaction, the quintessence of panic and of phobia. It is not the natural reaction to the mispronunciation of a name, which is more likely, in normal circumstances, to provoke a laugh—but the name that the Child of Ocean mispronounced was a true name, a name of power, whose connection with the thing it named was more intimate and more significant than the arbitrary representation of an object by a group of utterable sounds. The names of the child's evocation were vibrations that she had to sense and reproduce, and to amplify in the reproduction, by means of a sensibility analogous to mine . . . and I have to presume that my own sensibility enhanced my own perception of her song.

That accidental sensibility enhanced my oblique insight into her nature and identity, but it also enhanced my oblique insight into the nature and identity of the being with which she had entered into magical communion during her sojourn on the isle that the insensitive Captain Cook had dubbed Booby Island, the significance of its symbolic rock art being quite opaque to "enlightened" European eyes. It provided me with a glimpse—only a glimpse—of the entity dubbed "Cthulhu" by voices almost as insensitive as Captain Cook's. And that is what provoked the reflexive scream, because that incomprehensible glimpse seemed to be the quintessence of a particular species of horror.

I admit, frankly, that I am ashamed of that reaction. I am, after all, Auguste Dupin's friend and Jeremiah Reynolds' cousin. I had heard both of them commenting on the possible nature of Cthulhu. I also had personal experience of other strange and alien songs, most significantly the song of the flameflower I had heard in the bowels of Mont Dragon. I had an intellectual apparatus that could and should have allowed me to react in a different way to the glimpse of Cthulhu that I obtained via the child's song and the child's possession. But in the crucial moment, I could not do it.

The scream was not mine alone; it was a scream in chorus, echoing through space and time, the summary reaction of many human minds and voices; but it was my scream too. Dupin was there, playing his own part in the concert, but he did not have my sensibility, the intimacy of my relationship with the singer and the song; whatever glimpse he obtained of Cthulhu was more distant, more detached—not as distant as the echo that Cousin Jeremiah heard while merely bearing witness, but still detached. I was the privileged seer, the one with the opportunity to grasp a modicum of understanding—and I failed.

All I produced, in my reaction to the mispronunciation, was an echo of a scream: the scream that shattered the Mahatma's long-brooded but brittle scheme and put an end to the spell that held the Rue de l'Hirondelle and all its inhabitants in thrall.

There is a sense, I suspect, in which that mispronunciation might have saved the world from the transfiguration that the evocation was intended to bring about, albeit by means of an imported incoherency that could not work entirely to the world's advantage. I cannot get the idea out of my mind that the spoiled symphony must still have had an effect on the weave of perceived reality, albeit one that none of the planners involved intended. More than one of them—the Mahatma certainly, Anton possibly and perhaps even Dupin—must have thought that in spoiling the symphony, the child and I had spoiled the world as they would have liked to repaint it, and marred it even in its existing, unsatisfactory condition . . . but even if that had been, in a strictly literal sense, *our fault*, it was not something for which we could be held accountable. She, after all, was just a child, and I was just a fool.

But I, for one—perhaps the only one—do not regret what I did while I was in my capsule of nowhere and nowhen. I regret what had happened in my study and thereafter when I failed to save the life of Jana Valdemar and her unborn child, but I don't regret what happened when my sounding-board intensified the Child of Ocean's bum note. I rushed in where no angel would have dared to tread, and merely screamed when a calmer and more disciplined mind might have been able to make precious observations, and I'm ashamed of that dereliction of intellectual duty, but I'm not sorry.

And whatever argument anyone might put to me, I won't ever be sorry.

I wish I could say that nobody died as a result of that tiny catastrophe, and I suppose I have to admit that it was partly my fault that two people did die, but I'm not sorry that it turned out that way. I'm glad, in fact, that the Mahatma was one of the two. So far as I know, Addhema simply returned to the darkness from which she had emerged, and Angria took his ghost ship back down the river, all the way to Honfleur and the Ocean beyond, with his ghostly crew still intact and still capable, at propitious moments, of further acts of modest piracy, but they couldn't die, because they were already dead; the Mahatma had been alive, and he collapsed and died in the room on the first floor of the house in the Rue de l'Hirondelle.

There was some controversy after the fact, I believe, regarding the cause of his death—not to mention his identity—but I'm not in any doubt personally. Some might say that his spell, having failed to achieve its objective of massacre and liberation, had rebounded upon him as violent spells are reputed to do, so that he died of thwarted obsession. Almost all immortals, I had been told by a source that might or might not be reliable, fall prey to obsession and are consumed by it, to the point that there is nothing left of them but obsession: a vulnerable condition, and one more reason why so-called immortals are not immortal at all, but merely living in a hiatus of suspension, becalmed or marooned in death's waiting-room. Personally, though, I believe that he died of the effects of cold. No matter what uncanny powers of resistance his body had, and no matter what kind of fakir pride he had, it simply is not possible for a man to walk the streets of Paris in a winter like that of 1848 in flimsy sandals. His arrogance betrayed his immortality. He could not keep the literal chill of death at bay indefinitely.

All sorts of similarly trivial questions remained unanswered, of course, and undoubtedly preoccupied Dupin for months after that fateful night. Some of them even preoccupied me, in the moments of our earnest discussions, but not overmuch. I like to think that I can retain a sense of proportion regarding such matters, relegating trivia to the true measure of their triviality.

Did it make a difference, I have sometimes wondered, that Prospero's violin was accustomed to playing echoes of Will Maccabee's dance of the dead and Abbé Appollonius' improvised harmonies of hell, as well as Prospero's own scholarly compositions? For what it may be worth, I think it did, just as it made a difference that the dulcimer that Meg had given Dupin had been similarly practiced and possessed. The Mahatma, if he had thought about that, undoubtedly considered that mechanical memory to be an advantage, a pair of aces in his own hand, but in fact, it was to Dupin and Anton that the instruments lent their collaboration, and to Dupin and Anton's variant compositions.

My own part was entirely secondary, an echo of an echo, but it had to be my hands that supplied it, in collaboration with Prospero's violin, just as it had to be the little girl who had sojourned on Booby Island—Cthulhu's child—who supplied the vocal accompaniment. The girl, unlike me, was not untrained and unpracticed in the use of her voice, but all her training and practice came to naught in the end. Amélie Lacuzon had very little magic, by comparison with the Mahatma, and she had only been with the child for a matter of hours, but she had had time enough to do what she needed to do, and—more importantly—a furious determination to do something to preserve her own child, as she considered him to be, from the threat that she felt was suspended over his head. She could not read the *Necronomicon* inscribed in the child's flesh, but she could sense what it was, and although she could not oppose it with magic, she had another means at her disposal. Anyone else in her place would probably have hesitated to employ it, but not her. She acted entirely on her own, because she knew that if she had told Dupin what she intended to do, he would have forbidden it.

Her death, too, was controversial as to its cause. She didn't drop dead as soon as she had committed her crime, and when she began to sicken while Dupin was trying to return her to my house in Saint-Germain's carriage, he did not attribute her debility immediately to the failure of the Mahatma's spell, because he did not know, at that point, what she had done—she did not make him any confession—and she had been through tribulations enough in recent months for there not to be any cause for astonishment that she might have been overtaxed by it all. But I knew, because I had been in harmony with the child, and although I did not fear that the child might tell Dupin, or that he might interrogate her with sufficient intensity to make the discovery, I decided, after a time—even I am capable of hesitation when the occasion seems to warrant it—that he was entitled to know.

I thought he would understand, whether he approved or not, and he did.

Madame Lacuzon had taken the Child of Ocean away from my house because, like the Breton sailor aboard the *Excelsior*, she had immediately recognized a few terms in her incoherent jabber that seemed to be poorly-pronounced names—specifically, terms that reminded her forcefully of our confrontation with Oberon Breiz. That had led her to make the investigation that enabled her to sense the secret hidden and embodied in the child's flesh. She already mistrusted Saint-Germain, and when the other magician had turned up at the door, she had thought it a matter of the utmost urgency to get the girl to Dupin as soon as possible.

To that end, she had immediately set off for the Louvre, but she had been followed as soon as she left the house by more than one of the men set to keep watch on it, and had thought it wise to take evasive action. When she realized that the bravo was on her track as well as a police spy and an agent of the Holy Office, she hid, in a place where Dupin was bound eventually to come in search of her. She had already cast protective spells on the quilted jackets that a seamstress of her acquaintance—an associate of the so-called Sorority—had made for Dupin and me, and she had cast a similar one on her own coats, one of which Madame Bihan had given to the little girl to replace the ill-fitting pea-jacket that Jacob Pym had given her. The spell was elementary, and not very powerful, but Madame Lacuzon thought that it would help to keep the girl safe from occult investigation until she could make contact with Dupin.

At first, she had tried to employ the delay she had obtained in assisting the girl to communicate, having discovered that her larynx was magically enhanced and her hearing especially acute, but as soon as she realized that those abilities might be employed in an evocation of the *Necronomicon*, remembering the danger that Dupin had been in when the shoggoths had materialized in Paris and in Brittany—a danger that he had only just contrived to avert in the nick of time—she made up her mind, and decided to strangle the child. She did not even hesitate over the decision to murder an innocent child, who could not know what kind of infection she was carrying.

Unfortunately, or fortunately, the action was not so easy to perform. Although the old woman was strong, for her age, and the child was weak, the *Necronomicon* was also in play, and equipped with an instinct of protection. It resisted the strangulation, successfully . . . and Madame Lacuzon was forced to abandon her attempt, which she was unable to renew by a different means because Dupin arrived, thinking mistakenly that he had shaken off all of his followers.

The girl did not understand what had happened, let alone why, and had misconstrued the grip on her throat as a game of some sort, a tease. She did not think that it had done her any permanent harm, and in simple terms of injuring her respiration, it had not—but the pressure the old woman had exerted, although slighter than she had intended and swiftly interrupted, had deformed the larynx slightly. In any other individual, that slight torsion would have had no perceptible effect, but the capacity the girl's vocal cords had to produce the sounds necessary to the evocation was already stretched to the limit. The apparatus was too delicate, and Madame Lacuzon's clumsy hands, even opposed by the force of the *Necronomicon*, were a fraction too brutal. And in the course of the subsequent evocation, the girl had choked momentarily—only momentarily, but sufficiently, given the amplification provided by my sensitivity—and her voice had "broken," as voices sometimes do . . . routinely, in their natural development, at the onset of puberty, and not only in male children.

Sometimes, I tell myself that it might have happened anyway, that the child was a flawed instrument, by virtue of her heredity—but I can't bring myself to believe that. I believe that Madame Lacuzon did enough, when she attempted to murder the child—only just enough, but enough—to hurt her . . . and, incidentally, to prolong her own precarious existence by a few more hours. And I'm not sorry.

I suspect—I hope—that the child will never sing again, with or without the aid of the *Necronomicon* in her flesh and the future tutelage that she will certainly receive, but I'm certainly not sorry about that. In fact, I'm glad. And I think that Amélie Lacuzon would have been glad too, even had she known for certain that her attempt would cost her life. She had not given birth to Dupin, but she had become his nurse, his surrogate mother—or his true mother, in her own estimation—and she would have made any sacrifice to protect him from a perceived threat.

Perhaps she was a fool, but I, for one, am not going to hold that against her memory.

XVIII

THE MUSIC OF TIME

I cannot describe the music that we played on our enchanted instruments or the incantation that the Child of Ocean sang. The words available in my vocabulary are not adequate to the task. Those who heard it at close range—the people that the Mahatma had assembled to "bear witness"—all agreed that it was remarkable, but they could not describe it in any but the most impressionistic terms, and they differed markedly in their appreciation of it.

Prospero opined that it was disappointing, albeit technically accomplished, while Meg, his housekeeper, simply declared that she had not paid any heed to it; they both reclaimed the instruments they had lent to the performance, without any objection being raised and without any difficulty; I had been released into Parisian space-time as soon as I had played the final chord. Prospero opined that, in his prime, he could have done "much better"—by which he meant that, in spite of the spoliation of the chorus, he could have attained some kind of rapport with Cthulhu, which would have granted him an invaluable insight into the nature of that peculiar entity, and greatly enhanced his theoretical understanding of the cryptography of music.

The reincarnate Comte de Saint-Germain said that he did not dislike the music, but that he had heard better at the

Conservatoire, let alone the Opéra. He was not in the least ashamed of having made a belated bargain with the Mahatma, and did not regard that decision as treason. Like Prospero, he represented his actions as a matter of scholarly research, with the additional excuse of diplomatic necessity. His former self, he claimed confidently, would have done exactly the same thing, I believed him. Reincarnation is rumored to offer unlimited opportunities for reform and redemption, but cynics would doubtless argue that once a charlatan, eternally a charlatan.

Paul Lacroix approved of the innovative qualities of the music and the song, but said that he found the overall effect more than a little incoherent and also a trifle distressing. Ever a professional critic, he opined that it was not the kind of performance that could ever become popular, although it would undoubtedly appeal to a small number of esoteric esthetes. He refused to believe that Addhema had been a vampire, or a ghost, insisting that she must simply have been a prostitute hired by the Mahatma for the purposes of his imposture. He also insisted that I had been magnetized by "the fakir" and subjected to induced hallucinations—to which, in his opinion, I was especially prone because of my colorful imagination and my "impressionability." He did not go as far as to stating baldly that I was a weak-minded fool, but I did not need any magical rapport to know which way his thinking was tending.

Lucien Groix opined that the music was rather unpleasant, and that it would have required a choreographer of genius to design a ballet to fit it, which even Marie Taglioni would have been unable to perform. Like Lacroix—but with less excuse, in my opinion—he tried hard to rationalize everything that had happened, insisting that the shot he had fired at the Mahatma has simply missed and that the misdirected one his sergeant had fired had only failed to kill me because I happened to have a book in my pocket, which had absorbed and distributed the force of the impact. He had the mind of a policeman, ready to accept any improbability, however absurd, rather than admit what his pig-headed conscious mind dismissed out of hand as an impossibility.

Sergeant Bernard said that he preferred livelier music and more melodic folderols.

The cousins Pym could not agree with one another. Arthur declared the music to be a work of genius, undoubtedly magical in its inspiration and its potential effects, and probably capable of evoking Cthulhu if played more competently—for which reason he was glad of the mistakes that had been made in its execution. Jacob, by contrast, dismissed it as unmelodic rubbish, and flatly denied that he had been possessed or hypnotized when he had drawn his gun, insisting that he had only done so in defense of my liberty of action, like a good American. He opined that the Child of Ocean might make a satisfactory music hall performer when she was a little older, with better material and the aid of a competent vocal coach.

I did not have an opportunity to solicit opinions from Angria or Addhema, who disappeared into the nocturnal mist along with Anton, presumably dissatisfied by the lack of an evident Apocalypse. I only regretted not being able to hear Anton's opinion at length, although Dupin was far more regretful, thinking—correctly—that Anton could have told him a great many things of interest, being not merely immortal but someone capable of possession by the beings that Blaise Thibodeaux called "eternals"—superhuman products of the far future. I think I understand, though, why such individuals are even more given to obsessive secrecy than humbler immortals and magicians.

Cousin Jeremiah told me that he did not like the symphony at all, and that it jarred his nerves, but that it clearly had the capacity to induce interesting hallucinations which might offer interesting insights into the nature of the universe, if they could be properly decoded. He explained that it had been obvious to him that I was hallucinated, and that he had tried to prevent me from going into the witch-house because her feared for my sanity, knowing that—unlike him—I did not have a scientific mind or any great strength of character. Unsurprisingly, he spoke at far greater length than anyone else about what he had learned—or thought he had learned—while "bearing witness" to what he insisted on calling the Mahatma's experiment. He pontificated about it a great length, in a competitive spirit, partly because he was stimulated by the presence of his own sounding-board, Arthur Pym, and partly because he wanted to impress Dupin—which I think he succeeded in doing, although Dupin was not a man to admit such a thing, and insisted as ever, in reserving his own judgment.

"As I told you before," Jeremiah said, "the inhabitants of the world within the hollows beneath the Earth's surface, products of an evolutionary sequence quite distinct from the one that produced and shaped life on the surface, include creatures possessed of consciousness and intelligence, who communicate routinely by means of sonic vibrations, although they are probably also sensitive to other kinds of vibrations, to which humans are normally insensitive. They are aware of the existence of surface organisms, and have undoubtedly attempted to make contact with them, by means of vibrations that can occasionally be perceived as strange sounds and exotic music, but are more often only perceived subconsciously. Those vibrations can and do provoke hallucinations, but the art of shaping and guiding those hallucinations will take a long time—a very long time—for the transmitting and receiving minds to master.

"It would be a mistake, I think, to describe the most intelligent inhabitants of the underworld as 'cephalopods,' but they probably do have a certain physical analogy with the surface species for which we employ that term. In saying that they are the most intelligent underworld species I do not intend to decry the very different creatures that some surface folklore calls flameflowers, but if one looks at the lore of human legendry with a discerning skeptical eye, it is the species that bear some physical resemblance to cephalopods or hydras, possessed of prehensile 'tentacles,' that have clearly made the most assiduous efforts to establish communication with the minds of surface species.

"Unfortunately, human minds are as yet too primitive to react to those attempts in any reasonable fashion; their instinctive reaction is one of horror and terror: a reflexive scream and recoil. Minds capable of reacting in a more rational fashion are, as yet, rare. In future, they will doubtless become more numerous and more competent, but I fear that progress will be slow."

"With strange eons, though . . ." I hazarded.

"Indeed," he said. "Even the mindless recitation of mantras like that might eventually make some contribution to the furtherance of a rational attitude. Even screams of horror, repeated sufficiently, might eventually evolve into something more contemplative and more constructive. Over time, the reflexive recoil can be suppressed, and the experience of contact with strange vibrations can become a source of intelligent fascination. People sensitive to such vibrations might, and should, in the fullness of time, begin to decrypt the communications they receive from the minds of the Underworld. One day, it will be possible for a few of us to look entities like the one we call Cthulhu in the face, so to speak, and see them as they really are."

"But before then," I suggested, "a great many of us might simply go mad, especially if they actually make the effort to aid in that decryption."

"Undoubtedly," Jeremih agreed. "That is the price of progress. The improvement of species, physically and mentally, is a process of winnowing. Life requires an abundance of death, in order that the most capable can prove their worth. We ought to regard horror and terror as necessary tests of endurance for the armor of intellect and the defensive strength of consciousness."

I did not argue with him; I resigned that duty to Arthur Pym, and left Dupin to referee the contest, until the two of them left France, Arthur bound for the South Seas, like his cousin Jacob, and Jeremiah for America. Neither of them lingered for long in Paris, considering it, for the time being, to be an exceedingly hostile environment. In fairness to Jeremiah, however, he was the only member of our strange company not merely willing but eager to take responsibility for the Child of Ocean. He wanted to subject her sensibility and her voice to scrupulous scientific investigation, and to track their development as she grew older.

Nobody opposed his desire to take her with him to America. I was presumably not the only one who had qualms about condemning the poor waif to life as an experimental guinea-pig, but Dupin pointed out, very reasonably, that it would guarantee that she would always be fed, treasured and pampered, as well as given a assiduous education—and what chance would she have had of achieving that in any other custody?

"As forms of exploitation go," he opined, "it is certainly preferable to slavery and prostitution, and perhaps to marriage. Would you rather she fall into the thrall of a magician like Edward England, and suffer the fate of Ysolde Leonys?"

He did not cite the example of Jana Valdemar, who had eventually fallen into the relatively benign charge of the magnetizer Pierre Chapelain, but I cited it to myself, and had no hesitation thereafter in condoning Jeremiah's appropriation of his "subject."

The parting of our various ways was, in fact, accomplished without any evident drama. When Jeremiah and the Pyms set forth for Le Havre in something of a hurry, joining a more general exodus from Paris precipitated by the inevitability of the Revolution and fears of a cholera epidemic, Lucien Groix thought it diplomatic to follow their example, presumably going to rejoin his family in his natal province.

Prospero and Meg, on the other hand, decided to stick out the time of turbulence on the Île Saint-Louis—unwisely, I thought, and as it eventually turned out; they both died in the Val-de-Grâce of cholera and were buried, probably together, in a mass grave. I never found out what happened thereafter to Prospero's instruments, although I suspect that Saint-Germain might have obtained possession of them somehow, ostensibly on behalf of the Harmonic Society.

Lacroix, inevitably, joined the Republicans directing the barricades. So did Saint-Germain, once he was certain which way the wind was blowing, initially pretending to be a staunch supporter of Lamartine—a claim that the poet and presidential candidate refrained diplomatically from denying—but soon nailing his colors to the Bonapartist mast instead.

Sergeant Bertrand was killed, but whether he was attacking a barricade at the time or defending one I never discovered.

Oddly enough, it transpired in the course of our numerous brief conversations that no one had noticed my temporary absence from the world. When I fell back through the portal into the corridor of the witch-house, the general assumption of those down below was that I was returning from upstairs, while those who came downstairs apparently assumed that I had been there all along. I told Dupin what had happened, in full detail, but I think he simply assumed that I had been hallucinated and direly confused; given that the suspicion had been voiced even within the hallucination, I was in no position to defend my own convictions, and did not press my case very insistently. He did not deny what I told him about the child's history and Madam Lacuzon's attempted murder, but I suspect that he considered it secretly as mere delusion . . . and who could blame him for that?

At any rate, Dupin and I hunkered down again, in company with the Bihans. We had a hard time, but we did not starve and we were not arrested or attacked. I replaced the *Necronomicon* on my bookshelves, next to the *Resonances du Temps*. It is still there, but I have never opened it. Nor, so far as I know, has Dupin.

The Revolution swept through Paris swiftly, and took its course, which is too well-known to require description here. Dupin refrained from claiming that the symphony in the Rue de l'Hirondelle had any effect on that remarkable course, which quickly seemed to have been inevitable. "It was the inertia of history," he opined. "The people made their choice in a free election, and suffered the consequences of their poor judgment. There was no compulsion of any sort involved. Even Lacroix admits that, in spite of his dire disappointment."

"So," I said, "all that was achieved, by means of Anton's subversion, your improvisation and Madame Lacuzon's hasty action," I judged, when we had time to discuss the unfolding situation, "was a nullification of the harm that the Mahatma intended to do. All that the sum of your efforts produced was a massive anti-climax."

"All that *our* efforts achieved," he corrected me. "You might have played your part unwittingly, stumbling around in your usual blind and confused fashion, but you were an intrinsic part of the weave. And let us not be too modest in laying claim to the anti-climax. Saint-Germain and Prospero will never agree with me, but at the very least, we surely reduced the scope of the catastrophe. Things could have been a great deal worse, believe me."

"They might yet become a great deal worse," I observed, at the time. "Food is still in direly short supply in the city, and the various epidemics that are rife here have not yet peaked."

"That is not Cthulhu's doing," said Dupin. "If the people and the politicians had only listened to Raspail and his colleagues, the worst of the epidemics could have been averted. His prophecies had a far saner basis than the lunatic dreams of the Convulsionnaires and other victims of bad bread, but no action was taken. No one was ready to listen to reason. A day will come, though—perhaps not soon, but it will come . . ."

"Because of what we did?"

"No, because sanity and sanitation are bound to win in the end, no matter how stubborn the fight against science and sewerage turns out to be. That is the tide of history, which flows fundamentally in the direction of enlightenment in spite of all its crazy fluctuations. All we could ever do was to attempt to harmonize our own actions with that underlying march, but that is what we did; we played our part, to the extent of our ability. If it was an anticlimactic part, so be it; there is much to be said for mild anti-climax, no matter what Romantics might think. There is sometimes scant virtue in quietude, but there is none at all in wanton destruction."

Such was always his philosophy, and that was evident enough in the explanations he gave me of his conduct during the confusing prologue of our adventure. When he had quit the Harmonic Society's headquarters, after a brief interview with Jacob Pym, being anxious about my disappearance, he had rapidly contrived to elude the agents of the Sûreté and the Holy Office set to watch him, but not the Mahatma's Thugs and phantom servants. He had guessed correctly where Madame Lacuzon was hiding, but he had led the Thugs and the ghost pirates to her hiding-place. Unable to mount any effective physical resistance, he had allowed Saint-Germain's carriage, already on the way to the rendezvous in the Rue de l'Hirondelle, to collect the two of them, and had bided his time, assuming that he might yet have an opportunity to employ his esoteric knowledge to deflect the Mahatma's scheme. When he saw me with Prospero's violin, even before he saw Bertrand's shot hit me without killing me, he knew what he had to attempt, and was hopeful that he could outwit the magnetic influence of the Mahatma and the lamia, so he had pretended to play along.

He has always refrained from saying so explicitly, but I am convinced that he believes that I simply played the symphony where I stood, in the corridor of the witch-house. I suppose it is conceivable that I did, but I will never believe it. I know what really happened. Had I elected to rid myself of the *Necronomicon*, as the Dweller with the Eyes of Fire demanded, I suppose things might have worked out differently, but because I hung on to it, Cthulhu and its minions were able to secure the performance of the symphony composed by the Mahatma—and also the subversive symphonies composed by Anton and Dupin, until the choral part of the litany went awry.

There is a sense in which the treacherous book was only thwarted by its failure completely to neutralize Madame Lacuzon's attempted strangulation, but I ought not to minimize the part that Dupin played, even in the haste of his improvisation. Naturally, he explained to me at length what he had tried to do, the reasoning behind it, and the esoteric knowledge that he had, unknown to Cthulhu's agents.

When Prospero and his housekeeper had handed over the precious instruments to Dupin and me, the Mahatma and Prospero had both assumed that it was a straightforward matter of substituting one antiquarian student of exotic music, one dabbler in hellish harmonies, for another. The Mahatma and Prospero probably knew, or at least suspected, that Dupin had been a consenting instrument before, when he had played Erich Zann's violin in the house in the Rue d'Auseuil—and even if they suspected that the collapse of that house had not been an accident, they had automatically attributed it to an effect of the Crawling Chaos rather than Dupin's playing. They certainly knew that I had been an obliging puppet of the egregore at Du Potet's garden party. They had no reason to suspect, therefore, that Dupin and I would not play our parts—but Dupin had seen the situation quite differently.

Neither I nor Dupin ever had an opportunity to discuss philosophical matters with the Mahatma, so we were never able to obtain an explanation of exactly what he thought he was doing or why. Dupin told me that he regretted that, because he would have liked to discover what the magician understood by the concept of Maya, so fundamental to Hindu religious thought, promiscuously translated into English as illusion, appearance, power or the principle that conceals and disguises what really exists. As a simple man, I make no attempt to grapple with such subtleties, contenting myself with agreeing with the judgment that the world as human consciousness interprets it is, if not actually deceptive, at least oversimplified, and that, in order to render it graspable, human imagination imposes on "reality" a rigidity and a permanence that it does not really possess. Dupin, who was not a simple man, and had delved into the matter more profoundly, had an approximate notion of what the Mahatma must believe, especially the belief that by means of magic, the perceived reality of the world can be shifted, that there are entities that have the power to shift it, and that those entities are manipulable, to some extent, albeit uncertainly—even somewhat treacherously—by human beings, via the mechanisms of music and incantation; or, more accurately, by musical and incantatory resonance.

"He and his coreligionists are not alone in that, of course," Dupin reminded me. "In Europe, famously, Pythagoras observed the connection between musical resonance and mathematics, and jumped to the conclusion that if that relationship could be fully understood, the universe would become comprehensible. He might have been right, but it soon turned out that music and mathematics were both far more complicated, and far more mysterious, than he had initially assumed, or hoped. While the followers of Hinduism and Buddhism followed their own mystical paths in search of the heart of wisdom, the followers of Pythagoras and their descendants followed the path of mathematics and measurement toward more material rewards . . . but without ever reducing the fundamental mysteries to calculability. I cannot claim to have solved the problems involved, but at least I have a more sophisticated understanding than Pythagoras or the Mahatma of what they are, and that gave me confidence that I could modify the new reality that the Mahatma was striving to create, by modifying the music he had composed for that purpose. I knew that it would require an enormous intellectual effort, but I had attempted something similar before, with a measure of success, so I attempted it again. Perhaps I did not make any great difference . . . but how can I tell?"

How, indeed? I was, and am, in no position to dispute the issue with him. Perhaps he did have an effect, in the brief interval before the evocation of the *Necronomicon* was spoiled. Perhaps Anton and his far-futuristic possessor, the mysterious eternal, had an effect too, during that same interval. How can I tell? All I can do is speculate, probably foolishly.

Auguste Dupin, a human calculating machine if ever there was one, never attained the perfect wisdom at which he aimed his life's endeavor. By the time I met him, in fact, he already knew that his goal was far out of reach, and that no matter how hard he tried, he would never reach it—but he was not a man to despair. He knew that he could, at least, hope to get a little bit closer than all the predecessors on whose giant intellectual shoulders he could stand. He could not read all the books that already existed, and were still being written, but he could read as many as he could obtain, and try to make sense of their sum, insofar as there was sense therein to be made, in order that he might increase that sum a little further. He has always intended to write his own book, once he has done sufficient research, even though he is well aware of the fact that most of his predecessors had suffered the same fate as Blaise Thibodeaux, falling prey to old age, disease and dementia before completing their projects.

And he had also learned to play the violin.

He had never allowed that to become a vocation, let alone an obsession, partly because he knew what dangers lay in that direction. He had known Erich Zann and he had met the antiquarian who called himself Doctor Prospero, so he was familiar with the hazards of obsession, but he did not need such examples to warn him of the danger. He had learned to play with a reasonable degree of skill, enough to obtain a first hand appreciation of the magic, mystery and mathematics of music, but he had been careful to keep that magic and those mysteries, at a respectful mental distance, and he had never been able to solve the relevant mathematical equations.

He had also observed and taken note of the limitations of the kind of musical understanding that Prospero had, and the hazards of the kind of understanding that Erich Zann had. He knew, as almost everyone does, that there is a world of difference between simply learning to play musical notes correctly in a defined order and obtaining a real feel for and sensitivity to the music that they signify. He knew that the kind of scholarly fascination and expertise that Prospero possessed and pursued could sometimes be a barrier to an appreciation of the emotional resonances that the music was supposed to produce in its player and its hearers.

Prospero was a great scholar of music, and a technically competent performer, but he was not a great composer, no matter what judgment Paul Lacroix and Blaise Thibodeaux had made of the ballet music he had once composed for the Théâtre Moineaux before its destruction by fire. Erich Zann, on the other hand, had been a composer of great intelligence and originality—and because of that, paradoxical as it might seem—he had been unusually sensitive to resonances in space and time that the vast majority of his contemporaries could not perceive or appreciate: what he thought of, like many others, as the provision of his "Muse."

Auguste Dupin had not been a great performer, technically speaking. As a violinist he was not outstanding, merely average at best—but he did have an appreciative ear . . . appreciative, at least, to aspects of music to which many people are insensitive or inattentive. He understood the music of Erich Zann better than the vast majority of its hearers, perhaps better than Zann himself, and he understood the dangers within it, the extent to which it could function as a curse and a decryption. He understood how dangerous it might become when played by someone with the technical expertise of a musician like Prospero. So he had destroyed the scores that Zann had left behind, even while sympathizing to some extent with Prospero's judgment that it was an act of vandalism. Perhaps it had also been an act of vandalism for him to attempt to vary Zann's composition when he was blackmailed into playing it in the Rue d'Auseuil, and he admitted frankly that his variation might have been sadly inept, and might not have had the effect he intended on the irruption of the Crawling Chaos. One way or another, however, that irruption had been rechanneled in a fashion that the blackmailer had not intended or wished. The house had collapsed, and the possessed violin had been crushed.

Dupin was not at all sure, when the instrument was handed to him by Meg, that he would be able to do any more with the dulcimer, an instrument that he had not learned to play, but he thought he had a reasonable chance of achieving a similar disruption, an intrusion of disharmony if not an irruption of chaos. And he thought that he had understanding and sensitivity enough, once he got into the swing of the symphony, to be a little more creative than merely producing arbitrary noise.

"My problem," he told me, when he had had time to organize his thoughts, "was that I had no more idea than anyone else of what Cthulhu actually *is*. Some scholars interested in the problem, like your cousin Jeremiah, have managed to draw confident conclusions as to what it is not, and have become confident that it is not a kind of Devil, or anything that can be accommodated within any orthodox theological context—an important step away from the naïve assumption that it is simply an incarnation of evil, but only a small step—but that only gets us a little closer to the necessary comprehension. All his talk about the pseudocephalopods of the Underworld is pure speculation . . . but I can hardly deny its plausibility, having actually sung with a flameflower myself . . . an experience which greatly boosted my confidence that I might be able to intrude constructively in the music of the Mahatma's symphony.

"Contact with Cthulhu, even distantly, in the arena of dreams, has harmed a great many people, as we cannot doubt; inept attempts to comprehend or command it with the aid of the *Necronomicon* have too often proved fatal, with horrible results. It is surely a mistake, however, to assume that those effects reflect an intention on its part to do harm, and I have a certain sympathy with those scholars who, like Jeremiah, assume that if its latent power to affect the human collective unconscious can do harm, it might also be potentially beneficial, with the right guidance.

"You have heard me quote François Raspail's analysis of the logical consequences of his microbial theory of disease: that although microbes provoking nasty diseases are bound to be more obvious to our interested perception than those which do no harm or are beneficial, the latter must, in fact, be in the majority, because it is in their interests not to damage their hosts and even to promote their wellbeing, if possible. Well, the same argument applies to macrobes, if I might coin that term. It cannot be in their interest to wipe out their fellow beings, and might well be in their interest to preserve and protect them."

I was not entirely convinced by that argument, being easily able to see a relationship of dependency between hypothetical microbes and their hosts, but not between vaster entities and tiny commensals, but Dupin was adamant.

"Collaboration and mutual aid might not be easy of achievement by radically different organisms—it is difficult enough even among individuals of the same species, as our political struggles clearly demonstrate—but it nevertheless remains an ideal, productive of rewards if it can be achieved, and in order to be achieved, we need to understand what it is that we're dealing with. Among many other things, we need to understand what the Great Old Ones are, in order that we might collaborate in their endeavors, to the extent that we can."

Still unconvinced, I said: "But we need to understand cholera in order to wipe it out, not in order to learn to live with it and assist it in its projects. We need to understand entities like Cthulhu for the same reason: if not to destroy it, at least to hamper and thwart its operations. Isn't that exactly what you tried to do, with the aid of the dulcimer?"

"No, it isn't," he said. "What I tried to do, when I joined in with the Mahatma's symphony, was to employ the music beneficially. To judge by what you have told me, Anton was trying to do the same. In fact, even the Mahatma was probably trying to do that, albeit with a very different notion of the beneficial—which is another reason why I regret not having had the opportunity to discuss matters of philosophy with him.

"I was certainly trying to prevent the Mahatma's magic from unlocking the door of R'lyaieh *now*, but my ultimate ambition extended beyond that. I was composing intuitively, playing an unfamiliar instrument *by ear*, as they say, and perhaps ineptly—but I knew that the opportunity presented to me was not one likely to recur in the course of my lifetime, and that I had to try to do something constructive if I could. You have judged any effect that we actually had as anti-climactic, and I agree, but what I was attempting to contrive, with all my might and all my art, *was* essentially anticlimactic: to stimulate contemplative intelligence and a love of peace. I doubt that I could have achieved a splendid success, in opposition not merely to the Mahatma's more violent determination but in opposition to the momentary tide of history, but I certainly hoped for some small result, to lend some assistance to the more fundamental tide that will one day bring about an amelioration of the human condition, in spite of all the blind and confused opposition presently presented to that progress by human stupidity and bellicosity. Perhaps my attempt was impotent, as so many attempts to achieve a similar result have been, but I did try . . . and I felt that in trying to play in harmony with me, you were making a similar attempt."

Was I?

I suppose I was, even though I had not formulated such an intention consciously, being more narrowly focused on the problem of opposing the decryption of Cthulhu. I would like to think that, merely by harmonizing with Dupin, I might have been making a useful contribution to his effort, perhaps even amplifying it, just as I had amplified the discord that Cthulhu's child introduced into the incantation of the *Necronomicon*.

Did Dupin and Anton, in fact, have any effect, or did our good intentions go to waste? I wish I could say that time will tell, but it won't tell *me*. We have no way of knowing what would have happened had the symphony not been played, or had it been performed by different players. We have no way of knowing whether or not whatever happens in future might have been influenced by our modification of the music of time.

But we did try; and I do not want to minimize Auguste Dupin's endeavor by rejecting out of hand the possibility that it might have had an effect. If the intelligence and wisdom of men like him are, in fact, completely ineffectual in the course of human affairs, then the human world is a truly dire place. We must hope that the contrary is true.

And for what it might be worth, I did have one further hallucination or visitation that gave me a little perverse consolation, and a little unusual moral reinforcement.

When the first violence of the Revolution had died down, and a measure of quietude had returned to Paris in spite of the cholera panic, I was reading in my study one gloomy evening, with the aid of candlelight—Dupin was elsewhere, engaged in some research—and I saw Jana Valdemar's ghost again, seated in Dupin's chair.

"According to Addhema," I told her, "It was my fault that you drowned, my fault that you magnetized yourself and allowed your obsession to take possession of you."

"Addhema is a vampire, and not to be trusted," she replied. "All you did was feel sorry for me, for which I should have been grateful. And you tried to pull me out of the river, for which I should also have been grateful, although that was not my reaction at the time. I tried to make amends, on the Pont de la Tournelle, but I could not do it."

"I tried to follow your advice," I said, ruefully. "I tried to be careful, of all the hazards that you listed. If I failed, it wasn't your fault—but I'm not sure that my failure was absolute. I think I *was* careful, to some degree, and that I owe it in part to you. Can we forgive one another?"

"There's nothing to forgive," she said.

"Then why are you here?" I asked. "Have you come to issue more warnings?"

"No," she said, "although it will probably be reassuring for you to know that you're not in immediate need of any more, even though you still have the *Necronomicon* dangerously near to your heart and mind. Contrary to rumor, ghosts do not know everything—far less, in fact, than many living people— but some are sensitive to the echoes of time, and thus possess moderate gifts of prophecy."

"Including you?"

"Including me. Would you like me to lift a corner of the veil for you?"

What can I say? It's already established that I'm a fool. "Yes, please," I said, even though I was well-acquainted with the lore of legend and literature, which insists that no good ever comes of such requests.

"The Revolution will not have the intended result. Monarchy will return, although it will term itself Empire. The Empire will fall, and that will only be the first of three invasions and humiliating defeats that France will suffer in the course of the next century. The British Empire will collapse too, aided in its defeat by another ascetic Mahatma, and the Thugs' dream of expelling the British from India by slow strangulation will be fulfilled, with or without the aid of Cthulhu. America will then secure an Empire of its own, more subtle in its violence, and will take a great paradoxical pride in proclaiming itself, a nation founded on genocide and piracy, to be a beacon of liberation, equality and fraternity, entitled in consequence to rule the world."

"Dupin's hopes for a continuation and acceleration of enlightenment will be dashed, then?"

"Not at all. Human knowledge and technical expertise will expand more in the next century than in all of previous human history. Electric light and its multitudinous corollaries will transform the world, gradually but utterly."

All of that was interesting, in a way, but a trifle impersonal.

"And what will become of me?"

"You will remain what you are," she said. "The bullets of the Revolution and its aftermath will not strike you down, nor will cholera bacilli. Your eventual death will be an anticipated anticlimax. You will record your adventures, but few people will read them and no one will believe them. You will fade from human memory with a very commonplace rapidity, leaving no descendants or any legacy of ideas. You will not suffer unusually in life, but you will never be happy. You will, however, always be able to console yourself slightly with the thought that things could have been worse, at least for you, and that you will have done less harm to your fellow human beings than most of your peers."

"Good enough," I said—I have never set the bar of personal satisfaction improbably high. "Thank you for letting me know. Had you predicted success and splendor I would not have been able to believe you, but if you're an illusion, at least you give the impression of being an honest one. Are you satisfied with your own existential condition?"

"Of course not," she said. "No one ever encountered a happy ghost—but I console myself slightly, when the echoes of time permit me to be manifest, with the thought that things could be worse, at least for me."

"You don't regret life . . . or the life of your unborn child?"

"No. I have the gift of prophecy; I know what my life, and that of my child, would have been. I did the right thing. There is no reason for you to feel guilty, about the unwitting aid you gave me in affirming my decision, or your inability to pull me out of the river."

"I'll try to take that aboard," I promised, "but it won't be easy, even with the aid of the residual corruption of the *Necronomicon*, which hasn't made my heart any harder, alas, or my mind any more avid for dark enlightenment. Shall I see you again?"

"I doubt it," she said, "but the music of time has no shortage of ghosts, or incorrigible seers. You'd be wiser to forget me, but you probably won't."

"Probably not," I agreed, "but there's always hope in dementia and death." I was being sarcastic, but I'm not sure that she realized that. People often don't.

"Don't think that," she advised me. "Memories are precious."

She was bound to think that. What else did she have but memories, if she even had those more than intermittently?

She faded away, anti-climactically. Such is afterlife. I picked up my book, and carried on reading, until it was time to go to sleep.

THE END

Printed in the USA
CPSIA information can be obtained
at www.ICGtesting.com
CBHW021524010324
4848CB00040B/657

9 781645 251347